Praise for
Blood Slaves

"This is easily the best horror book I have read all year. . . . This was an entire experience."

@annywilkes

"This is American history with fangs."

@piperdoddslewis

"Redmond doesn't just tell a story, he delivers a reckoning."

@piasreadz

"*Blood Slaves* is more than a book, it's an experience. . . . 6 stars. . . . A masterpiece."

@shunny_reads

"*Blood Slaves* is the horror novel that we all need right now. . . . A masterpiece."

@elizabethandhermonsters

Blood Rising

Other Books by Markus Redmond

Blood Slaves

Blood Rising

MARKUS REDMOND

DAFINA
an imprint of Kensington Publishing Corp.
kensingtonbooks.com

DAFINA BOOKS are published by
Kensington Publishing Corp.
900 Third Ave.
New York, NY 10022

kensingtonbooks.com

All Kensington Titles, Imprints, and Distributed Lines are available at special quantity discounts for bulk purchases for sales promotions, premiums, fund-raising, and educational or institutional use.

Special book excerpts or customized printings can also be created to fit specific needs. For details, write or phone the office of the Kensington special sales manager: Kensington Publishing Corp, 900 Third Ave., New York, NY 10022, Attn: Special Sales Department, Phone: 1-800-221-2647.

ISBN: 978-1-4967-5319-9

First Kensington Hardcover Edition: September 2026

ISBN: 978-1-4967-5321-2 (ebook)

10 9 8 7 6 5 4 3 2 1

Printed in the United States of America

Library of Congress Control Number: 2026937442

Interior design by Leah Marsh. Map design by Cassandra Farrin, North American map courtesy of Kaldari and Halava/Wikimedia Commons. Adinkra symbols: drutska/Adobe Stock; Celtic cross and English coat of arms adapted from Wikimedia Commons.

The authorized representative in the EU for product safety and compliance
is eucomply OU, Parnu mnt 139b-14, Apt 123
Tallinn, Berlin 11317, hello@eucompliancepartner.com

To Michael Lord, who died so that
Kwadzo Okoro could live.

Please note the following trigger/content warnings:

Cultural abuse, emotional abuse, physical abuse, forced consumption of defecation, amputation, nudity, murder, racial slurs, hate speech, and violence.

Dear Reader,

If you are here because you joined Kwadzo and the Ramangans in the rebellion against "Big Jim" Barrow in *Blood Slaves*, thank you. You went through a lot to get to this point, and I sincerely hope you enjoy the next stage in the ultimate uprising.

If you are new to the journey, welcome. There is much to discover, and if you'd like to see how it all began, I encourage you to explore *Blood Slaves*, mindful of the much talked about trigger warnings, of course.

As I've stated before, *Blood Slaves* was born out of a rage that had been building within me for decades, one I wasn't even truly aware of. Because of that, writing the first book was the easy part. Now, for those of you who have read *Blood Slaves*, that might seem flippant, maybe even crass, but let me explain what I mean.

The anger I was feeling in 2020 was visceral, and it translated into the story immediately. I was writing through rage that was reignited regularly thanks to the state of the nation at the time.

But about two-thirds of the way through, I started to think differently about the story—or rather, I began to think of it exponentially. Immortals overthrowing a plantation would have a lasting effect. It would change things, and quickly. The biggest change was the most obvious one: The heinous violence rained down upon the enslaved would be no more. They would have time to breathe, to be, Kwadzo in particular.

If *Blood Slaves* is about the cost of freedom, *Blood Rising* is about the cost of power. I think we've all seen how wrong power can go, how dangerous it can be, if wielded by the wrong hands. One of my favorite lines in *Blood Slaves* comes from Kwadzo when Penelope's father tells him that, if killed by Kwadzo, he would die a hero. Kwadzo's answer?

"I'll be the one writing the history and I don't even know your name."

Yes, victors write the history, but what if the victors were the previously oppressed? What would history document if all the slaves were freed by vampiric power native to Africa in the early 1700s, decades before the Declaration of Independence was ever drafted? Would there even be a need for it? What events would happen? What atrocities could be avoided? Would new ones take their place? And would those new ones be worse?

Blood Rising moves the Blood Saga deeper into a burgeoning alternate history where immortal beings take power. What will they make of the world? What will things look like in the 1800s? The 1900s?

Now?

And who will rise against them?

No one gains power without opposition, after all. But what happens when such opposition comes from an unexpected place? So unexpected that it becomes betrayal? And ultimately, is betrayal one of the costs of power?

Thank you for joining me in this increasingly fantastical—and bloody—quest. I hope that *Blood Rising* makes you think about the nature of power, how it changes depending on who holds it, and what you do when you find yourself in its seat.

May only your loftiest ideals reign.

Welcome to the Blood.

Sincerely,
Markus Redmond

All that power done gone straight to your head. Your whole head!

—Gnima Konate, aka "Gertie," 1710

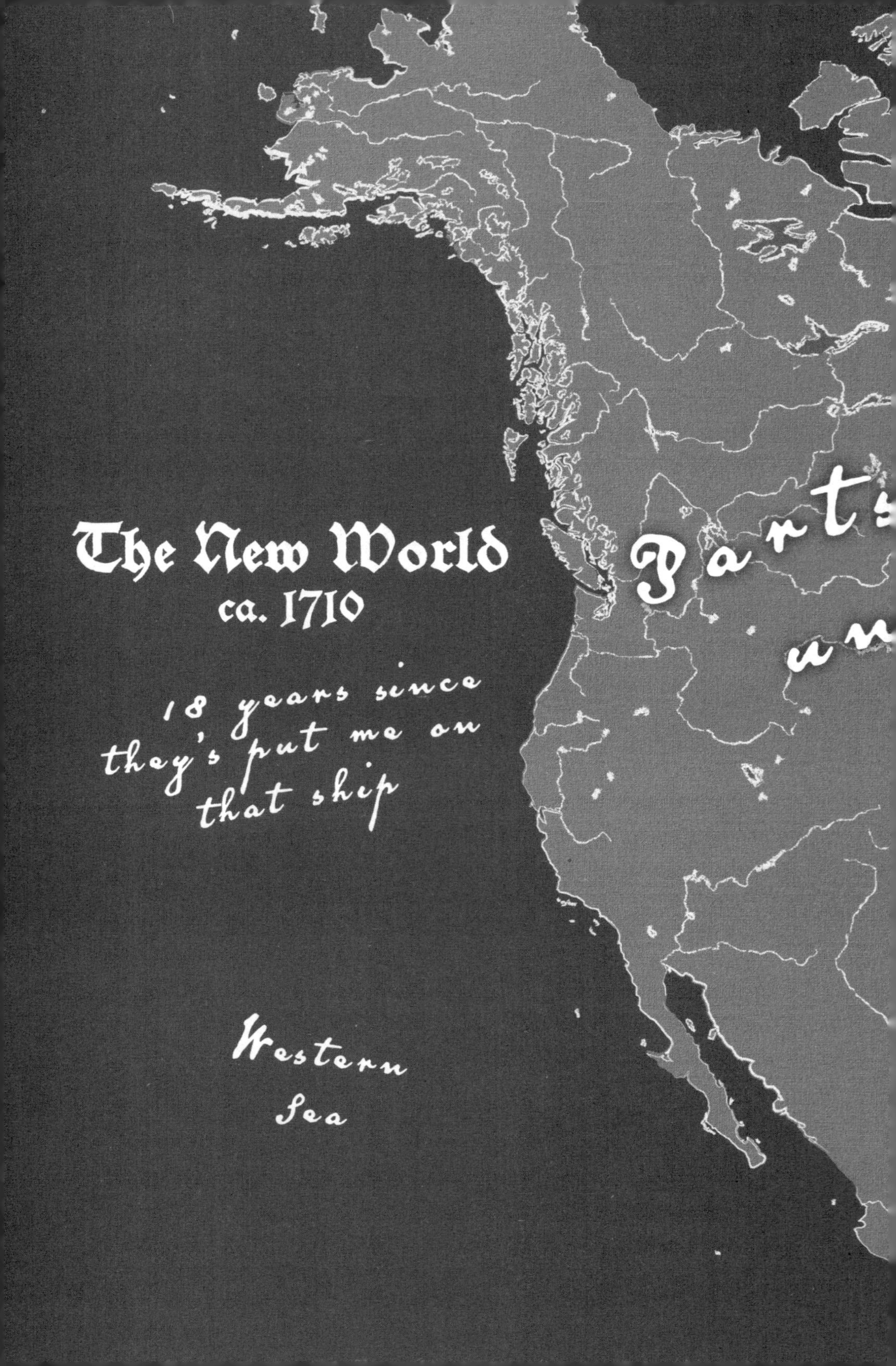
The New World
ca. 1710
18 years since they's put me on that ship
Western Sea

yet
nown
he North
Eastern Sea
Kingdom of Ghana
Land of Nez's people
Eastern Colonies
Carolina
Lakeside
Town Square
Crown Tavern
Peterson farm
~~Barrow~~ Crimson Plantation
Wilson Plantation

COME SIT A SPELL

Well, how do! Y'all come sit a spell. Kwadzo say I's the mistress of this here house now, so I reckon I is, but a month ago, I's was anythin' but. Y'all mighta heard 'bout me but I's Gertie, and this here hound be Charlie, and since Kwadzo done say what he say, I reckon I should be the one to tell y'all 'bout how all this here come to be.

I reckon y'all know 'bout Kwadzo 'cause of what he done, but back then, we's called him Willie. That the name Ol' Barrow give him when he bought him. Now Barrow was 'bout the meanest man on this here earth, but that Monroe, the overseer, was meaner, and he had it out for Willie somethin' awful. He beat on Willie something awful every chance he get; beat us all every chance he get, but Willie always got it the worst.

Willie thought it was always gonna be like that, but he ain't know what was comin'. Ain't none of us know. See, Willie meet Rafazi, who was doing shit work all by his lonesome. Lil' wisp of a thing, that Rafazi, compared to my big, strong Willie. But he say he the last of the Ramanga Tribe, so he can make Willie Ramanga. Now, ev'rybody know Ramanga weren't nothin' but myth, but it was evil myth. They say Ramangas is wicked, violent creatures that take your blood, and if they decide to make you one of they own, they feed you they's blood, kill you, and you s'posed to come back one of them. Ol' Rafazi ain't look like he got no power no way, but still, I warn Willie to stay clear of that evil. And if'n it was true, anybody know anythin' 'bout Ramanga know it weren't nothin' but evil. Killin' is evil and anythin' gots to kill to live, well, I ain't want nothin' to do with no evil, and I ain't want it for Willie neither.

But we was livin' with it all the same. And when Ol' Barrow snatch me up and force hisself on me, I thought evil was gonna kill me, but it save me. 'Least it try to. It turn out Rafazi really was Ramanga! He use his Ramanga speed—Kwadzo tell me later it called his blur—to pull me 'way from Barrow, but he ain't have all his power so they catch him and cage him up, and Barrow had his way with me, and make my Willie watch while he done it.

I think that what done put the idea in Willie's head to take Rafazi's blood and turn Ramanga. Now I tell him bold as I can not to, tell him he cain't die on me and our baby, tell him the very legend of Ramanga was wickedness, but he ain't listen. Not even after Rafazi's face get all twisted up with evil and he snatch Overseer Butch's heart clean out his chest and drink the blood right out it. Kwadzo still follow Rafazi out into them woods and leave me 'lone again.

And Ol' Monroe was the chief overseer, so when Butch and Willie and Rafazi went missin' all at the same time? Well, them beatins they give us only got worse. And what they done to po' lil' Fanna . . .

Anyhoo, Willie come back from them woods and say he done reclaim his true name, Kwadzo. Then he brung us all together and him and Rafazi offer us the chance to be like them, say he got him a plan to free us all with the power of Ramanga. Now, Minor, Tussy, and Irene, they's the first to wanna be turned but I beg them not to.

We all thought Ramanga was just a myth but now that we known it real, we ain't know what it would do to us. Only thing we known for sure was that it would make us killers, and I ain't have it in me to kill nobody. I know how bad we's had it, but killin' would make us just as bad as them white folks; worse, 'cause Ramanga live forever. That's a eternity of killin' just to live. I ain't know how to keep on lovin' Kwadzo knowin' blood done pass through his lips. I ain't never felt so 'lone in all my life. Derby try to fill Kwadzo's place, but I knew he never could. But I was just so alone . . .

Kwadzo and Rafazi took them that wanted to Blood out to the woods to show them how to use they powers to fight 'gainst Barrow, and Monroe, and the overseers, and the paddy rollers, and whoever else was gonna come for them. While they's out there, this ol' bloodhound come callin'. He had bit on Kwadzo earlier and Kwadzo snap his neck and leave him in the woods. But he had Kwadzo's blood in him, so he come back a Ramanga dog loyal to Kwadzo, so Kwadzo call him Charlie, and he been a good boy ever since. Ain't you, Charlie? You been a good boy, ain't you? He get a lil' protective of me and the baby some time.

Anyhoo, while they was in the woods, Barrow took us from the field to what Kwadzo say later was a church. Some evil ol' man get up there and talk 'bout somebody name Christ and how good he be, but that he was only for the white folks. He say we's weren't nothin' but niggers with no claim to nothin' in this life or the next. Then they stuff us back on top of one 'nother in a cramped wagon and Barrow start askin' where Kwadzo be. And I gets powerful mad 'cause it finally dawn on me that Barrow was 'fraid of what Kwadzo and Rafazi and the others had become. And I start wantin' them to come start the fight.

So, I tell Barrow that. And he punch me so hard it knock me out, and when I woke, he had me chained up inside the hot box.

That's when I finally know what Kwadzo been talkin' 'bout the whole time. I wanted to be good, wished for good, thinkin' being good would bring good. But not with Barrow and them people of his. They ain't had nothin' but hate for us. Hate is evil and they's evil through and through, and the only thing evil pay attention to is evil. Them intent on killin' gots to be killed to be stopped. So, I pray for Kwadzo to come save me, hopin' he still gots love for me, and he done it. Even though I was 'gainst him and Ramanga, he still come for me and his baby. Our baby.

Then him and all them that done took Ramangan blood run up on this here manor and, oh, child! I ain't never seen so much blood in all my life! They tore all Barrow's slave-ownin' friends limb from limb. Even tore up Mistress Barrow and her daughter, but Barrow was hidin' from the fight. Kwadzo found him alright, and he got his, but not before Kwadzo almost died again.

See, it turn out that blood is more than just blood to Ramanga. Love and hate be in the blood, one healin', one deadly. Barrow found that out, and knowin' how much hate Monroe have for Kwadzo, he cut up Monroe up and make him bleed all over Kwadzo. I thought I's gonna lose him, but Rafazi tell me that lovin' blood was the only thing that could heal him. My blood.

So, he drink from me. Drink so much I clean pass out, so I ain't see what all happen after, but Rafazi say Barrow set the manor on fire and my Kwadzo go rushin' in anyway. Say he run through the fire and got him a new Ramangan power, say he take the flames in his body 'til the fire was all inside him. And when he step out this here house, he spot Barrow and whoever else was left and blew all that fire out his mouth at them.

If I ain't seen him do it later myself, I reckon I wouldn'ta believed it either. He ain't show me with a whole lot of fire, mind you, but I seen him take a flamin' torch to his arm and watch the flame sink into his skin.

Well, once the fight was won, he took Barrow's head clean off and give it to the Natives to show they weren't in no danger from the man no more. They make a agreement to share the land and protect them, and now, here we be, livin' on the Crimson Plantation all together.

Now, I know y'all done probably heard all kinds of talk 'bout me, 'bout how I tried to get in the way of freedom and such; folks say I shoulda been more like Irene and not give Kwadzo so much trouble. Maybe they's right. But I was only thinkin' 'bout him and our baby. I love my Kwadzo with every inch of my heart and I ain't want a lick of harm to come to him. I ain't know evil could be used for good. But I done learned and I's gonna be by his side, but I's still me, now. If'n somethin' need sayin', I's gonna say it 'cause he gonna need me to. He gots more to do.

We's just one plantation in one colony. Kwadzo say there be thirteen colonies in this here New World, and they's all full of plantations and them plantations is full of slaves. They all needs to be free as us, and all them Natives need protectin' from them wicked white folk that come here, kill they kin, and steal they land, so Kwadzo got lots to do. And I reckon he gonna need to find that vile redheaded child, too. He say that evil child Barrow make me wait on durin' his house luncheon done bit on Fanna, so she might have the Blood. These white folks is evil enough without Ramangan power; ain't no tellin' what they'll do if they gets it.

But for now, y'all come on in here and gets y'all somethin' to eat. Charlie! Quit sniffin' on them people now, leave them be! I's sure they's done listenin' to me jibber jawin' and wants to get to readin' up on what all is goin' on now . . .

Prologue

In the Light of Day

The sun was coming up.

It was an inevitability she was well aware of, but it brought no solace to Penelope Callowhill.

No.

Knudsen.

She would no longer carry the name of a man who had hidden the knowledge of her real father from her. A poor excuse for a man who hid like a coward while her real father fought evil demon niggers until his last dying breath.

She was now—and would forever be—Penelope Knudsen.

She looked down at herself, kneeling upon the earth, covered in mud and blood, her dead mother lying before her, torn to shreds by her own hand. Penelope was dead, too, that she knew with great certainty. She still remembered the boot stomping down on her neck and the vile, metallic taste of blood in her mouth just before she took her last human breath and all went black. Then, she was engulfed in a brilliant redness. It surrounded her. It was all she could see, and it seemed to have no end or beginning. The blood in her mouth that had been vile and bitter became indescribably delectable. When she awoke, she was beset with dirt. She'd been buried.

In that moment, she felt the sensation of her breath catching, but there was no breath within her, just a remnant memory in her body. But worse, she had been made a part of the wicked scourge that plagued every decent white man and woman alive. She had ingested the blood of a demon nigger while trying to protect one of her own, and now, she craved the taste on her tongue with a hunger that was inhuman. Just like the ones who had afflicted her. They had made her one of them. They had turned her into a bloodthirsty demon monster filled with an evil craving beyond her control: one so sinful it made her take her own mother's life.

Her mother. She rose to the sound of her dear mother's voice, yet before hearing it, the most luscious of scents had awakened her senses. It did not occur to her that she was buried in the earth or that she no longer had any need for breath despite being conscious. She was overwhelmed by an intense hunger and a more scrumptious smell that she instinctually knew was blood. But the scent of this blood was even better, more compelling and desirable, unlike anything she had ever smelled before. And it was hovering just above her.

Only the sting of a fierce burning sensation against her leg cut through the crush of the blood invading her senses—the blade of her father's dagger. Her mother must have buried it with her. Even in her grief, Penelope surmised, her mother saw fit to give her child a piece of her true father. As her heart swelled with love for her mother, the scent filling her nostrils grew even sweeter as she carefully pulled the silver away from her skin with the blade's handle. It wasn't until she reached up through the dirt to grasp the person who contained the essence she so desired that she realized it was her mother. Somehow the knowledge made her even hungrier. In that moment, Penelope had no idea her eyes were red when she looked up at Anna. She had no idea she'd taken the form of a monster. All Penelope knew was that her mother smelled delicious and she could no longer contain her hunger.

Carrying her dear mother into the woods with superhuman strength and speed, Penelope feasted on Anna with reckless abandon. She felt drenched in her mother's love, which only spurred her on to drink more. Only after she was completely satiated did Penelope realize what she had done.

Now, she was hovering over the dead carcass of what used to be the woman who had given birth to her. She felt as if she had been sobbing for hours. Demon niggers had made her devour her own mother, taken her biological father just when she had come to know of him, and made her an orphan in a world overrun by them. Even one of them was one too many. Still, she had witnessed firsthand the power they possessed. There was no reason to believe that she didn't have the same power. She had experienced it. She died, yet she lived, and that made her immortal. And if she was, so could her white brethren be. She just needed to figure out how to make them like her.

The sun felt extraordinarily hot this early in the morning. It hadn't quite overtaken the sky, but it already felt like it was midday. Penelope's eyes went wide as flames broke out on her hands. She screamed as she shook them, a fruitless attempt at putting out the fire. They became as black as crow's feathers as the flame seared her skin. She fell back, and the fire spread across her form rapidly. The pain was nothing short of torturous. She screamed again until the flames burned through her neck and singed her vocal cords. She could feel her hair sizzling. Her eyes popped from the heat and melted away. Fire consumed Penelope entirely, burning her to a crisp. All went black.

She was dying.

Again.

Yet, she felt her senses go dormant within her, as if she were just about to fall into a peaceful nap, just like the last time she died. The overwhelming red tinge returned, and with it, peace. Penelope didn't know how long it took for her eyes to reform and open, but she felt a wave of rejuvenation wash over her. Slow at first, then growing in speed and intensity as the black char covering her form began to crack and fall away. The tightness around her eyes gave way first. She blinked and lifted her hand to wipe away the blackened crust. She peeled the scabs from her hands and, to her surprise, found her skin unharmed. Standing, Penelope brushed the rest of the burnt crust from her body. She could feel her hair growing out of scalp. She pulled away the scabs covering it and found her thick red tresses returning to their full length and luster as strands of them fell across her face. The fire had consumed her dress, and she became aware of her nakedness. She covered herself with the scraps of her mother's clothing, material she had torn to get to the blood she desperately craved.

Twice now Penelope had died, but she felt stronger than ever—powerful. She would harness this newly acquired power of hers and turn it on the demon niggers who had made her one of their ranks. Armed with this power and her father's dagger, she would make them pay.

She would make them.

All.

Pay.

One

Retribution

Kwadzo Okoro stood on the covered porch of his manor as night was quickly becoming day. The grand white façade of what used to be called Barrow Manor had been painted over in a brilliant crimson red. Much had changed in the thirty days that passed since the bloody battle waged inside the manor's walls. Still, vigilance was necessary. Ramangans were stationed around the perimeter of the property now, and Native warriors would take their place once the sun had arisen. The fighters of Ramangan Blood had warded off two blistering attacks from Lakeside townsfolk since the fall of Big Jim Barrow, and Kwadzo was sure there would be more. Still, there was a sense of peace in the knowledge that the man was no more.

From the handful of runaway slaves that trickled up to his doorstep in the weeks that followed the victory, he'd learned that a few other Lakeside plantation owners had perished in the manor battle. The slaves had heard rumors of vicious but triumphant Ramangans killing their masters. Some took the opportunity to run but were hunted down by overseers. Others remained too frightened to leave, and save for a very small number, most were even more terrified of the Ramangans. There was no telling what would happen as word spread beyond Lakeside, but Kwadzo knew he needed to stay ready for whatever was to come.

"'Twas a lovely night!"

Rafazi was dressed in a finely tailored suit with elaborate embroidery and in full Ramangan form. He used a spun-silk handkerchief to wipe the excess blood that trickled from his lips. The libertine disposition Rafazi had taken over the course of the past month amused Kwadzo to no end.

"How would you know?" Kwadzo chuckled as he shook his head. "You've spent your night in a bedchamber with women and blood."

"As I said, 'twas a lovely night."

They shared a chuckle at Rafazi's comment while he replaced his handkerchief. "Seems a shame to cover my skin with clothing. The Blood makes it glorious, especially in Ramangan form. Humans have such difficulty resisting the touch of it."

"And where did you get such finery?" Kwadzo asked, taking the lapel of Rafazi's jacket between his fingers to feel its smoothness.

"There are talented tailors among us, capable of far more than just whittling down Ol' Barrow's clothes to fit, which you seem perfectly fine with. The only finery you wear is that little trophy on your finger."

It was true that not everything in the manor was lost before Kwadzo extinguished the fire that raged through it. Even now, he wore the altered pants—held up by two straps of cotton the tailors had fashioned with brackets that attached to the waistband of the garment in the front and back to keep them in place—and ill-fitting shirt of the man who once called himself

Kwadzo's master. But the ring of ruby and gold was his favored prize of victory. The ruby on his finger shimmered in the waning moonlight, and as he always did since he claimed it from Big Jim's finger, he got lost in its sparkling redness. It reminded him that he would never be owned by anyone ever again.

"I prefer something that befits my station," Rafazi said, his words shifting Kwadzo's focus.

"And what station is that?"

"Master, of course."

"There is a part of me that envies you, Rafazi." Kwadzo laughed heartily.

"Envy is wasted energy, my friend. Being a leader does not mean you must lead every moment. Our people are strong. So are the Natives. They know what to do. You have earned the right to enjoy your victory."

Kwadzo didn't respond. Rafazi was no leader, he had said so himself. There was no way he could know the burdens that weighed on the head of a leader. Kwadzo gave silent thanks for Gertie. Only she could help quiet his mind, even if his quieting hers aided in the task.

"We come to stand guard."

Nez arrived with a large group of hulking Native tribesmen in tow. Kwadzo owed the young man a debt of gratitude. Had they not crossed paths and come to their mutually beneficial agreement, neither the crops nor the manor would have reached the level of repair they had so quickly. Working together, their collective peoples were a formidable foe against the colonists.

"There is still a bit of time before the sun rises," Kwadzo said to Nez. "Do your men need food or water before they stand guard?"

"No. Ready now. My people go to kitchen yard, offer blood," Nez said as his men assumed the positions of the guarding Ramangans, who languidly made their way back toward the manor.

"And, may I say, it is delightful," Rafazi said with a smile, one he tempered under the glare of Nez. "And we are extremely grateful to you and your people for your sacrifice."

Kwadzo clocked Nez's wariness. He had been instrumental in helping the chieftain of his tribe come to an agreement with Kwadzo for their peoples to share the land, and more than a few of their number had voluntarily gifted their blood in gratitude—and, Kwadzo suspected, in the interest of keeping bloodlust at bay. But trust between the two peoples, between Nez and Kwadzo, was still not absolute. It was clear that more than a few of Nez's people were not comfortable with Ramangans, and while things were steady now as the situation was mutually beneficial, there was no telling how long their alliance would hold.

"Please, Nez," Kwadzo said, hoping to help remedy the situation. "Do come inside. Let us feed you, quench your thirst with wine and ale."

A growl of pain sounded before Nez could answer. A blur rushed onto the porch and became a Ramangan, wincing in pain from his smoking shoulder. As the light of the sun began to break through, the remaining Ramangans used their blurs to escape its rays, racing into the manor as the Indigenous warriors stood ready in their place.

"Kwadzo? You hear that?"

Kwadzo focused his hearing as he looked out at the thicket of trees across the road from the manor with Rafazi. Kwadzo's eyes narrowed, and his Ramangan sight caught a group of five white men moving through the trees, armed with bows and arrows.

"It's another attack. Five of them in the trees," Rafazi said, his eyes now glowing red.

Nez's brow crinkled in confused awe. "How you see in dark?"

A grunt of pain came from the perimeter as one of the Native warriors fell to the ground, an arrow stuck in his chest.

Another arrow followed, this one slicing into a column on the porch mere inches from Kwadzo's face. As he pulled the arrow out of the beam, Rafazi backed away with a shudder.

"Silver . . ."

The arrowhead was indeed made of silver. Kwadzo resisted the urge to touch it, forgetting for the moment that silver had lost its effect on him ever since he had absorbed the manor fire. "Why are they using bows and arrows? The last two attacks came with fire, guns, and chants from far more than five."

"Maybe it's just a few angry small farmers. It doesn't seem like an organized attack," Rafazi said.

"I go with men," Nez said. "Capture white men. Bring them to you."

Kwadzo nodded as Nez rushed off the porch and collected the warriors guarding the front of the property to run after the white men in the trees.

"Come, Kwadzo," Rafazi said. "The sun is upon us."

He rushed inside the manor, but Kwadzo remained, his blood stirring. Something was off.

And then he smelled the smoke.

It was coming from inside the manor. Kwadzo spun, his blur racing through the house, which still had several rooms in a state of disrepair—including the parlor room, where two white men were throwing furniture on a pile while a torch-wielding third was setting it on fire. At the sound of screams, he saw three more white men swinging swords, keeping a few of the newly turned Ramangans who surrounded them at bay while the African humans tried to hide in their panic. The surrounded men swung frantically at those Ramangans only to miss their speeding blurs. Though those of the Blood escaped the blades, they would quickly reposition and hold the circle, effectively keeping the sword wielders contained. The five outside the manor had been decoys.

"Y'all demon niggers may be fast," one of the sword wielders shouted, "but this here silver's gonna cut y'all down to size and send y'all straight back to hell!"

Kwadzo felt the sting of a blade cut through his midsection before he looked down and saw the sword, covered in his blood, sticking out of him. He muffled his groans of pain as he heard five of the white men laugh.

"Ain't think we'd come for you in the daytime, did you, nigger?" the sixth man behind him asked, the one who had plunged the sword in his back. "Don't you worry none. There's more of us comin'. How's that silver feel, nigger? We gonna kill you and burn this place down with y'all inside. Then we gonna put things back the way they was 'round here."

"KWADZO!!"

Gertie's voice. She stood ten feet away from him, her face covered in shock and tears, staring at the blade embedded in him. Fanna was at her side.

"We gonna kill her, too," the white man behind him whispered.

Get Gertie somewhere safe, Kwadzo communicated mentally to Fanna, who disappeared with Gertie in her blur as a new throng of white men rushed through the house armed with rifles, torches, and blades. He could feel a heat growing behind him and clocked the confused faces of the white men rushing toward him.

"Why ain't the silver doin' him in?" one of the men behind him asked another. With a smile, Kwadzo took his Ramangan form—his eyes grew red as his brow extended over them, becoming engorged. His facial veins became visible beneath his skin; his jagged teeth and fangs came out of hiding, as did the razor-sharp edges on his fingertips. With his blur, he reached his talons into the mouths of the two men that used the most disparaging word to insult him and his people with and ripped their tongues from their mouths. As they screeched and sprayed blood from their mouths, Kwadzo stretched out his arms, thrusting his weight backward and falling into the fire, taking the two white men who were at his back with him. The sounds of the men screaming and of more white men running through the manor wreaking havoc were drowned out by his own shrieks as the fire overtook him.

The pain was searing. He shut his eyes tight and felt death take hold of the two white men at his sides as the clothing he wore burned away. The pain was intense but familiar, almost annoyingly so. His mind raced with thoughts of his people, of Gertie. But he could not simply lie here and burn. White men were rushing through the house—*his* house—who needed to be stopped. He knew it would be much longer before the pain from the flames would give way to a feeling of fullness. He felt the process within him accelerate as his body began to absorb the flames that engulfed him, and when he opened his eyes, his vision had gone a fiery orange.

Kwadzo was no longer covered in flames, though the bodies of the dead men behind him continued to burn. He was naked, but he didn't have time to care. He rose to his feet and looked down at the bright orange-and-red cracks crisscrossing the entirety of his skin. He tore the sword from his frame with a mighty howl and felt both his blood and fire repairing the wound. Fire once again coursed through his veins—he could feel it circulating through his blood, just as it had before, but this time it was different. This time, he was prepared for it. He knew what to do with it. The pain had been less than it was before, and the flickering orange in his eyes lessened when he wanted it to because he controlled it.

He could control all of it.

With flame bursting through his veins, Kwadzo opened his mouth wide until it filled with fire. He unleashed it in a ball, followed by another, and then another, aiming his flames at the white men who had invaded his manor. They screamed in torture as Kwadzo focused his balls of flame precisely where he wanted them to go, blasting the men in their knees, chests, and backs, careful to keep the flame away from his people, human or Ramangan, who did battle against them. The white men were few and his work was quick; there had been eleven men in total who had entered with malicious intent. Eight survived.

Kwadzo and some of the other Ramangans rounded up those survivors in their blurs and dropped them together in the center of the foyer, each of them moaning and whimpering as they did their best to pat out the flames they had been scorched with. The Ramangans were careful to stand back and away from the beams of sunlight now streaming through the windows at the entrance as the white men stared up at Kwadzo with awe and dread.

"It is not my intention to kill any more citizens of Lakeside," Kwadzo said, standing over them, nude, his eyes still flickering with orange flame, fire moving through the orange-and-red cracks covering his skin. "But a man has the right to defend himself in his own home."

"You ain't no man, and this ain't your home!" one of the men yelled, his voice shaking.

"I may no longer be human," Kwadzo said with a smile, "but this is most certainly my home. The sooner you and your people accept that, the better off we will all be. So, I urge you to do so."

Nez and the Native warriors came running into the foyer, dragging five battered and beaten white men with them and a new stream of sunlight through the open front door of the manor. Kwadzo and his Ramangans took another step back to remain shielded from the sun's rays as Nez, his warriors, and the defeated white men stared back at them, slack-jawed by Kwadzo's appearance.

"Your eyes," Nez whispered in near reverence, "carry fire."

The comment made Kwadzo acutely aware of his nakedness, but it was too late to make any attempt to cover himself. Instead, he blinked, causing sparks to flicker in his eyes.

"Yes," Kwadzo said. "It seems a new ability has presented itself. By the Blood of Gamab, fire runs through my veins, which also accounts for my lack of clothing." Nez and the Natives gawked at him while the white men they'd captured trembled. It was far too much to address now, and he had no intention of doing so. "Are these the men who attacked from the trees?"

Changing the focus was essential to Kwadzo. He was still getting accustomed to his growing powers, and he didn't have a full understanding of them. He could not afford to engage in discourse about them or what they meant with Nez. What truly mattered was that these white invaders, who had to be dealt with, had seen what he was capable of, and he saw this as an opportunity to send a message.

"Yes," Nez thankfully answered. "Trick us while more white men come."

"From the looks of them, your men have already taught them a valuable lesson. Thank you. You can let them go." Kwadzo was not surprised by the murmurs and gasps that rose in the room.

"You lettin' us go?" one of the captured men asked.

"Yes. And in light of this leniency, it would be wise of you to stop your attacks. You will never be able to truly fathom what was done to us on this plantation. Unspeakable things, savagery beyond measure, and we had no recourse against it. What we have become is the consequence of that savagery. Let the fate of the Barrows be your lesson. We do not aim to return the horror that was shown to us in great measure, but we are more than capable of doing so. We wish to find our place in society peacefully. But if you continue to attack us, you will be forced to reckon with strength and force far greater than your own. Now go."

The invaders began a collective scramble to leave. A few of them were fixated on Kwadzo's naked form and member as they went, causing him to shake his head. Seconds later, one of the humans placed a large tablecloth over his shoulders, with which he covered himself.

"You think they come back?" Nez asked Kwadzo.

The answer was one of inevitability.

"Yes."

Two

New Devon

Bartholomew Crabtree loved the sound of his wife's giggling. It was light and airy, endearingly so, and just a bit conspiratorial, like she was keeping a delicious secret. Of course, Bartholomew knew all of Constance Crabtree's secrets. He knew what made her laugh, what made her cry, what gave her pleasure.

"Again, my sweet?" he asked his wife as her giggles increased.

"Again, and again!" Constance shrieked with joy. Bartholomew smiled at her with glee. He was very much in love with his wife, her portly frame in particular. He loved how much of her jiggled when she was this delighted. Constance was both statuesque and Rubenesque. A slight man himself, Bartholomew reveled in the feel of her plentiful flesh and regularly smothered his face in her ample bosom. She would run her fingers through his dark, thin hair and giggle. Just like she was doing now as she handed him a jug filled with lime juice.

Bartholomew poured the lime juice over the bare back of the man who stood in front of him. The man's back was covered in open, bloody wounds and the initials *BC* were branded into his shoulder. The man bellowed out in torment as the juice seeped through his wounds.

"Scream, nigger, scream!" Constance shouted in glee, clapping her hand against a long, flat wooden spoon, giggling louder. It all brought Bartholomew a sense of joy. This was supposed to be punishment for a slave who had stolen sugarcane from the fields. Bartholomew was supposed to be angry about the theft, and on some level, he was. But he was far more jubilant at the thought of inflicting pain and humiliation than trying to teach his slave an unforgettable lesson.

Perhaps it was fitting. Bartholomew never reprimanded his slaves inside the manor, and certainly not in his dining room. It was an elegant space reserved for his most illustrious guests. Velvet covered the huge cherrywood table that sat under a crystal chandelier filled with lit candles, coating the entire room in a sparky golden glow. Each place setting was immaculate, complete with fine chinaware, polished silverware, and crystal goblets. It was certainly no place for a mongrel like Shep. Shep, the ingrate, stealing sugarcane from the fields and claiming hunger as his reason for doing so. Bartholomew had fed him just yesterday! Well, if the slave thought it was fine to take what did not belong to him, Bartholomew reckoned he might as well elevate the experience of Shep's delusion.

So, after an appropriate flogging for the offense, Bartholomew chained Shep's ankles up in bilboes that were bound to a chair at the dining room table. Shep's blood dripped onto his Persian rug, which was annoying but worth the frustration for what he had planned, and for the joy it would bring Constance.

"Thought you could steal from me, did you?" Bartholomew barked at Shep. The slave trembled from the torture Bartholomew was doling out, and the excess flesh on his plump body quivered almost as much as Constance's did when she giggled.

"You ain't fed me!" Shep growled back. "I's starvin'!"

"You! Ate! Yesterday!" Constance screamed deliberately, punctuating each word with a punch to Shep's head. "How dare you still be hungry, piggy!"

"No matter. We're going to remedy your hunger tonight. Hany, what is taking so goddamn long?"

In the corner of the room, a filthy female slave squatted and strained over a chamber pot. She was dark and disheveled; Bartholomew could smell her stench from across the room, and it only grew stronger the harder she strained.

"Woo-wee! Your shit stank, Hany!" Shep exclaimed despite his current position.

"You hush up, Shep!" Hany shouted in distress before Constance rushed to her, smacking the slave in the back of her head.

"Don't you shout in my house!" Constance snarled at her. "You're lucky to even be in it! You wouldn't be unless it was for my amusement, and your yelling is ruining my fun. Now do what you were brought in here to do and get it done quickly!"

The reprimand was followed by two plops, the sound of which returned the smile to Constance's face. Bartholomew winced as his wife waved Hany away and brought him the chamber pot.

"That is truly rancid," he said.

"Yes, it's perfectly fitting," Constance said, using her long wooden spoon to ladle out two logs of Hany's excrement from the chamber pot and placing them on the plate in front of Shep, who gagged at the smell.

"Well, what are you waiting for? I thought you said you were starving?" Bartholomew said, to the elation of Constance.

"You dare have the gall to steal from us yet turn your nose up to what we give you freely?" she asked gleefully.

"But this here is shit, boss!" Shep whined. "Stank shit! And it got some blood in it!"

"You eat it, or eat nothing at all," Bartholomew hissed as Constance poured the liquid remnants from the chamber pot into the crystal goblet next to the plate. "Now, pick up that spoon."

"A little something for you to wash down your shit loaf with!" She cackled.

"But boss . . ."

"Pick it up!"

The fierceness in Bartholomew's voice made Shep jump, and with a grimace, he picked up the piece of silverware. His hand shook as he moved it to the plate, and Bartholomew found himself cackling right along with Constance as the two hovered over the slave, anxiously awaiting his first bite. When it was finally taken, the couple erupted in laughter as Shep immediately retched across the table.

"Steal my sugarcane again," Bartholomew finally said, "and shit loaf is all you'll ever eat."

He took his wife's hand and led her out of the room while Shep sobbed over his predicament. He was Bartholomew Crabtree, for heaven's sake. The sugar plantation he owned with his wife was far and away the largest and most profitable one in New Dover—hell, in the entire province of Carolina. The only planter he knew of whose wealth and slave count rivaled his own was James Barrow a couple of towns over in Lakeside.

There had been rumor of an uprising at the Barrow Plantation; there was even talk that his slaves had somehow become possessed by demons, and still others had gone so far as to say the slaves themselves became bloodthirsty monsters—vampyres—who'd laid waste to the manor and the entire Barrow family.

Rumor so easily became the nonsensical, especially among slaves.

Still, any rumor of an uprising was dangerous. It was a well-known fact that niggers were ignorant creatures, so they could not be depended on to discern fact from fiction. If niggers heard about others revolting successfully, they would develop the idea that they, too, could revolt. Which was why it was important to Bartholomew and Constance to instill in their slaves a sense of reality.

That message was sent with clarity this night. Slaves talked among themselves. They would hear about Shep's punishment.

Neither he nor they would step out of line again.

Besides the jobs they were acquired to do, slaves were toys, vessels of amusement. So close to being human, and yet, not quite. Bartholomew found much enjoyment in pushing the boundaries of his perversions onto them and had found a kindred spirit in Constance. The daughter of a wealthy French planter, she too understood the entertainment value slaves possessed. She bored easily, but perversion kept life fun and full of surprises. Yes, a firm hand was necessary, but wealth and power were such grand privileges. They were not to be squandered by dour dispositions.

Perhaps if Barrow had come to understand this in time, he wouldn't be in the predicament he'd found himself in, whatever the truth of that quandary was. Bartholomew and Constance had sent an overseer to Lakeside to assess the situation. While he did not believe the poppycock about vampyres, demonic forces, and such, uprisings did happen.

If the account of this one was to be believed, this particular rebellion happened on the night of the Mistress Barrow's soirée. Owners of some of the larger Lakeside plantations were present and summarily slain along with the Barrows. Bartholomew surmised that though family members and even opportunistic overseers may have stepped in to take over unattended-to farms, he and Constance would have no problem appropriating the land and its slaves for themselves with a bit of persuasion. If Barrow really was dead, that left six thousand acres unaccounted for, not to mention a throng of slaves to be acquired. If there had been an uprising, he was certain he and Constance could set things right and add to their considerable wealth at the same time.

And have themselves a bit of fun in the process.

Three

Candlelight

The gentle glow of soft flames filled Kwadzo's field of vision as he stirred and opened his eyes. In this large bed, in what used to be Ol' Barrow's bedchamber, Kwadzo had been watching Gertie fall into a deep and peaceful sleep for several nights now. Though he no longer required sleep, closing his eyes while lying next to her sleeping form brought him serenity. He knew no greater joy than seeing the mother of his child resting, at peace, free, though she had not been spared from worry.

Nearly a week had passed since the last unsuccessful attack against them by the townspeople, and Kwadzo still found himself having to quell Gertie's fears. Each night since, in this bed, he would take her in his arms, place his hand on her belly, and assure her that all would be well. Sometimes, she would gift him with a taste of her blood. She would kiss his lips, and they would make love until she succumbed to slumber.

His eyes fixed on the lit candles illuminating the dark room. Fire was becoming as hypnotic to him as blood, though in a much different way. He felt at one with it, as if it were a piece of his very being existing outside of himself. It was a gift to feel so calm. He felt Gertie softly rouse from her sleep, stretching and wrapping an arm around his torso with a relaxed sigh. Charlie the bloodhound lay at their feet, his maw resting on her outstretched leg.

Charlie had taken to being at Gertie's side as often as possible ever since they'd taken over the manor. Kwadzo supposed the dog didn't think he was protection enough for his . . . Gertie. What was he to refer to her as? It seemed natural to him to call to her with something other than her name, something precious, a term of endearment and commitment, but he knew of none. He certainly hadn't heard any used by the white men he'd encountered. In truth, most seemed to loathe women. The only term he could call to mind was wife, but marriage had been an impossibility. However, they were slaves no more. He was the leader of a successful revolution. Could he not set new rules? Could he not now make her his bride?

Gertie shifted again, gently pushing herself up and off the bed before moving in front of a full-length mirror. Kwadzo chuckled at Charlie hopping off the bed to stand at her feet, gazing up at her inquisitively as she bunched her soft white cotton nightgown up beneath her breasts with one hand while she gently stroked her belly with the other. It had not yet begun to bulge with their child, but it was there and growing. Even now, he could hear his firstborn's heartbeat along with her own.

His firstborn and only child.

Until the end of time.

It did not seem plausible for new life to spring forth from death, so this child and Gertie would be the living proof of his humanity. They were a legacy he would outlive. But the woman he loved was here, right now.

"Not even you can resist your own beauty."

The gasp Gertie released in surprise returned Kwadzo's chuckle as he appeared behind her in a flash, placing his hands over hers, embracing the soft curve of her middle while Charlie unleashed a bark. Perhaps the hound had grown as fond of Gertie as he was.

"I done plumb forgot you don't sleep no more," she whispered while he nuzzled her neck.

"I enjoy resting with you both."

"Both?"

He smoothed a hand against her belly. She slapped it with a chuckle. "Hush now!" She ran her hands over his. "You's a big man. I's gonna have a big child." Gertie pushed her belly forward and Kwadzo laughed.

"You don't have to do that. Our son will make his presence known when he's ready."

"Our *daughter*."

Their eyes met in the reflection of the mirror with smiles. She leaned her head back against his chest. Kwadzo closed his eyes and pulled her closer. The feel of her against him, her smell, her presence, stirred his very soul. A soul. He wasn't sure if he had one anymore, or if he ever had—becoming a Ramangan shifted many of the ideas he had held before—but the bliss that consumed him now was something he wanted to hold onto for as long as he could.

"You wanna taste me?"

Kwadzo opened his eyes, and they glowed red in his reflection. He blinked several times, but his eyes retained their crimson glimmer. He was unable to hide his eagerness for her essence. Gertie reached back and placed her palm on his cheek.

"It's all right," she whispered. "That's just you havin' desire for me. I feels it, too."

His eyes pulsed, and her eyes became slits of passion in the mirror. He moaned as he pressed against her.

"You wanna taste me?" Gertie asked again breathlessly.

"Desperately," Kwadzo croaked with need. Her hand moved farther back, cradling his neck in her hand as she tilted her head to the side, exposing hers to him. His teeth grew jagged, his fangs wet with venom. He opened his mouth wider, but she stopped him.

"Wait just a bit now," she whispered. "I wants it to feel good."

The red in his eyes glowed even brighter, his fangs getting wetter. Once they were dripping with venom, Kwadzo rapidly dug them into Gertie's flesh. Her breath caught with the bliss the venom provided, and her eyes rolled as Kwadzo drank from her, pulling away before pain could set in. His eyes and teeth reverted to their human state as he licked his lips clean of her life force. She ran her fingers over the bite marks he left on her neck and stared back at him in the mirror. She offered the wetness on her fingertips to him.

"I will never be able to describe how good you taste," he said, licking her fingers and the marks he left on her skin clean.

"I taste better than anybody you done fed on?"

"You always will. It's your love. No one can ever taste as good as you."

Gertie stared intently at him in the mirror before her eyes shifted downward. Her fingertips grazed across his ruby ring, and he felt her shudder.

"What happened?" he asked. "Is it the baby?"

Gertie avoided his gaze and shook her head. Kwadzo's heart sank.

"Oh, Gertie," he began. "I'm so sorry. What this ring must mean to you. I'll take it off . . ."

"No." She squeezed his hand to keep him from removing it. "This here ring ain't the one Ol' Barrow punch me with, not no more. It's the prize my Kwadzo claimed for hisself when he take that evil man down and free us all. Weren't no other way. Rafazi walk 'round here in all his finery, you deserve some of your own for what you done. And you just love red ever since you took the blood."

Kwadzo's heart swelled. He kissed her cheek as she refocused her eyes on her own reflection. They seemed to glaze over, as if she were deep in thought.

"This here glass let me look at me any time I want," she said.

"And what do you see?"

"The pain from every day of toil I's made to work, but I see I's strong from survivin' it. And I see light and goodness, and joy. I see my yaay and baay, all my family, livin' through my eyes, showin' them you, what you done. How you makes me feel. I sees what you see when you look at me now. I look where you look on me, my eyes, my skin, my hair, my body, and I think it's all as beautiful as you do."

Kwadzo squeezed her just a bit tighter before slipping his hands around her belly, and she giggled in response.

"I sees love." Gertie smiled as she placed her other hand over his. "I sees life. I sees our child lookin' at me through my eyes, lookin' at you. This here baby see the good in you, and the happy in me. I feel her smilin' inside me. And it make me more happy than I gots right to be."

"No, Gertie. There isn't enough happiness in the world to match what you deserve."

Gertie's soft palm found Kwadzo's cheek as she turned to face him.

"I's happy, but I ain't fool enough to think I ain't never gonna know pain again. You done made us free, but we ain't safe from these white folks. 'Specially us that choose to stay natural. It's still their world, and free or not, we gots no place in it."

The crinkle of her brow was all too familiar. He saw it with every attack made against the manor. And though it was still their manor, he doubted the townsfolk would give up. They wanted vengeance for the Barrows. They wanted their normality restored.

They wanted his people dead.

And he needed a foolproof plan to ensure their everlasting freedom.

"We will make our place in it," he whispered to her, taking her face in his hands. "I promise you that. But until then, know that you are safe. As long as I walk this earth, you and our child will have nothing to fear."

Kwadzo kissed her, tenderly at first, then deeper, attempting to get lost in her for one more blissful moment before the concern of their situation clouded his mind. Their victory would be a shallow one unless something was done to cause a major shift in the status quo. They needed to be more than free. They needed to be accepted. Seen. They needed a place. They needed to find freedom for those still enslaved on other plantations . . .

A knock on the door pulled Kwadzo from his thoughts and his lips from Gertie's. Pulling on a pair of oversized breeches, he opened it to find a smiling Fanna on the other side. Gone were the rags she had worn as a slave. Over a long, white cotton smock she wore a red stay, and her hair was brushed back neatly. Kwadzo smiled. He thought she looked like a little lady. Standing behind Fanna, clutching the back of her smock, was a small Native boy, a few years younger than Fanna, peeking up at Kwadzo with a nervous smile.

"Hello Fanna," he said with a smile of his own. "Who's your friend?"

He chuckled as the boy ducked out of sight behind Fanna.

"That's Chev," Fanna said. "He's shy."

"Not so shy that he couldn't join you for a visit."

"He wanted to meet the fire god."

"The fire what?

"The fire god." Fanna giggled. "That's what Nez is calling you."

"I am not a god."

"They think you are."

"Who thinks I am?"

"Chev's people. They have a surprise for us, and they want to see you do what you did with the fire. Our people want to see it, too."

Young Chev's giggles could be heard from behind Fanna just as Gertie approached. Kwadzo watched Fanna's eyes light up at the sight of her.

"Is you causin' trouble, child?"

"No, ma'am," Fanna replied before hugging Gertie warmly. Fanna's eyes went red as she held her ear to Gertie's stomach.

"I can hear her little heartbeat."

"So, you think it's a little girl, too?" Kwadzo affected a faux frown. "It could be a boy, you know."

"But it ain't gonna be," Gertie said with a smile, "'cause she a girl. Ain't that right, Fanna?"

Gertie and Fanna laughed together while young Chev peeked around Fanna and caught Gertie's eye. Kwadzo watched Gertie soften even more as she took in the boy.

"And you is Chev."

The boy seemed to utter words involuntarily in his native tongue in response to Gertie, and his enamored gaze at her made Fanna giggle.

"What he say?" Gertie asked while Kwadzo smiled at the boy. He knew exactly what the boy had said. It had been said with an innocent kindness, almost with awe. And Kwadzo couldn't have agreed with young Chev more as the boy's statement translated immediately in his head.

How beautiful you are.

Perhaps my brother
would worry less if
you shared your blood
with me instead.

Four

With This Crimson Flame

Fanna and Chev led Kwadzo and Gertie through the first level of the house with Charlie in tow. A small group of Kwadzo's people milled about with anxious anticipation that was palpable to him. Most present were human, and as Kwadzo walked past them, he could hear the frantic beating of their hearts, see the respect on their faces, the near reverence in their eyes.

For him.

Kwadzo smiled back, receiving their quiet admiration graciously. He wondered if he was supposed to say something uplifting. Being a leader did not come naturally to him, especially when he wasn't in battle. He feared making one wrong move would result in him letting his people down. A young man of no more than twenty years stepped forward, his eyes shining, his smile broad. Kwadzo could hear the blood rushing through his veins.

"Mister Kwadzo, sir," the young man began nervously. "We done been talkin' 'bout ev'rythin' you done, and we ain't find no words to thank you proper, so . . ."

The young man spun around to the gathered throng with a nod before a collective and explosive cheer went up from them. The shock of it wore off quickly, and Kwadzo was left with a sense of pride so strong that he felt his chest swell. A small nudge on his side brought his attention to Gertie looking up at him.

"Mind your head now," she said with a funny little smile. "If'n it get too full up with praise, you ain't gonna hear nothin' else."

He chuckled and put an arm around her shoulders as Chev whispered something in Fanna's ear.

"Come, all of you," Fanna said. "Follow us!"

The children ran for the back door, a barking Charlie chasing after them. Kwadzo, Gertie, and his people made their way out onto the back porch of the manor.

"Kwadzo!"

Nez was rushing toward him with a smile, and beyond him stood rows of huge, long tables lined up a few feet from the porch, illuminated by lit torches planted in the earth. All their peoples, Natives, Africans, and Ramangans—along with Doc Farkus and his wife, Rebecca, the only white folks present—sat together as a bountiful feast was being presented. Roasted deer, duck, pig, venison stew, and wild bass were pulled from several earthen ovens and placed on the tables along with onions and beans, spinach and cabbage, cornmeal with molasses, fresh cranberries, mussels with curds, and clams. Farther past the feast and closer to the rice fields was a long row of squat round houses made from tree bark and cedar wood. New houses were also under construction. More Africans were crossing the fields and making their way to the tables.

"What's all this?" Kwadzo asked, descending from the back porch with the others.

"My people grateful to you," Nez replied. "We give thanks with feast. We try before with white man, not go well."

"I'm sure this time will be different."

As the others began to fan out, Nez led Kwadzo and Gertie along the tables. Kwadzo was warmed by the joy on his people's faces and the camaraderie they were finding with the Natives. His heart smiled to see those of the Blood who'd fought valiantly and survived—Rosana, Juba, Rufus, Polly, Anita, and others—in celebration. There was an overflowing of goodwill this night, and it made Kwadzo beam with pride.

A few of the Indigenous tribespeople who spoke English served as translators, expressing sentiments back and forth between the two peoples, something Doc Farkus and his wife seemed to take special note of. Others simply seemed to connect over the aroma of the food before them.

An outburst of laughter drew Kwadzo's attention to the end of a table where Rafazi held court amid a huddle of four Native women, all of whom sipped from short mugs. Rafazi spoke in their tongue fluently, and in an animated fashion that brought another rise of laughter from the women. Kwadzo smiled and shook his head as Rafazi excused himself from them, taking a mug along with him.

"It is indeed a very good night tonight," Rafazi exclaimed, embracing Kwadzo with a face full of glee.

"Another one? You learned their tongue quickly."

"Well, my blood may not be as special as yours, but it is older. Age carries its own benefits." Rafazi chugged the contents of his mug as Kwadzo looked on with narrowing eyes.

"What is that you're drinking?"

"Fermented wine made from blueberries, they tell me."

Rafazi's imbibing puzzled Kwadzo. He now knew the glory of Blood; it left in him no desire for any food or drink he had ever consumed as a human. He glanced across the tables and took note of the others who had taken the Blood, all of whom stared awkwardly at the food before them.

"Does it have any taste?" Kwadzo asked.

"Well, no. But judging by the smiles on the lips of these Native women, I'm guessing it's delightful." Rafazi chuckled.

"Do not take much," Nez warned. "I trust no liquid that make fool of man. Or men who fool our women." Nez's eyes peered into Rafazi's. The veiled threat he'd issued Rafazi did not hide the fright with which it was given, and Kwadzo thought the young Native brave to have taken such a stand against Rafazi.

"I'm sure Rafazi is simply enjoying your generosity," Kwadzo said with a smile. Nez's apprehension spoke to the tension that remained between the two peoples, and Kwadzo would not allow it to fester. Perhaps tonight would present an opportunity to quell it. A quick look to Rafazi was enough to convey his intent.

"That, I am." Rafazi smiled good-naturedly. "Wine has no effect on me anyway."

Nez was approached by one of his tribesmen. After a quick exchange in their native tongue, the young Native excused himself and moved along, giving Kwadzo the chance to interrogate Rafazi.

"What are you doing?"

"Enjoying their generosity, like you said." Rafazi was waving and winking at the Native women he had left even as he said the words.

"Mind yourself, Rafazi. We still need their allegiance."

"I am aware of the situation, but this is a celebration, brother. I know you've been in bondage for more than half your life, but surely you remember what celebration is."

For so long there had been little to celebrate. Kwadzo had grown accustomed to pushing through his anxiety for the greater good, but now, even in the wake of his first victory, his worry found fertile ground once again. Unlike Rafazi, who grabbed a handful of fresh cranberries from a bowl and chewed with glee.

"Why are you eating? How are those of the Blood supposed to partake in this bounty?"

"Just because we don't *need* to eat doesn't mean we *can't*. Engaging in human habits can help us gain favor when we need it. Some will do nothing for you, some will get even better."

Gertie was blushing now, and Kwadzo could not look away from her as the lustful smile on his face grew.

"Looks like you two have already discovered one of them."

"Rafazi right," Gertie said with a smile. "The night beautiful, and I's powerful hungry. C'mon, now!"

"Listen to the lady, Kwadzo! Eat, drink, be merry!"

"For tomorrow we may die," Kwadzo grumbled in response. Among the books that hadn't burned in the manor fire was Barrow's Geneva Bible. Kwadzo had skimmed through enough of it to be familiar with Rafazi's chosen phrase.

"But not you nor I," Rafazi said with a wink, leaving Kwadzo little choice but to surrender to his smile.

"I want to sit with Gertie!"

The playful chatter of Fanna, Chev, and a joyfully barking Charlie broke through the banter of fellowship rising from the crowd. Fanna threw her arms around Gertie's waist, looking up at her with pleading eyes.

"Can Chev and I sit with you?" Fanna asked.

"Of course y'all can, child. Come on."

The children led her away to find seating as Kwadzo pulled Rafazi in close and lowered his voice with confusion. "Where does the food go when you eat it? I haven't passed anything since you turned me."

"Of course not," Rafazi said with a chuckle. "You're dead. There's no more waste. The Blood sustains and goes everywhere we need it to. Anything else consumed will just decompose to nothing inside of us. Except water."

"Why not water?"

"Blood is partly made of water. It refreshes the blood. I actually enjoy it myself when it's clean and fresh. Now, eat up."

Rafazi offered a new handful of cranberries to Kwadzo to punctate his point.

"Y'all comin'?"

Both men found Gertie smiling as she called back at them in anticipation. Rafazi gave Kwadzo a pat on the back. "Enjoy, brother."

"Rafazi? Wait." The sound of Gertie's voice stopped him, and Kwadzo felt a flush of anxiety as she rushed back and faced Rafazi. It wasn't a secret that the two of them rarely saw eye to eye, and Kwadzo couldn't afford any division in his ranks to show, especially in front of the Natives.

"I's happy I's alive," Gertie said to Rafazi, "and it 'cause of you."

"Me?"

"I's 'gainst the very thought of you from the start. And I knows I's unkind to you. But what you done, what you made Kwadzo, it save me and my baby, our baby, and put us here where we's can eat real food and be together, and ain't no overseer houndin' on us. I aims to thank you proper for savin' me, and I's sorry 'bout the way I done you before."

Rafazi's response was a simple one. "Brothers and sisters fuss all the time, don't they?"

Kwadzo blinked back happy tears. The two most important parts of what made him whole were now locked in a warm embrace. His shoulders dropped; his neck relaxed. They were happy. His people were happy. And in this moment in time, he was happy. They were not free of challenges, and there were others like them who suffered still, but those who had served on this plantation under Barrow's tyrannical rule, those who had been through so very much, they were free of bondage and oppression. Yes, there was work to be done, but his people deserved to enjoy this bit of grace. This was why he had made the choice to take the Blood.

If it took dying to feel this alive, then so be it.

"Kwadzo!"

Nez's second call to him was followed by a wave beckoning him to the end of one of the long tables where the Native stood next to the tribal chieftain, Chief Great Oak. Kwadzo eyed the elderly man with familiarity and respect. He remembered the man's sharp but kind eyes that took him in with gratitude when he presented him with Barrow's head. He also took note of the reverence with which the warrior tribesmen who surrounded the chieftain regarded him.

"Chief Great Oak has led tribe for many years," Nez began. "Has seen much devastation at the hands of white man. Never see them driven away by their slaves."

"They are slaves no more," Chief Great Oak said in his native tongue, taking Kwadzo's hand to shake. "I appreciate the kindness you have shown to my people."

"That feeling is mutual, Chieftain," Kwadzo answered in kind.

"These powers of yours," the chieftain said with a chuckle. "I have seen them, and still, they astound me. Our tongue flows from your own like you were one of us." With the aid of a carved wooden walking stick, Chief Great Oak stood, an action that brought silence from all the Indigenous people present.

"Our peoples have suffered from the arrogance and tyranny of the white man. Our sacred land was stolen from us. You were ripped away from yours. But together, we have found harmony on a full moon and reclaimed what is rightfully ours—land and freedom. It is this that we celebrate and give thanks with this feast tonight."

Despite not knowing the language, the passion with which Chief Great Oak spoke quieted Kwadzo's people, the meaning behind the unfamiliar words resonating with them. One of the tribesmen presented the chief with a single eagle feather. The chief then held the feather high over Kwadzo's head, garnering a few gasps from his people.

"The eagle is sacred to our people," Chief Great Oak said, once again addressing both peoples. "The feathers of the eagle symbolize the strength and courage of the Great Spirit. I raise this feather to you now and wish for your continued bravery."

"Chief Great Oak bless Kwadzo with courage and strength for long time to come," Nez said to Kwadzo's people in translation as Kwadzo regarded the chieftain with respect.

"I will do all in my power to keep our peoples safe for all time," Kwadzo said to the smiling chief, who placed a hand of solidarity on his shoulder while a tribesman brought a long staff with thick bristles on its end to Nez. After receiving a nod from Chief Great Oak, Nez poured oil onto the bristles from a jar.

"To our people," Nez said, "fire cleanses, make new. We light staff with fire to honor Great Spirit, give thanks for new beginning. We never have honor of fire god to light staff. We ask you light flame with your fire. Show unity of our peoples."

Kwadzo could feel the eyes of everyone on him as Nez handed him the staff. His shoulders hunched with embarrassment. His fire power was becoming more familiar to him, and though he was gaining more control of it and reveled in the power he felt when flame raged within him, it was still new and unpredictable. This speaking of him as a figure of divinity did not sit well with him.

"Nez," Kwadzo said, tight-lipped. "I am *not* a god."

"I see flame burn in your eyes. Eyes not lie."

"Nez . . ."

"It is because his blood is special," Rafazi said as he stood beside Kwadzo. "It is unlike any other of this world and capable of much, even absorbing fire. He will be happy to light the staff for the Great Spirit."

"What are you doing?" Kwadzo hissed at Rafazi.

"This is their way of making us a part of one of their sacred traditions. You said it yourself: We need their allegiance. Our new beginning starts here."

Rafazi was right. Kwadzo was their leader. This was undoubtedly the first of what he surmised would be many choices made as the leader of a revolution for the good of his people. He'd chosen to enter an alliance with the Indigenous tribe. Perhaps fulfilling their request would be the first step toward lasting trust.

"Kwadzo!"

Doc Farkus's voice cut through the crowd as he and his wife rushed toward him. They were an odd sort, he short, meek, and timid with a thin mop of silver left on his head; she tall and a bit boisterous with long white hair shooting down her back from a black pointed hat that she seemed to always be wearing. Doc Farkus was the lone white survivor from the battle for the manor.

Though he maintained his home—in which he also practiced medicine—in Lakeside, he had taken up temporary residence with his wife, Rebecca, on the plantation grounds to see after the health of Africans and Natives alike, at least those who wished it—a condition of his being spared. He also looked after Gertie closely, ensuring that her health and that of the child remained strong.

To hear the doctor tell it, Farkus was the premier physician in Lakeside, if not the entire province of Carolina. However, whenever he returned to his home in town, he'd found that the residents were not happy with his choice to lend his talents to Africans and Natives, which accounted for his spending more and more time on the plantation. Kwadzo suspected they would have been even more unforgiving to discover his fascination with all things Ramangan.

The doctor and his wife were keenly interested in the ways of the Blood—it was their main reason for wishing to stay in the manor—but Kwadzo wasn't much help in that regard. He knew little of his powers himself, and Rafazi hadn't been inclined to share much knowledge with them, so they were left to their own observations. Still, they never overstepped and seemed to understand and accept their place within the hierarchy.

"Kwadzo, please, what exactly did Rafazi mean by 'absorbing fire?'" Doc Farkus asked.

"Is this a new power?" Rebecca asked. "We've heard the tales of you breathing fire on Barrow and his mates and that you burned them to white ash, but we thought those were tall tales. Were they true?"

Kwadzo could see the annoyance in Nez's eyes at their presence and did not wish to delay his decision any longer than necessary.

"Yes," he said simply, and the couple's eyes went wide.

"You must tell us how!" Doc Farkus exclaimed.

"I'll show you and everyone else. But you both need to stand back before this interruption is considered rude."

Kwadzo's stern look was enough to cause the Farkuses to retreat while he turned his attention back to Nez.

"I am not a god," Kwadzo reiterated, "but in order to light this staff, I must first be consumed by fire."

The declaration created a hush in the night air. There were varying levels of apprehension at Kwadzo's words, but none higher than Gertie's.

"Kwadzo!"

She worried for him so. He gave her the calmest smile he could to put her at ease.

"You stay clear now," he told her. Wringing her hands, she allowed the Farkuses to pull her back, and others took that as a cue to do the same as he took on his Ramangan form. With glowing red eyes, he signaled the tribesmen toward him. Two of them pulled lit torches out of the ground and moved toward Kwadzo.

Those of the Blood among them rose to their feet and took on their Ramangan forms, but Rafazi's raised hand kept them at bay. They watched as their leader balled his hands into fists, shut his eyes, and nodded to the tribesmen. They tilted their torches and set Kwadzo ablaze.

He could feel himself screaming in torture as the clothing he wore burned away in the flame. He could hear Gertie crying, Charlie barking. He also heard the accelerated heart rates of those who looked on, the blood pumping faster through their veins. But the pain abated even faster than it had before, and that familiar fullness in his veins took hold. Behind his eyes, orange seeped into the bright, brilliant red, calming him, and when he opened them, the red tint of his Ramangan vision was quickly replaced with an orange one.

Gasps rose from those gathered. It was the first time most of them had seen this transformation of his, and through the balls of flame that roared in his eye sockets, he could see their orange-tinted faces full of shock, including Gertie's. The tears in her eyes offset the smile on her face, one full of love and wonder. He felt ten feet tall.

Proud in the nakedness that exposed his fire-filled veins, he took the staff from Nez with a powerful calm. "This fire," he said, "is fueled by Ramangan Blood."

The orange flames in his eyes became red the moment he said the words, and a red tint filled his vision, brighter than ever. The cracks across his body shifted to full-on red as Kwadzo felt the flames fuse with his blood. He held the staff before him, and from his mouth he released a stream of flame onto its bristles—pure red flame. It created a brighter fire than anyone present had ever seen. Its red glow reached high and wide, completely illuminating the area, rendering the other torches that lined the tables useless. It was the first time he had produced red flames simply by wishing them to be so.

"With this crimson flame," Kwadzo said, raising the lit staff high in the air, "we give thanks and solidify the unity of our peoples. We will stand together for all time under this crimson order, and celebrate this land and our freedom!"

At his words, a mighty cheer went up from the Africans, the Ramangans, and the Natives alike as the flame of unity burned even brighter over their feast of freedom.

Five

Seneca

The glow of the crimson flame continued to burn high and bright as the united peoples ate and drank their fill. The Africans entertained the Natives with music from their homemade instruments, and those who could remember sang songs from their homelands in their native tongues. Older Africans taught young Natives to clap along to the rhythm of the tribal sounds; young Africans led older Natives in dance to the music. Even Doc and Rebecca Farkus were included in the revelry.

The night was thick with joy, and Kwadzo feared his face might break from laughter. After everything they had been put through by Barrow and Monroe, they deserved every moment of this frivolity. They had more than earned it. He had felt so triumphant in his declaration of unity that his nakedness had momentarily escaped him until Fanna's blur had rushed toward him carrying garments that used to belong to the man who called himself Kwadzo's master. Back in his human form, he now sat at Chief Great Oak's table—the chieftain to his left and Gertie to his right—tugging at the ill-fitting clothing despite it being tailored to fit him better. Perhaps it was time to heed Rafazi's advice and have the seamstresses create something new for him.

Kwadzo surveyed the merriment until his eyes finally landed on Gertie. Gertie. How beautiful he had always found her to be, but even more so now. With the glow of red and moonlight against her dark cheeks, she had a radiance all her own, especially this night. He told himself that it had something to do with the child she carried, but in truth, this radiance had been with her ever since he had taken the manor. With it came a look of awe sharpened by fear each time she looked at him. Gertie had seen him die and come back to life. She'd seen him command an uprising, and now, she had watched him burn and survive unscathed. Yet she never removed her eyes from him. Even now, as she gazed up at him, alongside everything else he saw in those eyes, the love she felt for him still shone through. It pumped through her veins. He could smell it.

"I ain't never seen nothin' like what you done," Gertie whispered to him, her hand clutching his. He worried for her state of mind. She had seen and endured many things through his transformation. She had every reason to run from his side, but the scent of her love still filled his nostrils.

"Do I scare you?" he asked.

"All the time."

She pulled Kwadzo close and kissed him tenderly, and he felt it stirring his very soul. He could hear her blood rushing through her veins, the smell of her love engulfing him, causing blood to flood his loins for her. He could see no one else.

"You thirsty for me?" she breathed into his mouth, her eyelids heavy with desire.

"Always," he moaned, questioning his ability to restrain himself.

"Please," he heard the chieftain say. "Eat."

The sound of his voice broke Kwadzo from the cocoon of Gertie, and he smiled his embarrassment as he searched for a way to decline the offer without offending the chieftain.

"His kind does not partake of food as we do. Only blood."

The soft, smoky voice came from the statuesque Indigenous woman who stood across the table from Kwadzo. Nearly six feet tall, she towered over Nez, who stood next to her with a perturbed look across his face. Her long raven hair stretched down the length of her back and framed the delicate softness of her face, which almost contradicted the strength apparent in her physique. She carried a twinkle of mischief in her deep brown eyes that was directed squarely at Kwadzo.

"There are some among us who have willingly given of our own blood to suffice their needs," the woman continued in her native tongue.

"And we are grateful," Kwadzo replied in kind before turning to the chieftain. "Your people are in no danger from us. We only take what is offered to us and never by force."

"My understanding was that you fed from animals," Chief Great Oak said, his brow crinkling.

"Human blood makes them stronger and lasts longer in the body," the woman interjected before switching to English for Kwadzo's benefit. "Or so I have been told."

Her eyes bore into him so that he felt Gertie's grip on his hand tighten.

"You speak the white man's tongue as well?" Kwadzo asked the Native woman.

"Who do you think taught it to Nez? Though his speech still needs improvement." Nez glared at the woman so fiercely that it spoke of familiarity.

"I am Seneca," she said, "elder sister of Nez."

"Seven minutes older," Nez grumbled. Kwadzo made a mental note of their twin status and allowed himself a little chuckle at their bickering. It reminded him of his own departed sister.

"I wish to thank you for your efforts in helping our people by offering you a taste of my own blood," Seneca said, ignoring her brother.

"No!" Nez objected.

"Why do you worry, brother? I am offering my blood willingly. I am not being forced. And I will be in no danger. Kwadzo has said so himself."

"Perhaps it would be best for me to decline," Kwadzo said as the siblings squared off. Gertie's grip tightened on Kwadzo as Seneca returned her eyes to him with a slow smile.

"Perhaps my brother would worry less if you shared your blood with me instead."

Her boldness took Kwadzo aback. Ramangan Blood and power were reserved for *his* people—no one who wasn't African had ever asked for it before. He was still concerned about the young white girl who had inadvertently consumed Fanna's blood. Ramangan power had to be controlled, contained, if they were to ultimately succeed.

"I'm sorry," Kwadzo said. "We only share Ramangan Blood with our own people."

"Yet we share our land with you," Seneca countered. "We share our land, our blood. Surely that makes us worthy of sharing your power."

"Ramangan Blood is sacred to us."

"And yet, our chieftain bestowed his highest blessing to you with a feather as sacred to us as the land we now stand on."

"Land y'all couldn't keep!" Gertie barked. Her nails dug into his skin as her voice got louder. "Ol' Barrow would *still* have it if'n it weren't for Kwadzo! And them white folks stay off this here land 'cause of *Ramangan* power. That's the only reason you can walk 'round here like you is, makin' demands!"

"All right," Kwadzo said, placing a firm hand on Gertie's shoulder. Confrontation was exactly what he didn't want. Gertie's chest heaved, but Kwadzo shook his head and she calmed herself.

"This not your place," Nez said to his sister. "Our peoples united by flame of fire god!"

"Is that true?" Seneca asked Kwadzo, ignoring Nez. "You are different than the others, more powerful. But are you truly a god as my brother believes?"

"It not your place to speak!" Nez said, facing off against her again. "You have no use for power!"

"I am perfectly suited for the power! I am twice the hunter you are, and three times the warrior!"

"*Enough!*"

Chief Great Oak slammed his walking stick against the table, punctuating his pronouncement. "Brother and sister are not to bicker like this. We are celebrating. Our peoples have united for the good of this land. We will honor one another. Seneca, you will show respect."

Seneca stepped back from Nez and nodded politely to Kwadzo. "Forgive my boldness."

"Boldness," Kwadzo said, "is a virtuous trait to have. Do not apologize for it."

With a smile, Seneca offered her nod to Gertie as well. "I believe it no easy task to be the woman of a god. But having seen him, in all his glory, I imagine your rewards are great."

Seneca walked away as calmly as she had approached, leaving Kwadzo with concern.

"Who is that?"

Ekow had moved next to him. Ekow Tetteh, one of the first Kwadzo turned who, like him, reclaimed his given name, had his eyes firmly planted on the departing Seneca. One look to Ekow revealed his craving for the woman as he tilted his head upward.

"Her blood," Ekow said. "It smells amazing. And what a lovely vessel it's contained in."

"Control, brother," Kwadzo managed to say, but his mind swirled with the potential problems that Seneca, and others like her, might cause. Though an accord of unity had been struck between his people and the Indigenous tribe, true trust was something that would need to build over time. The power of Ramangan Blood was sure to be envied, but he could not allow it to fall into the wrong hands. Those who had already been gifted the Blood, turned Ramangan during war, could not be helped, but now, even among his own people, the gift of the Blood could only be given after careful consideration. He could not risk anyone possessing Ramangan power and having an agenda adverse to the one he was establishing for the good of his people.

Clarence and Derby were two such examples. Clarence, the Barrows' former dutiful house slave, seemed to remain in mourning over the deaths, and Kwadzo knew that Derby, who most likely still had designs on Gertie, would take the opportunity to strike against him if one presented itself. There was no doubt in his mind that Clarence would rush to the whites and gift them the Blood were he given it. Considering the brutality they had already exhibited without it, Ramangan Blood in white bodies would be a catastrophe he couldn't dare to imagine.

Once again, his thoughts returned to the young white girl who had bitten down on Fanna's leg and taken in her blood in battle. It had been a month, and in that time, he had not heard of or seen any white person of Ramangan Blood, nor had Fanna spoken of sensing the girl's presence. Perhaps the girl was somehow still alive and had no idea of the power inside of her. Or maybe she had died, turned, and the sun took her since she would have had no knowledge of the power's limitations.

Either way, she needed to be found.

Six

A Free Woman

Gertie sat on the edge of the bed looking down at her shoes. They were pitiful excuses for footwear—dirty and worn down, plain black leather, with the tattered soles separating from the top of the shoes. They were shoes she had worn in the rice fields, and they had always been too big for her feet. She had often removed them when she worked since they proved to be more cumbersome than anything else in the wet paddy.

With the luxuries of not needing to work and living in the manor, she had taken to walking around with her feet bare. And though she found comfort in the option, there was something about it that slightly annoyed her. She couldn't quite determine why, it just did. It also occurred to her that she had never seen a pair of brand-new shoes up close, and that today, she wanted to. Like Kwadzo, she had been wearing the altered clothes of the Barrows, but she had seen the flashy attire the seamstresses had crafted for Rafazi at his request and wondered what it would be like to be adorned in finery custom made to fit her.

With shoes to match.

She was, after all, a free woman now. But Gertie was not used to such freedom of thought. She was used to surviving. Every day. Hour. Minute. Second. She was used to the ache in her back from being hunched over picking rice stalks, the cramping of her hands from stitching up cuts in the sick house, the anxiety that came from being within whip's length of Overseer Monroe almost constantly. There were few pleasantries in her former life, but she was never without something to do. As demeaning a purpose as it was for her to be productive for Ol' Barrow's sake, it was still a purpose.

Now, she felt idle.

Gertie swept into the manor's study with a quiet smile. It was as if there had never been a fire here. Behind the large wooden desk he sat, poring over a menagerie of books and papers while Irene and Ekow looked over his shoulder. The man she had met as Willie had become Kwadzo—leader of a revolution, freer of his people, an immortal with the power of a god, and also the father of the child growing inside of her. There was nothing about him she didn't love. He had kept every promise he made to her and then some. He was the reason she now had the luxury of feeling idle, but idle she still felt.

Despite all he had become, *she* was still just plain Gertie. In Mauritania, her homeland, her clan was governed by the rule of a maternal abosom. Their women were revered, unlike the way of the white man in this world. Gertie was smart; she had picked up the white man's tongue as spoken by the overseers much quicker than the others she was first enslaved with, though listening to Kwadzo speak now reminded her of how much more she had to learn.

But learn she could.

Why had the man she loved chosen to teach Irene and Ekow instead of her?

"Gertie?" The sound of Kwadzo's voice made her jump. "Everything okay?"

Gertie felt her tongue grow heavy when she tried to form a response. "I's fine," she finally said, smiling through the anxiety pounding in her heart. "Y'all look like y'all's workin' hard. Eyes all narrow, look like steam might come out y'all's ears any minute."

She offered them a nervous laugh and clocked the polite smiles from Irene and Ekow as she shifted her weight from one side to the other. She felt a bit more useless now than before.

"Well, I ain't gonna be no bother," Gertie said, backing out of the room.

"You're never a bother," Kwadzo said. He gave a nod, and Irene and Ekow swished past her in their Ramangan blurs so fast she shivered from a cold chill the wind of their speed produced.

"I ain't never gonna get used to how fast y'all move," she said with another nervous chuckle she had hoped to be able to keep in; Kwadzo's silent smile did nothing to calm her. "Well, I done disturbed you plenty."

"You didn't disturb anything. We were discussing ways to move forward."

"With what?"

"Lots of things, including the best way to free those who remain in bondage. It won't be the same as interrupting a soirée. So many plantations in so many colonies; we cannot fail them. But in the immediate future, we need to figure out a way to sell our crops. The rice and cotton are growing back at a faster rate than they ever did with Monroe running things."

"That's 'cause folks ain't slavin' no more. Folks work harder knowin' they's gonna get paid for their toil."

"We've got to be able to sell the crops in order to pay anybody. But no one seems willing to do business with us. Doc Farkus is familiar with some of Lakeside's merchants, but no one's willing to talk with him about our crops."

"'Cause he ain't the one in charge. You is."

"I suppose I am. But their business hours don't agree with me anymore."

"Who say you gots to do business when them white folks do? These here crops was the best crops when Barrow was 'live. Ain't nothin' changed 'cept he dead, and the crops is even better. They's still in need of 'em. They can't hold out forever. You make them do business the way you wants to, when you say."

He looked up at her with eyes so warm and gracious, it was hard to believe he was dead. He listened to her, and she could see the appreciation for her words in his smile. It was a fleeting moment of usefulness that she already felt slipping away along with his smile.

"What's wrong, Gertie?"

The words were said with such loving care that she accepted the invitation of his outstretched arm, which curled around her middle as she moved to sit on his lap behind the desk.

"Ev'rybody in this here house gots somethin' to do but me." She could hear the pout in her voice. She wasn't proud of it, but it was genuine.

"You are doing something," Kwadzo said with a chuckle. "You're doing the most important thing."

Gertie slapped his shoulder with a frown. "Don't you dare say growin' our baby."

"Is that not important?"

"It ain't all I can do. I's smart."

"I know you are. You just gave me a dose of your wisdom."

"Well, I gots more. I can help more than I done. All I's do now is sit 'round and get wait on. Folks bring me food if'n I wants it, clothes when I needs 'em . . ."

"What's wrong with that?"

"It ain't *for* me, ain't 'cause of me. It's 'cause of *you*. Girls wantin' to get my blessin' to let you feed on them." Her pout returned, and Gertie felt her face twist in a cringe.

"We've talked about that," Kwadzo said softly. "It's a necessity. Besides, I feed on men, too."

"*I* gots the best blood for you."

"Yes, you do. But you and the baby need it more. And even if I could take it, I'd run out of it far too soon."

"See? I can't even be the only one to keeps you fed, and won't nobody let me do nothin' else 'round this here house." She grimaced at the sound of her pout becoming even more pronounced, but there was little she could do about it now.

"You've done enough, Gertie. What's wrong with you relaxing? You've been working your whole life . . ."

"So's ev'rybody else. I can do more. You got Irene and Ekow in here book learnin', readin', to read, I could learn readin'. I need to do *somethin'*, Kwadzo. All this sittin' 'round 'bout to make me lose my mind."

Gertie breathed. She had never been afraid to let her feelings be known to Willie, but she was still adjusting to Kwadzo. She knew he was the same person, but he had gone through an unimaginable change. He had become a larger-than-life character to everyone, including herself. She could feel his love for her even as he was creating this brave, new, and different world—a world where, outside of being the mother of its fearless leader's child, she was unsure of her place.

"Gertie," he said softly, "you're free now. If you want to learn to read, I'll teach you. There is no question that you're smart. You're smarter than I am. More than smart, you're wise. If I was smart, I would've listened to you."

"If'n you listened to me, you wouldn't have done all this here. You wouldn't have set us free."

"We're not all free."

"Not yet. But we will be. You gonna see to it."

"And you are a part of that happening."

He placed a hand on her belly, and despite her current irritation, the touch made her smile.

"This child, our child, will be the first one born free in the world we are creating," Kwadzo told her. "This is the beginning of something brand new for us all—a truly new world. One in which you can do anything you want to do. You don't need my permission. If there's anything I can help with, I will. All you have to do is tell me what you want."

For reasons unknown to her, only one thought flooded Gertie's mind. "Shoes," she said. "I wants me some new shoes."

THE YELLOW GOWN WITH its floral embroidery pattern fell to the floor despite the alterations the seamstresses had made. Gertie felt glad to be shorter than the deceased mistress of the house. Because of her height, the gown covered her tattered shoes. Her own feet were too big to fit Charity Barrow's shoes and too small to fit her daughter Virginia's, so she would take her threadbare shoes for one last wear on her first real trip into town, one where she wasn't being stuffed into a wagon and led to her doom.

Given her relationship to Kwadzo and considering his status as leader, Gertie surmised she was probably the new mistress of the house, even if Kwadzo hadn't taken her hand in marriage. Perhaps it was better if he didn't. A man like Kwadzo, given his status and power, could take as many wives as he wanted if he were so inclined. There was no shortage of willing women, both Africans and Natives. Most could barely conceal their lustful aspirations, and some didn't bother to.

But Kwadzo showed no signs of succumbing to any of their charms. He had much to attend to, but she was nearly always by his side. It was what he wanted and what she preferred. One day, she would grow old and pass on. She reckoned he could do whatever he wanted then. But for now, she wanted him all to herself.

Gertie wrung her hands in front of the standing mirror in the master bedchamber—*her* bedchamber—as Irene worked behind her, folding her hair into a lace hat that matched the gown. *Her* gown. She had worn the clothing of her dead ancestors before, but this was different.

"You are a stunning vision, Gertie," Irene said, her reflection smiling at Gertie in the mirror.

"Don't feel right. Wearing a dead white woman's clothes," Gertie declared.

"They took much from us," Irene said. Gertie suspected the woman was wearing the shirt and trousers of the dead Thomas Barrow. "Taking their clothes for ourselves is no different from taking the manor."

Though Irene's reasoning made sense, it didn't alleviate Gertie's anxiety. The true reason for her concern still lingered. She met Irene's soft gaze in the mirror when she felt the young woman's hands cover her own.

"There's nothing to be nervous about," Irene told her.

"Them white folks ain't gonna wanna see me movin' through they's town, buyin' things."

"Doesn't matter what they want. Not anymore. We battled and won. They're going to have to accept that sooner or later, because we aren't done."

"What if they won't accept it today?" Gertie's breath caught with her true fear. Irene turned Gertie to face her and gently tightened her grip on her hands.

"Every time they've tried to come and take this manor, they have failed. They are well aware of our power, and they know that anything they do against us in the daylight will be answered in the night. They don't have to like us. They fear us. If even a single hair on your head is touched, they'll have a fire god to contend with." Irene's soft giggle brought on Gertie's. Her assuredness was beginning to rub off.

"And you won't be alone," Irene continued. "Doc Farkus's wife will be with you. They wouldn't be foolhardy enough to attack one of their own kind in broad daylight. And even if they are, Kwadzo found the three biggest, strongest, and bravest humans among us to escort you all to the cordwainer."

"What that? I's s'posed to be gettin' shoes. I gots to go to the cobbler."

"Cobblers only fix shoes. Law says they can't make them. You'll have to go to the cordwainer for that."

Gertie could only blink back at the smiling Irene with a twinge of jealousy. Between being a former house slave and now a Ramangan, she wondered how much more Irene knew about the world than she did.

"Kwadzo found out from Doc Farkus," Irene said with a gentle shrug, as if she could read Gertie's thoughts. Gertie wondered for a moment if she could. Ramangan Blood was still such a mystery. It made Irene so vicious and powerful she could tear a man to shreds, and yet here her touch was incredibly gentle as the woman fixed her hair. There was no trace of the monster she was capable of being on her face.

"Don't you miss nothin' 'bout bein' 'live? Bein' human? Food? Sunshine? Nothin'?"

Gertie watched Irene's smile fade and felt guilty for pressing the issue.

"Only thing I miss in this whole world is my mama." Tears welled in Irene's eyes even as her gleeful smile returned. "But now, thanks to Kwadzo, I won't have to miss her for much longer. He's going to free all the slaves, and I'll do anything to make sure she's one of the first."

"Wish I had me a purpose strong as you."

"You do."

Gertie rolled her eyes. "Ain't talkin' 'bout the baby. 'Course I's gonna love the baby . . ."

"I'm not talking about the baby. Kwadzo speaks for those of us of the Blood, but you represent the rest of us. The humans who deserve to be free just as much as we do. You going into town, dressed like a proper lady, that will show them we are not the simple savages they think we are. Now, they get to see a beautiful African woman in their presence. Not a slave, but a lady just as beautiful as any proper white lady. Kwadzo has shown them our strength. You will show them our grace."

No words came to Gertie, only happy tears.

What need do we have
of their society?

Seven

Grace

The sensation Gertie felt as she stepped outside of the manor was overwhelming. Yes, she had spent most of her time working outdoors, but this was much different. The hot sun beating down on her on the paddy was replaced by a pleasant summer breeze wafting through the trees. Instead of squinting from the brightness of the sunshine, her eyes were open and relaxed under the shade of the lace hat she wore. The sour scent of the water on the rice paddy had been exchanged for the aroma of jessamine flowers, and the sound of her feet sloshing around in that water no longer rang in her ears. In its place was the cheerful chirping of birds.

The comfort of the dress she had worn when she'd served lunch to the Barrows with Irene had felt awkward enough, but the fabrics she was adorned in now were a cut above. The gown was so soft against her skin that it made her feel even more out of place. It didn't help that the small tapestry bag hanging from her wrist on a chain handle, one of Mistress Barrow's possessions, was filled with money that once belonged to the man she used to call Master.

When he gave her the money, Kwadzo offered an explanation that aligned with Irene's rationalization for her wearing the clothing: The Africans who had slaved away in the fields were the ones who had made the money Barrow claimed as his own; with him gone, it now belonged to them. Gertie supposed neither of them were wrong, but she still felt like she was carrying stolen goods.

"Might I say you look lovely in that gown, Miss Gertie," Rebecca Farkus said. "Far lovelier than that, that, that shabbaroon Charity Barrow!"

The woman nodded with a proud smirk. Gertie had no idea what a shabbaroon was, but she suspected it wasn't a compliment. Rebecca had made no secret of her disdain for the Barrows or her fascination with the Ramangans, and though she had yet to be cruel, Gertie remained wary of her. If she could turn on her own kind so easily, how long would it take for her to turn against the Africans?

"I am most contrite if you find my language crude," said Rebecca, who awaited Gertie on the porch steps in finery of her own.

"I thanks you kindly for your honey words, Mistress Farkus," Gertie said, "but I ain't understand none of them other words you say."

Rebecca laughed. It was a good-natured laugh, one that Gertie didn't feel diminished by.

"My goodness me!" Rebecca said. "You must forgive me. I remain amazed at how much was kept from you and your people. A shabbaroon is an unpleasant word for an unpleasant person, someone mean-spirited, which Charity Barrow certainly was. And to be contrite is to be sorry, which I truly am if my words offend you."

"No, I's fine," Gertie said with an amused smile. Rebecca seemed genuinely concerned for her. Perhaps the trip would be more pleasurable than she thought.

"If I may be so bold, the yellow suits you. I find your hair to be even more becoming. The contrast in tones of your hair and skin against the color of the dress is simply divine. And your hair—it looks so terribly soft. Might I touch it?"

"Why?"

"Pardon?"

"Why you wanna touch my hair? You wants me to touch your hair?"

"I suppose not."

Rebecca's smile dimmed, which amused Gertie even more. She'd found it to be such an odd request, and her questioning it seemed to relieve the woman of her interest in Gertie's hair.

"I agrees with her, Miss Gertie. I thinks yellow suit you just fine."

Gertie recognized the young woman smiling next to her, also dressed in altered fashion, from the paddy, though she had never known the young woman's name. Her round cheeks dimpled when she smiled.

"I's Sadie," the young woman said before motioning to another young African woman next to her. "This here's Poppy. I don't reckon you know us, but we knows you. Irene done told us to come 'long so's we's can look after you."

"Look after me?" Gertie asked.

"Yes, of course!" Rebecca exclaimed, her smile beaming once more. "They are to serve as your lady's maids. They're here to tend to you, which is only fitting. You have become the mistress of the house, after all."

The mistress of the house. The notion had been said aloud by someone other than herself. Somehow, it felt less awkward than the clothes she was wearing.

But they were starting to feel less awkward as well.

"I reckon we's all gonna have to look after each other," Gertie said as Rebecca led them to a horse-drawn carriage. Three tall, burly men in livery suits stood in front of it. One of them opened the carriage door for the women, and they all climbed in.

The ride into town was a bumpy one, but once in the carriage, Gertie began to feel a bit like a proper lady, even in her shabby shoes. When the landscape that passed by through the window gave way to farms and houses, Gertie's hand-wringing returned. It grew faster when she caught sight of townspeople: the three-point hats of the men and the colorful parasols of the women, shielding them from the sun. Merchants of all kinds selling and trading wares, fruits and vegetables, fur pelts, and the like. And each face that caught sight of her was filled with more fury than the last.

She swallowed back a lump in her throat as the carriage passed by the auction block in the town square where Africans were being sold: their eyes darting around, their limbs wrestling with heavy chains, their naked bodies covered in sweat, their hearts choked with fear. She remembered when it was her on that block, her family dead, voices shouting at her in a tongue she couldn't understand, the weight of the metal confining her, the fear and loathing and helplessness coursing through her simultaneously.

Her heart wept for them. But the good was coming. That she knew. She chose to take quiet solace in that knowledge and returned her thoughts to the purpose of her trip. As the carriage passed a manor where slaves were tending to the front lawn, a group of white men, thunder clouding their faces, rushed over the fence with iron crowbars and chains, charging for the working slaves. Gertie's blood began to boil.

"This is a disgrace! An outright disgrace!"

While Gertie appreciated Rebecca's impassioned sentiment, she was wrong. This was well beyond disgraceful. This was a disgusting display of violence, and no one was doing anything to stop it. These poor men and women were being punished for Kwadzo's victory. It was the most cowardly brand of vengeance she had ever witnessed. Her eyes grew dark, and her sorrow was replaced with a fury she could not contain. She punched her fist against the roof of the carriage.

"Stop!"

Before the carriage came to a complete stop and despite Rebecca calling after her, Gertie was stepping out of it. If she could not free slaves herself, she could at least stand in the way of those bringing them harm. She ran to the fence as fast as she could while townspeople passing by glowered at her action.

"Stop!" she yelled at the white men. "Leave them be!"

A splatter of blood sprang from the head of a slave struck with an iron crowbar; it landed on Gertie's face. The man wielding the weapon stepped over the slave's body and moved toward her with a menacing growl.

"I'll be damned if I let some Negress tell me what to do! 'Specially a thievin', lyin' Negress like you!"

"And I'll be damned if I allow you to lay a hand on her!" Rebecca said, having rushed to join Gertie. "This isn't even your land! These people have done nothing to you!"

"They ain't people!" the man shouted as his band gathered around him. "And since you and Doc Farkus done abandoned your own for them blackies, I reckon y'all ain't people no more neither."

"How dare you, sir!" Rebecca said. "My husband and I are citizens of Lakeside, just as everyone living on the Crimson Plantation is, the same as the Barrows were."

"What in tarnation is going on out here?"

The mistress of the house exited the front door to take in the scene. Confusion covered her face as Gertie turned to her.

"These men, they done took it upon theyselves to attack these poor folks for no good reason," she said as the mistress frowned.

"How dare you look me in the eye and speak to me in such a manner!" the mistress growled. "My slaves are no concern of yours unless you've learned your lesson and are ready to get back to work where you belong."

Gertie was left dumbfounded as the white men cheered the mistress on for her comment.

"Have you no caring at all?" Rebecca asked the mistress. "Even if you are ignorant and evil enough to regard human beings as property, do you truly care nothing for your own property? Have you no desire to stop the action of men who would destroy your property against your will?"

"The slaves are none of my concern. My husband tends to them along with the overseers."

"Well, where are they? I should hope they would be willing to protect your husband's investment."

"They are tending to the ones in the fields. These are the house slaves. When my husband returns from his travels, he will be made aware of all, including the abomination that happened on the Barrow plantation."

"So, you are willing to let your own slaves get beaten by men who are of no consequence to you?"

"I don't know what's worse: niggers or nigger lovers," the man spat at Rebecca.

"Slaves are slaves," the mistress said. "They are tools that are easily replaced."

"All due respect, ma'am," the man said to the mistress, "all the niggers 'round here need to be put straight after what happened. Them niggers killed Barrow, killed his whole family, killed the good Minister Easton, they killed the goddamn governor! Left us without no direction. They killed planters and left slaves without masters. Now these slaves get to thinkin' they can just do as they please? No, sir! We got to do somethin' 'bout it, but instead of stickin' by your own people, y'all just up and joined them! Seemed to a lot of us that y'all wouldn't be needin' that house of yours no more. So, we burned it down."

The man's laughter was joined by the band of white men behind him. Rebecca stared back at them in wide-eyed shock, and Gertie shook her head. Rebecca and her husband were now hated purely because of their association with her people. It seemed the loathing of Lakeside residents knew no bounds. A crowd was forming, watching the proceedings, but not one of them bothered to intervene. The men's laughter ended, however, when Rebecca, her face red with anger, spat in the face of the man who had taunted her.

"You little, little man," she hissed.

"Looks like you need some correctin', too," the man growled, and the band of white men moved toward her, rowdier and more aggressive. The girthy Africans who piloted the horse and carriage stepped in front of Gertie and Rebecca to form a protective wall.

"I don't care what powers you demon niggers got," the man hollered out at the Africans who towered over them. "You *all* gonna die today! Come on, boys!"

"Stop it! Stop this instant!"

The voice, sharp but soft and very feminine, stopped the men, and Gertie turned to the onlookers to find its owner. An auburn-haired woman who Gertie figured was no older than she was emerged from the gathered throng. She was dressed from head to toe in the finest silk, but her presence seemed to stoke the ire of the men more than Rebecca's did.

"Is there some sort of nigger-lovers meetin' happenin' we don't know about?" the man said, mocking the auburn-haired young woman, who seemed to ignore the comment out of concern for Gertie.

"Are you all right?"

Despite the warmth in her voice, the gentle touch of the young woman's hand on her arm made Gertie jerk away involuntarily. It had completely caught her off guard. She recognized the compassion she was being shown, but it was coming from someone she did not know, and certainly not someone from whom she expected such kindness. The young woman's brow seemed to crinkle with true worry.

"You poor dear; of course you're not," the young woman said. "How frightened you must be." Gertie blinked as the young woman fumbled in the small pouch she carried and pulled a clean handkerchief from it. "Are you hurt? Is this your blood?"

With the groans and whimpers of pain from the injured slaves ringing in her ears, Gertie had grown annoyed with her own inaction. She may not have had Ramangan Blood, but she could still stand by her people. She would not let them suffer alone. So, she tore a strip of fabric from her gown.

"No, ma'am," Gertie told the young woman. "But they needs help more than me."

Gertie took a step toward the lawn only to have the white men block her path.

"Where you think you goin', Negress?"

Her heart pounded, but Gertie remembered what Irene had said.

You will show them our grace.

To Gertie, grace was just another word for doing good. No matter what happened to her, she had to do good. So, she took a step around the men to get to the lawn, and they intentionally boxed her in.

"Let her through."

The young woman's command went unheeded.

"The governor is dead," the man said to her. "You ain't got no say 'round here."

"Perhaps not," she said with a smirk, "but you forget that my father is Lord Proprietor of this land. And in my grief over my dearly departed husband, the violence visited upon Doctor and Missus Farkus's home, and the accosting of slaves which do not belong to you, I may find myself strongly suggesting to him that some of the land grants you all benefit from be rescinded." The young woman moved to Rebecca and clasped her hands in dramatic fashion. "After all your husband has given to the citizens of Lakeside, and this is how he is repaid. I am so sorry."

"And now, these men would have me fear for my very life for simply accompanying those who showed us kindness," Rebecca responded in equally dramatic fashion. "Had it not been for the generous nature of the victorious slaves of the Barrow Plantation, we would be left unhoused."

Gertie had no idea what the two white women were doing or why they were doing it, but it wasn't helping her help the injured slaves. She made another attempt to get to the lawn, and two men blocked her path just before two of the African men stood in front of her.

"Move or get moved," one of them said.

"Why you uppity . . ." One of the white men raised an iron bar to attack, unfazed by the size of the Africans. But his wrist was caught and twisted by one of the towering African men so sharply that the bar fell to the ground. The white man whimpered as he dropped to his knees in pain, unable to break free from the man's grasp.

"I been just itchin' to hurt me a white man for a long time," the man said with a sneer while Gertie took the opportunity to rush to the man whose blood she had been splattered with. Taking his bleeding head into her lap, she quickly wrapped her piece of torn material around his head wound. With a path to the lawn cleared, the two young African women who accompanied Gertie moved to help the other wounded slaves as best they could. Soon, Gertie was joined by the auburn-haired young woman and Rebecca on the lawn while the white men glared in angry silence.

"Might you be willing to spare Doctor Farkus?" Gertie heard the young woman ask her. "There are other physicians, but none as good as Doc Farkus, and also, I can't be sure what their reaction will be to this particular situation, and these people need immediate attention."

Gertie looked to Rebecca, who was diligently helping the others, and found the woman staring back at her in silence. She realized then that Rebecca was respecting her as the mistress of Crimson Manor—it was Gertie's decision to make. Turning back to the young woman, Gertie gave a nod and watched as a fire rose in the young woman's hazel eyes.

"Is there any among you good enough to rush back to Barrow Manor and fetch Doc Farkus?"

The vigilantes and the crowd answered her request with silence until one of the white men spoke out.

"Let them niggers go back and get him!"

"So that these women are left unprotected from the likes of you?" the young woman spat back. "Shame on you! Shame on all of you!"

"No! Shame on you for speaking up for them," one of the men said. "These demon niggers done changed everythin', and now this Negress is walkin' 'round in Mistress Barrow's clothes! If we don't keep the rest in line now, ain't no tellin' what will happen!"

Murmurs of agreement began to rise from the crowd, but the young woman turned to address them all.

"It seems you all have forgotten why you came here. Most of you came for freedom. Political freedom. Religious freedom. Economic freedom. But while you were pursuing your freedoms, you took them away from the people you call your slaves."

"Slaves ain't people!" a shout came from amid the crowd, followed by a wave of vocal concurrence. Gertie kept her eyes fixed on the young white woman, who seemed to stand even taller in the face of the opposition.

"If they are not people, then they are something far stronger, and dare I say, better, far better than how they've been treated. After what happened on the Barrow Plantation, we should all consider ourselves lucky to still be alive. I barely escaped the wrath of their leader and his fire. Yes, the rumors are true: One among them spews fire from his mouth. Had I not run when I did, his flame would surely have ended me.

"And yet, he did not pursue me until my end. I found justice in his actions. It is true I have been outspoken in my disagreement with the enslavement of the Africans, both here and in the Old World. With the power these Africans possess, they would be well within their rights to turn the tide on us, yet every one of you walks free. That is by their grace—grace, all things considered, we certainly do not deserve."

Loud murmurs of disapproval rose from the crowd as the young woman knelt next to Gertie.

"Pay them no mind," she said as Gertie looked up at her. There was an earnest sincerity in the woman's eyes that Gertie could not let go unmentioned.

"Thank you kindly for what you say 'bout us," Gertie said.

"It's the least I can do."

"All I's wanted was some new shoes," Gertie said lowly, half to herself.

"My name is Sarah Collins. I am—was—the governor's wife." Sarah extended her hand, but Gertie's were full and occupied applying pressure to the head wound of the maimed slave. Sarah shook her head, and Gertie smiled.

"Of course. Forgive my ignorance."

"I reckon you ain't accustomed to this sort of thing."

"And it pains me to think you are. I do not share my late husband's sentiments, or those of many Lakeside citizens for that matter, on many things, which led to more than a few household disagreements before my husband's demise," Sarah said with a chuckle. "My goodness, with the governor gone, I fear I am no longer Sarah Collins. I suppose I don't know exactly who I am anymore. May I?" she asked, presenting her handkerchief to Gertie once again.

This time, Gertie nodded and allowed Sarah to wipe the blood from her face. She was gentle, careful, thorough. The two women locked eyes for the duration of the process, and Gertie felt something akin to the sensation of safety in Sarah's presence. There had been plenty of hateful shouting since her appearance, but no one else had been attacked. Not yet, anyway.

"There. That's better," Sarah whispered.

Gertie was once again at a loss at being the recipient of this woman's tender kindness. This white woman of some obvious note had helped her. She was a world away from Charity and Virginia Barrow. She surmised that Rebecca did not share the same station as Sarah and the Barrows, and she wondered how three women from the same social circle could be so very different.

"I reckon without a husband you can be whoever you wants to be." Gertie shrunk a bit in discomfort at the intense look her words elicited from Sarah.

"I suppose so," Sarah said, as if coming to a revelation. She paused before shifting her shoulders and emitting a small, nervous laugh. "Well, I do hope I've fostered enough goodwill that you won't want to drink my blood."

"Oh, we ain't all of the Blood," Gertie said. "Most of us is livin' humans, same as you."

Sarah's shoulders relaxed, and she released a long exhale. "That's good to know."

"I's Gertie."

Sarah smiled. "Nice to meet you, Gertie."

"You say you escaped my Kwadzo's flame?"

"You there!"

Their attention was pulled to a grand red carriage led by two black horses that came to a stop in front of the lawn. The carriage door opened, and Gertie found her brow raised in surprise once again. Before her was an African man, dressed in even finer materials than Sarah was. His skin was clear and dark, his jaw chiseled; he somehow looked both youthful and mature at the same time. Gold shimmered on his fingers as he remained cloaked in the shade of his carriage. He leaned a touch forward on an onyx cane with a ruby knob handle.

"I heard your call and sent my emissary to find the Barrow Plantation to fetch this Doc Farkus. Has there been a successful uprising here?" the African man asked.

"Why, yes," Sarah said, her brow crinkled in confusion. "Thank you . . ."

Her words trailed off as Gertie, having placed the slave she was helping in Rebecca's care, stood to get a closer look at the man.

"What plantation you from?" she asked.

The African man laughed hard and deep. It was not a menacing laugh, but his smooth and mysterious voice made it jarring.

"Dear lady, I have never worked on any plantation. I am a free man from New France."

"New France? Ain't that in the North?"

"Very much so."

"And you know 'bout us? The uprisin'?"

"I sensed a shift, shall we say, and came to see if my premonition was true."

Gertie took note of how clear his speech was. She figured it to be a by-product of his freedom. Still, her brow furrowed at the long, new word. She didn't dare try to repeat it.

"Beg pardon?" Gertie asked instead.

"He means to say that he has had an intuition," Sarah whispered in her ear. "A feeling that something was different here."

"How you gets a feelin' 'bout somethin' so far 'way from where you be?" Gertie asked.

"I would love to pay you and your people a visit and meet the man responsible for your successful revolt. I believe we have much to discuss. In the meantime, I have every confidence that my emissary shall find the doctor and bring him directly. Till we meet again."

With a smile, the African man closed the door of his carriage. Gertie watched it travel away, her head spinning. It had been quite an eventful trip already. She told herself that it would be some time before she decided to venture out again.

Eight

One of Us

Kwadzo felt his jaw tightening. There was much to discuss. The destruction of the Farkuses' home and what to do about it, and them. The Africans he'd emancipated from Lakeside after white men attacked them, and the ordeal Gertie had been put through while witnessing the attack. Then there was her strange encounter with a white woman who claimed to have escaped his flame, and a mysterious free African who he was fairly certain was connected to the equally obscure white man who came to the door of Crimson Manor, alerted him to the news of the slaves being attacked, and requested the assistance of Doc Farkus. There was also the matter of the redheaded girl who had ingested Fanna's blood that he still hadn't told anyone about.

Yes, there was much for the council to discuss. But not all the council members were present in the room where they met. Kwadzo was still waiting for the most important member to join him and the rest. The one who could provide the most insight, the one who had been of the Blood the longest.

The one who had made him.

"Ain't got no respect," Gertie muttered next to him. He was inclined to agree with her, but he didn't have the luxury. Leadership was a new concept to Kwadzo, and he needed guidance.

"I'm sure he'll be here soon."

"Shall I go up and remind him?" Irene asked.

"No," Gertie barked. "Don't go get him. He know where he s'posed to be, but he laid up with them girls just bitin' on them and drinkin' they's blood like he ain't got a care in the world . . ."

"Enough!"

It was sterner than he had intended, but Gertie's frustration with Rafazi mirrored his own. He owed his maker everything, but he was also appointed a leader by him. Kwadzo had no idea where the boundary was. Was he to lead his maker along with everyone else?

Nez entered the room, followed by Seneca. "More of your people come," Nez said.

Kwadzo felt the woman's eyes on him just as he heard Gertie's blood quicken.

"Why you no tell?" Nez asked.

"I didn't exactly know they'd be joining us."

"Must tell!"

"What?"

"You have to let us know when you bring in more people, Kwadzo," Seneca said, casually looking around the room. "Three or four showing up here is one thing, but this was a decision you made without us."

"You can't just come walkin' up in here! This here a council meetin', and you ain't on the council! 'Sides, he ain't got to tell *you* nothin'!" Gertie growled.

"Yes, he does," Seneca replied calmly. "We made an agreement to share the land and all it provides. That includes food, clothing, shelter."

"That makes sense," Ekow said, gazing at Seneca with soft eyes. The sight made Kwadzo roll his own.

"As I've said, I didn't know they were going to be joining us. Gertie saw them being attacked on her trip into town, and I had them brought back here for their safety."

"Are they staying?" Seneca asked.

"As I said, they were brought here for their safety, and I will no longer leave any of my people in harm's way. They say they worked on the Peterson farm, so I suspect Mister Peterson will seek their return. We have many things we need to discuss."

"Very well," Seneca said as she took a seat at the table next to Ekow, who seemed very pleased with the development.

Both Gertie and Nez protested Seneca's action, but it was Fanna who caught Kwadzo's attention. Sitting at the end of the table, she furrowed her brow, and her eyes went red for a moment as she rubbed her temples as if she were in pain. The moment seemed to pass as quickly as it came, but it gave Kwadzo pause. There was an ever-so-slight stirring in his blood that dissipated quickly as well.

Had she just sensed the girl and not known?

Before he could approach Fanna, Rafazi's blur raced into the room, and he was standing with two women when it settled: one African, the other Native, both with arms wrapped around him and giggling incessantly. The Native raised an arm to his mouth, and with a smile, Rafazi bit into her arm. The eyes of every Ramangan in the room flashed red.

Including Kwadzo's.

They reverted to their human hue when Gertie smacked his arm a bit harder than he thought was necessary.

"Took you long enough," Gertie murmured at Rafazi.

"Forgive me. I was unaware that I was to keep the timetable of someone who is not of the Blood," Rafazi said. Kwadzo's heart fell at the diminishing goodwill between Gertie and his maker.

"*I* am of the Blood, Rafazi," Kwadzo said, his frustration getting the better of him.

"And I am here," Rafazi responded, with a chuckle copied by the women with him.

"We have much to discuss," Kwadzo said as Rafazi sat. His companions took their places on his lap.

"Then, let's discuss," Rafazi said. All eyes turned to Kwadzo, and the tension in the room rose.

"Your father seeks you, Halona," Seneca leaned forward to say to the Native woman on Rafazi's lap in their native tongue. "Perhaps it's time you return to him."

"You seem as comfortable here as me," Halona retorted in the same language. "There's no need for me to go if there's no need for you to."

"Both of you need to go!" Nez said. "All of us need to. Now!"

"I disagree," Seneca said, her eyes on Kwadzo. "I find it odd that Chief Great Oak has not been invited to this discussion. If decisions about what goes on here are being made in this room, it is only fair that our people are represented. Don't you think, Kwadzo?"

"I have no objection," Rafazi said. "After all, Gertie is not of the Blood but sits with the council. Why shouldn't Seneca?"

Kwadzo knew it wasn't what she wanted to hear, but Rafazi's comment kept Gertie quiet on the matter of Seneca, and having said his piece seemed to keep him silent and refocused on his female acquaintances. With neither Seneca nor Halona moving, Nez stomped out of the room.

"Well?" Rafazi asked, his gaze now focused on Kwadzo. "What is so urgent?"

"I sent Gertie into town today with a group of our people, and things did not go well. Slaves were being beaten . . ."

"Surprise, surprise," Rafazi interrupted before nuzzling the neck of the giggling African woman on his lap. Kwadzo swallowed back his frustration. He was certain that Rafazi would come to understand the seriousness of the issue once he'd heard the entire story.

"Gertie tried to stop it and found the aid of a white woman."

That statement got the attention of everyone in the room, including Rafazi.

"She say her name Sarah Collins," Gertie said. "Say she the governor's wife."

"The dead governor?" Rafazi asked.

"She say she was here the night Kwadzo took this here manor from Ol' Barrow, say she got burnt by Kwadzo's flame but run 'way. She help me and Rebecca keep them men away so we's could help them 'til Doc Farkus come."

"Those white folks are making them pay the price for what we did here," Irene said.

"Which is why I had them brought back here," Kwadzo said. "But I suspect liberating them in such a manner will have repercussions."

"Well, how many do you plan to liberate to this land?" Seneca asked. "Because at this rate, we will run out of food and space and need to go to battle to gain more."

"'Course there gonna be more battle, you dumb girl!" Gertie barked. "They's still sellin' us. I done seen it. They's still bringin' us here and sellin' us off on the block, like Kwadzo ain't done a damn thing to set it right!"

"And you think my people don't suffer?" Seneca asked harshly. "You think we haven't lost people to the white man's violence and hate? And do you think we did nothing but cower in fear until Kwadzo came along? My people have been fighting these colonists long before you were even born!"

"Both our peoples have suffered," Kwadzo said calmly but firmly. "And both our peoples need to be free, no matter the plantation or the tribe."

"So, how do we do it?" Ekow asked.

The question turned Kwadzo's eyes to Rafazi, who stared back at him in silence. Kwadzo's blood heated up with anger. He had assumed that Rafazi would be the one guiding and advising him along. But he wasn't. Kwadzo shook his head with quiet realization. Rafazi had called himself a coward, someone interested only in their own immediate yearnings. It was the reason he survived the plague while the rest of his kind perished, and it had afforded Kwadzo the opportunity to successfully topple Barrow and his acolytes, but now the real work had to begin.

One plantation in one town was one thing. But there were more colonies in this New World and countless plantations. While Kwadzo was lighting the crimson flame of freedom in celebration with his people and the Natives, countless Africans remained in bondage.

Gertie was right: They did all deserve to be free from the violent control of the colonists—the Indigenous tribes included—but waging ambush after ambush to do so would be costly and bloody. Kwadzo knew that taking such a relentlessly ferocious course of action would make them the savages they were already thought to be. This new world, for better or for worse, would have to be shared in a civil manner. Respect would have to become the new order of the day, and for him to earn it, he had to show that he could run the plantation just as well as Barrow did, if not better. And that meant selling crops.

"I'm not exactly sure," Kwadzo said in answer to Ekow, "but more bloodshed will only bring even more bloodshed. They should, however, respect money. We'll find this Peterson and buy their freedom from him. We'll show them that we can conduct business as they do. Once they see that we can, we'll secure a merchant for our crops. Between that and our power, they'll have no choice but to accept our presence as equal to theirs."

"Except we aren't equal," Rafazi said. "Their blood is our food. They don't consider the animals they eat equal to them. Neither should we."

"Not all of our people are of the Blood," Kwadzo replied, as if he were being tested. "They need to respect the humans in our numbers as equals. We need to be better than these white colonists *and* the Ramanga of yore. They know our force. Now, we will show them our savvy."

Kwadzo saw approval on the faces of everyone in the room. His eyes sought out Rafazi, but his maker was preoccupied with the neckline of the African woman on his lap. A low red hue emanated from the Ramangans again as the African woman moaned from Rafazi gently biting into her neck. While he drank, her hand found its way into his pants while Halona nibbled at his ear.

Was Rafazi completely uninterested in the freedom of their people? This plan and the path toward it were, after all, his.

"Forgive me, brother," Rafazi said, pulling away from the woman's neck and wiping the excess blood from his lips with a finger he promptly sucked, "but I fear I'm needed elsewhere." He rose with the women and started for the door.

That's when Kwadzo's own vision went red.

"We are not done."

"You seem to be," Rafazi said. "You've identified your problem and came to a solution. Just as a leader does."

"There is still the question of how we should approach the Lakeside population, how we should house the new ones, how we will accommodate more . . ."

"Where we's gonna put Doc Farkus and his wife?" Gertie interjected while Kwadzo took her in with confusion. "They done burned they's house down. They ain't gots nowhere else to go."

Amid the heated discussion, this fact had slipped Kwadzo's mind.

"One thing at a time, brother." Rafazi once again turned for the door.

"There is also the matter of the free African Gertie met in town."

Rafazi's attention had finally been captured. "What free African?"

"Ain't say no name," Gertie said. "But he was wearin' finery like the rich white folks got and had him a big ol' fine-lookin' carriage. Had him a stick with a red stone on the top of it, like the one on the ring Kwadzo took from Barrow, but bigger. Said he had him a feelin' 'bout the uprisin'—said he was gonna send somebody to come get Doc Farkus."

"I think that someone he sent is the white man who showed up here and alerted me to the situation in town. Which means, at the very least, he's rich enough to have a white servant," Kwadzo added.

Gertie nodded. "Say he from a place he call New France."

"What do you mean, he had a feeling?" Rafazi asked, suddenly very focused.

"He say he knew 'bout what happen. Say he had a feelin' there be a shift."

Rafazi's cavalier demeanor was gone. A look of genuine concern clouded his features, and oddly enough, it relaxed Kwadzo. He had thought Rafazi was past caring about the continued plight of their people, but clearly, he just needed something to drag his attention away from his baser instincts. Finally, his maker had returned to him.

"Don't worry, brother," Kwadzo said with a smile. "We will find him, I'm sure. A free African in Carolina will be hard to miss."

Rafazi was already backing out of the room again, but Kwadzo still needed his guidance on perhaps the most important issue of all. "There's also the matter of Fanna's spawn." Both Fanna and Rafazi turned to him with wide eyes, so he addressed Fanna first. "In the heat of battle, you were bitten in the leg by a young white girl. You kicked her away and continued to fight, but before you did, she ingested your blood."

"A white girl took the Blood?" Rafazi's eyes were red now, his nostrils flaring.

"During the heat of battle, I believe so, yes," Kwadzo answered.

"Why haven't you told me about this?"

"Because we were in the thick of the fight and Barrow had to be dealt with."

"He's been dealt with for a month now. Why haven't you told me?"

"You've been a bit preoccupied for the past month."

The two men were standing face to face now, red glowing in both their eyes. The room was deathly silent save for the rapidly beating hearts of the humans in the room, and Kwadzo suspected that, were his heart still a living one, it would have been beating twice as fast as theirs. This was the first time he felt Rafazi's anger directed toward him, and despite his smaller size, it made his maker ominous. Fear wasn't something Kwadzo had felt much since taking the Blood, but there was definitely a sense of it running through him now.

"All right, now, y'all; that's enough, now," Gertie said, but neither he nor Rafazi moved or looked away from each other. It had become a battle of wills, one that added to Kwadzo's exasperation. Here he had been made leader, and yet, the one who had bestowed him with the responsibility, who showed no interest in the position himself, was now questioning his authority. In battle, choices must be made, and Kwadzo had made the choice that would free his people. The white girl was collateral damage, and she would be found and dealt with, but he would not cower now.

"So, a white girl has the Blood, but my people are denied it?" Seneca's question broke the silence and turned Kwadzo away from Rafazi, but it did not remove the red from his vision.

"The white girl's attack was a casualty of battle. It was not anticipated. The Blood was not gifted," Kwadzo explained.

"It was stolen," Rafazi said as he moved to Fanna. "Like they steal everything else." Fanna blinked in fright as Rafazi leaned in close. "Can you sense her, child?"

"Sense her?" Fanna stuttered softly.

"Do you sense her?" Rafazi barked, making Fanna jump before Gertie moved to pull her away from him.

"You ain't got no cause to be yellin' at po' Fanna! She fought just as hard as you for this here freedom, you leave her be!"

"Leave her be?" Rafazi asked incredulously. "Have you forgotten how brutal the white folks were when they were just humans? This girl could be turning them in Lakeside right now!"

"It's been a month, and we've heard nothing of the kind," Kwadzo said with a tempered tone. As he calmed and regained control of himself, his red vision cleared. He was chosen to be leader; he simply needed to act like one. And that meant maintaining order. "Gertie saw nothing when she went into town. But I agree, she must be found. She may still be alive, wandering around alone in the wilderness."

"Or she's dead," Rafazi said.

"And if she is, she is clueless, hungry, and without guidance. And if she has truly turned, she needs to be brought home," Kwadzo said.

"Brought home?" Gertie asked with a crinkled brow.

"If she took in enough of Fanna's blood to die and turn, then she is of the Blood. She is one of us."

Kwadzo couldn't believe the words he'd said, but they were true.

Go back to Hell!
I will show you
no mercy!

Nine

Disregard of the Father

Rafazi feared he'd made the wrong choice.

The very notion of this white girl ran afoul of the legacy of Ramanga. Yes, there were those who had sold the Blood at a premium to Europeans and others outside of the Tribe, but there was always a gain for the Tribe. This time, the Blood was ripped from one of their own—stolen. And now, after centuries of absence, the one he'd chosen to lead this new Tribe, the one spawned from his very blood, was intent on embracing the thief.

It was a horrible way to have his night interrupted.

There had also been much talk of all that Kwadzo had done. Kwadzo. There would be no Kwadzo if it hadn't been for him. It was his idea, his blood, that made all of this possible. That seemed to have been so quickly forgotten. And while he was content to remain in his bedchamber indulging in willing women and feasting on their blood, respect should still be shown for who he was. Rafazi Yeboah, father of the New

Ramanga Tribe. His blood should be revered. He shouldn't have to lead for his contribution to be appreciated and highly esteemed.

Feared.

Even by the leader.

"It was not my wish for this girl to have the Blood, Rafazi," Kwadzo said to him, "but if she carries it, that is what she is. If she has turned, she has the power to be our adversary or our greatest ally. We have to find her and welcome her."

The red in Rafazi's eyes cleared upon hearing Kwadzo's words. As much as he was annoyed by the treatment he'd received, his progeny's reasoning did make sense. Still, he was in no hurry to acquiesce. Though Kwadzo had stood strong, Rafazi had sensed not only his fear but that of everyone else in the room.

He had centuries on all of them. All their ages combined didn't even add up to a third of his entire existence. They all needed to be reminded that their fear of him was well placed for a little while longer.

So, he kept silent and let Kwadzo continue.

"It could be advantageous to have one of our Blood among them," Kwadzo said, a hopeful lilt to his voice. "We'll teach Fanna to use her binding to help find the wayward girl." He braved raising a hand and resting it on Rafazi's shoulder. "The path forward requires a unified front, brother. I understand you may not wish to accept the girl, but doing so might serve the greater good of us all."

"She could be killed," Rafazi offered curtly. "That would be a simpler solution."

"You cain't kill no child!" Gertie protested. "Kwadzo right. If'n she got Ramanga blood, then she Ramanga. You cain't kill your own kind."

There was no point arguing with her. Kwadzo would side with her reasoning, as it aligned with his own. Once again,

Rafazi feared choosing him was misguided. After everything he'd been through, was Kwadzo so naïve as to think he could achieve his goals without bloodshed? Even this system Kwadzo had implemented of having humans donate a little of their blood at a time would eventually grow tiresome. They were creatures of bloodlust. They would soon be yearning for the hunt. Just that one trait had taken him centuries to gain full control over.

They weren't human anymore. Human reasoning hadn't defeated Barrow, violent power had. Killing was a necessary part of the path forward, as Kwadzo called it. The girl was not just a child: She was a child with the capacity to spread Ramangan power to the ones who had oppressed them for at least a century.

Their very existence depended on bloodthirstiness. So would the white girl's, and anyone she gave the Blood to.

"We must gather everyone," Kwadzo continued. "We've basked in our first victory long enough. Plans must be made to find the girl before the white folks do and start freeing the slaves on the other plantations."

Kwadzo's voice was filled with such fervent purpose that it made Rafazi chuckle. "Basked in our victory long enough? We just *finished* doing battle. Honestly, Kwadzo. You are making something very easy much harder than it needs to be."

"What do you mean?"

"As I've said, we just finished doing battle. We won. And each time they try to retaliate against us, they lose again. By now, all of Lakeside, all of Carolina knows this. All you need to do is send one or two of us of the Blood to a plantation in the dead of night, have them turn as many as they can, and repeat there what we did here. All you needed was me. Trust me, no plantation's slaves will have to fight as hard as we had to. We will terrify the white folks into submission."

"I fear there is too much brutality in your plan."

"Were they not brutal to us?"

"Those who were have paid the price. But if terror buys our freedom, it really isn't freedom at all. Now, come. There is much to do."

Rafazi stiffened at being given an order.

He had assigned Kwadzo as *their* leader because *they* needed leadership.

He didn't.

As night began to fall, Kwadzo stood at the front of the newly refurbished great room in the manor with the eyes of several women, both African and Indigenous, on him as he fed from the neck of one he did not know. It hadn't escaped him that a good number of women clamored for the opportunity to feed him. Some bit their bottom lips, others licked their lips, but all their faces were awash in adoration.

All but Gertie's.

Over the course of the past month, several of the humans, both African and Indigenous, male and female, had volunteered to give of their blood to the Ramangans to help keep them nourished and prevent them from rampaging. They had been instructed to tap the shoulder of the Ramangan who fed from them at the first sign of light-headedness to ensure their safety and quick recovery.

To keep things civil, Kwadzo, in conjunction with the council, set ground rules:

Ramangans were instructed to dislodge as soon as they were tapped.

Ramangans assigned to protective patrol of the manor were to space out their feedings three days apart to keep them at top strength should they need to wage battle.

Ramangans who worked in the fields at night or in the house were to space their feedings six days apart.

A small percentage of the livestock was set aside for feeding as well, and Ramangans, if they were feeling particularly ravenous, were free to roam the wilderness and feed on whatever animals they could find. This also kept them sharp and ready for battle. Some even returned with extra animals for the flock.

No Ramangan was to go into Lakeside and feed on its citizens.

All of this was well and good, and Gertie understood the necessity of the situation. But she took exception to so many of the women offering their blood to Kwadzo, especially since he had to taste their flesh to get to it. To eliminate jealousy, who he fed from was her decision. There were far more women begging to be fed from than men, and more often than not, Gertie was left unhappy with her choice.

The African woman he was feeding from now had begun to moan, and she wrapped her arms around his neck as Kwadzo dislodged his fangs from her. She gave a pout as he released her, and he found Gertie, her arms crossed, pouting just the same. It was all he could do to hold in his amusement.

"I *need* blood. I *want* you. There is a difference," he said to her softly, wiping the excess blood from his lips before leaning in to kiss her. But Gertie's arms remained crossed, and her pout lingered.

"There better be."

With a smile, Kwadzo stole a kiss from her cheek and watched her fight against the smile it had given her. That was all he needed before he addressed those who had gathered; even more people were crowding into the room.

"My people!"

They fell into silence, and just like that, Kwadzo had their rapt attention. "Our time of celebration is over," he began. "For as we rejoice, all through the colonies our people still suffer in bondage at the hands of men who claim them as nothing but property. Our freedom means nothing as long as they remain enslaved."

Murmurs of agreement rose from the group. Kwadzo began to walk among them with searching eyes. "At the same time, this Blood, our Ramangan Blood, was taken in by someone who has stood against us."

Kwadzo stood in front of Fanna, her eyes wide with worry as murmurs rose again.

"During the battle for this plantation, a young girl bit into Fanna's leg and took in her blood. A young white girl. If this young girl has died, she has turned. And that makes her one of us."

As the group of Indigenous and African people raised their voices in dismay, Seneca stepped forward. "We have all suffered and fought the white man on this soil," she said, addressing the Natives, "but now, a white daughter carries Ramangan Blood while our people have been denied it. Should this girl pass along the Blood to her people, it could mean devastation for us all."

Her indignation was met with a wave of accord from the Natives present before she turned to Kwadzo. "This presents a danger to all of us. The girl must be found at all costs. To be most effective, I say a select number of us be gifted the Blood so that we may contribute to this endeavor."

Immediate objection rose from the Africans, which was met with equal opposition from the Natives. These two peoples, who days ago celebrated their united bond, were now rising in conflict against one another.

"ENOUGH!" Kwadzo's roar restored quiet. "Fanna is our best chance at finding the girl. It is her blood she carries." Kwadzo moved to Fanna, who stared back at him with quaking eyes. "There is nothing to fear. You've done nothing wrong. But you are her maker. If she has turned, you can sense her—something like a disruption within you. Have you felt anything like that?"

"A few times I've felt my head pound," Fanna said. "But it quickly goes away."

"We will gather a group together to search for her tonight. Rafazi will go with you and teach you how to use your mind-bending powers to locate her."

"My presence on the hunt is unnecessary," Rafazi said, calmly but with intention. "I'm no good in a hunt. I can teach the child what she needs to know, send her on her way, and watch over things here at the manor."

Kwadzo was slow to respond. The tension building between him and Rafazi was clear to him, but he could not let that show to his people, and especially not to the Natives. Their alliance could rise or fall on the strength or weakness of one wrong word, one wrong look, one misplaced gesture. He couldn't afford that. He needed all of them.

"Good." Kwadzo nodded, gritting his teeth. "You will teach Fanna what she needs to learn, and I'll gather a group together to look for the child."

"I will join the search," Seneca volunteered as others stepped forward to be chosen.

"Very well," Kwadzo said to her before turning his attention back to Rafazi. "While we search, take a group of our people with you to the Peterson Farm . . ."

Rafazi chuckled with raised brows. "I see you have come to your senses. I will take two of the strongest we have in the Blood here and we will lay waste . . ."

"No, brother," Kwadzo interrupted. He could see the fury in Rafazi's eyes, but he kept his composure, mindful not to raise his voice. Rafazi was baiting him into conflict, but he had to rise above it and be the leader he had been chosen to be.

Even if that meant defying his maker.

"Not only will we free our people, but we shall do so in a way that will grant us a peaceful transition into this society."

"What need do we have of their society? We could slaughter the lot of them all and create a new society. A Ramangan utopia."

"And you would have us in battle forever? Killing them all would make us no better than them and would thrust the existences of our humans into constant turmoil. No, Rafazi. Like it or not, we are all on this land now. Just as we share with the Native peoples, they must also learn to share. Yes, they will be resistant, but I believe the best way to start the process is by speaking their language."

"Do we not already?"

"I mean money. We will use Big Jim's fortune to buy the slaves on the Peterson Farm, the ones already here and all the rest, give them their freedom, and have them join us. You'll serve as my representative."

"*Your* representative?"

The room became deathly still as emotion finally found its way into Rafazi's voice. His roaring response hung in the air. Kwadzo was searching for a way to keep his own emotions in check and out of his voice, but he didn't have to respond at all.

"I will go."

Irene stepped forward, her eyes shimmering with hope. "I can represent you at the Peterson Farm, but I worry for my mama on the Wilson Plantation. I fear for her after what we did, just as much as I do for all the others."

"I fear for them all, too. Everyone is watching," Kwadzo said. "We have to make sure this is done right. The Wilson Plantation is much bigger than the Peterson Farm."

"I reckon money means the same to them both, and buying slaves at either plantation sends the same message."

"It's more than that, Irene. We need to learn to do things, handle business the way they do."

Rafazi scoffed audibly at his statement, but Kwadzo chose to ignore it.

"We have to show them that we are forever changed, that we cannot be treated the way we have been in the past ever again. We have to establish our place . . ."

"I learn fast, Kwadzo," Irene insisted. "Perhaps Doc Farkus or his wife can shed light on how best to negotiate."

"I believe I can offer a bit of assistance in that regard," Doc Farkus spoke up from the crowd.

"And if that Gavin Wilson won't come to terms, I'll bend his mind," Irene said.

"No," Kwadzo said. "If we just go around bending their minds, we'll be no better than they were. We will stay at war. They fear us now. If we are to truly thrive, they must come to genuinely respect us."

Rafazi's chuckle made Kwadzo ball up his fist. A way of keeping himself in control.

"We are superior to them in every way," Rafazi said. "Who cares if they respect us or not? They should bend to our wishes or be drained and be grateful for either!"

"We will not become what they were," Kwadzo said firmly, "and we will not be what Ramanga was."

"We are Ramanga. *Brother.*" Rafazi spat the word. Kwadzo did not know why he had become the target of such scorn, but there was no time to explore it.

"I have no doubt as to who we *are.* It is what we *do* that is my greatest concern now. This manor, this plantation, is ours now, cloaked in crimson, and from this Crimson Plantation, we will remake the world. But we cannot do that if we don't know what the world is made of. Learning their ways helps us create better."

"Like I said, I learn fast." Irene never flinched. Her determination was as clear to Kwadzo as Rafazi's obstinance.

"Very well. Tomorrow, you will take Doc Farkus and a strong show of force with you to the Wilson Plantation. Bring your mother home along with the other slaves."

"Tomorrow? During the day? But the sunlight . . ."

"They do their business in the sunlight. So must we. Besides, we cannot let them know the sun is our weakness. Have the seamstresses prepare cloaks for you and those of the Blood you take like Rafazi's. It won't hurt to have other humans with you as well. Tonight, I will go into town with a contingent. I will seek out Peterson and pay him for the slaves myself."

"The Crown Tavern is where the men gather," Rebecca called out to him. "A gathering place for libation and doing business. Among other things."

"Very well. I will gather a group to go to this Crown Tavern. This should give me the opportunity to also secure a merchant to sell our crops. When I return, we will set out to search for the girl."

Murmurs of agreement spread through the crowd. When Kwadzo turned to find Rafazi, his maker had already left the room.

Ten

The Governor's Widow

The soft breeze of the night air did nothing to cool the burn of anger swelling in Kwadzo. Despite having no knowledge of how to be a leader, Kwadzo took up the mantle Rafazi handed him and led his people to victory. He had done everything Rafazi asked of him.

So, why did it now feel as though his maker was against him, at odds with the very position he'd bestowed upon him? For now, concerns about Rafazi would have to wait. There was business to attend to back inside the manor. In the parlor room, which had been refurbished since white men had attacked Kwadzo in it, he gathered Ekow from the council along with Polly, a young woman who had fought and survived the battle in the manor, and Samson to accompany him into town.

Samson—so named for his massive size and muscularity—was new to the Blood and eager to play his part in the ongoing revolution. Having gone into town with Gertie earlier, he'd asked for the Blood upon their return and Kwadzo willingly gifted it to him. He turned in record time and made for the perfect intimidating Ramangan specimen. Well over six feet tall, with a tuft of well-cropped hair on his head and unbelievably broad shoulders, Kwadzo thought Samson's presence might be enough to keep things from getting out of hand.

"I've got the money," Ekow said as he approached Kwadzo with a large canvas bag. He opened it and looked inside along with Kwadzo. "Think it will be enough?"

Kwadzo did not know. He had no sense of finance in this New World, of what price was paid for goods or people.

"I suppose we'll find out. I intend to buy those here and the rest Peterson owns."

"Maybe I should get more."

With a nod, Kwadzo sent Ekow away in his blur while he turned to the others in his entourage. "Our goal here is simple," he told them. "We are buying Peterson's slaves, making our intentions known, and securing a merchant for our crops."

"What if they want a fight?" Polly asked, red flashing in her eyes. Over the past month, she had proven to be a rambunctious sort. While her enthusiasm for their cause was admirable, Kwadzo knew she had to be kept in check.

"We will not give them one," he said flatly. "They have failed against us time and time again. Samson's presence should remind them of that."

"All that power and you still ain't nothin' but a uppity nigger."

Ever since their victory, and despite it, Clarence, always accompanied by Derby, taunted Kwadzo on a continuous basis. His words never truly affected Kwadzo, though he did marvel at the man's undying devotion to a dead master. Especially since he'd made no attempt to leave the Crimson Plantation, unlike others who had taken the opportunity to run after Kwadzo's victory.

"Shut up, Clarence!" Polly snapped. "Always got something to say and every word is dumber than the last!"

Kwadzo looked at her sternly, and she quieted herself. "If your freedom displeases you, Clarence, you may use it to leave this place as your small friend Bitty did. Derby is welcome to enjoy the same," Kwadzo said. "Perhaps the reason you don't is because you are aware that your devotion would not be rewarded were you to do so. Or perhaps Bitty is simply braver than you both."

"Whatever ungodly thing you be gonna get took to Hell by the white man's Lord one way or another," Clarence retorted.

It wasn't uncommon for Kwadzo to find Clarence in the study searching through the books that hadn't been burned for his new favorite: the Geneva Bible.

"Gertie was right," Derby said. "You is evil. Ain't no tellin' what wickedness you done used to bend her mind, but she need releasin' from the likes of you."

"I'm sorry you feel that way, Derby," Kwadzo said, his voice calm even as the red entered his eyes. "I considered you both to be my people, but you should know there is only so much of your insolence I will take."

Derby shook visibly from Kwadzo's ominous stare, which was then turned on Clarence. "And should I hear you use that vile word again, I'll have little choice but to remove your tongue."

"What vile word?" Clarence asked, his head high but his quaking voice betraying him.

"If you don't know, perhaps you should refrain from using any words for the time being."

A sudden knock at the front door of the manor captured the attention of all. A second series of knocks sent Kwadzo to the door in his blur. Blinking the red in his eyes away, he opened the door and was confused to find a white woman.

"Oh, hello."

She was alone, which he also found puzzling. Her breath caught at the sight of him, and her hazel eyes shook noticeably from what Kwadzo presumed was fright. Her auburn hair seemed luxurious though a bit disheveled, and she seemed a bit out of breath. The finery she wore spoke to wealth, but there was no carriage awaiting her; there was only his own, formerly Big Jim Barrow's. Had the woman walked here? In her hands, she held a medium-sized box, which he suspected kept her hands from shaking.

"I believe a Miss Gertie lives here?" she asked after clearing her throat.

"Who are you?"

"Oh, yes, right. Of course. My name is Sarah. Sarah Collins."

"Sarah," Kwadzo said, finding his smile. "The woman who helped Gertie."

"Yes, yes . . . or at least tried to. You are the one, aren't you? Mister Barrow's . . . well, I mean to say, the leader of the rebellion. The one who can breathe fire."

"You know me?"

"I know your power. I was an unfortunate victim of it. I was here that fateful night and I barely escaped your fire . . ."

Turning to her side, Sarah lowered the top of her dress, nearly dropping the box she held to expose the back of her shoulder. Her skin there was blistered and red, proof of her claim.

"You were here," he said.

"I was," she said, covering herself. "I was the governor's widow. You burned him to death."

"I burned several people that night."

"You certainly did."

"And I suppose you've come for some form of retribution."

"No! No, the furthest thing from it. My husband and I very much disagreed on the very nature of enslavement. I was against it. *Am* against it."

"I've got the money."

Kwadzo found Ekow standing next to him holding a much larger canvas bag while he stared at Sarah with glowing red eyes. He watched her shudder in fright before snapping his fingers in front of Ekow, causing the Ramangan enough shock to send his eyes back to their human hue.

"This is Sarah," Kwadzo told him. "She's the one who helped Gertie."

"Forgive me," Ekow said. "I meant no harm. It's just . . ."

"The scent of new blood tends to excite us," Kwadzo explained.

"I see." Sarah audibly sighed in relief. "Might I ask what's inside the bag?"

"We are going into town to buy the slaves of the Peterson Farm," Kwadzo told her.

"The same ones who were attacked."

"And all the other slaves on his farm. I'll be granting their freedom. I'll also be securing a merchant for our crops. They've grown by leaps and bounds."

"You'll be heading to the Crown Tavern, then. I could go with you."

Such a peculiar woman. All the other white folks who had come to the manor since he'd taken it were violent. But this woman had not only come to Gertie's aid in front of her own people but had also somehow made her way out here, offering assistance. It went against everything he'd ever seen from her kind. And because of that, he didn't trust it—or her.

"Why would you want to?" he asked.

"Your rebellion has shifted the tide . . . might I know your name?"

"Kwadzo."

"Well, Kwadzo, Mister Peterson has returned from his travels and will most likely be found at the Crown Tavern, but I fear it will not be the most welcoming place to you and your people. Perhaps I could help mediate so you can accomplish your goal."

"Until we can find the girl, this one's just as white as the rest of them," Ekow whispered to Kwadzo with a shrug.

Kwadzo stared into Sarah's eyes and found only sincerity. But he had to remain cautious.

"Please," Sarah said. "At the very least, you would be providing me with travel home. As you can see, I have no horse or carriage."

"You walked here?" Kwadzo inquired. Sarah nodded. "Why?"

"No one in Lakeside was willing to accommodate my trek here."

"Why did you come here?"

"In all the commotion, Miss Gertie never got to go to the cordwainer." Sarah opened the box and revealed it contained a pair of lovely shoes of brown, stout leather with golden buckles at the top. "I guessed at the size. I do hope they will be to her liking."

Eleven

The Business of Change

The ribald sounds of drunken shouts and curses seeped out of the Crown Tavern as Kwadzo's horse-drawn carriage approached. The two-story structure was large but less impressive than he had imagined.

"Why do they shout so?" Kwadzo asked Sarah, whose blood was pumping fast with fear—evidenced by the red, hungry eyes of Ekow, Samson, and Polly on her. With her gaze on the tavern, Sarah never noticed. Kwadzo's warning look to the Ramangans fixed their expressions. "What are you afraid of?"

"Quite frankly, everyone in that tavern," Sarah sighed. "I'm afraid I will not be welcome in there, either."

"We've never been welcome here," Kwadzo said.

"The Lakeside citizens," Sarah began, turning to face Kwadzo, "for the most part, see you and your people as thieves and murderers now."

"I gathered that from the attacks on the manor."

"With my husband dead, there's been little effort put toward keeping order. And with my history of opposing slavery . . ."

"You're worried for your own safety."

"I suppose you find me weak-willed." Sarah let out a sad chuckle.

"We are all dealing in newness," Kwadzo said. "And with a little effort, those who wish to will find their footing. Those who don't, won't."

Sarah looked back at him with eyes full of wonder. "I've never heard an African speak as you do. It makes me wonder how you could have been enslaved at all."

"I am different now than when I arrived on this land. Stronger. Everyone in this carriage is. I think it's time the rest of Lakeside found that out. Shall we?"

Kwadzo tapped the roof of the carriage, and in seconds, the driver opened the door and let Sarah out. Kwadzo and his Ramangans followed. He kept his eyes on Sarah the whole time. Perhaps she was an ally. Maybe she was leading them into a trap. He wanted to believe the former as she stopped in front of the tavern's door.

"So long as you stand with us," Kwadzo said, placing a gentle hand on her shoulder, "no harm will come to you."

"Thank you, Kwadzo. I fear I will need your protection quite immediately."

She pushed the doors to the tavern open, and they found the patrons inside at a fever pitch. There were two levels filled with men cheering boisterously, lit by candles and lanterns. The ground floor was a large, mostly open space with a bar filled with mugs, kegs of ale, and bottles of spirits. Long tables and benches had been pushed to the sides, allowing the men to form a crowd in front of a haughty-looking man and woman who stood on a table at the front of the room. Kwadzo found them to be an odd pair: he, small and slight, leaning forward on a black walking stick; she, towering and corpulent. The men clapped and shouted at them.

A few bar maidens, all dressed in simple and short white frocks, milled about delivering mugs of ale to the men while a few hounds followed them around. Ekow lurched back at the sight of one of the hounds, an involuntary reaction rooted in his past. Kwadzo placed a hand on his back.

"Easy, brother," he whispered. Ekow nodded as Kwadzo looked up at the balcony on the upper level. The men up there were behaving similarly, with the added endeavor of groping the bar maidens that served them. Perhaps being farther away from the main event left them prone to distraction. The bar maidens certainly didn't seem to enjoy it.

"Yes, friends, you've suffered a terrible plight," the slight man called out over the cheers, causing the men to settle. "Much has been taken from you at the hands of mere niggers."

"Not just niggers," someone in the crowd called out. "Demon niggers!"

"Demon niggers that stole my slaves!" another shouted.

Mumbles of agreement rose from the crowd, but they softened when the slight man raised his hand.

"Now, now, friends," he said. "I understand the strain that comes from an uprising, especially one that robbed men of status and importance from you. It can play terrible tricks on the mind. Having spoken with some of you, I've learned that not only have farms and slaves gone unattended in the absence of their masters, but your very leadership was snatched away. Your governor, your slave patrol captain, your minister. I ask you: How can a community thrive without the proper spiritual guidance? It cannot! Your doctor . . ."

"We ain't lose Doc Farkus," another cried out. "He chose them niggers over us!"

The mutterings of agreement grew stronger and louder.

"Now, now, friends," the slight man called over them again, "let us not lose sight of who is to truly blame here."

"I believe that would be me."

Kwadzo stepped forward, causing all the patrons and bar maidens to turn and stare at him and his associates. He could feel the blood in the room shift, and the scent of fear overwhelmed his nostrils. Venom coated his teeth, but he had to stay in control. They all had to.

Remain calm, he communicated telepathically to the Ramangans with him. *We are not here to feed or to kill. We must show them restraint. They are no longer in control of us.*

"I see familiar faces among you," Kwadzo said, slowly making his way through the crowd, inching toward the man and woman standing on the table. "Some of you have tried, and failed, to attack our manor."

"Ain't your manor!" someone shouted, and yells of agreement rose again. Spurred on by each other, the cries grew louder and Kwadzo heard them out, waiting for them to reach a crescendo.

"QUIET!" he finally roared. He still was not used to how loud he could make his voice, but the call, akin to the roar of a lion, was enough to silence the tavern entirely. The instantaneous result made him feel even more powerful, and calm within his power. A quick look to his fellow Ramangans told him they felt the same.

But Sarah's fear was just as intense, maybe more so. She placed herself as close to Kwadzo as she could without touching him, something he took note of with appreciation as he looked up to the slight man and rotund woman.

"Your faces are new," he said to them both, and they stared back at him with wide-eyed wonder.

"Well, I do declare!" the woman said. "Never in my life have I heard anything quite like it!"

"That boy is uppity as all get out!" the man said.

"And loud," the woman said.

"Yes, dearest, the boy is quite loud, indeed."

"I have not been a boy for quite some time," Kwadzo said, a bit confounded. His roar had triggered fear in all the Lakeside citizens. Of this, he was certain. But he could smell no fear coming off these two.

"Ornery, as well, I see," the man said. "You must be the one they're all in a tizzy over. Now, do you know they think you're a vampyre?"

Vampyre.

The word unsettled Kwadzo. It was the word Monroe had said in reference to him during the battle in the manor when he'd wielded his silver sword. In the heat of battle, there had been no time to investigate the term. He'd heard both Irene and Gertie say they'd also heard the word used by Monroe in reference to those of the Blood. He'd never heard Rafazi use the word and it had only been spoken by the white folks, so he paid it little mind. He did not understand its meaning, but it had been spoken with certainty, as if a descriptor, as if the man knew of what he'd become. Only instead of Ramangan, he'd used this word.

Vampyre.

He had come to know that he could sense his own kind. At least, he believed he could. There was a certain stirring in his blood that ceased when he was exclusively in human company, but that could have just as easily been a feeling of camaraderie, an intimate knowing from a shared experience: a sense of death as opposed to one of life.

Life, however, was all he got off the slight man and rotund woman, and gauging by their appearances, he would estimate they were into their fifties. They certainly hadn't lived long enough to have known of a Ramangan, not when the Ramanga Tribe had been wiped out centuries ago by plague.

Or so Rafazi had said.

"He's no vampyre," the woman said, climbing down from the table and rushing to him with fists at the ready. "He's just a regular, ordinary nigger! See?"

The woman slammed her fists against the sides of his head with such considerable force that it set off a slight ringing in his ears.

"That usually makes them fall down," she said. "Why haven't you fallen down?"

He was proud of his fellow Ramangans for keeping their calm, and he chose to do the same and not retaliate. He could very easily have morphed into his Ramangan form and coated the tavern's walls with this woman's blood, but that would not help him accomplish his goal. Besides, the ringing in his ears had already subsided.

He had to keep his eye on the prize.

"I say, this one possesses a useful fortitude," the man said, hopping down from the table to join the woman. "I can see now how a rebellion against Barrow could have been won. He's strapping, well built. He'll make an excellent addition to the coffle."

"Yes, he would," the woman said.

"I imagine now that you've had your violent little outburst, you and the rest of the niggers on Barrow's land find yourselves lost and without direction," the man said. "You've no idea what to do with yourselves, which is probably why you had the gall to come here. Shameful. Well, none to worry. What you need is a new master to set you straight. It's all the wayward niggers left without masters need. I'm sure once I have a chance to assess the plantations left without planters, we'll take control of them and put things back in order. Constance and I will fix everything."

"Constance?" Kwadzo asked the man, who responded with laughter.

"How silly of me," he said, "to use so many words in such quick succession, thinking your feeble little brain would be able to understand. CONSTANCE-MY-WIFE-AND-I-WILL-TAKE-OVER-BARROW-LAND-BE-YOUR-NEW-MASTERS."

His speech had become so unnecessarily loud and slow, Kwadzo thought the man was soft of mind. It was also clear that he didn't understand the situation he was in.

"We are not in need of any master," Kwadzo said to the man. "We are free, and the Barrow Plantation is the Crimson Plantation now. It belongs to us."

The man and the woman, Constance, broke into laughter so hard and loud that it didn't take long for the rest of the folks in the tavern to laugh as well. The Ramangans looked to Kwadzo with confusion. He could only shrug in response, but he did notice that the scent of fear, which had been so profound before, had greatly diminished. He had no idea what to make of these two, but he would not allow them to deter his mission any longer. It was time to get on with the business at hand.

"Is Peterson here?" he called out above the laughter.

"I'm Peterson."

The fear that remained in the man who stepped forward made him smell delectable. He looked to be of forty years, and his knees seemed to wobble as the laughter died down.

"Are you afraid?" the slight man asked him. "Are you not the one who said your slaves were stolen?"

"Well, yes."

"And yet you stand in fear of the slave who took your slaves?"

"But Mister Crabtree . . ." Peterson whined.

"Please. Bartholomew," the slight man offered.

"Bartholomew, you don't understand . . ." Peterson attempted to explain.

"No, sir! It is *you* who does not understand! This is nothing but a slave nigger. One who has forgotten his place but will return to proper form once I throttle him like so!"

Bartholomew swung his black walking stick to strike Kwadzo, who yanked it from his grasp, flipped it, and smacked him across the face with its tip before placing it under the man's chin. In response, Constance charged for him but halted with a gasp when he flashed his eyes red at her.

"Consider yourself lucky I do not wish to practice harm this night," Kwadzo said, turning his attention back to Bartholomew. "I did not think I would have to say this again, but I suppose it cannot be helped."

Bartholomew grabbed the walking stick, and Kwadzo allowed him to take it back. But when he raised it to strike for a second time, Kwadzo took hold of the man's neck and lifted him off the floor.

"Unhand me!" Bartholomew choked, a plea ignored as Kwadzo leaped up onto the table Bartholomew and Constance had been standing on, the man still twisting and struggling in his grasp.

"Citizens of Lakeside," Kwadzo began. "I imagine you are all going through a period of adjustment, given recent developments. As you know, you have tried and failed in your attempts to retaliate against those changes, and, as I've stated before, I have no interest in killing any more of you indiscriminately. So, my suggestion to you all is to embrace these changes, because what you had grown accustomed to regarding my people and the Indigenous tribes from whom you pilfered this land is no more. The purpose for my visit is threefold. First, Mister Peterson."

Kwadzo gave a nod to Ekow, who handed off the canvas bag to Peterson. Constance pointed a finger at Kwadzo with a frown.

"You release my Barty this instant!"

"Very well."

Kwadzo opened his hand and Bartholomew dropped, first onto the table, then the floor, gasping for air.

"You are an unruly nigger!" Constance said as she rushed to a struggling, coughing Bartholomew. "And anyone with ears can tell you've been in your master's books, reading! Which is against the law! You will hang for this!"

Kwadzo completely ignored her in favor of Peterson.

"As I'm sure you are aware, men raided your land and attacked your slaves without provocation. My Gertie was witness to it, as was Sarah, your deceased governor's widow. Those slaves were brought to our plantation, and it is there they will stay. In the bag, you will find the funds with which to pay for those slaves, and enough for the remainder of your slave coffle. They will be collected from you first thing in the morning. Have them ready."

"Wait a minute," Peterson said, turning to Sarah. "They killed your husband, and yet, you stand with them?"

All eyes turned to Sarah now, including Kwadzo's. It would be a brave thing for her to voice the same sentiments she'd shared with him at the manor, but he could not fault her if she lost courage. Their success did not hinge on Sarah's loyalty. But one way or another, her words would tell him exactly where, and with whom, she stood.

"Her misplaced sentimentality is just an ailment of the feeble feminine mind," Bartholomew said as he got to his feet and caught his breath. He winced after a hard pinch from Constance. "Not something my dear wife suffers from, you understand, but there could be no other explanation for this woman's chosen affiliation. Well? Have you nothing to say for your treacherous ways?"

"You, sir, are not my husband nor my father," Sarah said, her voice quaking. "I owe you no explanation as to my life, my choices, nor the company I choose to keep."

"Nigger lover!" someone shouted out. Laughter and agreeable cheers rose.

"Second," Kwadzo called out over them, "I have decided that this ugly name will no longer be used in reference to my people."

"Are you making demands, boy? Have you clean forgotten what you are?" Bartholomew asked. "Now, you heed *my* words. The good people of Lakeside have had enough of your savagery and foolishness."

Kwadzo stared back at the man, dumbfounded. Mere seconds had passed since he'd held the man in his grasp, one he could have tightened to the point of tearing his head from his body. And yet, he'd retained the gall to speak as he did. Kwadzo had already broken his promise to not indulge in violence, and this Bartholomew character was making it increasingly difficult for him to keep his composure.

"You, and the black lot with you, are thieves and murderers, but most of all, you are slaves," Bartholmew spat. "Your very presence anywhere except for the field of your master is illegal, especially one who has led a revolt like you have. You have claim to nothing. Strutting around wearing your master's jewelry, sending your females into town wearing their mistress's clothes, and waving around your master's money does not make it your own.

"Now, you may think because of your freakish *nigger* strength and the fact that someone, perhaps this *nigger*-loving traitor to her race, taught you a few civilized words that I would stand in fear of you. But you don't scare me none. Because you are nothing but a *nigger*. And a *nigger*, is a *nigger*, is a *nigger*. Now, these folks may think you're some kind of powerful demon . . ." A giddy Constance handed him a rifle and clapped with excitement as her husband aimed the gun at Kwadzo's head. "But I reckon a bullet to the head will send you right back to Hell."

Do not turn, do not react. Not even with the red in your eyes, Kwadzo telepathically told the other Ramangans. He was speaking to himself as much as he was to them. He could not have this night erupt in violence. Not, at least, until he had accomplished what he'd set out to. The tavern was deathly still and silent, but despite the angry white faces surrounding him, Kwadzo could smell their collective fear rise again. It stirred his hunger, but he kept control of his reaction, both to it and to the weapon pointed at him.

Control was key. He had survived much, but he was unsure of what a bullet to the head would do. He was equally unsure of the mob's knowledge of silver. Though it no longer seemed to affect him, it would surely endanger his present company if they chose to attack. Blood would spill on his first foray into society. White society.

Despite his power and victory, it was still *their* society, and in it, he was a monster. It was a perception he had to change if he was to fulfill his ultimate goal, and splattering this man's blood all over the tavern floor would be counterproductive. Still, if Bartholomew persisted with his rifle, Kwadzo would be left with no other choice.

"Yes!" Constance squealed. "Call him a nigger again! It irks him so! Call him a nigger and then blow his brains out!"

"Not in here you won't."

A second rifle barrel was presented, only this one was pointed in the direction of Bartholomew and Constance. Holding the gun steady as she descended the stairs was a woman of fifty years or so and dressed in red silken finery, her blonde-and-gray tresses wrapped in a decorative bun atop her head. Her face was awash in rouge and lipstick. The men present made way for her respectfully.

"I don't care who you are or how much money you spend, ain't nobody killin' nobody in my tavern," the woman said. "It's all I got left since my husband passed on and I intend to keep it, so if anybody does any killin' in this here establishment, it's gonna be me." She moved closer to Bartholomew.

"My dear madam," Bartholomew said, never taking his eyes or aim off Kwadzo, "has it escaped your memory the stranglehold this beast put me in but a short while ago?"

"The way I remember it, you swung for him first. Besides, you still alive, ain't you? And that Governor Collins was a bastard who never thought he had to pay for what he took 'round here, but his missus always had a kind word when she saw me, so I reckon she's a fair judge of character."

"Well, it seems we have yet another nigger lover in our midst," Bartholomew sighed.

"I've loved two things in my lifetime, my husband and money. Now whatever happened up on Barrow's farm don't make no nevermind to me. I wasn't fancy enough for the man to give me the time of day, and I wasn't dependent on him to put food on my table, so I ain't ever thought one way or another about him. But I reckon if he was beatin' on me all the livelong day, I'd want me some retribution, too. So, I would lower that rifle if I were you, Mister Crabtree," the blonde woman said, keeping her gun trained on Bartholomew. He submitted to her order while she turned her attention to Kwadzo.

"Now, I've heard the rumors about what happened out there, what you done, what you are. Vampyre, red-eyed demon, fire-breathin' monster—don't make no difference to me. If what they say 'bout you is true, well, that's the kind of power I'd be stupid to cross. Now, if I recall, you said you had a threefold purpose for comin' here tonight. I done heard two. I suggest you get on along to three and be on your way."

Kwadzo smiled. "And whom might I thank for such hospitality?"

"They call me Kitty Greer," the woman said.

"A pleasure, Missus Greer. I am Kwadzo Okoro." Kwadzo gave her the warmest smile he could, and she reciprocated. He had a feeling that Missus Kitty Greer might be helpful in his mission as it progressed. So far, she had been far more useful than Sarah.

"Lastly, then," Kwadzo said, addressing the crowd, "our crops have grown ripe for harvest, and we wish to secure a merchant to sell them."

"Don't nobody wanna buy from no nigger . . ."

Before the man could finish his sentence, Kwadzo had blurred through the crowd and then behind him, grabbing his tongue. "As I have stated, this word will no longer be used. If it is uttered, its speaker shall have his tongue removed." The tavern once again fell silent in awe of Kwadzo's speed. "But I suppose it would be unfair to remove this tongue before Bartholomew's. Shall we consider this a warning?" The man whose tongue he held nodded, and Kwadzo released him. "Now, then. Who will do me the honor of becoming my merchant?"

The quiet was unfathomable until Sarah stepped forward.

"Mister Josiah Browne," she called out. A portly, balding man with glasses gasped and jumped near a corner of the room. "You conducted Barrow Plantation business with Monroe, did you not? You know all the exporters, and I suspect, considering how profitable the plantation was, you gave him the best prices."

"Well, yes," Josiah groaned, "but that was Monroe and Mister Barrow. This is . . ."

"These are the same crops from the same land, only farmed better and more efficiently," Kwadzo offered.

"How so?"

"Because these crops won't be harvested at the end of a whip."

Josiah was sweating. Kwadzo surmised he felt pressured to do what the mob wanted him to do, and the danger he felt were he not to go along with their wishes plagued him. His eyes darted between his compatriots and Kwadzo. The scent of fear increased and Kwadzo could only assume the man was also considering what he would face if he did choose to work with the Crimson Plantation. "I don't conduct business at night. That's my time to be with my wife and family."

"And yet, here you drink, your wife and children nowhere in sight," Sarah said, which garnered her a smile from Kwadzo.

"I find I focus better at night," Kwadzo said.

"No good Christian, no God-fearing man anywhere in all the colonies, would be foolish enough to discuss plantation business with a slave," Bartholomew said with a scoff.

"Be that as it may, Missus Greer notwithstanding, there are many people who do depend on the crops from what used to be the Barrow Plantation, and if memory serves, my husband often spoke of how much Lakeside and even its neighboring towns benefit from what those crops bring in terms of goods and services," Sarah said. "Those crops are the same under the new plantation, so there would be no reason that they wouldn't carry the same value. What Kwadzo is asking would simply continue the profitability we already enjoy from them. Or would you rather allow petty prejudices to cause the entire town to suffer?"

Josiah opened his mouth in protest, but no words escaped his lips. The look on his face and the faces of the others had softened considerably, which told Kwadzo that Sarah's words had resonated. When she turned to him, her brow raised in question, Kwadzo gave her a nod and a small smile. In response, Sarah bared her teeth with a smile of her own.

"Very good, then, Mister Browne," she said with strength in her voice. "Shall we say Friday night here for the two of you to discuss this business in depth?"

Josiah's eyes were directed at the floor, but he nodded.

"And Mister Peterson," Sarah continued, "if I am not mistaken, the state of your farm has become dire, has it not? Before his passing, my husband told me selling off the land had become a serious consideration for you. I would imagine the money presented to you for all your slaves would go a long way in helping keep your family afloat while you search out a new profession. So, I trust you will have them ready as Kwadzo has requested?"

Mister Peterson, also with his eyes downcast, nodded.

"Excellent," Kwadzo said. "We will take our leave and bid you all goodnight." He extended his hand to Kitty Greer, waiting out her trepidation before she placed her delicate hand in his. Indignation filled the eyes of the white men, who looked on as Kwadzo gingerly kissed her hand with a slight bow. "Thank you for your kind hospitality."

Kitty Greer's cheeks flushed red, and she turned away from the men, concealing a smile. Turning toward the exit, Kwadzo motioned for his companions to follow.

"You may think you have won, but you have not," Bartholomew called out.

"For a people who risked life and limb to travel across the sea for weeks on end to build a new world for themselves, you are oddly resistant to change," Kwadzo said with a chuckle. "But change has come, and there is nothing any of you can do to stop it. For the good of your health, I suggest you accept it."

"I still have a question," Constance said. "I want to know. Are you a true demon or not?"

"We are Ramanga," Kwadzo said. "Immortal power runs through our veins."

With that, he took on his full Ramangan form and his fellow Ramangans followed suit, their eyes gleaming so brightly that a red hue illuminated the space as a collective gasp rose from the gawking crowd. The delicious smell of communal fright grew even stronger, but Bartholomew's eyes were as wide as the smile on his face.

"I don't believe it," Constance said breathlessly.

"My God, what a specimen," he said. "I swear on all that is holy, I will find every way that exists to kill you and use them all to make you submit to my will. You will go down in history as the greatest slave I have ever broken."

"Or," Kwadzo said, "you will simply go down."

Once again, Kwadzo could feel the rage rising in his blood. He was certain it would be satisfying to torment this little man and his large wife until they were on their knees and giving him an explanation of this new "vampyre" term: what it meant, where it had come from, who knew of it. Or, perhaps, his questions would be better reserved for Rafazi. For now, his mission here had reached its conclusion. There were more things to attend to. He needed to remove Sarah from this place safely and find the girl before sunrise.

So, with a nod, Kwadzo and his companions left the tavern without further incident.

Twelve

This Greater Power

The voice inside her head was driving Penelope crazy—it had been calling to her for hours. No matter how fast she ran, she could not shake its unrelenting echo. The voice was soft and feminine, but not one she recognized. Though she continued to run from fear of it, she found it increasingly harder to ignore.

Girl? Girl, where are you? I need to find you!

There was something authoritarian about the voice, and a part of her felt as though she should submit to it. But she fought that impulse and ran, using her extraordinary speed to escape into the dark wilderness.

She had no idea where she was. She only knew she was starving. Time seemed to move much slower ever since she was plagued by this voodoo curse, and though her new instinct had led her to feast on the blood of animals—she didn't dare go into any towns being the abomination that she now was—it was never enough. Nothing had satiated her hunger the way her dear mother's blood had.

Still the voice loomed. Up ahead of her, Penelope spotted a fisher cat climbing a tree. It was plump in size, which meant it was a male and full of blood. Perhaps a fresh serving would mute the voice that plagued her. The fisher cat hissed at Penelope as she approached. The animal scampered up the tree in retreat, but it was no match for her speed. Within seconds, Penelope had scaled up the tree trunk and snatched the animal up. She felt herself transform into her monstrous, demonic state before she tore through the fisher cat's thick fur and lodged her sharp, jagged teeth into its skin. The animal shrieked its death as Penelope sucked the life force from it.

Girl! Hear my voice!

She shut her eyes and gulped down the blood, willing the voice out of her consciousness, but it was no use. The voice only grew louder.

Girl!

Penelope dropped the drained carcass, jumped from the tree, and took off at inhuman speed even deeper into the wilderness. Fright seized her entire being, but that only made her run faster.

I feel you running! Stop!

The command halted Penelope against her will. She wanted to run but felt compelled to stay still, as if her body was no longer under her own control. She squeezed her eyes together, balling her hands into fists.

"Move," she told herself. "Run!"

Yet she remained. What was this voice and its power over her? She was certain it had something to do with what she was now—the evil thing those slaves had made her—which could only mean the voice calling to her belonged to that of a slave. That realization opened her eyes and replaced her fright with anger.

"You do not control me!" Penelope yelled into the night, still unable to move. "You're just a good-for-nothing slave nigger!

And there isn't a nigger alive that will ever control me! You hear me?"

Penelope's limbs loosened at her proclamation, and she laughed with abandon as she launched herself forward at her fastest speed yet. She rushed through trees and foliage until she could sense that the sun would soon be rising. She stopped in a clearing but knew that the sunlight would bring her to a standstill she could not avoid. There was no doubt in her mind that she was being chased at the very least—and in the most sinister scenario, hunted. She could not allow herself to get caught. She didn't know why the Good Lord had given her these demon powers, but the best use she could think of for them was turning them against the slaves who had snatched away the only life she had ever known.

They had to be stopped, and she was the only one who could do it. She just needed to figure out how this dark power worked . . . then she could build an army like her, an army of Whites to fight by her side. With their superior intellect, they would easily defeat the demon niggers and send them to Hell where they belonged. She would free the good White people of Lakeside from the tyranny of those evil slaves.

Samuel Knudsen was the bravest man in all of Carolina, maybe in all the colonies, and she was his daughter. Penelope realized then why God had allowed this wickedness to befall her. Now that He had called her father home, she was the only one strong enough to rid the province of the nigger evil. Regardless of the black wickedness within, her father's blood still ran through her veins. She would call upon his strength to help guide her in her quest, and she would succeed. Once she had done that, surely the Good Lord would return her to her pure form and free her from the diabolical curse that she had been placed under.

She had been chosen.

First, she had to survive her hunters and the sun. And she

would need to find presentable clothing. Her body's new reaction to sunlight would burn up the stitched-together rags that covered her now. So, she began her search for a safe haven. If she could find a place to hide and avoid burning, perhaps it would keep her hidden from the ones she sensed were hunting her.

A new but familiar scent filled her nostrils. She realized it was an aroma the same as her own: the smell she had picked up even since she had become the evil she was. Salty, earthy, and mixed with the faint, neutral rust scent of blood. She felt it odd that it wasn't an unpleasant smell, but whatever it was that shared her aroma was getting closer. The darkness in the sky was beginning to give way. She spun to continue her search but instead found *her*—the very same slave girl she'd bit to stop her from attacking a White man in the Barrow Manor. She remembered her teeth breaking the skin of the slave girl's leg, the blood that seeped into her mouth, blood she had swallowed.

The voice in Penelope's head was hers. She knew it instinctively. The cause of the blasphemy she had become finally stood before her. Penelope's eyes went red with rage.

"Don't!"

She turned to find *him* standing behind her—the slave who had killed her father. There were two more of their kind to her left and right who kept their distance. Penelope was completely surrounded. Penelope could feel the slight shift of temperature in the air telling her the sun was getting higher in the sky, but she reached into a wayward pocket from her rags and presented her father's dagger anyway.

"You," she seethed, facing the big slave who had stood behind her. "You're the nigger that killed my father!"

His eyes shifted toward the sky, telling her the sunrise was a problem they shared.

"We're not here to hurt you," he said, his voice low and gentle.

"You've already hurt me! You killed my daddy, and that little niglet turned me into a bloodthirsty monster evil enough to kill my mother! She made me a demon just like you!"

"None of that matters now, child. What does matter is that you are one of us."

"I will *never* be one of you!"

"You already are!"

Penelope turned again to find the slave girl she'd bit walking toward her. She frowned at the sound of her voice, the one that had been in her head all this time, taunting her, controlling her.

"If you don't like what you've become," the slave girl said, "you've got no one to blame but yourself. You bit *my* leg, you sucked up *my* blood, then you ran into the heat of battle and got yourself killed."

Penelope's face was hot with anger, but tears formed in her eyes. There was nothing she could deny in the slave's speech.

"Now that you are of Ramangan Blood, you cannot go back."

The big slave took his place next to the slave girl while the others among them changed form and became monstrous. She blinked back tears with realization—did she look as ghastly as they did?

"The life you remember living in Lakeside is gone," the big slave said.

Penelope shook her head. She could find no words to convey the sadness and anger coursing through her being.

"You are no longer human," the big slave said, taking a step closer. "You're one of us. We've come to take you home. Teach you what you are, show you how to use your powers."

Penelope leveled her father's dagger at him. "You really think I would go along with you after what you did? You think I would forsake good, Christian White folk for demon niggers?"

“Look at yourself!” the slave girl hollered back. “You’re a demon nigger now, too! The white folks won’t want anything to do with you!”

“Fanna!”

The slave girl lowered her head at the big slave’s scolding tone. He took another cautious step toward Penelope.

“We didn’t track you all this way just to hurt you. And as far as killing your father goes, rest assured, he killed me first.” Penelope’s brow crinkled at this while the big slave looked up to the sky.

“There is no time for me to explain now,” he said with urgency in his voice. “I cannot bring him back, and for that I am sorry. But you will exist forever now. And forever is a long time to be alone. Come with us.”

“How dare you! How dare you ask this of me! You’ve taken everything from me! EVERYTHING!”

Penelope shut her eyes as tears rolled down her cheeks. The speech of the slaves was as clear as her own, and the only thing that made sense was nonsensical—the blood. Ramangan Blood, he had called it. The name sounded even darker than their skin, like it had come from the Devil himself. She refused to be in league with the Devil and shook the very thought from her mind. She was an agent of God, given devilish power to fight fire with fire to rid the New World of the evil scourge of the demon slave niggers.

“I will not be alone,” Penelope said, her eyes glowing red as she felt herself transform into her monstrous state. “I will take this power back to the good people of Lakeside, and I will build an army of White men and women in my image, and we will destroy every last one of you!”

She lunged for the big slave with the dagger, but he disappeared from her field of vision in a blur, and she fell to the ground.

“We don’t have time for this!”

She got to her feet and found him standing behind her.

"I do not want to hurt you, child. The sun is coming up, and if we don't get you to shelter, we will all perish from it!"

His statement made Penelope pause just as two horses arrived carrying savage Indians, a male and a female. The scent of their blood made her mouth water. Humans. And she was so very hungry.

"You found her," the female Indian said. "Is she coming back with us, or has she chosen to die in the sunlight?"

Penelope's mind churned. Her reaction to the sunlight was atrocious and painful, but she survived it every morning.

"I don't die."

"Of course, child. You are already dead," the big slave said.

Penelope smiled. For all their posturing, she knew something they didn't. Or was it that she possessed an ability they did not?

"Do you fear the sun, slave?" she asked. "Because I don't."

"Have you not felt the effects of the sun on your skin?"

"I have. And every day, I rise from my burns and scabs anew."

The demon slaves turned to each other, their eyes wide with concern. Penelope's smile grew broader. Soon, she was laughing with realization.

"You cannot survive the sunlight!" Penelope jubilantly exclaimed. "The Lord's Light destroys you, yet it renews me!"

"Kwadzo," the female Indian said to the big slave. "What is she talking about? Your people of the Blood hide from the sun."

Penelope's laugh grew louder now, echoing across the clearing as the first of the sun's rays began to peek out from behind the clouds.

"The Lord's Light kills you but renews me!" she repeated. "I truly am an agent of the Most High!"

She stood in the path of a ray of sunlight, and the skin on her arm began to sizzle.

"There's no time to waste!" the big slave screamed in panic. "We need to get you out of the sun!"

He reached for her, but she pulled him toward her, and they both screamed as the sun burned their skin.

"Every morning, His sun cleanses me by fire! Frees me of my sins and makes me whole again! New! I am holy and you are evil, and God has given me your power to defeat you with it!"

The big slave pulled away from her, and the others of his kind, save for the girl she'd bitten, leapt high into the air only to plunge down, their fists pointed at the ground. They punched through the earth and burrowed beneath it to escape the sun.

"That's right!" Penelope laughed as she moved more of herself fully into the sunlight, the skin on her arms and face bursting into flame. "Go back to Hell! I will show you no mercy!"

With one last look to the big slave, the slave girl plunged herself into the ground. Penelope cried out in pain as her left eye popped and burst from the fire that was beginning to consume her face. Before she lost her right eye, she looked to the big slave, the only one who remained, steam rising from his shoulders and head as he took solace under a tree branch and its leaves.

"And you," she hissed at him through the righteous pain coursing through her. "Your destruction will be the most delicious of all!"

As he followed the others like him into the ground, she gave herself to the sun, God's Holy Light, bearing the unimaginable pain it brought, awaiting the wave of rejuvenation that was sure to follow.

Penelope awoke and wiped the burnt crust from her eyes to find her body covered in scabs of black char once again. She was alone in the clearing. Peeling the scabs from her face, she smiled with renewed purpose. She was more powerful than the demon slaves who had cursed her with this power, which only cemented her superiority over them. Her mind was clear. Under the protection of sunlight, she would share her greater power with her people and conquer the demon slaves once and for all.

Thirteen

Cruel Memory

Irene savored the taste of blood on her tongue. It belonged to Sadie. Irene had approached Sadie with the glory of the Blood along with her sister, Poppy. It was a fact few knew about the two; Irene supposed they refrained from exposing themselves to stay together. Though Sadie had refused the Blood, she believed in the cause it was being used to fight for. During the manor battle, Irene had the opportunity to save them both from an attacking white man. After their victory, Sadie and Poppy had become Irene's constant companions, offering her their blood whenever she wanted it.

Though many men had shown their eagerness to give their blood to her, Irene almost always refused. She found the blood she'd extracted from females tastier than that of the males. She presumed this was because, for the most part, females had been more pleasing to her eye. She had certainly cast admiring glances at both Sadie and Poppy in the past. It seemed odd to Irene that the girls, both a few years her senior and who had held higher positions in the house than she had, were attending to her in such an acquiescent manner. But nothing was as it had been before.

Sadie moaned beside her, and Irene closed her eyes as her teeth produced more venom and she bit deeper into Sadie's arm. Sadie was sweeter than her sister, and the flavor called to mind Kwadzo's musings about the love he tasted in Gertie's blood, describing it as beyond the best flavor Irene could ever imagine. But as delectable as Sadie's blood was to her now, she knew she was not tasting love. The only love she'd ever known had been snatched away from her years ago.

She had not seen her mother since Gavin Wilson sold her off his plantation to Big Jim Barrow. She wasn't even allowed to say goodbye to her mother, Cecilia. Overseer Eli simply yanked her away and loaded her into Barrow's carriage, where Big Jim wasted no time busying his hands with her body.

She was only ever to refer to Overseer Eli as such even though the man had fathered her. It was an order he decreed upon learning of their relation. Overseer Eli never regarded Irene as his daughter, though her mother made her aware of their kinship as soon as she was able to understand it. Irene found out later this was to ensure that her younger self would obey the man implicitly and without familiarity, something Cecilia hoped would keep her daughter from harm. The distance Overseer Eli kept was such that Irene did not even know the man's last name. The only kindness he'd ever shown her was keeping quiet about her to Gavin Wilson, which allowed her to be raised by Cecilia. Once Irene was old enough to be put to work and registered with the plantation owner, Overseer Eli was just as hard on her as he was on any other slave, in fact, more so.

Cecilia would physically freeze up whenever Irene made mention of Overseer Eli. He was a brutal man in the cotton fields, and even worse out of them. One night, Irene witnessed him assaulting her mother with a level of sexual violence that left her paralyzed with fear. When he was done, Cecilia's arm was broken, her body bloody and bruised. She was too weak to walk on her own power. As a tearful Irene helped her mother back to slave village in the dead of night, she uttered only one sentence.

"Now you know how you came to be in this world."

Through it all, Cecilia doted on Irene. She defended her fiercely against those who condemned her because of her light skin and European heritage. She held her when the pressure of the cotton field brought her to tears, found moments of joy with which to laugh with her, even when Overseer Eli's viciousness against her was unrelenting. Irene had no idea how much more of his ruthlessness Cecilia could endure and often wondered if he had succeeded in murdering her mother. If he had, she vowed to tear her father to shreds, for he would have taken the only love she had ever known away forever.

Given the ferociousness she had seen and suffered at the hands of men, Irene thought it impossible for her to find love with one of any heritage, and though she had felt attraction, she had yet to encounter the spark of true ardor with any woman she'd known. She wondered if she would ever taste love for herself as Kwadzo had.

Sadie's tapping on her shoulder opened Irene's eyes and she realized Doc Farkus, sitting across from her in the carriage between Anita and Polly, was speaking to her.

"I say, maybe I should do the talking."

Irene released Sadie's wrist and wiped the excess blood from her lips as she peered back at Farkus with confusion.

"Traditionally," he said, "business is not discussed with women, let alone Negro women. As it is, the man will most likely be disinclined to discuss the matter at all. It may help to see a familiar face first."

"You mean a white face," Polly said.

"A white, male face," Anita added.

"Didn't Kwadzo say that word was no longer to be used to address us?" Polly added.

"No," Anita retorted, "he said no one could say '*nigger*' to address us. He said 'Negro.'"

"I don't know. Coming out of his mouth, it still sounds like nigger. Maybe we should let Kwadzo know."

"Enough!" Irene said, the haze of her tranquil feeding lifting as Polly and Anita went back and forth. "There's nothing to let Kwadzo know about. And while I appreciate your concern, Doc Farkus, your presence here is meant to facilitate my negotiating, not replace it. However, a familiar face may very well ease my arrival. Especially here."

The carriage slowly came to a halt, signaling their arrival at the intended destination.

"Take the men driving the carriage and get Mister Wilson to the door," Irene said to Farkus, who nodded and grabbed the oversized canvas bag on the floor of the carriage. Irene's foot kept it where it was. "Just get him to the door."

"A show of good faith might go a long way in achieving your goals," Farkus said, never taking his hand off the bag.

"And a bag full of riches could go a long way in helping you achieve yours," said Irene.

"I beg your pardon. Do you know the sacrifice my Rebecca and I have made to help your people?"

"Sacrifice?" Polly scoffed. "You forget I was there when you begged for your life. Kwadzo took mercy on you."

"A mercy I may not have afforded you," Irene said. "You have helped our sick and given aid to Gertie in her pregnancy, but you had no choice. Now, you have nothing else. Your home is no more, and your people regard you as a traitor. But with a big bag of money, you could start anew, and with a tale of woe delivered to Mister Wilson, you could share what you've learned of the Blood with the people of Lakeside and reclaim your place with them."

"And against us," Anita was quick to point out.

"You do not trust me," Farkus said.

"Not as long as your hand is on this bag, I don't."

Farkus relented, and Irene took hold of the bag.

"I do understand there has been a way of doing things," Irene said, "but things have changed, and they will continue to do so. The best your people can do now is grow accustomed to it. So, as I said, take the men and get Mister Wilson to the door. I'll take care of the rest."

With a nod, Farkus exited the carriage. Irene listened as three sets of footsteps moved away. Anita and Polly cracked with laughter.

"You had that man terrified," Anita said. "I could feel him shaking against my shoulder! I reckon no woman has ever held dominion over him like that before."

Irene was neither amused nor empowered by her exchange with Farkus. Her power came from within, from the Blood, from the years she'd struggled in servitude to nefarious forces and survived. The difference now was that, thanks to the Blood, men like Farkus could no longer deny her power. He couldn't, and neither would Gavin Wilson.

"Sadie, take a look outside and tell us where Farkus is."

She obeyed Irene's command, and the Ramangans were careful to scoot back to avoid the small stream of sunlight that entered the carriage from Sadie leaning out the open door.

"He walkin' up the porch steps with the mens now," she reported.

"How far away is the porch from here?" Irene asked her. "Is it shaded?"

"It is. And it only look to be 'bout ten feet 'way."

"Ten feet. That's nothing," Polly said.

"Any time in the sun is something," Irene said.

"With our cloaks, we'll be fine. Plus, with our blurs, it'll be like no time at all."

"Sadie," Irene said, "Tell me when a short white man with a graying beard comes to the door."

The phantom feeling of her heart rate increasing seized Irene as the minutes passed slowly and she waited for Sadie's report.

"There he go," Sadie finally answered. "And he don't look none too happy."

"All right. Don't leave the carriage."

Sadie nodded to Irene, who then did the same to Anita and Polly. Donning their newly fashioned cloaks, the three Ramangans blurred up onto the porch, but not without the wince of pain on their faces and steam rising from their shoulders. Irene could hear Gavin Wilson arguing with Doc Farkus at the front door in the presence of the two tall and brawny Africans with him, but his words ceased as Irene, Anita, and Polly appeared on the porch. Irene locked eyes with the man, who went pale.

"What in tarnation?"

"Good morning, Mister Wilson," Irene answered him, forcing her lips into a smile.

Gavin's eyes narrowed as they refocused on Doc Farkus.

"How dare you!" Gavin growled at Farkus.

Irene stepped between the two white men to stand directly in front of Gavin Wilson, raising her voice.

"Perhaps you didn't hear me, Mister Wilson. I wished you a good morning," she said, but Gavin only blinked back at her in silence. "I believe the proper etiquette when someone bids you a good morning is to bid them one back."

Irene shook her head as Gavin looked past her and at Farkus again. Despite being in the presence of true power, he was intent on dealing only with the other white man. Not only could the muscular Africans pummel him into the dirt with ease, but he would also have been nothing more than a light snack to the three Ramangans before him. This realization was not only lost on the man, but he stood proud in his ire, safe in his perceived superiority because they were all darker than he was.

In that moment, she was astonished at how powerful the color of skin really was to white folks. Even more astonishing was the idea that the only thing possibly more powerful to them was the contents of the canvas bag she held.

"You take yourself and these niggers off my property, Farkus," Gavin huffed. "The gall to bring them to my doorstep in the first place after abandoning your own people for them. Look at you, standing with slaves . . . You are a disgrace to your race!"

Apart from Farkus, all Gavin Wilson saw before him were slaves. And slaves, all of them, were beneath him, which kept him from seeing their power. Irene decided it was time to show it to him. Taking her Ramangan form, she grabbed Gavin's face and trained her glowing red eyes on his.

"You do not talk to him," she hissed. "You talk to me."

Now, Gavin's heart pumped, and the aroma of fear filled Irene's nostrils. This, she thought, was more like it.

"Do you realize that I could kill you where you stand?" she asked him, her anger rising. This was the man responsible for her woe, the one who thought her less than human, the one who sold her away from her mother and into the evil clutches of Barrow just so he could have his way with her. The one who allowed the villainy against her mother to persist. "I could command you to take your own life and never lift a finger."

"Kwadzo said no mind bending!" Anita called to Irene, but it did nothing to lessen the intensity of her fury.

"Remove your filthy hand from my person!" Gavin seethed at her through squished lips.

"Brave in the face of your fear. Impressive. As you wish." Irene obliged Gavin by hurling him to the floor. Returning to her human appearance, Irene hovered over him.

"You think you can scare me?" Gavin yelled, scooting back from her. "I've heard all about you demon slaves and the evil you've done! You're still nothing but a bunch of worthless niggers!"

"I would refrain from using that word again," Irene said evenly.

"Or what?"

"Do you truly wish to find out?" The red flashing in her eyes seemed to quiet him. "Now, then. We are here on business for the Crimson Plantation."

"I've heard of no such plantation."

"You just have. The Barrow Plantation is no more. Crimson stands in its place." She opened the canvas bag, revealing the plethora of notes inside. "We are here to buy your slaves, starting with Cecilia."

Gavin's body trembled before his eyes flashed with anger. "Caesar!"

A shocked African, who looked every second of his sixty years in his proper livery suit and with the crown of his head free of hair, rushed to the door, his eyes wide with shock at his master on the floor of the porch and those who stood over him.

"Fetch Eli from the field and tell him to bring the other men and their rifles!" Gavin said to Caesar as he rose to his feet, but Caesar was frozen in place staring back at Irene and her companions.

"We represent the Crimson Plantation," she said, sweetening her voice as Caesar's bottom lip quivered. "We are the ones who took the Barrow Plantation, and we're here to give you your freedom."

"They will do no such thing, Caesar!" Gavin said. "They may be ornery, but deep down, they still know their place. Now get Eli."

"But they the ones killed Mister Barrow," Caesar croaked.

"Get Eli!" The older house slave lingered, his eyes jumping between Irene and Gavin. "NOW!"

Finally, he ran off. Gavin opened his mouth to speak, but Irene's words cut him short. "You live because Kwadzo does not wish for you to die. I am here at his behest and in his stead to negotiate the sale . . ."

"How dare you! How dare you set foot on my property with your master's stolen money speaking of business. How can a slave conduct business with stolen money? A female slave at that?"

"I suppose the same way a man can claim to be the owner of land he stole."

"You are a slave, girl! You know nothing of business! Do you honestly think that because this wayward doctor taught you a few proper words, you can deign to speak to me as if you know me? As if we are equal? Well, upon the arrival of my chief overseer, you shall take your final breath so that you can return to the pit of Hell where you belong. The entire lot of you!"

Irene peered into his eyes with intention. Did he really not know? Had he completely forgotten? Had she meant that little?

"You don't even remember selling me, do you?"

"Why in the hell would I have any recollection of a damn slave?" Gavin scoffed.

"I suppose you're right." Irene chuckled. "I was the same as a cane knife or a serving spoon to you when I was here . . . just a thing. And like you said, you have no recollection of me, so it wouldn't matter to you that you ripped me away from my mother or that my father is your chief overseer. I was just a few welcome extra pounds for your haversack. Yet when I offer you money for slaves now, you take offense."

"The money is not yours."

"The hell it isn't! I earned it! *We* earned it! Every penny! Me, on my back, because that was what you sent me there to do!

You took money for me to be defiled by a fat pig! Barrow deserved worse than what he got. I reckon you're no different."

Realizing her words had stirred up more emotion than she had intended to show, Irene calmed herself once again. She made a mental note to herself. Perhaps skin *was* held in higher regard than money.

"It doesn't matter," she said to Anita and Polly. "He doesn't hear my words, and he will not conduct business—not with me or any of us. He only sees skin he considers inferior to his own. Take the money and Doc Farkus back to the carriage."

"What are you going to do?" Doc Farkus asked.

"Mister Wilson has made it abundantly clear that he will not accept our money for his slaves. Which I take to mean they are already free. I've but to collect them."

Without another word, Irene's blur raced past Gavin and into the house.

Fourteen

Cecilia

Within seconds, Irene had made her way through to the back end of the house. The sting of heat on her skin told her that she had stepped out the back door and into the sunlight. She tried to call out to Caesar as he rushed toward the fields, but the sunlight fast became unbearable. She jumped back into the safety of the house and listened as the small sizzle of the skin on her face stopped.

She took stock of the small group of house slaves who had gathered to watch her while keeping their distance. Kwadzo had given her a very specific mission, but it had not gone as planned. Gavin Wilson had changed the rules of engagement, not her. Besides, Irene had a mission of her own—to free her mother from this wretched place. That is, if she was still alive. She would apologize to Kwadzo and do whatever he asked of her to free the rest, but regardless of whatever else happened on this day, she would not leave Wilson's plantation without her mother.

Fear registered in both the eyes and blood of the house slaves, but before she could offer them calming words, a rough hand clamped onto her forehead from behind just before the searing sting of a blade sliced across her throat. Her eyes wide with surprise, Irene gagged as blood gushed from the new gaping wound in her neck. She stumbled forward and raised her hands to cover the wound, but the blood kept coming, flowing from her as hot as lava.

"Silver, you hateful demon nigger slut! Die!"

Gavin's voice.

Falling to her knees, weakness overtook her. She could feel her body shutting down until her vision went blurry, then black.

IRENE FELT HER BODY shut down. The silence that engulfed her was such that she thought she'd gone deaf. She'd lost all sense of time; she couldn't tell if it was seconds or hours that were passing, or even days. She felt as if she had died, but she knew that she was already dead. Yet, her consciousness remained. Upon this realization, the field of vision behind her eyes became a blinding red, and a new realization overtook her. Yes, she was already dead, but she had just been killed. She also understood that because Ramangan Blood had made her immortal, this murder would be temporary.

Movement still eluded her, but the silence was beginning to lift. Muffled voices echoed in her ears, the fiery pain in her throat returned, and her heart pulsed in the same way it had when Ramangan Blood first awakened her, a throbbing that recharged her system before settling to a hum that somehow remained vibrant within her, though deadened. The red behind her eyes throbbed and pulsed as well, returning awareness to her, and with it, an unmistakable feeling consumed her entire being.

Rage.

Opening her eyes, she found herself face down on the floor, blood pooling beneath her. Red pulsed in her vision as she felt the wound in her neck begin to heal, and words became clearer.

"What are you all standing around for staring? Put this good-for-nothing demon nigger in the ground," she heard Gavin tell the house slaves.

Gavin Wilson.

The essence of her yearned for vengeance, and her body ached for blood.

And only his would do.

Irene felt the speed of her blur return as she rose to her feet and spun on him, wrapping a hand around his neck and rushing him against a wall. Her eyes burning red, she lifted and tightened her grip. Gavin's mouth was agape in shock as he struggled against Irene's grasp, his legs dangling helplessly below him.

"I killed you," he croaked out while trying to free himself from her clutches, his eyes fixed on the actively closing wound he had cut across her throat.

"I was already dead. You murdered me."

Irene released her former master long enough to free his neck before pulling him in close. She took on her Ramangan form, bared her jagged teeth and fangs, and used them to rip into the man's neck. She drank from him deeply, feeling his blood accelerate the healing of her neck. She was aware of the house slaves watching. She wanted them to see her dominance over this mere mortal who ruled their lives. She wanted them to see how weak and helpless he was in the wake of her power.

She wanted them to watch him die.

Gavin's skin went gray as the life force was drained from him. Irene dropped him on the floor in a lifeless lump, the sound a slight interruption from the pumping of blood that filled her ears.

"You are one of them, no?"

There was a French lilt to the voice. Irene didn't know how she knew that, but its resonance calmed her. With blood still dripping from her lips, she turned to find the house slaves staring at her, shivering in fright.

"The ones the white folk whisper about. The demon slaves of the Barrow Plantation."

Irene studied the girl who had bravely stepped forward, her dark skin bright and flawless and her warm, pale blue eyes quaking with fear. Irene surmised the girl to be just a few years older than her, but her voice, posture, and speech made her seem much more refined than the others. Or perhaps she was simply distracted by the girl's shimmering eyes.

"I have never seen an African with eyes like yours," Irene said.

"I have never seen a demon."

"We are not demons, and it is no longer the Barrow Plantation. It is the Crimson Plantation now, and it belongs to us. We are no longer slaves. Some of us are of Ramangan Blood."

A collective gasp of recognition rose from them.

"C'est impossible," the blue-eyed house slave said.

"Your master is dead because of Ramangan power. Do you not believe your eyes?"

Soiled in blood, Irene reverted to her human form and took a step toward the young house slave, who jumped but did not move away.

"Do I frighten you?"

"Oui," the house slave said. "Just as you frightened our master and his friends."

"They attacked us."

"They have failed. Those of us who work in the house, we hear the master and men he has hosted speak of you with trembling when they do not believe we are listening. They fear that what befell Mister Barrow will befall them as well."

"And so it shall." Irene smiled. "What is your name?"

"Antoinette."

"Your master is dead, Antoinette. That makes you free. It makes all of you free. None of you have anything to fear from us."

Irene stopped short when Antoinette, her blue eyes glazed over, reached a finger out to touch the blood on her face.

"My father," Antoinette said, "he will tell the overseers of you. They will kill you for what you have done."

Irene smiled. "I am already dead. Eli cannot stop what is coming."

"You know our overseer?"

"He is my father." The declaration chilled the air in the room. "The slave called Cecilia is my mother. I came here to buy her back, to buy the freedom of you all, but Gavin Wilson refused our money. There is nothing Eli can do to me, but he can kill my mother for what I've done to his master. I have to save her before that happens, but the sunlight will end me."

Antoinette and the house slaves gawked at her. She understood the shock they must have been experiencing, but time was of the essence.

"The gift of the Blood can belong to you. The power you bore witness to can be yours. If you help me, we can return to Crimson Manor and I can introduce you to Kwadzo, our leader. He will free us all, but for now, I must get to my mother before Eli gets to me. I need your help."

Antoinette traded looks with the other house slaves before taking Irene's hand and leading her to a full standing suit of bronze plate armor in an adjoining room.

"It was his prized possession. He says it dates back to 1550s Sweden. It may protect you from the sun, but it is very heavy."

"Not for me."

"It would not fit you; you are too small."

"It will have to do."

"Then you must hurry. When the mistress returns from market with their children . . ."

"Don't worry. There is no one to keep you here any longer. Gather those in the house together and go to the Crimson Plantation. You will be safe there. Leave by way of the farm so that you won't be stopped by townsfolk."

"But the overseers . . ."

"Will be far too busy with me. Go."

"Caesar, my father. Please save him."

"I will."

THE BULKY METAL WAS slowing her down. Irene couldn't tell she was still moving extraordinarily fast because she was not used to the cumbersome armor. There was more of it than there was of her, and she found herself tripping over her steps a bit as she went along. It was hot inside the suit, but it was nothing compared to the burning she would have felt without it. The sweet, musty smell of freshly burnt sugarcane in the air brought back memories of her mother, spurring her on. She knew Kwadzo would not be pleased by this turn of events, and she had no idea what the fallout from her actions would be, but they could not be reversed, and it would all be for naught if she didn't rescue her mother.

Spotting Caesar making his way toward the fields through the visor of the helmet, she rushed forward and stopped in front of him.

"Caesar," she said. Sweat dripped down his face as he gasped and stumbled back in fright.

"Caesar," Irene repeated, eyeing him through the slits in the visor. "Don't be afraid. Your daughter Antoinette helped me put this suit of armor on."

"But Master . . ."

"He is your master no more. I killed him. You and your daughter are free. Everyone on this plantation is. You have nothing to fear."

"But you do . . ."

The tremble in his voice and the wide-eyed look on his face gave her an idea as to who was behind her. The click of a rifle hammer behind her head removed all doubt.

"Take that helmet off. Now."

Irene heard two more clicks before she turned around to face Eli and the overseers behind him, all of whom aimed their rifles at her.

"You have already lost," she said calmly. "Your master is dead."

Eli's face twisted in rage. He fired his rifle at her, and his overseers followed suit. Irene remained in her position but felt herself take on Ramangan form beneath the armor that served as a shield from the bullets for a cowering Caesar behind her. She then leapt over Eli and kicked him to the ground in the process. Despite the clunky metal, she moved with such speed that neither of the other overseers had time to fire off more shots before Irene's strength punched the metal gloves of her armor through their chests, killing them both instantly. Moving over Eli, she snatched his rifle away and held her metaled hand at his neck. She glared at him through the visor slits, her red eyes glowing fiercely.

"You're one of them demon slaves, aren't you?"

With the sun at her back, Irene reverted to her human form before opening the visor to expose her face. Recognition registered on his face, and it brought tears to her eyes.

"I am the fruit of your loins, Overseer Eli."

Recognition turned to fear, and then to disgust in Eli's eyes.

"No," he said. "My seed ain't make this. Whatever you are now is an abomination of evil."

"Evil you should fear."

"Evil or no, you're still a slave. And a slave ain't nothin' to fear."

"Is every white man blind?" Irene chuckled incredulously. "Do you not see your men dead before you by my hand? Do you not see the power I possess? Do you not understand that I will decide whether you live or die?"

"I reckon this is all about you tryin' to save your whore of a mother."

"You flatter her, Eli. Whores are paid."

"Yeah, well, if she ain't already dead, she's about to be."

"Then I no longer have any use for you, Father."

Irene punched Eli with all her might, sending the metal glove through his skull. Tears filled her eyes, both at the act and at her mother's fate. She had once again reverted to her human form.

"You really killed Master?"

She turned to find Caesar still trembling behind her.

"What will become of us?" he whimpered.

"Kwadzo will lead us all. But I have to find my mother."

"Your mother is here?"

"Yes, Cecilia. She works in the fields here. Do you know of her?"

"She suffers in the sick house from consumption with the others."

"Show me."

Caesar pointed in the distance, then let out a yelp at being lifted onto Irene's back. She sped through the fields toward the sick house at the edge of the property. He banged on her back plate as she reached the entrance.

"I can't go in," he told her, and she released him before walking into the small space filled with the sick lying in cots. They moaned their pain like an eerie symphony of death, and Irene could smell the sickness in the air. They were pressed up against one another, making their conditions worse. She removed her helmet and began to search their faces.

"Put that helmet back on your head, child," a familiar voice croaked behind her. "You'll catch your death in here."

Irene spun to find a shell of a woman, once vibrant and beautiful, staring back at her with yellowed eyes. Irene fell to her knees at her side as recognition registered in the woman's eyes.

"Irene? Baby?" Cecilia muttered.

Irene no longer felt the need to hold back her tears as she took her mother's hand in her metal gloves.

"Mama . . ."

Cecilia took note of the blood on the metal gloves. Weakly, she tapped her knuckles against the armor.

"Child, what you done? How you get all this metal 'round you?"

"I'm something more, Mama. I can free you."

"What good freedom gonna do me now? I ain't long for this here world, but now I can go happy."

"No, Mama!"

"I never thought I'd see your face again, child. This here, layin' eyes on you one last time, was my only prayer. I loves you, my girl. You 'bout the only good thing this life done ever give me."

"Before they took me away from you."

"That ain't nothin' we gots control over. We's cursed in this here world, and if'n you don't put that helmet back on your head, you gonna be cursed 'long with us, if'n Massa don't get you first for doing whatever it is that you done."

Cecilia was seized with a coughing fit that broke Irene's heart. Once she was able to get control of her breathing, she spit out blood. Irene wanted her mother to be alive, but not like this. This was no kind of life. She had waited so long to reunite with her mother, only to find her teetering on the brink of death. Irene fought to form words through her sobs.

"Your master . . . is dead, Mama. I killed him."

"How in the world . . . ?"

"He sold me to Ol' Barrow, Mama. Have you heard what happened there?"

Cecilia's brow crinkled, but she nodded her head. It made Irene beam with pride.

"I was a part of it, Mama! I was in the revolt. I helped win it. And now I'm taking you back with me."

"No, child. There ain't no need for me no more."

"You're my mother. *I* need you."

She could no longer ignore the thought that had consumed her since the second she stepped foot in this place. These people, worked literally to death, could all be made whole again. Better than whole. And she could have her mother with her forever.

"I can save you. I can save all of you."

"How?"

Irene removed the metal gloves and slit her wrist with a Ramangan talon.

"I can make you what I am."

Fifteen

Seven

The sun shone brightly, and Rafazi could feel its warmth. He sat shirtless in a wainscot chair by the back door of the manor, one leg hung over the chair's right railing, nursing a mug of blood, surrounded by his current harem. The African and Native women had been so eager to service him that he'd begun cycling them in and out, retaining his favorites while tasting new blood that appealed to him. However, the six of them brought him no solace now as he reclined, watching his people move back and forth, into and out of the house. He could see the sweat on their brows, smell the heat in their blood from their exertion. It made him shake his head.

All that fighting for freedom and still they worked themselves ragged.

Now that the Peterson slaves had been collected, the manor was filling up. It was almost fully repaired and the land was being cultivated again. More squat round houses had been built, the cabins in slave village had been reconstructed into larger, more comfortable housing, animals were tended to, food was prepared, and all in a very short period, thanks to Ramangan Blood. Still, from where he stood, Rafazi figured they were working just as much as they had before.

Only now, they were laboring for Kwadzo.

He had been just an insignificant slave named Willie until Rafazi saw fit to gift him with the power of Ramanga. Rafazi felt himself snarl at the thought of them all bowing down to him the way they did. Next to him, Willie was merely a child. Thirty-some-odd years on this planet was no comparison to seven centuries of existence. Rafazi had seen the Mali Empire rise to power and fall, celebrated with abandon during the Golden Age of the Swahili Coast, feasted on French blood during the Seventh Crusade. *He* was the one who had survived the Plague; it was *his* blood that kept Ramanga from being wiped off the face of the earth. But one measly battle won against a fat fool, and now Kwadzo thought he was in a position to give him orders.

Yes, it was Rafazi who appointed Kwadzo the leader of the new Ramanga Tribe, as he did not wish for the responsibility of leadership himself, but he deserved more respect for his position than he was being given. He had done his part. He had provided the ultimate tool of war in Ramangan Blood. So, if he now wanted to indulge his wantonness instead of waging war, he should be thanked and revered for his invaluable contribution to the cause and left to his own devices without comment or interference.

He certainly was not there to serve as anyone's representative.

"Sure could use a lil' more help 'round here," he heard Gertie say.

He closed his eyes and bit his tongue. The only person who had grown more annoying to him than Kwadzo was Gertie. She had nearly ruined everything with her arrogant objections, and now, here she was, pretending not to enjoy everyone bending over backward for her because she carried Kwadzo's baby. Did she think she was somehow special? She was not the only pregnant woman on the land. It was his venom that had saved her life, yet she felt justified in speaking to him as if he were beneath her.

"Ev'rybody workin' hard to make this here place a home for all of us," she said as she approached. "'Cept you and these here womens done took up with you."

During the height of the original tribe, he would have ripped out her tongue, turned her upside down, and drained her from her mouth for speaking to him with such disrespect and in such a haughty tone.

"You don't realize what Kwadzo done for you, do you?" she had the audacity to ask him.

Rafazi could feel indignation rise in his blood as a red tint clouded his vision. He rose to his feet.

"What *he* did for *me*?"

He could smell the fear seeping into Gertie's blood, but she remained defiant.

"His blood made you whole again," she said, her voice cracking.

"And my blood made him what he is! My blood gave him his power! I was the one who told him how we could be free and how to do it. My blood is what made all this possible, and it was my venom that saved your life when he nearly killed you."

Gertie's jaw tightened even as her eyes quaked. If he wasn't so infuriated, he would have been impressed.

"So, you gots power. So what?" she said. "Power ain't all. Lion got power, but it still get hunted. Kwadzo mind make him a leader. You ain't got what it take to be no leader."

"I've earned the right not to be! You've been drawing breath on this earth for barely twenty, thirty years? I spent centuries in the dirt, little girl, avoiding an unspeakable plague that ended every one of my kind, feeding on creatures of filth to sustain myself and the power in my blood, so that it could rise again. Kwadzo was just a cog in my destiny. If it wasn't him, it would have been somebody else. But if it wasn't for *me*, you both would still be in that field, you would've been Barrow's new whore, and you never would have laid eyes on that baby inside you. I handed you *all* the path to freedom, and that gives me the right to do whatever the fuck I damn well please without permission, or interference, from you, Kwadzo, or anyone else!"

Rafazi watched Gertie shudder from the roar in his voice, but its full effect was cut short at the sound of commotion coming from the front of the house. Blurring to the front door, he found it open, and in its doorway stood a frazzled and panting white woman being held back from entering by two Native warriors. She had blonde hair that was frayed and dirty. Her blue eyes shook with both fright and desperation. The finery she wore was speckled with dirt and her own perspiration. She was a young thing, younger than Gertie but perhaps older than Irene. Her eyes found Rafazi's and he allowed his to revert to their human state.

"These Indians refuse to let me in," she said breathlessly.

"They're not Indians," Rafazi said. "Why do you want to come in?"

She swallowed and sighed while Rafazi studied her. She was a fair beauty, her skin supple, her complexion as creamy as fresh buttermilk. There was a generous swell beneath her bodice, and he found himself imagining what further treasures were hidden beneath the rest of her dress. Her blood was rich with fear, but there was another element he could detect within it.

Desire, if he wasn't mistaken.

"We have been most unkind to you," she said. "My family held slaves. I was aware of how they were treated but paid it no mind. I was raised to believe it was just the way things were."

"And now?"

"I realize the error of my ways. Many in Lakeside, like my family, seek retribution, plotting against you."

"But you do not."

"No! Once word spread of your conquest, I voiced objection to my family's opposition to your revolt and was cast out. I have come to believe we must pay penance for what we have done to your people. I wish to pay true penance to you."

As she spoke, the quality of her voice calmed. It became less labored but breathier. The fright left her gaze and was replaced with a look of hunger, but Rafazi suspected it was not for food.

"And how do you suppose doing so?" he asked her, taking a step closer to her, careful to stay out of the path of sunlight streaming through the doorway.

"It is my understanding that you nourish yourself with the blood of humans."

"Some of us, yes."

"Then I wish to give myself over to you. My blood, my body. I give it all as atonement for what my people have done to you. My family and those like them stand in defiance of your power, unrepentant and unwilling to accept your place as our new master. I, however, willingly submit to it. Please, you must free me of them. There is no place else for me."

Perhaps she was sacrificing herself in the hopes there would be no more bloodshed. Perhaps she simply did not wish to be on the losing side. Neither mattered to Rafazi. Here this white woman was submissively casting her eyes downward. The action pleased him as much as her words of acquiescence. This was the kind of devotion he had been waiting to be shown.

What an excellent addition to his harem she would make. The thrill of extracting her blood, parading her around as his willing servant; what better way to exercise his freedom and trumpet the beginning of the end for every slaveholder in the New World?

Securing a white woman into their fold, having "one of them" on their side, and making her his personal emissary to do any bidding necessary with humans on his behalf without having to go hunting through the wilderness to corral her would show Kwadzo that their revolution was everlasting. That they would all fall under Crimson rule. Perhaps then he would find a way to enjoy the spoils of the victory as well.

"Release her," he said to the Native warriors in their tongue, and they followed Rafazi's command. A small smile crept across the woman's lips as she took her place in front of him. For good measure, Rafazi flashed his eyes red at her and made them pulse, not enough to bend her mind, but just a touch to mesmerize her. She was still a white woman he didn't know. There was no sense in being careless. Her breath caught at the sight.

"What is your name?" he asked her.

Offering her hand, she gave a slight bow, just enough to offer a more advantageous view of her décolletage.

"Lily," she said, her voice now as soft and light as morning dew.

"What you think you doin', Rafazi?"

Once again, the grate of Gertie's voice threatened to split his eardrums.

"Who this here? You cain't be lettin' in nobody unlessin' . . ."

"You led a gaggle of slaves into this house, did you not?"

"But Kwadzo say . . ."

"It is *my* blood that runs through Kwadzo's veins! You can abide me or be drained by me."

Her face twisted in fear and anger, but the fear won out. Gertie left the room in a storm, and by the time she was gone, Lily was standing even closer to him, her breath heavy, her smile sultry.

"What would you have me do first? Master?"

In an instant, his harem had grown to seven.

Sixteen

A Disruption in the Blood

Moonlight flickered across the clearing as Kwadzo emerged from the earth. The coolness of the air soothed him. Hours ago, deep in the ground, he'd felt a rumbling in his blood, an eerie sense that there was disruption in his bloodline. Some sixth sense, deep in his core, allowed him to sense everyone he had turned. He could *feel* them somehow, sense their existence—and to a lesser extent, he could also perceive those turned by them. It was an inner understanding of their presence, giving him the ability to intuit whether any of them were in danger and communicate telepathically with them if necessary.

The sound of horses racing toward him in the distance was not enough of a distraction from the disturbance in his blood. It was different from anything he'd felt before. It was something more than those his blood had spawned, and yet, it was tied to them. Or, at least, one of them. It was an almost malignant force he felt, so disquieting that it churned his stomach in knots while he waited underground for night to fall.

Still, it remained unfamiliar, and there were very real concerns that troubled him, the most immediate of which being his failure to bring the young white girl into the fold and her claims of surviving the daylight. One could never know what special ability Ramangan Blood would bring. Rafazi had told him stories of an ancient Ramangan who possessed that very power. The girl had made it clear she was an enemy, and a formidable one she would be if she truly could walk in the sun.

Though he didn't see how. The sight of her grotesque disintegration in the sunlight was etched in his memory. He could not see survival beyond that, but there was no pile of dust where she had stood. Her blood had registered within him the moment they met, and he still felt her presence.

The girl's existence was certainly a dangerous thing, but he was sure that the rumble in his blood had nothing to do with her. No, this force felt akin to a contamination in his bloodline, in his very essence. It was something completely unknown to him, which made Kwadzo worry that whatever it was might pose an even more serious threat than the girl did. Still, he maintained his calm as the others climbed out of the earth. He couldn't let them see his anxiety.

"Good. You're back." Seneca brought her horse to a stop in front of him as Nez halted his horse beside hers. "We have problems."

"What of the girl?" Kwadzo asked.

"Girl speak truth," Nez said. "Sun burn her, scorch her skin black so we start back to land, then her blur rush past. We chase, but she disappear. Too fast."

"We searched for hours, but there was no sign of her. We came back here to see if you could track her again. But that's not all," Seneca added.

Kwadzo groaned and winced. The disturbance in his blood had become an ache, one so blinding that it sent him to his knees, making his body seize up in agony. He wrapped his arms around his torso, but it didn't help.

"Kwadzo!" Fanna cried, rushing to his aid.

"Something's not right," he croaked, curling into a fetal position.

"We've got to find her," Fanna said.

"Yes." Kwadzo nodded. "But this is something else. My blood . . . I can feel something wrong in my blood . . ."

"Can you move?" Seneca asked as she gently pulled his arm around her shoulder and helped him up to his feet. He could hear the pumping of her heart grow quicker as she held him up, just before he was snatched from her grasp by Fanna.

"I'll take him, and make sure he gets back to *Gertie*," Fanna said, the pitch of her voice punctuating Gertie's name. He could speculate on this exchange, but there were more important things at hand.

"Can you feel her?" he managed to ask Fanna.

"We will find her, Kwadzo," she said, "but we need to make sure you're okay and that our people are protected."

"Wait." Kwadzo addressed Seneca before Fanna could blur him away. "You said that wasn't all. What more is there?"

Seneca's eyes moved from his to Fanna's, and Fanna glared back, her eyes red.

"She's taking you back, isn't she?" Seneca scoffed. "Why ruin the surprise?" She clicked her tongue and tapped her heels into her horse's flanks before turning and racing away with Nez following suit. The distraction of the exchange seemed to lessen the pain in his blood.

"What was that about?" he asked Fanna.

"Nothing," she huffed. "Shall I carry you?"

"Not just yet."

With a firm grip on his hand, Fanna led him through the woods as they blurred forward together, and the others followed.

"Fanna, focus your mind on your blood," he said as they raced alongside each other now, his pain dissipating further. "Do you feel any new presence?"

Fanna came to a stop and shut her eyes. "I feel her, but I don't discern anyone new of our kind."

"Don't lose her."

"I won't. Let's go."

Their blurs resumed, taking them back to the edge of the Crimson Plantation property, which was surrounded by lit torches. Across the rice paddy, there were a lot more of his people roaming around, albeit in a hurried fashion. It must have meant that Irene had successfully negotiated the freedom of the Wilson slaves. His smile was only temporary as his blood churned again, doubling him over in pain.

"Kwadzo!"

"Do you hear that?" Kwadzo could hear a low and ominous growling moving toward him, but he was in too much pain to move. The closer it got, the more the ache in his blood worsened, though it didn't seem to affect Fanna or any of the others. The rumble in his blood moved to his head as the growling became an immensely foul roar and two grotesque creatures sprang out from the wilderness. Their sudden presence sent Kwadzo and Fanna tumbling backward, along with the Ramangans traveling with them.

They were what he had been feeling; Kwadzo felt it instinctually. He could smell that they were of the Blood—Ramangan, but mutated, deformed. Their brows extended further than a normal Ramangan's and curved downward, nearly obstructing their eyes, the red in them burning with a high and consistent intensity. The veins in their faces were more pronounced, so much so that they protruded. Their muscles were so thick that they caused them to hunch over, making them quadrupedal. Both their hands and feet had the appearance of animal paws and were rotated inward and downward. They were feral, like wild beasts.

"What are they?" Fanna asked, a tremble in her voice.

"They are of the Blood, like us," Kwadzo said. The two beasts roared again and lunged forward.

"Stop!"

The sound of Irene's voice stopped them both cold and they sat back, docile, obedient to her as she approached. "Where have you two been? I've been looking everywhere." She petted both beasts on their heads before looking up at Kwadzo with tears in her eyes.

"I'm so thankful you're back," Irene said. "I've made a terrible mess of things. I killed Gavin Wilson."

In a daze, Kwadzo listened to Irene's bloody tale as they crossed the fields and headed toward the manor. She spoke of Gavin Wilson's arrogance, his "killing" of her, her going out in the sun under the protection of armor, her vengeful freeing of his slaves, her killing of the overseer who fathered her, her choice to save her mother from dying from consumption by gifting her the Blood, and her choice to save all the others dying with her in the same manner.

The sheer number of new faces that walked the property—their desperate stares, their eyes soaked in hope—made it hard for Kwadzo to focus completely on Irene's words. He had gleaned enough to know they had followed Irene from Wilson's farm and she had declared him their savior. It was not something he could refute or take back, not now. Their "master" was dead, and they were on his property. They were his responsibility now.

"They all wanted to be turned, but the sun was still out."

Irene was still talking, and he fought to bring his focus to her words.

"Who wanted to be turned?" he asked.

"Everybody in the sick house with my mama." He finally looked at Irene's face and found it twisted with despair. She wrung her hands and darted her head in every direction as they walked, as if she was sure something would go wrong any second.

"And you gave all of them the Blood?"

"They all would've died of consumption without it. But they rose quick, and the hunger set in even quicker. I tried to keep them under control, tried to keep them inside until nightfall, but some ran out into the sun and burned up. I still had the armor on, so I went out and collected a few hogs for the rest. But when I came back, some of them had fed on each other, and they came to be like these two."

"What happened to the rest like this?"

"They ran off into the sun."

The deformed Ramangans remained tame by Irene's side as she pleaded her case.

"They can't seem to talk, but they understand what I tell them. And they do what I tell them, which is good, because they are so much stronger and faster than we are. I waited until nightfall and brought the ones who survived back here so that we could protect the humans among them."

Stepping into the manor, there was more chaos and more humans; some he recognized, many he didn't, crowded together, their murmurs of concern ricocheting off the walls.

"I sent the ones from Wilson's farm that I turned out to feed on the hogs and livestock to keep them away from the humans," Irene was telling him as he struggled to wrap his mind around the situation. "I'm so sorry, Kwadzo. I didn't mean to kill him, but I just . . ."

The sight of Gertie in the crowd caused him to speed through the horde to get to her. They embraced and he felt some semblance of normalcy, which was what he needed to admit the turmoil of his ordeal and deal with the result of Irene's botched mission.

"Are you all right?" he asked her.

"I's fine," Gertie answered. "Irene done freed more."

"That she has, but not in the way I would have preferred. She killed their master."

"She what? She ain't say nothin' 'bout that; that ain't no way! You need to punish her!"

"Punish her?"

"Yes, Kwadzo! I know y'all got powers, but there need to be rules. You cain't have none of y'all just goin' 'round killin' however they please. We still ain't all free, you barely gettin' started, and now, she done gone and killed they's master and brought his slaves here? They gonna come for all of us, for what she done."

"I'm afraid the lynch mob is being assembled as we speak."

He saw the recognition on Gertie's face as the man approached them, having made his way through the throng and into the manor. The finery he wore, the brightness of his white teeth set against his dark skin, all of it was secondary to his scent.

The man that stood before him was Ramangan.

A Ramangan he had never seen before.

A Ramangan that wasn't supposed to exist.

All you do,
all you are,
is because of me.

Seventeen

The Free African from New France

"I am Jenue," the man said, extending his bejeweled fingers for Kwadzo to shake.

"He the one I met," Gertie said. "The free African from New France."

Kwadzo studied Jenue's demeanor; his face was calm, the grip of his hand sure, confident. He was comfortable in his form, like it had been his for a very long time.

"It is an absolute pleasure to see you again, dear lady," he said with a nod to Gertie. "I do hope it's not too much of an imposition, me taking advantage of the disarray to find my way in."

Turning his smile to Kwadzo, Jenue brought a joyful lilt to his voice akin to the way a proud father would speak to his son. "I assume you to be the new one, the one who led these people to their victory."

Kwadzo became fixated on the ruby in the man's cane knob, and in turn noticed that Jenue had become fixated on his ruby ring. His mind whirled with questions he had no time to ask.

"You mentioned a lynch mob," Kwadzo said instead.

"Yes, well, Missus Wilson raised quite a fuss after returning home to find her husband dead and her slaves gone," Jenue said with a small chuckle. It struck Kwadzo oddly, as he didn't find anything funny about the situation.

"So, she rushed to tell her tale of woe to the townsfolk gathered at the Crown Tavern, and it was decided rather quickly that you were the culprit. They were all set to march down here, pitchforks and torches at the ready, an odd couple leading the charge: a slight man and a much, much larger woman. But they were stopped by a filthy girl child with an extraordinary tale of her own, one of gaining demonic powers from slave niggers, her words, but being afforded an even greater one by their god, one that allows her to walk in the sunlight. She believes she has been sent by their lord to be their savior from your evil clutches."

The girl. She had made her way back into town. Kwadzo bit his inner cheek to help prevent any panic from showing on his face. Then he remembered that he was speaking to a Ramangan. He felt gnawing begin in his head, a probing through his mind. He knew the foreign mental presence belonged to this man, this Jenue, but found that he could fight against it easily. Still, his concerns were stacking up. There was a powerful Ramangan from Africa in their midst, one that he had no link to, one that should not exist. Rafazi was the last of the original tribe.

Or so he'd said.

What else was Rafazi keeping from him?

"How would you know any of this?" Kwadzo asked, his voice harder than it needed to be. "Free or not, they would not welcome an African into their meetings."

"My emissary, of course. The same one I sent here to collect your doctor. I had him slip into the tavern so he could report back to me. I've left him in my carriage; I had no idea what your temperament for white folks would be. I would suggest getting one of your own as soon as possible, though; they can be quite handy. At any rate, the girl's story bought you a bit of time—she's a chatty little thing with a bit of a god complex, and as you can imagine, her mere presence is raising all kinds of questions, but . . ."

"Has she turned any of them?"

"I doubt it. They're far too spooked. It will take some convincing to even get them to believe what she says is true. Though the odd couple seemed rather intrigued with her, and they seem to have a fair amount of sway with the others. I daresay a course of action must be decided upon and quickly."

"What he talkin' 'bout, Kwadzo?" Gertie asked, but he was not of the mind to explain anything right now, especially in front of Jenue.

"Would you excuse us for just a moment?" Kwadzo whisked himself and Gertie away in his blur. As they traveled, he could hear her barrage of questions about who he thought Jenue really was, where he was taking her, what he was going to do about Irene, but he couldn't focus on anything but confronting Rafazi. He would make Rafazi tell him everything he'd been hiding before deciding what his penance would be for lying. Gertie was right. There needed to be a set of rules and consequences for not following them.

Eighteen

Unwelcome Guests

When Kwadzo and Gertie burst through the door of Rafazi's bedchamber, they found a young, blonde, and very naked white woman on the bed, moaning in ecstasy, covered in bite marks that tiny streams of blood trickled from, with Rafazi's head buried between her outstretched legs. So indulged in her erotic display was she that she didn't even react to the intrusion. Kwadzo's eyes went red as he heard Gertie gasp at the sight before them.

"Our house lies in chaos, and I find you here? Do you not hear what is happening downstairs, or are you just willfully ignoring it?"

The blonde woman looked up at Kwadzo, her eyes half slits of lust. She giggled as Rafazi mumbled at her womanly gate.

"He says his concentration is on other things at the moment," she said in between heaves and gasps.

"Who is this woman?" Kwadzo's voice had become a low, ominous growl.

Rafazi held his position, smirking over his shoulder at Kwadzo, his face smeared with the woman's essence.

"My guest."

Rafazi returned to his current proclivity as the woman moaned, and Gertie gagged. This could not stand. It would not. With all the chaos happening downstairs, the very real danger they were in, his mentor was here, between the legs of a white woman he did not know. How Rafazi could have welcomed her into the manor, given everything they had been through, was beyond him. There was no telling if she had been sent to the house to gather more information for the citizens of Lakeside who were actively plotting their demise.

With the plethora of beautiful women on the land now, both African and Indigenous, many of whom had already willingly given their feminine gifts to him, Rafazi chose to indulge someone who could very well be an enemy, someone whom Kwadzo had not approved. Where did she even come from? Why was she here? And why was Rafazi so insistent on being insolent? Rafazi may have abandoned the cause for true freedom, but Kwadzo had not, and he would let nothing, not even Rafazi's lack of restraint and logic, take him and his people off the path. He had reached his limit with Rafazi's defiant attitude. It was he who had made him the leader, and he intended to lead.

Kwadzo zipped to Rafazi, grabbed him by the neck, and hurled him across the room. Before he could stand, Kwadzo hovered over him again, then picked Rafazi up and held him against the wall by his neck.

"Release me," Rafazi said, his eyes now glowing red and pulsing.

Kwadzo shook with anger and his brow crinkled in frustration, but he did as he was told.

"Step aside."

Despite the rage he felt boiling in his blood, Kwadzo was obedient once again as Rafazi moved toward the white woman in his bed, who was quaking in fear and covering herself with the bedsheet. Kwadzo was flummoxed as to why, when he had set out to exert his authority over Rafazi, he'd instead become subservient to him.

"Because I am still your maker," Rafazi replied, as if he'd heard his thoughts and responded directly to them. "You seem to have forgotten that. All you do, all you are, is because of me. I hold dominion over you."

"You said I had to fight it to be the leader you wanted me to be."

"I did. But can you?"

"Quite an impressive display, Rafazi, but I daresay we do not have time for it."

Jenue's presence in the room returned Kwadzo to his own faculties. He suppressed the urge to tear Rafazi's throat open when he saw that his maker was frozen in the face of Jenue. All the power Jenue possessed, the centuries of his existence, they were all etched in the shock painted across Rafazi's face.

"Who are you?" Rafazi said, his voice trembling. "You should not be."

"And yet, I am," Jenue said. He found a chair and sat, crossing his legs comfortably. His demeanor had become even more relaxed as he stared at Rafazi, whose distress became more pronounced by the second.

"You've made an excellent choice with Kwadzo here," Jenue said, his voice as soothing and calm as a cup of warm tea. "I can still smell the remnants of his human blood, and even in its diminished form, it still carries an exquisite bouquet. Of course, he has much to learn, and he must find a way to get better control of his scions," Jenue continued, his voice changing rapidly from calm to a frightful growling storm, "because I see no cause as to why a child against us of absolutely no consequence would be claiming to possess our power, or why the strong among our number would be allowed to become part of the Wretched!"

His agitation had brought him to his feet, and now, at the apex of his fury, Jenue was hovering in the air over Rafazi, his eyes a deep, pulsing red. Gertie rushed to Kwadzo's side, clutching his arm as he took a tentative step forward.

"Who are you?" Kwadzo asked of Jenue, who never took his burning eyes off Rafazi. "Why have you come here?"

"Because of you, dear Kwadzo. Your act of valor alerted me to Rafazi's continued existence, and I couldn't pass up the chance to say hello to an old friend."

Another Ramangan, one that Rafazi knew of, had been walking the earth all this time. All his stories of staying buried to survive a dreaded plague to preserve the tribe, all his posturing about being the last of his kind.

Lies.

Here, hovering in the air in an angry, inhuman perch, was a Ramangan he could sense was far more powerful and much older than Rafazi was.

"You said you were the last one," he hissed at Rafazi, his own eyes now red with anger.

"If it's any consolation," Jenue said, "he hid like a coward and offered no help to his kind as the plague and silver warriors took them, one by one. It stands to reason that he would believe he was the only one."

"I do not know you!" Rafazi screamed, the sting of tears beginning to fill his eyes.

Jenue seemed to expel a pocket of air, air that surrounded and blew around him as a metamorphosis began, the likes of which Kwadzo could scarcely believe. Jenue's hair began to grow, large puffs of it kinking up, then lengthening out, then straightening themselves in long strands before twisting over themselves, until a rich, black, and luscious mane of glorious locks cascaded down his back. The bones in his face began to crack audibly as his features shifted, becoming softer.

Feminine.

Beautiful.

The cracking of bones grew louder and more frequent, but Jenue never seemed to react, with pain or anything like it, to the changes. The chest expanded until two full, womanly breasts became apparent underneath the shirt. The waist softened and curved, and along with the pronounced round suppleness of the hips and bottom, created an unmistakable and undeniably appealing female form.

The pure shock of the transformation was enough to cause the white woman in Rafazi's bed to scream out in fright right before she fainted and fell over on her side. Kwadzo and Gertie stood with their mouths agape, and Rafazi's eyes went wide with recognition and reverence as Jenue's soft eyes returned to their human state. The air dissipated, and Jenue, irrefutably now a woman, gently descended until she was standing on her feet again. Her clothing had become ill-fitting with the drastic change in her physique.

"Jenue," Rafazi whispered.

"Kneel before your maker," she said with a smile, her voice now soft and floral, sounding nothing like it did in her masculine state. The female Jenue did not resemble the male in the slightest. The only feature they seemed to have in common was the rich dark tone of their skin. Rafazi never hesitated. Bowing his head, he took her hand and dropped to his knees.

"How?" Rafazi asked, his eyes cast downward in a gesture of respect.

"I never let you see my man. I took too much pleasure in your subservience to my woman."

"How did you survive the plague?"

"We fought the warriors who came for our fallen, but many fell prey to the plague, too many. When our numbers dwindled, we fled to Rus with the Vikings. We remained in the cold and drank only the blood of the young, those too new to be touched by the world beyond their villages."

"You fed from children?" Kwadzo asked.

"One does what one must do to survive in dark times. And they were indeed dark times. The burden became too great for the others. They let the sun take them. I suppose others could have survived—those who traded gold for blood in Old Europa and Anatolia. Among those with me, only I held fast, stealing and hording until the darkness finally gave way. Centuries of silence, darkness, and then I felt new blood. *Your* blood, and Ramanga rises again. Now, it must be preserved. Come, Kwadzo. Time is short."

There was so much to take in. Watching man become woman, Rafazi's submissiveness in the face of his maker, an ancient Ramangan still in existence who fed from children to survive. But there was no time to explore any of it. The enemy would be at the gates. Jenue was right.

Time was short.

Nineteen

UNCERTAIN TRUTH

Following Jenue downstairs, back into the bedlam that spun there, Kwadzo could not seem to take his eyes off her. Mere moments ago, she was a man. Despite the urgency of the hour, questions continued to swirl in his mind about her, her history, this mysterious ability to transform genders, Rafazi's history and how she had come to turn him, the origin of Ramangan Blood, the truth of what he now was.

"I can sense the chatter in your brain," Jenue said, looking back at him with a half smile. "You would do well to abandon it for the time being."

"Can you bend my mind?" he asked her.

"No, but not for lack of trying."

Jenue's smile reached its fuller extension, which told Kwadzo the questions in his mind had made their way onto his face.

"Ramangans cannot bend the minds of other Ramangans," she began, stopping midway down the stairs, "a fact I have tried to conquer nearly my entire Ramangan existence. A maker can make one she's turned obey her command, but only if she is the direct maker. Of course, one turned can ward off a command if one's mind is strong enough. After centuries of practiced focus, I've gotten to the point where I can get a sense, a general leaning of thought. Of course, the Ramangan mind is strong. It senses mental intrusion and blocks it, so the best I can get is . . ."

"Chatter."

"Yes, chatter. Your chatter seems to be in distress. Or it could just be the shock of having watched a man become a woman before your very eyes."

A nervous titter escaped Kwadzo. He looked away from her in embarrassment.

"There will be time to teach you more later, but we must ready ourselves."

"Can you feel any new presence?"

"My blood has run through multitudes, but when our numbers shrank, my senses dulled. After centuries of silence in the Ramangan realm, your presence was like a spark of light in a darkened cave, but it only told me that Rafazi's blood had been active. The farther removed from the turned I am, the harder they are to sense. You would feel anyone new before I would."

Kwadzo did not feel any new presence, but he stirred in worried expectation.

"If you don't," Jenue said, "then we have more time. But we shan't waste a moment of it."

"My God . . . it's you!"

Kwadzo and Jenue stared back at Doc Farkus, who was gawking up at Jenue, much to the chagrin of his wife.

"Many, many moons ago," Doc Farkus continued, "I encountered you in Sopron. You tasted my blood. You haven't aged a day! Unlike me . . ."

Jenue smiled softly. "*A véred csokor ismerős. Talán egy második ízlelés felidézi az emlékeimet . . .*"

But Kwadzo pulled her back as she leaned toward Farkus. "You just said we have no moments to waste. You can sample his blood again later."

"You understand Hungarian?" Jenue marveled.

"I understood enough of what you said to know we don't have time for it."

"Remarkable!"

Kwadzo ignored Jenue's curiosity as he took in the frenzy of uncertainty on the main floor of the manor—the former slaves of two plantations, along with those who had toiled this land under Barrow's rule, those native to this land, as well as Ramangans, some who had fought alongside him, and those new to the Blood—until he spotted Irene. Several of those who he assumed were from Wilson's farm approached her with panic on their faces, fear she, in turn, took on, the crinkle in her brow deepening with every person who besieged her.

She became his point of focus. Kwadzo closed his eyes and spoke to her mind first before mentally connecting with all the others he had turned. Soon, they served as extensions of him as they successfully quieted everyone in the manor.

"My people," he began as all looked up at him on the staircase. "First, I say welcome to those of you who have come to us from the Wilson and Peterson plantations. Your time under your so-called masters is over, and never will you go back to the life of servitude you were subjected to. Your home is now here at the Crimson Plantation. I will admit that we were not entirely prepared for you. Be that as it may, we shall make appropriate accommodation available.

"There are, however, pressing matters to be dealt with first. There exists a white girl with our power, Ramangan power. We found this child and tried to bring her into our fold, but she rejected us. She has the power to turn white folks with her blood and send them to us in retaliation. This child has run back to Lakeside and most certainly shared this knowledge with its citizens. We must be prepared to fight toe-to-toe with others who can match our power, and the humans among us must also be ready with weaponry that can extinguish our kind, fire, and silver.

"This freedom we enjoy was hard fought, but I'm afraid the fight is far from over. Those of the Blood will take watch at night, as always, and they, like the humans who volunteer themselves for battle, must be armed with fire and any silver we have here. They must also be mindful of it so as to protect our number."

An older man stepped forward and looked up at Kwadzo. His voice carried a French accent. Standing next to him was a genteel young woman with striking blue eyes who resembled him.

"Kwadzo," he said with a bow, "I have come to this property at the insistence of the one called Irene. She has promised me and my daughter Antoinette safety and freedom under your rule."

Rule. The word sounded so official when the man had used it, as if he were speaking to royalty. Kwadzo wondered if that was what he had become, or if Jenue would respond to the term. The power she possessed certainly spoke to that type of respect, but she remained silent, her eyes on him, awaiting his response.

She was acceding to his position.

"As I've said, our freedom is not yet absolute, and we will need more to step up and protect it. But I will do all in my power to honor Irene's promise to you and your daughter, sir," Kwadzo said.

"Then I am happy take up arms in the fight to come," the man said. "I failed to step forward in courage earlier today, but I would like to show my daughter that her father is a brave man, capable of fighting for her freedom."

"Don't be silly, Papa," Antoinette whispered to her father. "You are all I have."

"If you will have us as well, then this is the beginning of a new chapter for all of us," Kwadzo said. "Those of you of the Blood, take positions around the outside of the manor." Several blurs escaped through back and front doors. "I would like Native warriors with arrows to join them. Douse your arrows in oil and flame so that any attack is met with the onslaught of fire. Any of you who remain human who would like to join the fight, now is the time to stand . . ."

"I feel her. Here."

Fanna's interruption was abrupt, but her eyes were red with knowing. Kwadzo leapt from the stairs to join her, and they moved through the crowd to the front porch of the manor with Jenue in tow.

There, standing patiently between two Ramangans, was the redheaded white girl, just as filthy and tattered in rags as she'd been when he encountered her in the woods just a night ago. He studied her closely, her hard stance, her cold eyes. He chose not to speak. She had come to his door after rebuking him. Slowly, the strength in her countenance began to give way. Her shoulders slumped, her lips quivered.

"They have rejected me," she said with a whimper.

"Your Blood is our Blood," Kwadzo said to her. "Does this remain so? Or have you shared of your Blood with them?"

She lowered her head and shook it. Kwadzo tried to sense her sincerity, but just as Jenue had said, a Ramangan could not bend the mind of a Ramangan. Jenue had also said that a maker could make one she turned obey a command. Fanna was newer in the Blood than he, but she was this child's direct maker.

"Fanna," he said, "command her to tell the truth."

"Tell the truth, girl."

The girl's hard eyes returned when she glared up at Fanna, but they soon filled with tears. She opened her mouth twice to speak, but no words came out. Her eyes flashed red, and she shook her head again, her limbs trembling.

"In the wilderness," the white girl said through gritted teeth, clasping her hands together, "a man took my blood but perished in the sunlight."

"And when you returned to Lakeside?" Kwadzo asked. The white girl's eyes flashed red again when she looked up at Fanna for a second time, but Fanna held the girl's gaze with her own red-eyed glare. Kwadzo's lips curled. He was proud of Fanna's tenacity as a maker as tears finally made their descent down her progeny's cheeks before she groaned, then exhaled as if exhausted. Kwadzo believed she was losing her fight against Fanna's command.

"I showed them what I was," the girl stammered, her speech slow, "and they said . . . they said they wanted no part in the partaking of nigger blood." The word rankled Kwadzo's ears, but he let her continue as her distress seemed to worsen. "They said they would not be beholden to a little girl, that my power was meaningless."

Her shoulders shook as she lowered her head and openly sobbed in front of everyone. Kwadzo turned to Fanna, whose eyes had returned to their human state. There was sympathy in them.

"I have no home with them anymore," the girl said. It looked to Kwadzo as if she was gathering courage. Still, he remained silent. "Forever is a long time to be alone, but as you've said, we share the same blood now."

With trembling limbs, she bowed her head to him and knelt. "Will you still call me home?" the girl asked.

Kwadzo could feel Jenue's eyes on him, but this was what he wanted. To bring this white child into their fold, to keep her from turning the whites with her blood. But he could hear Fanna in his head.

I do not trust her, Kwadzo, her voice said in his mind. *She called us evil and vowed to destroy us, to destroy you.*

It was most likely true that her return to the Lakeside townsfolk had sparked conversation about their demise, about ending the Crimson Plantation, and probably about this girl's hand in that proposed destruction. Still, here she stood—alone. It was entirely possible they had rejected her for the very reasons she claimed, and the rejection could have been the flicker of change in the girl. Kwadzo was certain Fanna had made her tell the truth, but it was also possible to tell the truth without telling the *whole* truth. He turned to Jenue, who simply shrugged.

It would be his decision to make. So, he decided he would choose hope and grace. Grace. The thought caused him to smile. He imagined Gertie would be proud of him, that she'd approve of a choice made with the thought of goodwill rather than suspicion. If this girl's presence was indeed a ruse, he was confident she could be contained among them.

But if her motives were sincere, she could be invaluable.

"What is your name, child?" he asked her.

"Penelope."

"Well, then. Come, Penelope."

Twenty

A Fox Among Wolves

Kwadzo felt an immediate shift in the tide of his people from the moment he walked Penelope into the manor. A sea of frowns, silent and angry faces dark with betrayal, glared back at them. Even Charlie the bloodhound, after a thorough sniffing, only seemed to tolerate the young girl's presence.

"I do not trust her, Kwadzo," Fanna reiterated, and before he could respond, she was on the girl, her hands a blur, searching Penelope's person while the young girl protested the invasion. Fanna yelped and pulled her hand back, the tips of her fingers sizzling. Kwadzo reached into the pocket Fanna had found on the girl's clothing and retracted a silver dagger by its handle. He remembered it as the one that had temporarily killed him during the manor battle.

"You give that back! That's my daddy's blade!" Penelope protested. Kwadzo responded by holding the blade to the girl's throat, silencing her while simultaneously bringing the manor to a standstill as all looked on.

"This is the child that took Fanna's blood in battle," Kwadzo said to the crowd. "Her father took this dagger to my throat believing it would end me. Neither he, his dagger, nor his daughter are a threat to us anymore."

Kwadzo's words did nothing to fade the ire on the faces staring back at him. He took them in, looking through the crowd in search of better words, words that would provide solace. When they didn't come, his eyes began to seek out Rafazi. He hoped that once he saw that the girl had been found, his maker would offer assistance as to how to handle the situation. But Rafazi was nowhere to be found in the crowd. In disappointment, he turned to Jenue.

"Will you alert Rafazi that the girl has been found?" he asked her.

"I scarcely believe the news would remove him from his bedchamber of blood and flesh," Jenue said, chuckling, further stoking Kwadzo's frustration. "People are fickle. Once you determine the correct course of action, they will revere you once again. Your decision will be met with my support."

The trouble was he had no idea what the correct course of action was, and Jenue's words led him to believe she didn't either.

He was aware of the contradiction he was putting on display by accepting her in the fold, but after all, she was still a child. Yes, he had learned of her vicious words at the luncheon Barrow had forced Gertie to serve, but he was certain they were the product of beliefs ingrained in her from birth and that her actions were but a reaction to events he played a part in, justified or not. In truth, the girl had done little that had harmed his people, and the idea of somehow turning Penelope's thinking around was something he believed would be a monumental step forward toward cementing their place in society, perhaps even becoming the first gesture in a peaceful coexistence between his people and hers.

"Why you bring that horrible girl in this house?" Gertie snapped, having found him in the crowd to confront. The eyes of his people caught them.

"We will discuss this away from prying eyes," Kwadzo said in a low voice. "Fanna, take her to the cellar. Chain her up. Get Irene to help you. Just in case."

As Fanna did as she was told, Kwadzo quietly steered Gertie into the study where they would be alone.

"She is of the Blood," he said to her, closing the door. "She was out there alone in the wilderness."

"She evil!"

"She's just a child."

"She a evil child! Them words that come out her mouth! She look Irene dead in the eye and say she just folly, a mistake. Say just one drop of nigger blood make you a nigger, say any white blood she got was forever tainted, say she should be fed to the hounds if she ain't workin'. That's who you let in this house!"

Kwadzo stared back at Gertie, her nostrils flared and her hands balled up into fists. It felt like the days before the Blood when she seemed to challenge his every decision.

"First, you tell me to punish Irene for killing a white man, but now you're mad at me for welcoming a white girl who is of our Blood? You have always been the one saying that the best we can do is to be good. To be different in power from the white folk. You can't pick and choose with your compassions, Gertie. You're either compassionate or you're not."

"In power?" She sucked her teeth and hunched her shoulders. Her eyes carried a look he had never seen directed at him before. She had been angry with him. Disappointed. Disagreeable. Sad, worried for him. But this look was new.

It was one of disdain.

"Power?" She scoffed. "All that power done gone straight to your head. Your whole head! Is you so blind and drunk on your *power*, oh great Kwadzo, that you cain't see this girl bein' here ain't nothin' but a trap? And I tell you this here, it done already worked. They done sent that girl here to get you, and she gonna get you, too. She done already got you, 'cause you cain't even tell you done already fell into they's pit for you!"

"What would you have me do, Gertie? Kill her? She's already dead!" He could feel the anger surge anew in his veins before he closed his eyes and pleaded with it to subside. He marveled at the turmoil this one child had already stirred up.

"I'm well aware that her surrender may not be what it seems," Kwadzo said, lowering his tone, "but if she said that Irene's father's blood was tainted by her mother's, then it stands to reason that this girl's blood got her thrown out of their world entirely. It's not just African blood in her veins, it's Ramangan Blood. They're terrified of us having it, but now, one of their daughters carries it. As much as they hate us, I can't imagine they can make any sense of that, let alone be willing to accept her. I would never have chosen for her to have the Blood, but her having it could become a bridge between us all. I won't give up the chance to try and make that happen."

"You so worried 'bout this child; what you need to be worried 'bout is freein' the rest of us like Irene done!"

"And yet, you want her punished for killing a slave owner when you know Barrow had to be killed for us to be free. You can't have it both ways, Gertie."

"All I know is she done what you s'posed to be doin'. 'Least she got her mind on what's important!"

"Then maybe she should be the one leading!"

They had not fought like this since their victory. Kwadzo felt a pit in his stomach. Gertie stood right in front of him, but she felt miles away. Still, he was the leader. He was in control, not her.

"That girl may have volunteered to come here so she could get back into their good graces by spying for them," he said, calming his voice again, "but she'll learn nothing we don't want them to know. In the meantime, she will be here, like it or not, among her own kind. She will learn the truth about what she is, about who we truly are. She will be shown kindness. Perhaps if we show her good, good will find its way into her heart. Or has your staunch belief in doing good above all else left you?"

His words seemed to have taken a bit of the steam out of her ire, but it remained as she crossed her arms aggressively.

"I gots my eye on her. And you," Gertie huffed as he led her out of the study and into the cellar.

Penelope waited patiently as Irene and Fanna locked iron shackles around her wrists and ankles while Kwadzo, Jenue, Doc Farkus, Nez, an agitated Seneca, and an equally upset Gertie looked on. The shackles were affixed to chains that were bolted to the wall, but the young white girl did not struggle against her restraints. The dark dankness of the underground space—crowded with farming tools and rice sacks with only two small flickering lanterns—barely registered on her stony face.

Her eyes lifted and met Kwadzo's blankly. What she had experienced in the wilderness all by herself was still a mystery, but the girl seemed built with fortitude, which kept his suspicions piqued.

"What did they send you here to do?" Kwadzo asked her.

"I told you," Penelope sighed, "they cast me out."

"Perhaps she does not deserve the grace we have shown her," Seneca said before a nudge from Nez quieted her.

Kwadzo turned to Fanna, whose eyes were red.

"Speak the truth, girl!" Fanna barked, which caused the girl's eyes to go red as well.

"I am!" she seethed. "And do not take that tone with me, you little Negress! It's your fault I've become this abomination!"

"*You* bit *me*!" Fanna growled back.

"Some truth is not the whole truth," Kwadzo said, keeping his calm.

"Are niggers hard of hearing?"

In his growing frustration with her, Kwadzo began to lunge for Penelope until he felt Jenue's strong hand on his shoulder, stopping him. Had he the ability to take a breath, he would have.

"Speak that word again, and you will lose your tongue," Kwadzo said, flashing his eyes red at her.

"Which word?"

"If you wish to keep your tongue, perhaps be mindful of all the words you speak from here on out."

"Do not ask the truth of me again. I have already told it to you."

"What did they send you here to do?"

"How dare you!" Penelope took on her Ramangan form to scream at Kwadzo. In turn, he transformed as well and blurred to both lanterns, absorbing their flame through the flesh of his hands before grabbing the girl by her throat.

"What did they send you here to do?" he roared, sending the girl shuddering as flame now flickered in his eyes.

"They sent me into the lion's den to spy!" Penelope relented painfully. "They want to destroy you, and they want me to tell them how, but first, they wanted to see if you would reject me, too."

"Your maker commanded you tell the truth when you arrived at our door," Kwadzo said. "Why did you lie? *How* did you lie?"

"I *didn't* lie," Penelope moaned. "I felt the compulsion to speak of all I'd encountered, but I fought against it. But the things I said were true. The things they said to me were said."

"The girl is formidable," Jenue whispered to Kwadzo, and he agreed. The power the Blood had given her was both impressive and infuriating.

"None of it matters anymore," Penelope said. "There is nowhere I belong. Everything I had, everything I ever was, is lost. Even if I were to complete their task, I will still be of your blood, which they despise! There is no hope for me!"

Her façade fell away as she reverted to human form and set about blubbering incessantly.

"Theatrics aside," came Jenue's whisper, "I sense the despair in her to be genuine."

"She cannot be trusted," Fanna said, her eyes pulsing red. "I feel her despair, too, but I sense no fear."

"You will discover who you truly are here, Penelope Knudsen," Kwadzo hissed in her face. "And so shall we."

KWADZO DECIDED TO HAVE Penelope moved into the small storage room that Irene used to occupy when Barrow was in charge and had silver cuffs made for her. Irene was ordered to stay in the room with her—part of the penance for her transgressions was the duty of babysitting their new charge whenever she wasn't confined.

At daybreak, Penelope was taken to the covered porch by Doc and Rebecca Farkus for observation while Kwadzo, Jenue, Irene, and Fanna watched. They questioned her about all manner of things about her existence before asking her to step out into the sunlight. For several days, they would watch her full transformation, hoping to gain some kind of information that could help others of the Blood survive in the daylight, an effort Kwadzo was keenly interested in considering there was battle ahead, but it was to no avail. Irene would clothe her afterward and give her a nip of animal blood for sustenance and to accelerate the healing process.

At night, Penelope was trained in the use of her powers. As her maker, Kwadzo instructed Fanna to be her primary teacher while he supervised, forcing the two to learn together under his own tutelage. Gertie would sit under the stars and watch them, her eyes fixed on Penelope, Charlie the bloodhound at her side.

When her training hours were completed, Penelope was put to work in the fields at night along with humans and other Ramangans, who used their speed under the light of the moon to hasten the cultivation of the crops. She was met with scornful looks and hateful words by nearly all she encountered. Kwadzo allowed it. He wanted her to suffer their words and taunts just as Gertie and Irene had suffered hers.

"I put her with my mother," Irene told Kwadzo, blurring up to him as he watched over the field with Gertie by his side and Charlie the bloodhound at her feet. Penelope's skin provided a stark contrast in the moonlight against those whom she worked alongside, the bulk of them refugees of Wilson's plantation. "The others may mock her, but my mother will keep them from doing her harm."

Since her return from the Wilson Plantation, Irene had taken to wearing breeches instead of dresses. Kwadzo presumed they were formerly Barrow's son's, but he noticed they were a part of her ever-evolving nature. Gone was the tortured, put-upon house slave, demure in all her dealings and trapped between her dual heritages. She remained respectful toward him and mindful of his disapproval about how she handled things at the Wilson farm, but she showed no remorse for it. In fact, she walked more assuredly in the wake of it, her head held high. Kwadzo believed her wearing of breeches was the outward sign of her increasingly confident attitude.

Still, in this moment, he could feel her hesitancy, but he chose not to respond to it.

"I'm sorry, Kwadzo," she said after a long moment, her voice cracking. "You put your trust in me, and I know I did everything wrong, but I was so angry at that man already, and then he killed me—or he thought he had. I wanted him to pay. I wanted them all to see that he was weak and that we are strong." She stopped short, braving a look toward Gertie before finding her speech again. "I've heard the rumblings that you wish me to be punished for killing, Gertie . . ."

Kwadzo held up a hand, silencing her.

"You flaunted your power. You used your force as theater for your own glory. That is not what we do. We fight, yes, but for freedom."

"I needed to save my mother."

Kwadzo nodded. "I know how important your mother is to you, and I know that you were put in an impossible situation, that I put you in an impossible situation. I never should have sent you back to the man who sold you away from your mother. But we now have chaos of our creation that must be controlled."

They stood in silence for a moment. Only the sounds of the autumn breeze, the shuffling of feet in the earth, and the swift, continuous tearing of lint from cotton bolls surrounded them until Irene found new words to speak.

"Would you like to meet her, Kwadzo?"

Their blurs arrived in front of Cecilia and Penelope, who had pricked her fingers on the boll again; the blood on her fingertips told the tale.

"Careful, child," Cecilia told her. "Don't go so fast."

"I thought the whole point of us doing this was that we were supposed to go fast," Penelope sulked.

"Don't matter how fast you can go, if'n it be somethin' you ain't done before, the goin' gonna be slow."

They both looked up at Kwadzo and the beaming Irene.

"Mama," she said. "This is Kwadzo."

Cecilia stood and took his hand. "Thank you, sir," she said, and he shook his head.

"No, ma'am. Thank you for joining us. You being here is a great comfort to Irene. Have you not had a chance to be gifted blood by one of our willing humans?"

"Oh, no, sir," Cecilia said sheepishly. "I's s'posin' you can tell on account of my talkin'. Don't seem right to be suckin' on nobody's blood that's 'live and ain't done me no wrong."

"I wouldn't have a problem with it," Penelope huffed.

Her comment was summarily ignored. Once the observation of her transition in the sun was completed, Penelope was only allowed hog's blood for sustenance—never human blood—and it was brought to her in a jar; she was not permitted to drain an animal herself. She was fed once every six days. There was no sense in making her stronger, especially when she exhibited a power neither Kwadzo nor any of the other Ramangans in the tribe had.

"Irene say a fight gonna come," Cecilia continued, "and I reckon takin' blood in a fight should suit me just fine."

"It would be our good fortune to have you by our side in battle," Kwadzo said.

"I know my Irene was wrong what she done to Ol' Wilson, but my girl gots her a good heart."

"Something I see she inherited from her mother. You're one of the few to show kindness to little Miss Penelope here."

Penelope rolled her eyes, and Cecilia gave a warm chuckle. "Well, I know what it be like to have ev'rythin' you know taken 'way from you. I reckon you do, too."

"That I do."

"'Sides, this child only know what they done taught her. Maybe we's can teach her somethin' new."

"Something better. Isn't that right, Clarence?"

The former house slave hovered nearby with Derby by his side, both looking worse for the wear after weeks of sleeping in the field. Their self-imposed isolation from Kwadzo's leadership left them ostracized by everyone else.

"It's hard sleepin' when y'all work through the night," Clarence said even as he locked eyes with Penelope. "Young Miss Callowhill? Is that you? What in blazes is you doin' out here, child?"

Penelope rolled her eyes for a second time and took on her Ramangan form, causing Clarence to squeal in fright and fall back into Derby, sending them both tumbling to the dirt.

"What y'all done? Don't you know what's gonna happen to y'all for giving this innocent white child demon-nigger power?"

"That's enough, Clarence," Irene said. "Find somewhere else to sleep before Kwadzo takes your tongue. And take Derby with you."

She flashed her eyes red, causing Clarence to scurry off, pulling at Derby to do the same. Derby hesitated, glowering at Kwadzo.

"I still ain't 'fraid of you, *Willie*," Derby said.

"Kwadzo. And yes, you are. I can smell it."

Clarence successfully pulled Derby away, and Kwadzo noticed Penelope watching them go. Her shoulders shook, and when she turned back to her task, he could see she was smiling. It was a small smile, but a smile all the same. Looking up, her eyes found his and for the first time, he shared a smile with the girl: his first shared smile with a white person.

Against better judgment, he chose to see it as a good omen.

Twenty-One

An Invitation

Early mornings were usually a time to quiet his mind in the warmness of Gertie's flesh and the scent of love in her blood.

But here had been one distraction after another that prevented calm from taking hold, mostly because they postponed the freeing of slaves from the other plantations.

Though she had murdered the plantation owner in the process, only Irene had successfully liberated other slaves purposefully. She had botched the mission terribly, but oddly, no one from Lakeside had come for her head. Outside of Rafazi's exercise in defiance, Penelope had been the only potentially threatening white face that had visited the manor, a fact that also left him on edge. And while Gertie's presence did relax him a bit, the aroma of her ardor had become a bit diminished, as it always did when they were at odds. At least he could take solace in the scent of their child, still untouched by worldly concerns. A knock on the door of the bedchamber spun his head to the source of the disturbance, where he found Seneca slowly stepping into the room.

"I believe it customary to wait for a response to your knock before opening the door," he said to her in a hushed but authoritative tone, his eyes burning red.

"There are pressing matters," she said, undaunted by his eyes. "There are questions about the fate of the white girl among my people. The bond we entered with you was founded on the idea that we would be kept safe. Many no longer feel safe with her in our midst."

"In all honesty, Seneca, neither do I." Kwadzo's eyes returned to their human state as he sat up. Thankfully, the intrusion hadn't woken Gertie, and he was grateful Seneca had hushed her voice.

"My people are also puzzled as to why you have welcomed this white girl into your bosom while we, who have been loyal to you, are still denied the power of your Blood."

"Your people? Or you?"

Seneca frowned and looked away. He shook his head at her small tantrum.

"This has been addressed," he told her softly. "Regardless of her theft, the Blood makes her one of us. We cannot afford her betrayal."

"I would be a much better candidate for the Blood than she will ever be."

Her pout was purposeful, and it amused Kwadzo.

"And why is that?"

"Because I would revere it and you!"

Seneca's eyes shimmered with emotion as her voice rose. He felt the weight in his head grow, adding Seneca's admission to the list of things that plagued him. The silence that followed was excruciating. The only answer that would satisfy Seneca's request, he was not ready to give.

"The mother sleeps well."

Her eyes shifted, and the urgency drained itself from Seneca's voice with a sigh. He turned to take in his sleeping love. Perhaps one more moment focused on Gertie would give him the clarity he would need for the day ahead.

"Your love for her in spite of your power is admirable."

"Should a man not show love when he feels it? And why should power dictate it?"

"Many here desire you, would gladly lie with you despite her. But you, a fire god, remain in the bed of a love you know you will outlive. It is admirable."

There was a warm smile on Seneca's face now, soft, welcoming. He had seen a similar smile on many women in the manor. He chose to ignore them, just as he chose to ignore Seneca's now.

"You don't believe me to be a god," he said.

"I don't believe you *not* to be a god."

Kwadzo shook his head while her smile grew warmer. He suspected it was not a smile Gertie would take kindly to.

"You spoke of pressing matters. Is there more than your concern over Penelope?"

"A white woman is at the door. She asks to see Gertie."

In seconds, Kwadzo's blur took him to the covered front porch of the manor, where Sarah Collins stood in a coat-and-skirt street suit of pink silk chiffon broadcloth with embroidery and lace decoration, from the lacey hat on her head to the parasol she held at her side. In the distance, an elegant carriage awaited her at the entrance of the property. Her hazel eyes shimmered from fright as she shifted her head back and forth between the two muscular Africans standing to her left and the pair of Native warriors to her right on the porch before finally resting on Kwadzo's appearance.

"Oh my," she said, her body responding to his sudden presence with a jump. "This doorway was empty but a moment ago." She leaned back, taking in the manor's façade. "I must say, the red is very bold. Striking. A bit thrilling, actually."

"And I see you have reestablished suitable transport for a lady of your station," Kwadzo said, nodding toward the carriage.

Sarah chuckled as if embarrassed. "Oh, yes. Well, in the wake of my husband's demise, my father saw to it that his good name would not fall into shame from my, shall we say, lack of acquiescence. I'm ashamed to admit it, but in the past, luxuries had a tendency to tame my tongue."

"I don't get your meaning."

"My life has never been my own, you see. I lived under the rule of my parents until I married, then I lived under the rule of my husband, the governor. Both they and he held slaves. It never felt right to me that a human could possess another human. But I was complicit in the practice as I saw no way to stop it, even as I benefitted from it. And, as I enjoyed the comforts afforded me, though my beliefs remained, my words were not much more than an occasional annoyance to my husband's ears.

"But then, by some miracle, you rose against James Barrow with a most frightening power. You conquered those who chained you and claimed the house you built and the money you toiled for as your own. If you can do that, I can make my words a little louder, say them with a bit more conviction. Still, with my husband gone, I see no reason why I shouldn't accept my father's extravagant attempts to keep me silent, whether they work to his benefit or not."

Sarah sucked in a large breath, having not breathed during her diatribe. She gave a nervous chuckle and her eyes went wide. The air was pleasantly cool, but there was moisture accumulating on her upper lip. She dabbed at it with the index finger of her gloved hand, and the familiar stench of fear made its way into Kwadzo's nostrils.

"You must forgive me, Kwadzo," she said quickly. "I fear you still make me quite nervous."

"My fire did nearly extinguish you."

"Had I perished, I would not have blamed you. You had no way of knowing I was on your side. You do know I am on your side?"

"You made your stance clear at the tavern." Kwadzo smiled assuredly, Sarah smiled back, and the scent of fear abated.

"Do Africans possess surnames?"

"Okoro. Kwadzo Okoro."

"Kwadzo Okoro. I shan't forget it." She chuckled, and her shoulders relaxed. "I trust Gertie approved of the shoes?"

Kwadzo had to think for a moment before remembering shoes Sarah had brought for Gertie before accompanying him to the Crown Tavern.

"Ah, yes. They were lovely, thought she hasn't had occasion to wear them as of yet."

"Well, then. Perhaps I can provide occasion this day." Sarah closed her eyes and took a deep breath. She exhaled and stood tall, but her shoulders drooped with a nervous laugh. "My goodness . . . I suppose I am quite nervous to ask what I've come to ask."

"Which is?"

She took a second breath and made another attempt to stand tall. "I would like to ask for the pleasure of Miss Gertie's company for a spot of tea and lunch. There is a wonderful little tearoom belonging to one Edna Livingston in the back room of her house overlooking her lovely garden. She serves the most exquisite teas, scones, and cakes; creamed chicken on toast, nut and preserves sandwiches. Pear and ginger salad."

"Why?"

"Well, because she is your wife, for one. That makes her the most prominent wife of the community to come, and this particular luncheon is for prominent wives—and, I suppose now, widows—of Lakeside who disagree with the laws as they stand. Considering what happened at the Wilson Plantation, I assume your work is not done. Am I correct?"

"You are, but she is not my wife. Your laws do not allow for it."

"After all that you've been through, you are still mindful of colonial law? That is quite admirable, Kwadzo, but laws will change. Much will, and I suspect your needs and desires will be reflected in those changes. What you've done, what you shall continue to do, will shift the course of the colonies. You've rung a bell that cannot be unrung. Try as they might to stop it, your position among us is not in doubt—it is imminent. There are a precious few that agree with me, but they do exist, and I think that they and your Gertie should get to know each other. Besides, given that and the little time I've spent in her presence, she seems to be a delightfully caring and charming person. Quite beautiful as well."

Kwadzo laughed. This woman wanted to make friends with his wife. His wife. A pleasing image of him and Gertie, standing together in brightly colored kente, adorned in gold jewelry and royal regalia, flashed onto the screen of his mind. It was a thought he wouldn't have dared think of before, but now, it was something he could hold onto, even look forward to. *Laws will change*, she had said. This was another thing that hadn't fully occurred to him, and the change would be because of him. With that being the case, would he be the one to change the laws?

But he couldn't get distracted from Sarah and her request. The last time Gertie left him, it was this woman who came to her aid, but danger surrounded them both. There was no guarantee that she could protect Gertie should anything happen, and the sun prevented him from doing so, but Sarah was providing an introduction into Lakeside society. It was a chance to garner respect and that could not be passed up. But first, he would need to secure certain assurances.

"Very well. All I will require to present this invitation to Gertie is a taste of your blood."

Sarah took a step back and exhaled involuntarily. Her breathing quickened and her heartbeat raced, but she did her best to smile, as if to keep her terror hidden. Several times she attempted speech, but no words were produced.

"There's no need to worry," Kwadzo said with a chuckle, and Sarah regulated her breathing with a laugh of relief.

"My goodness!" she exclaimed. "I was truly terrified for a moment!"

"It won't hurt, and it won't be much at all. In fact, it will be quite pleasurable."

Her smile was gone, and she was blinking back against the wetness building in her eyes.

"Think of it as a gesture of goodwill," he said. "You are asking me to entrust Gertie to you, to take her to a place she would have to go without me to keep company with those who are unknown to us. While you may be sincere, there are those who have come to this door who are not."

Sarah hesitated, and Kwadzo remained silent. He wanted to see where her mind would take her without his assistance.

"She is here, isn't she?" she finally asked.

"Who are you referring to?"

Sarah cleared her throat and swallowed. "Young Penelope Callowhill. I heard the Crabtrees hatched a plan to send the girl under the guise of peace. Kwadzo, if she is here, she cannot be trusted."

"I don't suppose she can be, but it is trust in you that I am most concerned with now."

"There is blood on the hands of the British who came to this land. We were invaders who justified our attacks by placing them in the name of God. And then you rose up with godlike powers. If you are meant to be our retribution, it is justice."

She took a third breath and stretched her neck upward, standing in decision. "By rights, you are the victor and the master of this property now, and if I wish to gain your favor and the pleasure of Gertie's company, I must bend to your will. How shall it be extracted from me?"

Kwadzo smiled as his eyes glowed red and pulsed. Sarah stared into them, mesmerized.

"You simply need to tilt your head to the side. I will do the rest. You will not be afraid of my appearance."

In a trance, Sarah did as Kwadzo said. He transformed and bit into the ivory skin before him. He heard her gasp as his fangs pierced her skin, then heard her moan as the venom in them set in and the tension in her body dissipated. Her blood was sweet with renewed fear, but he had no intention of indulging in it. He would take just enough to ensure the suggestion he would plant took hold. Dislodging from her neck, he found her eyes glazed over and a silly smile across her lips. He looked directly into her eyes and spoke with deliberate purpose. He was breaking his own law, but Gertie's safety was paramount above all else.

"You will protect Gertie with your life," he said, continuing to pulse his red eyes while peering into hers. "You will keep her safe and let no unpleasantness befall her. You will give her nothing but kindness and patience, and you will assist her with anything she might need on this outing. You will protect and defend her at all costs until you return her to me at sunset."

As she lingered in a haze, he reverted his eyes to human form and turned to the African guards. "Find something for her neck, a scarf. One that matches the colors she wears."

As they rushed into the manor, Sarah began to shake free from her trancelike state. Her fingers traced the punctures in her neck.

"Well, that was something," she said.

"How do you feel, Sarah Collins?"

"Well. Quite well, in fact. That wasn't at all what I imagined it would be. I can feel that my neck has indeed been bitten, but here I stand, right as rain. I might be so bold as to say that the tingle felt rather good!"

Kwadzo smiled.

"Wait here. I will do my best to convince Gertie to accompany you."

Our Blood is the
Blood of the gods.

Twenty-Two

Vanth's Imps

Kwadzo stood on the covered porch with Irene, Seneca, Fanna, and young Chev watching Sarah lead Gertie, dressed in finery, toward her waiting carriage at the front edge of the property.

"Are you sure she will be safe?" Seneca asked him.

"She'll be safe until sunset."

"Did you bend that white lady's mind?" Fanna asked him.

"Just a little. To protect Gertie."

"To protect her?" Seneca asked. "And what if she is overpowered by men who want to take Gertie and make her pay for what Irene did?"

"Their retribution for Irene's actions is already upon us."

Chev tugged at Kwadzo's hand, asking him in his native tongue when Gertie would be coming back. He assured the boy that she would return at the setting of the sun, something that seemed to satisfy him. He then grabbed Fanna's hand and the two skipped back into the manor with Seneca in tow. Only

Irene remained with him now, looking out at where Sarah's carriage once sat.

"She won't let Gertie come to harm. I could see it in her eyes," she said.

"You barely saw her eyes."

"She won't let Gertie come to harm."

Kwadzo was taken aback by Irene's staunch response, her eyes fixed and cold, as if he had offended her in some way.

"Will Gertie's wish prevail?" she asked. His mind swirled with so many things—not the least of which was Gertie's safety being out of his hands—that he had forgotten Irene's words as soon as she'd said them.

"How will you punish me?" she asked, her voice sharp enough to garner his answer.

"I don't know, Irene. Perhaps our immediate concerns should be focused on Gertie and Penelope right now."

She nodded and moved back inside the manor, which remained crowded with faces clouded with uncertainty and anxiousness. Kwadzo walked through them, examining their expressions with dismay. Those from the Peterson and Wilson plantations had been put to work in the fields now that the prospect for sales had increased thanks to the agreement he'd come to with Josiah Browne, but their existence here was not much different or better than it had been on the farms they'd been delivered from. They needed more food, more blood.

Just more.

"Tea with the governor's widow?"

Jenue was at his side, chuckling. "Your Gertie is moving up in the world."

Kwadzo never stopped his stride. He was in no mood to be teased by her. Between Penelope, Gertie, and the needs of the newly freed, he had plenty to concern himself with.

"Would you rather have this conversation with a man?" Jenue asked, keeping step. "Because I can make that so."

"Why are you here?"

The thunder of aggravation was apparent across Kwadzo's face. His stance was one of antagonism against an ancient Ramangan whose power he was sure could end him, but still, he stood.

"I have answered this question."

"You've answered nothing! It's no wonder you are Rafazi's maker, you talk and talk and talk, but you say nothing. You've lived for centuries in apparent wealth and luxury; I imagine without regard for anything or anyone else. You could have gone on for eternity doing the same. Why come here? Is eternity really that boring?"

"In a thousand years, you tell me."

Kwadzo moved away from her, shaking his head in frustration.

"Uneasy lies the head that wears a crown," Jenue called out. The words meant nothing to Kwadzo, so he never stopped walking. Not until Jenue was suddenly in his path.

"Have you not read Shakespeare?" Jenue asked. "Charming fellow. He was a friend. Begged for the Blood." Kwadzo stared back at her in an extended silence that soon became uncomfortable. "What?"

"I'm just wondering if you could be of any meaningful use here at all. You've done nothing but jest, pontificate, and drive Rafazi into a shell of himself I don't recognize, so I'm just wondering of what meaningful use you could be."

"You see me as being of no use to you?" Jenue scoffed. Kwadzo shrugged. "I am the oldest Ramangan in existence!"

"So claimed Rafazi. Until you arrived."

"I have lived on this earth for over a thousand and five hundred years. I am the closest connection you have to your origins. The knowledge I could share . . ."

"What is a vampyre?"

Jenue blinked and silenced herself. "Where did you hear that word?"

"Do you know what it means?"

"I have heard the word, yes."

"Then tell me what it means and why the white folks at the tavern would have used it to refer to us. Prove to me what use your hundreds and hundreds of years of knowledge are."

"Very well. In the ancient days," Jenue began, "we traveled far and wide, into parts of Europa, Anatolia, the Far East. We feasted on many. Some of the wealthiest of those lands, the Kingdoms of Dacia, Meath, England, and Scotland in particular, would offer us gold in the hopes that we would grant them the Blood and gift them immortality. They were the ones who first called us vampyres."

"So, white men were willingly given our Blood in exchange for gold?"

"The world was different then. The Tribe was different. I'm sure Rafazi told you of our disregard for anything besides our own pleasure and supremacy. Gold bought much pleasure. Of course, even as they purchased the Blood from us, they believed us to be attendants of the Devil. Not that they cared. Dying was a small price to pay to live forever. Sadly, their savagery knew no bounds before they took the Blood, so having it quickly led to their ruin. The gold they gave us far outlasted the lives they had hoped for."

"Why the word vampyre?"

"It took the efforts of many to settle on the term. When we moved through Italia, we learned the people there believed in a goddess they called Vanth, who guided souls to the Underworld. When they learned that our power came after death, they thought us to be imps, which was the word they used to describe the Devil's attendants. So, we became Vanth's imps. Over time, they morphed the two and started calling us vamps, which seemed to stick throughout most of Europa except for the east, where, for some reason, they started collectively calling us 'the upyr.' Eventually, vamps and the upyr melded together, creating 'vampyre.' No matter where we traveled, our true name was disregarded."

Kwadzo considered the information Jenue had presented, and while interesting, he found it pointless. It offered little more than an explanation of a curiosity. In truth, it didn't matter what they were called by the white folks. What mattered now was not only what they did but how they did it. Jenue, still, had offered nothing useful.

"An entertaining tale, Jenue. You must excuse me."

Jenue grabbed the retreating Kwadzo's arm, stopping him from walking away in the crowd. "Did it ever occur to you that those centuries of wealth and luxury, which you were quite accurate about, might have also been empty and unfulfilling? That it may have grown tiresome and utterly depressing to watch generations of friends, and acquaintances, and lovers grow old and die? That I might have longed for naught but to be among my own kind, only to discover that I was not as alone in this world as I believed myself to be?"

"Do you understand what is going on here, Jenue? What's at stake? For all of us?"

Kwadzo shook his head at Jenue's smile, which he found particularly annoying.

"Baako would ask me similar questions."

"Who is Baako?"

"Baako is why we exist."

Kwadzo fell silent. He didn't want anything to hinder Jenue's next words. *Baako is why we exist.* That simple sentence echoed in Kwadzo's mind as he peered at Jenue, awaiting more. What she spoke of now was history. *Their* history. It meant answers Rafazi couldn't provide.

"Has Rafazi not told you of Baako?"

Or wouldn't.

"He isn't the full story, but he is crucial to it. What else has Rafazi neglected to tell you? It's obvious he told you nothing of me."

"Jenue," Kwadzo said. "Penelope . . ."

"Was sent to us by the white townsfolk on a false mission of peace for some nefarious purpose that the governor's widow was not clever enough to learn. My hearing is as potent as your own."

"No . . . if she learns of our history, of what being of the Blood truly means at the same time as the rest of us . . ."

"A shared learning experience could bond her with the herd."

"Yes." This, Kwadzo thought, would be useful. If Jenue was willing to do it.

"She is no ordinary child, Kwadzo. Her blood is special; she survives the sunlight."

"But a child she is, still. Just as Fanna is. And Chev. What child does not like a good story? Especially when the story is about them?"

"The governor's widow is right. She cannot be trusted."

"Maybe she can be *made* trustworthy. Gertie accompanies Sarah Collins to Lakeside for tea. One of their daughters carries our Blood. These are strides toward unity. If we can gain understanding, maybe we can free the others without spilling any more blood."

"You forget what you are, Kwadzo. Blood spills to keep you walking this earth. To keep all of us walking."

"And knowing why is a story every one of the Blood needs to hear to go forward truly united. It could also settle the minds of the humans who suffer with uncertainty of the road ahead."

"I suspect now you are also speaking of yourself."

"Perhaps I am."

"Then you have found use for me after all."

Kwadzo ignored her ribbing but could not deny the smile crossing his lips.

"I'll have Penelope summoned, and we'll gather everyone together here, all of the Blood and any human willing to hear, African and Native."

"Very well. Shall I tell the tale, or shall my man tell it?"

"Have them both tell it."

Twenty-Three

Gamab, the Divine

Kwadzo and Jenue stood at the mouth of the manor's foyer looking out at the mass of Ramangans and humans that had assembled before them. Kwadzo spotted Irene pulling Penelope through the crowd. Trailing behind them, Irene's mother and her ever faithful pair of deformed Ramangans. They drew fearful stares, but they kept their heads down and the glow of their permanently red eyes stayed on Irene's back. Charlie the bloodhound leapt past them and took his place at Kwadzo's feet.

"Bring her up here, to the front," he called out to Irene, and soon, Fanna and Chev joined Irene, Cecilia, and Penelope, sitting on the floor at Kwadzo's feet.

"Thank you for welcoming Chev into your fold."

Kwadzo turned to find Seneca smiling at the young boy.

"He has struggled among our tribe ever since his parents died of smallpox. But I have never seen him smile more than when in Fanna's company."

"May he have many reasons to smile from now on," Kwadzo said as Seneca's eyes met his and they shared a smile, one that Seneca took her leave from abruptly, but Kwadzo was too focused on Penelope to give it much thought.

"I'm glad you're here," he said to Penelope.

"Better here than suffering in cuffs," she said, gingerly rubbing at her wrists, still reddened and scarred from the silver that had restrained her.

"You were sent here to somehow weaken us from the inside. After what we hear today, I think you'll come to realize that if we fall, you will as well. Our fates are intertwined."

Kwadzo smiled at the crinkle of confusion twisting up the young girl's face.

"My people!" he then called out to the mass. "This has been a time of great change for us, and more is to come. We are still learning what the Blood can do."

A shuffling on the stairwell brought Kwadzo's eyes upward where he found Rafazi, surrounded by his harem—the blonde white woman still among them—leaning over the railing and listening in. The smile he offered was not returned.

"Many of you remember the stories about the Ramanga Tribe of lore," Kwadzo continued, "and many of us believed them to be pure myth, me included, until the Blood forever changed me, as it has all of us, and some of you directly. We believed there were none left of that ancient number but Rafazi, but we have been sought out and found by his maker."

Amid a rumble of murmurs, Kwadzo nodded to Jenue, who stepped forward with the regality of a queen addressing her loyal subjects.

"I am Jenue, and I am indeed Rafazi's maker. I was born in the Kingdom of Aksum at the dawn of the third century, well before the Romans could lay claim to the luster of Alkebulan."

"Pardon," Doc Farkus said, raising his hand to be heard. "The Kingdom of Aksum, you say? And Alkebulan? I've not heard of these places."

"You wouldn't have," Jenue said with a smile. "You're far too young." A few chuckles rolled through the crowd considering the age of the good doctor. "Long before your ancient ancestors decided to venture into places they did not belong, the Kingdom of Aksum was one of the great powers of the world in the third century, far mightier and more beautiful than you could ever imagine. This was long before the Greeks decided to give the land a moniker no one native to it asked for, when the place you call Africa was called by its true name: Alkebulan."

While Farkus nodded at this knowledge, genuine curiosity flashed in Penelope's eyes before she shrugged and looked away, feigning disinterest. Perhaps this was working. Kwadzo gave Jenue a nod to continue.

"It was a time of kings and gods. There are those who claim the power of Ramangan Blood to be evil, but it is not. Our power is the power of the gods, our Blood is the Blood of the gods."

"There is only one God!" Penelope called out, garnering rumbles of contention.

"You British," Jenue chuckled. "After all your predecessors saw and did, it astounds me that you have clung to such a narrow-minded view of theology. You've abandoned the true mysticism of divinity for one diminutive but charismatic, I've been told, Nazirite who spoke of nothing but mysticism. What do you think all those miracles you all are so fond of reading about him performing were? Of course, you all changed his description to your likeness to help further the cause. Wise, but false. Power isn't good or evil, it is divine. Its measure is only determined by how it is used."

"So then why can't any of you survive in the sunlight like I can?"

"And why are there some with powers beyond the rest of us?" Ekow called out.

"And why would that white child be more powerful than any of us?" came the shout of another of the newly turned.

"And why would her having the Blood be embraced while my people are denied it?" Seneca exclaimed. The echoes of discontent had risen to a fevered dither.

"Friends, please," Jenue hollered out to no avail as their bickering escalated. She turned to Kwadzo. "They are your subjects. What would you have me do?"

His people had seen miracles of the Blood free them. Perhaps seeing a new one would make them settle down and listen.

"Show them your power," Kwadzo told her.

The crowd didn't notice at first. Jenue's eyes pulsing red did nothing to bring their attention back to her. When she began to levitate off the ground and expelled a breath from her mouth, a breath that grew into a fierce wind that whipped around her, sending her hair waving, the rattling stopped. When her long, thick twisted locks began unraveling in the wind and retracting into her scalp, her hair texture becoming denser and coarser, a silence fell over the manor. The faces of those watching were frozen in bewilderment and trepidation at the cracking of bone and the shifting of Jenue's facial and body features from soft and feminine to chiseled and masculine. The air subsided as he floated back down to the floor—Jenue was a man again.

Kwadzo watched Penelope marvel at the change and smiled to himself. Surely, this would open her mind beyond the paradigm she had managed to cling to even after becoming a Ramangan.

"How," she said, her speech stumbling. "You're not even the same person! You're a . . . a man! How is that possible?"

"You can survive the sunlight. Kwadzo can absorb and conduct fire. I can do this." Jenue formed his lips into an *O* shape, and the air began to stir in his mouth again before he quickly shut it. "This is my special power, this last vestige of life's breath that rebirths me each time I release it and breathe it back in. It changes me, makes me brand new. My very own breath of life."

"That's evil!"

The shout rang loud in the silence of the crowd and all eyes turned to its source: Clarence. With his eyes hard and his lips tight, Clarence pushed his way to the front of the flock with Derby in tow, waving a finger of accusation at Jenue.

"Ain't nobody can give the breath of life but the Good Lord, and you ain't him. No, sir! Now, I done listened to all this foolishness for long enough, and I ain't gonna let y'all drag poor Miss Penelope to the depths of Hell with you!"

Murmurs rose from the crowd, and Kwadzo stepped forward.

"That's enough, Clarence," he said. "You're upsetting the others."

"I'm upsettin' the others? This here heathen turned from a woman to a man, and *I'm* upsettin' the others? And you wonder why me and Derby rejected this wickedness? We keep our heads down and do our bit on this here farm 'cause there ain't nowhere else for us to go, but when y'all done gone too far sullyin' this innocent child of light, I ain't afraid to speak my piece on it!"

"Nothing was done *to* her," Fanna said, getting in Clarence's face. "If you had joined the fight for freedom instead of being intent on betraying your people, you would know that."

"That's enough, both of you," Kwadzo said. "Clarence, you've said your piece. Your interruption is over."

Clarence audibly scoffed, sucked his teeth, and rolled his eyes. "Nigger, you ain't my massa."

Every eye in the house turned to Kwadzo. Yes, he had decreed he would snatch the tongue of anyone who uttered the heinous word against his people, but he had also vowed to protect all who had suffered the horrors of bondage. Despite this, Clarence's affront had to be handled. He could not lose ground with his people, but he was unsure of what action he should take.

"Give him the Blood."

Rafazi's words only heightened the tension in the room as he descended the stairs. They were the first words Kwadzo had heard him speak since Jenue's arrival. His expression was blank, his eyes lazy, as if he was bored. Moving to Clarence, Rafazi grabbed him by the neck and lifted him off the ground while Derby quaked in his presence.

"You won't take his tongue, let alone kill him," Rafazi said, turning to Kwadzo without an ounce of urgency in his voice. "Even though he serves no purpose and has no intention of doing so." Clarence twisted in the grip, gasping for air. "The worst punishment you could give him is the Blood. He despises it and us, so why not sentence him to becoming the thing he hates the most? Let him live an eternity with the knowledge of his fate. Maybe in death, he'll become useful in this slave-saving crusade you haven't managed to start yet."

Rafazi was testing him and mocking him. In the presence of his maker, no less. Perhaps this was an act of defiance against Jenue. Or maybe he simply wanted to embarrass Kwadzo by pointing out his lack of action to their people. Neither mattered. Kwadzo now had two to deal with, and he had to do it swiftly but calmly. How he handled Rafazi, and how the elder Ramangan responded, would set the tone for Kwadzo's leadership going forward. Of this he was certain.

"Let him go, Rafazi."

"As you wish."

Rafazi thrust Clarence to the floor hard before planting a knee in his chest. He presented his talons and slit his wrist open. Clarence gagged as the blood spurt forth.

"Open your mouth."

"Stop," Kwadzo said, but Rafazi paid him no attention as he punched Clarence in the side of the head, forcing his mouth open.

And that's when Kwadzo moved.

His blur sped him up the stairs and into his and Gertie's bedchamber, where the silver sword Monroe used against him sat. He could see Rafazi holding his bleeding wrist over Clarence's open mouth as he sped back down the stairs. Never slowing, Kwadzo rammed into Rafazi. Righting Rafazi in his blur, he slammed his maker against a wall and placed the blade of the silver sword at his neck with all eyes on him. Rafazi's eyes were wide at the presence of the silver, but Kwadzo's hold was sure and steady, mere inches away from Rafazi's neck.

"We do not force anyone," he said, his voice even. "Do not make me raise silver against you again."

His point made, Kwadzo stepped back and lowered the blade. Rafazi's blur zipped away and up the stairs past his harem members, who all chased after it. A door slammed shut so hard it seemed to shake the entire manor. *Insolent child*, Kwadzo thought. He moved to the panicked Clarence, pulling him to his feet, and there, on his still-open lips and tongue, it was.

Blood. Rafazi's blood.

"You too late," Clarence whimpered before he began spitting profusely. He wiped roughly at his tongue.

"Maybe now you will learn the value in keeping your mouth shut." Kwadzo pointed the tip of the sword at Derby. "I trust you have no words of defiance to speak?" Derby shook his head frantically as he stepped back from the sword. Kwadzo then turned to two muscular humans. "Take Clarence to the cellar and lock him up."

"Will he . . . ?" Penelope's voice shook as Clarence was led away.

"As I've said, this is the Blood of gods," Jenue answered. "It does not take much. Once he perishes, his blood will be our Blood."

"Come, Rebecca," Doc Farkus said, grabbing her hand and chasing after the men taking Clarence away. "We must examine him!"

It should have been a very simple afternoon. Jenue's story of the origins of Ramanga should have opened Penelope's mind and renewed the reverence that everyone else felt toward the wonders of the Blood and the purpose of using it—not only to free their people, but to unite *all* peoples. Instead, there had been only chaos and derision.

"Perhaps another day would be better for you to tell your tale," Kwadzo whispered to Jenue.

"Nonsense!" came his boisterous response. "Now, more than ever, all of you must understand the truth of the power you are dealing with, where it comes from, and how it works the way it does. Take, for example, the man who stands before you now. I believe this breath of life that rebirths me comes from two things. First, my proclivities as a human. I find that this New World has discarded many of the indulgences of the Old, particularly the freedom of carnal pleasures. I would lie with both men and women regularly to great satisfaction. Not that I'm a braggart, but I built a most desirable reputation throughout Mazaber that served me quite well. My second belief is that this particular power was made possible for me because of the god our Blood comes from: Gamab."

"Gamab," one of the elderly Africans said with recognition. "The god of both sexes."

Jenue nodded "Yes. Many believe that the great god is both male and female and can take on the form of either at will. I believe the power of the one breath that remains within me is testament to that. It is not known what makes certain human blood special, but mine was, apparently, and I believe the great passion and yearning I had for both the feminine and the masculine carried with me in death, and the Blood gave birth to its manifestation in this power."

"Are you any stronger as a man than you are as a woman?" Irene asked.

"Physically, no. But, as you have seen, my female form is quite undeniable, yes?" A smattering of laughter spread through the crowd, and Kwadzo could feel the tension in his chest—and the room—start to slip away. Jenue's charm was salvaging the day. "My strength is equal in either form, but perhaps there is more power in my woman's form than in my man's. For obvious reasons."

The laughter grew as Jenue's eyebrows rose, his lips curled in a provocative way. Kwadzo enjoyed the frivolity Jenue's antics elicited, but a question was nagging at him.

"So, if your blood is special, your greatest emotion becomes manifested in your power?" Kwadzo asked.

"That is what I believe."

It made sense, then, that fire fell under his control. The fire he could not save his family from when he was a boy. Now, fire was no longer a hindrance to him. He wondered what connected Penelope to her power over the sunlight.

"What about these?" Irene called out again, pulling the two deformed Ramangans obedient to her forward. "They became so hungry after I turned them that they fed from each other, then this happened."

"There is great liberation when human and Ramangan blood mix," Jenue continued with a look to Charlie. "And apparently, when animal and Ramangan blood mix as well." Charlie barked and wagged his tail in acknowledgment, eliciting chuckles from the crowd. "It frees us from the darkness of death, though the price we pay to continue on is the essence of life. But the power of the Blood is rooted in death.

"When Ramangan Blood mixes with itself, the liberation is stunted. When this happens, we call the result the Wretched. Their existence is eternal like ours, but the darkness in their existence is more pronounced; it is far more like a waking death. They must walk the earth in this form for eternity. There is no longer any power of transmutation within them. They can only heed the word of their maker with no ability to communicate on their own. They are far stronger than we are. Your responsibility is great as their maker. Only you can harness their feral nature, and harness it you must. The Wretched are capable of untold violence and terror no other Ramangan can execute."

"What do you mean when you say that the power of the Blood is rooted in death?" Seneca asked.

"The origin of our power lies with the Blood that fuels it. The Blood of Gamab, the Supreme God of life, death, and seasonal renewal."

Kwadzo sat on the bottom step of one of the staircases with Charlie's head rested on his lap, giving Jenue the floor and his full attention to his story. He felt like a child again, sitting and listening to the stories of the elders of the village. The tales of Ramanga were always so dark, full of fire, blood, and brimstone, warning of the disastrous path of evil, but neither he nor anyone he grew up with had seen or known of anyone of the fabled tribe. Not only was he now a part of the legend, but he would finally learn the secrets of its beginning from another who had been there.

"There was a time in ancient Wagadou," Jenue began, "when the gods would grace the ground of this world with their footsteps."

He paused, and Kwadzo saw Penelope roll her eyes.

"Much like the Nazirite you hold so dear who treaded across water," Jenue said directly to her. She could not meet his gaze, and Kwadzo smiled as Jenue continued and the room became hushed in anticipation.

"Gamab was one such deity. One day, walking our realm in his male form, he saw Dula, a beautiful farm girl, lounging under a tall willow tree. Under its weeping branches was her favorite place to be. Gamab immediately fell in love with her. He aimed to seduce Dula and take her back with him to the Underworld, but she rejected all his considerable charms, telling Gamab that her heart belonged only to Amadi, her warrior lover.

"Enraged at being denied in favor of a mortal, Gamab took Dula to the Underworld by force, but Dula, being a living mortal, could not survive the world of the dead. Her presence there was against the natural order of things, and so nature, to correct the error, caused the energy of the Underworld to consume her, draining the very life from her. She began to deteriorate and deform, but Gamab was desperate to keep her as alive and beautiful as she was when he first saw her, so he began to feed her his own blood to restore her. Her lively beauty would return, but after four days, she would begin to fade again, so he would give her more of his blood, without knowing that by doing so, he was imbuing her with godlike power.

"After many moons of repeating this cycle, Dula began to calculate when she felt the strongest, and on a day when she was at her peak, she escaped the Underworld to once again enter our realm. It didn't take long for her to develop a hunger like she had never known before. She came across a matoke plant and gobbled up all its fruit but found it to be flavorless and wholly unsatisfying. It did nothing to fill the deep, empty pit inside her.

"She saw beasts and could smell something about them she never could before, and she realized that it was their blood. Blood, she found, was what she now desired. As she grew hungrier, her outer manifestation started to change, taking more of her deformed appearance despite the vitality she was experiencing—her brow engorged and extended, the veins in her face rose to the surface of her skin, her nails grew and became sharp like talons, her teeth grew sharp and jagged in her mouth; only the burning red in her eyes shone vibrant with the altered life force that coursed through her. The constant pumping of blood pounded in her ears; she could hear nothing else."

Kwadzo heard whispers of recognition floating through the crowd as Jenue continued telling the story in an animated fashion.

"When she could no longer bear it, she chased a hartebeest through the brush, an otherwise impossible task, except that she realized she could move at the animal's pace, and even faster. She tackled the hartebeest with ease and tore through its hide with her teeth and talons, guzzling its blood into her throat. She marveled at her newfound strength, and at the fact that, though it was far better tasting than the matoke, the hunger still gnawed at her.

"Her thoughts returned to her lover, Amadi, and she searched him out. When she found him, he smelled better than anything she had ever encountered. He embraced her with love, and she found him so irresistible she was overwhelmed with the urge to taste him, his tongue, his skin, his blood. Unable to control herself, the kisses she planted on his shoulder turned into bites that ripped through his skin, releasing the magical elixir flowing inside him. Nothing had ever tasted as good. She fed from him vigorously, savagely, until she realized that he was near death from her attack. Her heart ached with panic, but she remembered Gamab's method of returning her vitality. So, she opened her wrist with a talon and fed him her own blood, hoping against hope that it would revitalize him. But alas, he perished in her arms."

Everyone was enraptured by Jenue's tale. Penelope rubbed the back of her fist across her wet eyes with a frown, and Kwadzo thought back to her distressed words when they found her in the clearing. How she claimed that they had taken everything away from her. He knew she blamed him for the death of her father, but she did not speak of her mother. Had the woman's love for her child ultimately been the cause of her demise?

"Dula was distraught beyond measure," Jenue continued, "until Amadi's open neck gash began to heal itself before her very eyes and he miraculously awoke, his features mirroring her own monstrous peculiarity. He expressed a hunger he'd never known before to her, and she was overjoyed to have a partner in blood. Together, they raced the countryside, feeding on whomever they chose as lovers once again.

"Happily reunited with Amadi, Dula thought nothing of Gamab, but the god had followed her to the earthly realm and became furious at her betrayal. He summoned his power against her and Amadi and cursed the blood rushing through their veins with his otherworldly license, resigning it to darkness. When the lovers awoke the next day under Dula's favorite willow tree, the sunlight nearly burned them to death. They used their great power to burrow underground and save themselves. When night fell, they returned to the surface to resume their lounge under the tree, only to find Gamab standing over them. He tore a large piece of bark from the tree and cursed it as well, rendering the wood of Dula's favorite tree poisonous to her and all of her blood. Gamab stabbed her through the heart with a sharpened piece of the willow tree's bark, and it ended her existence, reducing her to a pile of dust beneath its branches.

"Armed with a blade of silver, Amadi used it to fight Gamab off in a fit of rage, but the great god stole the blade away from him, placing a curse on its silver to make it poisonous to all those of Dula's blood as well. Amadi barely escaped Gamab's attack but thirsted for vengeance against the jealous god for the demise of his beloved Dula. Racing through the villages along the countryside with his inhuman speed, Amadi went in search of the strongest men he could find to turn with his blood, so that he could build an army to combat Gamab and avenge Dula's murder. But even with his assembled army, Gamab proved to be too powerful to conquer. In battle, Gamab reduced Amadi and most of his turned to dust. Amadi's extinction was the revenge Gamab had sought all along, and the mighty god returned to the Underworld, vowing never to return to the land of the living again.

"Those of Amadi's blood who had survived the battle retreated to a small village in the north called Ramanga. Their thirst for blood, however, persisted, and the name Ramanga became associated with those who drank the blood of the living. They consumed the blood of all in the village, growing their number, and migrated west in search of more. They settled on Baako as their leader, the first of them turned by Amadi. Baako became my maker."

"What became of Baako?" Kwadzo asked.

"The symbolic crown he wore as the leader of the Ramanga Tribe soon became too heavy for him to bear," Jenue said. "The responsibility of his role as leader fought against the ferocity of his nature. He could not reconcile the two, so he rushed into the sunlight and burned until he was no more. But the tribe went on, savagely I might add, until the Great Plague. We were rudderless, without purpose, slaves to our desires. However, this new tribe of Ramangan Blood has a purpose greater than all who have come before you, and a leader who believes in it. My hope is that the unity he seeks does not run afoul of what needs to be done. If it does, I fear, like Baako, the pressure may become too great."

Jenue's eyes fell on Kwadzo as the leader contemplated his plan for Penelope, and the greater mission that lay before him.

Twenty-Four

Edna Livingston's Tearoom

The overwhelming aroma of jasmine hit Gertie the second Sarah led her into the house full of brightly colored flowers. They were everywhere, in vases, painted on the walls. Even the furniture cushions were covered in flowery prints. The tones and colors were so soft and feminine, she wondered if a man lived in the house at all. She noticed the house was much smaller than the manor she now called home. There was a white man wearing a suit, the kind Clarence used to wear, leading them through the house. Gertie found it odd to find a white man in a house-slave suit.

"Lovely to see you again, Madam Collins," the white man said to Sarah.

"And you, Geoffrey. This is my friend, Gertie . . ."

Her pause sent a surge of anxiety up Gertie's spine. These two white people were staring at her now, their faces clouded in question. Had she walked into a trap?

"What is your family name, Gertie?" Sarah asked her.

"Family name?"

"Yes, your family's name. Not Barrow, of course, but the name of your true family, the family you come from."

Gertie's heart rate decreased, and she blinked. It was a question she had never been asked before, not even by Kwadzo. She blinked again, fighting back the sting of grief welling up behind her eyes.

"Konate." Gertie stopped and released a little cough, clearing her airway, willing back her tears and the tremble in her voice. "Gnima Konate my true name." She shut her eyes hard, but it didn't work. Her mind overflowed with images of her family: mother, father, sisters and brother, cousins, aunts and uncles, and the deluge of their loss began to break free from her eyes.

"They's all died on the ship," she whispered, hoping the act would temper the sorrow simmering in the back of her throat. "They's put me up on the block and ain't wanna say my name, so they calls me Gertie. Ain't spoke my true name since."

She had averted her eyes from embarrassment, but she looked up to find that Sarah's eyes were wet with tears as well.

"You poor soul."

Gertie's tears halted when Sarah wrapped her arms around her. She stiffened. She had never been embraced by a white person whose intent wasn't to defile her, but there was a warmth coming from Sarah that felt genuine to Gertie, sincere. The tension in her body began to relax. The tightening of Sarah's arms across her back caused Gertie to close her own around Sarah's, and the intimate act gave her permission to release the sobs she was holding back so tightly in her throat.

She could hear Sarah sniffling behind her. "I'm so sorry," she said, releasing Gertie and brushing away her own tears with her fingers. "Shall we call you by your given name, then? Gnima? Did I say it right?"

She didn't know why it made her laugh, but Gertie was laughing. Maybe it was the legitimate effort Sarah put into the mispronunciation of her name that set her off, or the pure absurdity of the situation. Either way, Sarah was soon laughing with her, and that made her feel something approaching safe, comfortable. Even the white man smiled at their interaction.

"Gertie be just fine," she said, setting off another round of giggles.

"Well, this is quite unfair. You two having all this fun without the rest of us."

It was a large and robust woman who had addressed them. Tall and round with cheeks of jovial red, a pair of spectacles adorned her face, but they were not nearly as ominous-looking as the ones that horrible tall man from that building wore who had preached such dreadful words to the former slaves of the Barrow Plantation. This woman was immaculate in every way, from her perfectly coiffed raven hair with swirling streaks of silver running throughout it, to the elegant silk gown she wore, to her lovely shoes. Her teeth seemed too big for her mouth, as if they would pop out when she smiled.

"You must be the guest Sarah has been so excited about introducing us to," the big woman said. "I am Edna Livingston. And you are?"

Gertie peered up at the woman in awe. This was the second white person from Lakeside she had met that greeted her kindly. The intimidation she felt stole her voice from her.

"Her name is Gertie. She is the woman of Kwadzo Okoro, the man who usurped James Barrow and took his plantation."

Edna's eyes and smile grew wider, lighting up with what looked to Gertie like delight.

"Well, you *are* a special guest," Edna said to Gertie. "Kwadzo Okoro. How delightfully African. Well, Gertie Okoro, welcome to my tearoom. Please."

Edna gestured forward, and Gertie followed behind her. She hadn't bothered to correct the big woman, because the sound of hers and Kwadzo's names combined was something she had never heard before.

Gertie Okoro.

Husband.

Now there were three words she'd be saying silently to herself over and over for the rest of the day. Though she wasn't in full agreement with him on the issue of Penelope, she loved him dearly, and the fact that his actions had led her to be in her current position made her heart swell with pride for him.

Edna led her and Sarah into another room, perhaps more floral in design than the first one. The melodic sounds of a fiddle and flute playing together flooded her ears, and Gertie smiled at the older African man who played the fiddle while the younger white man playing the flute kept his eyes on her. In the center of the room sat a gracefully set table with five place settings, five petite porcelain cups and saucers with pink flowers on them, and a silver tier that held silver trays with tiny sandwiches on them. Next to it, a large platter filled with scones and cakes. She heard Edna tell the suited white man to ready the tea, and he scurried off.

Two women were already seated at the table—one about her age with blue eyes and long, silky blonde hair that she seemed to run her hand through continuously, as if she didn't regularly get the chance to; the other was close to ten years older, her face hard in spite of the luxury that adorned her.

"Ladies, you all know Sarah," Edna said as the women waved, "and this is her friend, Gertie Okoro. Her husband is the one who won the battle at the Barrow Plantation."

There were those words again. Gertie Okoro. Husband. Her head was starting to swim. If this kept up, she wouldn't need to say the words to herself repeatedly. She felt like she was smiling. She thought that if she were white, she'd be flush red.

"A new guest, I see," the hard-faced woman said. She seemed to want to smile, but her face fought against it.

"Yes, I trust you'll both make her feel welcome," Sarah said, leading Gertie to a chair and sitting next to her.

"Gertie, I would like to introduce you to Hester Holdsworth and Bridget Shenton," Edna said, taking a seat at the head of the table.

"How y'all do," Gertie said with the most respectful nod of her head she could muster.

"It's how *do* you do," the blonde woman, Hester, said, the pleasantness in her voice accented by a touch of condescension.

"I'm sure that if Gertie would had been given the same privilege of education and breeding that you have grown accustomed to, and most likely taken for granted, proper English would have been an easy feat for her," Sarah said.

Gertie stared at Sarah. She was leaning forward, her face flush, her voice half an octave higher than it had been before. The look on her face was one she had seen before, but only on Kwadzo's face. Sarah blinked before retreating into her chair and inhaling.

"My, my," Hester said with a chuckle. "I did not intend to offend our new guest. Nor you, Madam Collins."

"Well." The comment had reignited Sarah's calm stance. "Considering ours is her second language, I think she speaks it incredibly well. I doubt any of us would be able to master . . . Gertie, what is your native tongue?"

Another new question she had never been asked before. She wondered how much of herself she would end up revealing to these women.

"Zenaga," Gertie said. It registered no recognition in the room. Gertie lowered her head and smiled to herself in silent amusement. It didn't take much to stump these white ladies.

"There. You see? I doubt we'd be able to master Zenaga so easily. I've never even heard of it. Have you, Hester?"

Having finished her reprisal of Hester, Sarah smiled when the white man returned to the room with two more young white women who bore a resemblance to him. They carried large trays containing teapots, a slop bowl, containers for milk and cream, a tea canister, a sugar container, and tongs. Gertie was mesmerized by these white people, serving other white people like slaves; she had never seen such a thing.

Did white folks enslave everyone?

"I say, Gertie . . ."

She had been so taken aback by the white slaves that she hadn't heard the hard-faced woman—Bridget—ask her a question.

"I's sorry, ma'am. Was you talkin' at me?"

Hester covered her mouth to chuckle, and Sarah glared at her with prejudice.

"I asked how you did learn to speak as you do now," Bridget asked.

"From gettin' yelled at in y'all's tongue on the paddy for so long, I reckon," Gertie said matter-of-factly. "Weren't no book learnin' allowed, so anythin' I heard got told to me by the overseers, and they likes yellin' more than talkin'."

"Well, that makes sense," Hester said. "The overseers aren't educated either."

Gertie barely heard the words; she was awestruck at the sight of a white woman standing over her, pouring her tea. *Serving* her.

"Do you take cream or sugar, ma'am?"

Gertie didn't have the capacity to answer the question asked of her by the young white slave woman; she was far too flummoxed by the peculiar act of being asked it.

"You can have a little cream or sugar mixed in with your tea if you'd like," Sarah whispered to her.

"I ain't never had no tea," she whispered back.

"I enjoy it with a bit of both," Edna said with a smile. "I highly recommend it."

Her smile was contagious, and Gertie offered one of her own to her server.

"A bit of both," Gertie said, mirroring Edna.

"Very good, ma'am."

Gertie watched with fascination as her tea was prepared. The quiet respect she was being shown was a marvel to her. It rendered her speechless and the room quiet, save for the music and discreet sipping. Gertie tasted the concoction placed before her and found it pleasing to the tongue. Sarah was smiling at her. If this is what having tea was, music, lovely scents, pleasant décor, and being served by white folks, Gertie felt that she could come to like it very quickly.

"The very reason I agreed for Sarah to have you join us was to get to know you, Gertie," Edna said, setting her cup down. "Mother tongue and languages aside . . ."

"Who will be next?"

Gertie blinked in confusion at Bridget's abrupt question. That trapped, nervous feeling bubbled up inside her again.

"Next?"

"You'll forgive Bridget's lack of couth, but truth be told . . ." Edna leaned forward in an almost conspiratorial fashion. "There are those of us in certain quiet circles who stand in absolute marvel of what your man has accomplished. There aren't many of us, mind you, but we know a change in season when we see one."

"Is that why you got white slaves?" Gertie asked her. The women all chuckled.

"They aren't slaves," Edna corrected her. "They are indentured servants. Even the Negro."

"What that mean?"

"Geoffrey and his family wished to come to the New World but hadn't the money to do so. It was the same with Andres. He was born free in France and worked as a sailor but found work scarce when he went to London. My husband and I learned of his plight, befriended him, and decided to pay for the passage of all four of them when we came to the colonies, and now they are here working off their debt."

"Missus Livingston and her husband do not hold slaves," Sarah said with a smile.

"Mister Livingston is a merchant," Edna said. "We have no land to till, no children. We have no need for slaves, so we carry no ill will toward those who make up their population. The more slaves a person holds, it seems, the viler they are toward them. Rest assured, Gertie, the women before you have no desire to see slavery continue."

Indentured servants, free Negros, white folks being cordial . . . Gertie's head was spinning.

"We are straying from the point of conversation," Bridget said.

"She's quite right," Hester huffed. "But I would also like to point out that some of us just flat out did not like Mister James Barrow. Strutting around town like a peacock, lording his wealth over everyone. What happened, well, perhaps he had it coming."

"Everyone knows it was you all who conquered Gavin Wilson and his plantation," Bridget insisted. "So? Who's next?"

Gertie turned to Sarah as the pit in her core returned, throbbing inside her with a growing panic. How stupid she had been. There was no desire to become friendly. She was here to be interrogated. To whose benefit or what true end she did not know, but she would not expose her people with any information these women sought out. There was no telling who they had promised it to or who was waiting for it. It was a good thing Kwadzo hadn't openly shared what his plan was outside of rehabilitating Penelope.

"I don't rightly know," Gertie said.

"You must know something," Bridget insisted, but Gertie remained silent. Bridget chuckled, lightening her tone. "My goodness, Gertie, this is not an inquisition. Edna's husband is a merchant with no need of slaves; Hester's husband is a chandler who refuses the use of slaves."

"He doesn't trust them to learn the trade properly," Hester said. "Candles are too important to leave in the hands of niggers, he says."

"My husband owns the Shenton farm," Bridget said. "He grows tobacco. It's not as huge a plantation as Barrow's was, but he does have slaves. The holding of them isn't my decision, you see. I am not included in my husband's business decisions. Nonetheless, your people will come to free those slaves, and when they do, I don't want to be in the path of your husband's fury."

Gertie studied Bridget's face. She could very well not want to be in the path of fury, or she could be looking to find a way to set a trap for Kwadzo.

"Kwadzo say my only job is to rest and mind this here little one growin' inside me."

The women all sat back in silence, their faces blank—all but Sarah, who was beaming.

"Gertie! You are with child?"

"Yes, ma'am. Cookin' me up a little girl right now." The two women shared a smile as Sarah placed a friendly hand on Gertie's shoulder while Gertie's hands wrapped across her belly.

"How lovely. A child of the future if ever there was one. And it is the future I believe the man is concerned with. Having spoken with him myself . . ."

"You spoke to him?" Edna asked Sarah.

"Why did he kill Mister Wilson?" Hester inquired.

"Kwadzo ain't aim to kill nobody," Gertie quickly added in an attempt to defend Kwadzo against the accusation.

"So, he simply didn't mean to kill Mister Wilson after freeing his slaves? Was it an accident?" Bridget asked.

"How could it have been an accident?" Hester countered. "He drinks blood. Human blood."

Gertie stammered, looking for a response that would not incriminate her husband. There was that word again.

"He drank of me and yet here I sit drawing breath," Sarah said to the gasps of the other ladies. They were all leaning forward now, wide-eyed in shock. With a smile that looked almost prideful to Gertie, Sarah removed the white silk scarf that adorned her neck and revealed the bite marks—a jagged horizontal wound bookended by two deeper, circular puncture wounds. A smattering of verbal shock broke out among them as all the ladies rose to inspect Sarah's wound more closely. Gertie shook her head. Just a couple of months ago, her people were invisible to these women. Now they were fussing over a Ramangan bite.

"Did it hurt?" Edna asked.

"There was a pinch, but it quickly gave way to a sort of euphoric feeling. When it was all over, I just felt tingly. It was quite delightful."

"I don't think delight was what the men who died in the manor felt," Hester said.

"Perhaps it depends upon the pressure applied," Sarah said. "Kwadzo's bite was quite gentle."

"Is that true?" Hester asked Gertie. The women were staring at her in anticipation of her very next breath. She sipped her tea. It did nothing to assuage the women's eagerness.

"If'n he don't wants it to hurt," Gertie said coarsely, feeling rushed to swallow and answer, "it won't hurt."

"Yes, but why did it feel *good* to Sarah?" Bridget asked. There was no way Gertie would tell them about the venom. They could not know anything more about Ramangan power than they already did. She caught Sarah looking at her and the woman's smile faded, as if she could sense Gertie's discomfort.

"I suppose it's not our place to know," she said to the women firmly.

"Yes, but . . ." Hester pressed.

"It is not our place!"

The increased volume in Sarah's voice wasn't a yell, or even a shout, but it was emphatic enough to bring back the silence that had left the room.

"Killing may not be his purpose," Hester said finally, "but Gavin Wilson and his overseers are nonetheless dead."

"A terrible shame for his widow and children," Edna said as the other women nodded. "And that poor Penelope." Gertie bit her tongue to keep herself quiet. "Has anyone tried to contact Robert Callowhill to tell him the fate of his family? Rumor has it he escaped the fire and disappeared."

"Is it really true that your man breathes fire?" Bridget asked Gertie.

"Perhaps the power Kwadzo possesses is relative to the rage he feels," Sarah said bluntly, saving Gertie the trouble of responding to Bridget's question. "Had he and his people not been treated so horrifically he may have never developed such justified ferociousness. However, what's done cannot be undone. Life continues on, merchants and exporters continue to conduct their business. The plantation is still fruitful. Josiah Browne himself has begun trading with Kwadzo. He has no choice. None of us do. This is a new world, one we all must adapt to."

"My husband said that the manifest for the crops Josiah traded was forged with Mister Barrow's signature to keep up appearances," Bridget said. Gertie took mental note of this; she would need to tell Kwadzo of the underhandedness he had been subjected to.

"My mind keeps going back to little Penelope. Does anyone know where Mister Callowhill is?" Edna asked. Gertie's lips tightened. Perhaps they were unaware of just how vile the child was.

"It's rumored he left for the North, Philadelphia," Hester said. "My husband said Edward Taylor had business in Delaware. He and Robert were quite friendly. Perhaps he took a letter or found a postrider who could locate Robert and deliver a message."

The room fell silent, and the women turned to Gertie with expectation in their eyes, willing her to say something, anything, on the matter. She kept quiet but remained on guard. She looked away, sipping her tea.

"My brother was caught in one of the attacks on the manor after the revolt," Bridget said, breaking through the hush. "He said the demon slaves had them cornered and could have easily killed them, but that the leader, this Kwadzo, I imagine, let them go, saying they meant no harm to us, that they only wanted a place in society."

"Do you really think it possible? Slaves a part of civilized society?" Hester asked.

"They are not slaves," Sarah said. "Not anymore. Never again."

"And we ain't demons neither," Gertie said as she felt Sarah's hand clasp hers under the table. It was a gesture she appreciated as much as the words Sarah had spoken. It made her feel less alone in this place.

"So, you *are* one of them. Do you too drink blood?" Edna asked.

"No, we ain't all take the Blood. Most of us is human, just like y'all."

"Then how does it work, exactly? The power your husband and the others like him possess. I suspect that if they'd had it all along, they would have used it long ago. How does it come about?"

Gertie could feel her chest tighten as the questions were flung at her faster than she could think of excuses not to answer them.

"That is an excellent question indeed."

The sound of a male voice stopped the music from playing and stunned the women silent once again. A cloud of dread darkened the room as the owner of the voice stepped inside. The man, slight of build with thinning hair, was followed by a towering and overly stout woman whose bulbous bosom seemed to enter the room before the rest of her did. They both carried sinister smiles, and behind them came more men, enough of them to do something unspeakable if they chose to.

Gertie's vision blurred as she began to feel faint. She'd been right after all. She had indeed been drawn into a trap. She refrained from turning to look at any of the other women at the table, including Sarah. She had to find her focus if she was going to figure a way out of this room unscathed. She was sweating and fighting to control her breathing, but her anxiety was winning. She could see the mouths of the small man and the large woman, but their words were drowned out by the loud, incessant beating of her own heart.

The danger and despair she felt coursing through her was the same as when Barrow had locked her in the hot box, but it was still daylight. Even if she called out to Kwadzo now like she did then, he would still have to wait for nightfall to rescue her, and she didn't know if she would have that much time. She felt uncomfortably warm when the man knelt, putting his face directly in front of hers, clearing the haze in her ears until his words became clear.

"Have you gone deaf, slave? I asked you a question."

"She hears just fine," she heard the large woman say, a lecherous inflection in her voice. "Give me some time with her alone. I'll make her talk."

The woman's fat hand reached for Gertie, but another reached across her and slapped the hand away.

"How dare you speak in such a vulgar manner in the presence of decent women!" she heard Sarah shout.

The slight man's eyes looked past Gertie to take in Sarah, she presumed, but she was too frightened to turn her head to find out.

"What right do you have to ambush Missus Livingston's house like this?" Sarah asked with prejudice.

"You are mistaken, Widow Collins," the slight man said. "This isn't an ambush. We're here because of the good Missus Holdsworth."

Out of the corner of her eye, Gertie watched Hester stand. She threw her napkin down and glowered at Sarah.

"That's right. I told the Crabtrees that you were bringing this good-for-nothing nigger here in our midst!"

"Hester," Sarah said with surprise in her voice. "You are one of us."

"I was never one of you! Harboring affection for filthy niggers in secret, none of you are any better than they are! I told my husband straight away when this kind of talk began, and he told me to play along. We told the good Crabtrees about it, and they came up with a plan to catch you all, capture this Negress, and put an end to this nonsense. I hope you're all burned at the stake!"

Hester disappeared from Gertie's field of vision, and she felt the slight man's rough hand on her chin, forcing her face to turn back to him.

"Now, then. Dear Missus Livingston will tell us the names of everyone else in this little band of dissenters so that they can all be punished for their treasonous ways, and you will tell us everything we need to know about the demons among your kind so that when they realize you are missing and come to rescue you, we can defeat them. It doesn't take much to triumph over you niggers. Vampyre or otherwise, you are still inferior to us."

Gertie had been in this situation before, and she had survived. That fact caused her fear to give way to her anger.

"Y'all the one that sent that little spy to our door. What happen? She ain't deliver nothin'?"

His hand was squishing her cheeks together. She couldn't move her face while his grew redder.

"Your orneriness knows no bounds, does it? Now, you are going to tell Constance and myself everything you know, and maybe I'll just hang you instead of skinning you first."

"Unhand her!" Sarah yelled from behind her before a ruckus broke out, one that gave the slight man pause. Turning her head, she saw Sarah struggling against the fat woman, who gave a howl before she lurched and fell back, clutching the side of her generous belly. Sarah had a knife in her hand, blood dripping from its tip. The slight man rose to his feet and swung his fist wildly above Gertie's head, shouting out at Sarah. Gertie remained seated and saw that his crotch was now at her eye level. In that moment, Gertie decided to throw a fist of her own. With every ounce of power she could muster, she shook off her shock and rammed the full force of her fist into the slight man's nether region. She heard the wind leave his body in a defeated wheeze as his hands dropped to the area and he collapsed in a heap.

A knife-wielding Sarah helped Gertie to her feet. She could now see the room—the weighty woman on the floor bleeding from her side, two men tending to her as she cursed, while two more men skulked ever closer while that slight man whimpered like a child, rolling on the floor below them, unable to form words. Hester was gone, and Edna and Bridget both seemed petrified until Bridget rose to her feet.

"Forgive me, Edna!"

With a grunt of force, Bridget tilted the table up and over, sending its contents flying, and for the moment, blocking the pathway the intruders had to Gertie and Sarah. The women took the opportunity to run while the two lurking men made their way over the toppled table and its fallen contents. Gertie and Sarah rushed out of the back of the small house and ran around it for Sarah's horse and carriage. Her man was no longer in the box, but the horse and carriage remained and were joined by a second horse-drawn carriage and several other horses.

"Get inside!" Sarah yelled to Gertie as they ran for it. "You must remain safe!"

"What 'bout you?" Gertie asked, noticing one of Sarah's eyes was swelling up.

"I'll ride us back to Crimson Manor!" Sarah was already climbing into the box as Gertie shut the carriage door. Just outside the window, the two lurking men were running out of Edna Livingston's house toward them.

"Sarah!"

Gertie tumbled backward as the carriage jolted forward before picking up considerable speed, growing farther and farther away from the men mounting horses to chase after them.

Twenty-Five

A Leader Anew

Gamab.

The name rang familiar and true in Kwadzo's ears. Offerings were made to the god by the elders of his village. His parents both feared and revered Gamab, the director of the very fate of all of mankind. The great god loomed large in his early years, but now it seemed he was much closer to the powerful deity than any of those spiritual and holy men.

Gamab's blood ran through his veins.

If the Blood of Gamab, this godly blood, strong enough to renew him from death and lead him to victory, surged through him, did it make him a god as well?

The question filled him with a proud calm, though he dared not speak the answer he'd decided upon. He had been so concerned with how to handle the white humans, conducting business in the manner *they* had to show his capacity for learning and applying *their* knowledge to gain *their* respect . . .

plus his ridiculous mandate to refrain from the use of the divine mind-bending powers to be fair to *them*.

The Penelope situation: the mental effort of figuring out a way to sway her so she would become the catalyst for uniting the enslavers and the formerly enslaved. How to proceed with freeing those still enslaved by appealing to the business acumen of those who still held them, offering more currency to avoid more warfare and allowing such consideration to postpone the work of liberation. Finding a way to show them that he and his people were worthy of a place in their society.

As if they had ever taken a single second to consider the thoughts and feelings of him and his people while they were beaten, raped, and terrorized.

Never truly realizing that he, a Ramangan, was a member of the dominant species. His role was *not* to bow down. He had been branded the leader of the new Ramanga Tribe. Rafazi clearly had no desire for the position, and Jenue—far more powerful than him and probably the eldest Ramangan left in existence—had shown no interest in usurping him, and he was the only one who could.

Uneasy lies the head that wears a crown, Jenue had warned him.

Perhaps.

But Kwadzo now saw that he had not fully embraced his position as leader nor who he had truly become. All the power stored within him—more than any human could ever dream of having—and yet he allowed the so-called supremacy of the white colonists to continue to have a say in his behavior. An ever-expanding intellect filled his brain, one that would grow far beyond that of any human, if only by virtue of the fact that he would outlive every human alive by infinity, and he was still taking into consideration *their* rules and laws.

He had been going about it all wrong.

It was not how a god conducted himself.

His vow not to return to the ways of the original Ramanga Tribe would stand. He would not return to the white folk the same brand of draconian malice they had perpetrated against his people, but he would no longer allow for the decrees of mortals to dictate his thinking. He could do whatever he wanted. Make new rules. Carve out a new society, one that placed his people in the seat of privilege and him in the seat of power.

It was time he put on the crown.

He watched his people mill about with the Natives, discussing the history Jenue had relayed to them all. Many of them cast harsh eyes toward Penelope. The girl was still sitting on the floor, rubbing her fists against her eyes. He moved to her and felt the eyes upon him grow, listened as the chatter dulled.

"Now you know what you are," he said to Penelope even as the girl looked away from him with a sniffle. "You were right. Your blood, like mine, is divine. There is nothing evil about it."

Penelope's eyes were wet and red when she turned to him.

"And yet it caused me to do evil! Despicable evil!" The words escaped her as she broke down in heaving sobs before she could regain control of her tongue. "This blood filled me with a hunger so wicked it forced me to . . ." She gave way to heavier sobs, unable to continue.

"You consumed your mother."

Penelope's mouth gaped open, and her eyes went wide at the words; even in her grief, Kwadzo sensed a relief emanating from her.

"I didn't mean to," Penelope confessed. "I couldn't stop; she smelled so good, better than anything I have ever smelled, it was too much, I didn't even realize . . ."

"What you smelled," Kwadzo said to her softly, "was her love. Ramangans can smell true love in the blood, and it is the sweetest scent you will ever know. Unmistakable, undeniable.

What happened wasn't your fault. You had no idea what you had become, no idea the power you possessed or how to use it. You succumbed to the hunger, just like every one of us of the Blood has."

Penelope's brow furrowed and she shook her head. "What I did was evil."

"No, child. You were just unknowing. You were hungry, scared, and alone."

"I shall be alone for all time."

"You will only be alone if you choose to be. You are in the very bosom of your people. The Blood running through you goes beyond skin. This world separates us by skin, claiming good and superior for the lighter and calling it white, while claiming evil and inferior for the darker and calling it black. But what does skin matter between us when *our* Blood, the true source of our eternal power, is the same? Understanding that is the path to true freedom for all. If you can release your allegiance to your skin, you can be a part of giving freedom to my people across the colonies so that the one true power can reign and bring peace to all who dwell under my rule."

Penelope blinked and Kwadzo smiled. He felt so clear of mind. This was how a leader spoke.

"*Your* rule? You want to free all the slaves, and then take over?"

Everyone's attention was now rapt, and Kwadzo was grateful for it. He was speaking a new world hierarchy into existence for the very first time.

They needed to hear every word.

"The antelope runs free in the wild, but does he not fear the lion? It is the natural order. We will be just, but those of us of the Blood will rule by the Blood," Kwadzo said. "And I will lead us."

He felt a firm hand on his shoulder. It was Jenue's man, smiling down on him like a proud parent.

"Those of us of the Blood, you said," Penelope replied. "I am of the Blood. Does that mean that you will share this power with white people?"

Penelope's question brought the Ramangans, Natives, and Africans—that is to say, humans of Alkebulan descent—present to a deathly standstill. The quiet was such that her words seemed to echo off the walls. Kwadzo surveyed the room and locked eyes with Seneca, her breath stuck in her throat, awaiting his answer.

"I have learned a great deal about how this Blood has been distributed in the past," Kwadzo began. "Wealthy in the East and Europe traded fortunes for it, and it brought them to their ruin. Time will no longer restrict us, but it remains the only measurement available to determine what will be. Penelope's thievery of Fanna's blood cannot be undone. By the Blood, she is Ramangan, but she must still answer for her treachery."

"Treachery?" Penelope asked as Kwadzo pulled her to her feet. "What treachery?"

"By your own admission, you have conspired with our enemies to enter our walls and spy on us."

"How can I be accused of treachery when I told you what was asked of me? And of what use have I been to my people when I have been kept prisoner here with no way to contact anyone in Lakeside or beyond? And you still have not answered my question."

"She's still stolen from you," Seneca called out. "She took blood that was not hers to take. For that, she should at least be made to taste silver."

Uproarious agreement rang out from the crowd. The shouts were quieted by Kwadzo raising his hand.

"This girl is our greatest challenge. She resists our camaraderie, and yet, she is capable of great service to our cause. Her punishment must be fair."

"Seem to me she done punish herself already."

Kwadzo recognized the voice immediately. Fuddle, who had toiled with him on the rice paddy and endured more than his share of violence and humiliation at the hands of Monroe and the Barrow overseers, stepped forward from the crowd. There was a hobble to his gait from Monroe having broken his leg, but Doc Farkus's attention and a bit of Ramangan venom had been helping it along nicely. His face made Kwadzo smile. Fuddle had chosen against the Blood, but their time in bondage together made the freedom they shared all the sweeter.

"Speak your piece, brother," Kwadzo said, and Fuddle stood a bit straighter as he took the floor.

"Well, sir," Fuddle began, "this here child done kill her own mama, ain't got no kin to speak of, her childhood and riches gone, and she here with us niggers who she hate."

Grumbles of disapproval went up from the throng, and Fuddle winced as Kwadzo narrowed his eyes at him.

"Don't hurt me now!" he shouted. "I know we ain't s'posed to say that word no more, but y'all know she still think it!"

"What is your aim, Fuddle?" Kwadzo asked.

"I reckon all she got left is the promise of gettin' back in them white folks' good graces. Them white folks was just so awful to us, but I used to hope 'gainst hope one of them overseers would find favor with me. Ain't happen much, but when they did, I thought I's just 'bout the luckiest nigger . . . oh . . . sorry, Willie. I mean, Kwadzo . . ."

"You are only speaking of the past, not from malice," Kwadzo said, shaking his head with a touch of amusement. "Finish your thought."

"Well, I reckon the promise of that white folk light be all she got left. They hate her blood, but if'n she brung them somethin' they can use to hurt us, they would shine it on her again, and I reckon she figure that be 'bout the best thing could happen to her now. So, I say we takes it from her."

Penelope's sharp gasp preceded several more as Fuddle captured everyone's rapt attention now.

"She ain't know what she stole when she stole it, but she done stole it, and she cain't gives it back. I say, make her choose it fully. She say she ain't give none of thems the Blood, maybe she did, maybe she ain't, either way, I reckon they sent her here 'cause they's hopin' to win 'gainst you, and I reckon she come for the promise of them takin' her back in. So, I say, we march this here girl back to town with the strongest Ramangans we got, take her to town square, and make her rebuke them and pledge her allegiance to us!"

Cheers were coming forth from the people now, and Penelope's eyes danced with tears. "No!"

"Don't matter if she means it or not, she just gots to say it. That'll make them white folks hate her much as they do us. Make her tell them what she done to her mama, and make her tell it in Ramangan form! Just like Rafazi say make Ol' Clarence what he hate, only punishment fit for that child is *they's* hate!"

An uproarious ovation swept over Fuddle. As he received claps on the back and unyielding praise for having come up with an unanimously accepted penalty for the girl, Penelope grabbed hold of Kwadzo's hands, pleading with her cries to spare her such denouncement.

"Your reaction to it tells me it is a fit punishment," he told her. "You will do it."

"I won't!"

"The time has come for you to make a choice. You do this and choose us, or deny us, become our enemy, and seal your fate."

Several took on their Ramangan forms and stepped forward

to surround Penelope, their red eyes pulsing down at her. She did not bother to take on her own Ramangan form; instead, dread filled her eyes as she turned back to Kwadzo.

"You said you would not force anyone," she beseeched him. "You are forcing me to do this! Are you not a man of your word?"

"We force no one to take the Blood. You took it upon yourself to snatch it away from Fanna in a fit of rage. You were not forced. Now, you must make a decision. These are simply the terms of making it. You are free to accept or reject them. The choice is still yours."

"But it is an impossible choice!"

"Yet it is one you must make. But know this. Should you choose against us, we will show you no mercy and our wrath against you will be tenfold, for you will have forsaken your own Blood."

She released her sobs in a torrent of sorrow as she crumpled to a heap at Kwadzo's feet. The crowd cheered, and Kwadzo nodded. It was not the determined stance he'd hoped she would come to, but there was an eternity for her to come to her senses.

"We will free our people," he called out above the jubilation, "and we will rule this land!"

The collective shout that followed was blistering. If it hadn't been for his Ramangan hearing, he never would have heard the front door of the manor bust open, or the frantic running steps of two people, or the panicked call that came from the sweetest voice his ears had ever known.

"Kwadzo!"

Faster than he thought she would be able to move, Kwadzo found a panting, sweating Gertie rushing toward him. Sarah was in her wake in a similar condition. So frenzied were they that neither woman seemed to notice the celebration surrounding him or the groveling Penelope below. Kwadzo could hear the blood racing through their bodies, their hearts pounding with acceleration.

He could smell their fear.

"Kwadzo," Gertie wheezed, fighting for breath to speak. "There's gonna be trouble!"

From now on,
mind your thoughts.

Twenty-Six

Penelope's Gambit

Penelope had to collect herself. She had been sent here with a mission but still had not figured a way off Mister Barrow's property to report back to the Crabtrees as she had been instructed. Of course, it was and always would be Mister Barrow's property to her, no matter what the slaves claimed. They were far more structured than she had counted on, however.

When her skin wasn't being singed and blistered by silver cuffs, she was in the fields at night under the watchful eyes of a plenitude of slaves, Ramangans, and Indians as they farmed the land or built new cabins for the overflow of slaves stolen from the plantations of Mister Wilson and Mister Peterson, or guarded the borders of the property in case another attack occurred.

Ramangan. Loath as Penelope was to admit it, there was no question that she was one of them, and as such, she could no longer bring herself to refer to them as demons anymore. In doing so, she'd be calling herself a demon, albeit an even more powerful one who could survive the sun. Still, she fought to cling to the idea that somehow, some way, she was God's vessel to rid the world of those like her of darkened skin.

Her unique position on the property didn't help. All eyes were always on her, whether in the field or the manor. There were no consequences for berating her, and the slaves not "of the Blood," as it was referred to, were fully protected by those that were—a fact she discovered when she did strike out with her talons after an unsavory comment was flung her way. She found herself hurled across the room by a Ramangan, three, maybe four times her size, knocking her head against the wall so hard that everything went black. She awoke in her silver cuffs.

Worst of all, she had learned of no specific plot as to what their next move might be, just the overarching villainy to take over. Still, this was the first meaningful agenda she had heard, and she needed to figure out a way to escape before they forced her to lie and make a spectacle of herself.

Penelope had been making mental notes about the structure of her time on the plantation, searching for blind spots to make her escape. She pushed fleeting thoughts that the very slaves in the manor might have gone through the same circles in their own heads when Mister Barrow was in charge out of her mind. Empathizing with slaves was a waste of her time, a by-product of her weak femininity, Mister Crabtree had told her. He had warned her to remain mentally strong, and she was determined to stay on course.

However, it was beginning to occur to her that a better opportunity had not presented itself to Penelope than what was happening right now. Gertie's return with Missus Collins had thrown the house into disarray. She didn't know why Missus Collins was there, but it somehow made sense that she was. Her support of the slaves was well known—many believed her a traitor to her own kind. Kwadzo had disappeared with the two of them, and there was much rushing around. Mobilization was taking place, and the daily structure she had witnessed up until this point had broken down.

In her very real grief over what they had planned for her, she hadn't heard any instructions given. All she knew for certain was that this plan of Kwadzo's to overtake white society needed to be stopped. The slave had gone mad, likening himself to a god because of some ridiculous made-up story about some underworld creature who tried to claim some nigger woman for his own and failed.

Kwadzo may have thought himself a leader of gods, but she had the power to stop him. She could do what he couldn't. The thought occurred to her that she could escape back into town amid the chaos, but the sun was still in the sky. She would burn up before she took two steps, and who knows what they would do to her in her charred condition.

At that moment, a clearer plan emerged. There were four other white people in the house now: Doc Farkus, his wife Rebecca, and the young white woman Rafazi had been hiding in his bedchamber, the one who showed her face on the upstairs balcony during Jenue's ridiculous story. If she could get each one of them to take her blood, they could escape the manor with their collective power and spread it among the strongest men in Lakeside. Missus Collins would be the hardest of the bunch, but she was sure that once presented with the facts, the governor's widow would see the error of her ways and take a stand to preserve their way of life as her husband had intended. It was only right. She was, after all, a white woman.

She was still on her knees on the floor as everyone rushed around her. No one seemed to be watching her, and while there was much traffic around the staircase that led to the cellar, there was no one on the staircases that led to the second story. She had seen the contention between Rafazi and Kwadzo, and she reasoned the former might support her going against the arrogant demon slave he had made. Or perhaps she could turn the white woman in the harem, and together, they could make an escape. Either option was better than the one Kwadzo had presented.

After a count of three to gather courage, Penelope dashed for the stairs in her blur.

Twenty-Seven

Not My Master

He dares put silver to *my* neck?!"

With one punch, Rafazi had reduced the cherrywood chest at the foot of the bed to kindling. The bedchamber vibrated with his anger. No; anger wasn't a strong enough word. Rage was more fitting. His vision pulsed with burning red, and he was in full Ramangan form.

"He was nothing but a pathetic, miserable, broken slave before me. If it hadn't been for my Blood, none of this would have been possible. None of it!"

He could see the fright in the eyes of the members of his harem, all except Lily. Her chest was heaving, her mouth slack, her eyes quaking with arousal. Rafazi zeroed in on her. He could smell the licentious bouquet of her essence. His fury was fueling her desire.

"The fat old whip-cracker who used to own this place . . . Kwadzo would have been killed by him if it wasn't for me."

"I've no doubt," Lily breathed, taking a step toward Rafazi.

"He would have discovered Gertie's baby and killed him just because he could."

"Of course he would have. You saved Kwadzo from death itself."

They moved closer to each other with every word, a dance of provocation.

"I made him what he is. Not Jenue, me! Instead of taking my power and crushing his enemies, he speaks of justice and fairness, yet he puts silver to *my* neck? I am his maker! With one word, I could command his destruction!"

"He doesn't deserve the gift you've given him. It is an unbearable travesty against you, Master."

With a heated growl, Rafazi pulled a gasping Lily in close and bit deeply into her neck. She winced in pain, but soon her eyes went cross, and she embraced him as his venom seeped into her skin. She was panting now, pressing herself up against him. Retracting his talons, he reached under her petticoat and slipped two fingers into her wanton insides. A breath of passion escaped her as the warmth of her quim tightened around his digits, and she squirmed against him. He pulled away from her, his mouth wet with her blood.

"Leave us!" he barked at the rest of the harem, all of whom made a hasty retreat. Once they were alone, Rafazi felt Lily's tongue assaulting his lips, lapping at her own blood and moaning torridly while doing so. Her willingness to engage so passionately with him in Ramangan form only fueled his fire for her.

"He does not exist without you, Master," she mewled, and he groaned lustfully in response. It sent a thrill to his loins every time she used the word in reference to him. "Perhaps it is not in him to be the leader."

"He grows weaker by the day. If he isn't careful, Jenue will usurp him, and I will not fall under Jenue's command. Never again. I want her gone!"

"But she is your maker, Master. What can you do?"

The thought of the cruel and disgusting punishments he suffered at her hands made Rafazi shudder. In response, he felt Lily pull him closer.

"If Kwadzo can fight you off, you can resist Jenue's control just the same, and once you do, Kwadzo will not challenge your lead. It should be you, anyway."

"I do not wish to lead."

"Then what do you wish, Master?"

Lily yelped with delight as he hoisted her onto the bed. He watched the curves of her figure quake in the aftermath of her fall and climbed atop her as the crimson left his eyes, and he reverted to his human form.

"No," she whispered. "Ravish me as you truly are. I wish to feel your velvety dark and monstrous skin everywhere."

Rafazi tore his shirt from his body and once again took on the form afforded him by the power of the Blood.

Having satiated their lust, Rafazi had returned to his human form and Lily released soft pants as they lounged on the cool bedsheets, a thin sheen of sweat covering her. Their respite was broken by the bedchamber door being flung open. Lily draped a sheet over her naked form with a squeal as a blur sped to the bed and revealed itself to be Penelope.

"You dare come into my room?" Rafazi snarled at her. The girl's complexion went pale, and her face turned sour at the sight of his nudity. She looked away and Rafazi chuckled.

"Perhaps if you had known your place, your childish eyes would not have had to witness what a man and woman do in privacy."

"The sheets retain our decency, Master," Lily said, throwing a sheet over him. "But she looks troubled by something other than us."

"I am, ma'am," Penelope said, her eyes on her feet.

"Well, speak, girl!" Rafazi barked.

"I fear it is something I must speak to the lady about alone."

"Do you not know that I am her master now? Say what you've come to say or get out."

"I cannot!"

"You are trying my patience, girl!"

He studied her as she looked at them. He sensed her disturbance, and though he could not bend her mind, he could feel that whatever was troubling her might also be of concern to him.

"There is bedlam downstairs," she finally said, folding her hands in front of her. "It started when Gertie returned."

"Gertie," Rafazi huffed. "The woman cannot rest until she's laid a sufficient amount of turmoil at Kwadzo's feet."

"Yes," Penelope said, her voice growing surer. "He seemed to be in great distress when she returned. And now, the whole house is under duress. He has decided to send me to the town square and force me to pledge my allegiance to him and forsake my people for all time."

"This is why you saw fit to burst into my room? Did you think I would shield you from your fate?"

"He put silver to your throat when you are the one who made him. He does not respect you, and if he does not respect you, he will respect no one. You cannot wish for such a man to lead your kind."

He had no immediate response. Twice now, a white person had shared with him a derogatory sentiment of Kwadzo that he agreed with. He had lifted his progeny up and made him a leader, and in return, he'd been humiliated in front of all the others, and with Jenue's approval. If things continued in this manner, he had no idea what would become of him under Kwadzo's Crimson rule. Despite the complaints he had about his maker, Jenue had shown no interest in taking Kwadzo's position as leader, even though it would have been an easy task for her. If anything, she had replaced *him* as Kwadzo's counsel and confidant. In truth, for as long as he'd known her, Jenue was never interested in leading. She had been, however, very influential to those who did. Perhaps she was dissuading Kwadzo against him. Either way, Jenue's presence did not bode well for him and may have even played a part in his progeny having put silver to his throat.

The girl was right.

"He wants to cast me out," Rafazi said with revelation.

"A slave spoke out against him, and he put silver to *your* throat, Rafazi!" Penelope said with urgency. "He's gone mad with power! Do you think he will let you continue if he's allowed to go on this way? He will not listen to wise counsel, and no one who opposes him will be safe."

"Who says I oppose him?"

"Why else would he have put silver to your throat? He must be stopped."

"Stopped?" Rafazi laughed. "So that the white folks can put things back the way they were?"

"Nothing will be the way it was ever again," Penelope insisted. "The Blood runs through *my* veins when it's not supposed to. He wants me to be the catalyst for unity, but I won't do it. I refuse to forsake my people."

Penelope took on her Ramangan form and thrust her hand out toward Lily.

"Please, Miss, come! The despair of this new reality has led you astray, but you do not have to lay with this monster ever again!"

"What is this?" Rafazi asked.

"I will give you my blood, and together, we can free the Farkuses from their tyranny and give them the Blood as well."

"Do you think I will allow this?" Rafazi asked with a chuckle of disbelief.

"We'll have the power to escape to Lakeside," Penelope continued, ignoring Rafazi, her speech getting faster, "and we can build an army of immortal white soldiers to conquer Kwadzo before he puts his plan into action. But we must act now!"

Rafazi took on his Ramangan form and flashed his eyes red at Penelope.

"You have uttered the last words you will ever speak!"

He was ready to launch himself across the room at her but felt the soft hand of Lily on his chest. The action halted his race to rage.

"Everything the girl has said about Kwadzo will come to pass if you kill her, Master," Lily said, calmly, softly.

"Miss, please!"

"Put your hand down, child," Lily told Penelope. "I have no desire to take the Blood."

"But you would live forever!"

"Perish the thought. I have no intention of doing that either. I've decided that I want the remainder of my life to be of finite intensity, and my Master has seen to that."

She was kissing him now, and Rafazi gave in to her embrace. He would never have believed that a white colonial woman would turn out to be his most loyal companion, but there she was, in bed with him, rejecting an offer from one of her own kind to turn against him. There was safety in her lips, her embrace. So much so that he reverted to his human form.

"How can you engage so with him?" Penelope asked, her face twisted in disgust.

"I'm sure you were the apple of your father's eye," Lily said. "But such affection is resolved only for girls. The fate of a woman in this world is a harsh one. I have never been a slave, but I have certainly never been free. I have been beholden to men since I have entered this world. Not a single choice I've made was my own until I chose to come here. If slaves can garner otherworldly power and murder their owners, then anything is possible. Even what I truly want."

"And this is what you truly want? *He* is what you truly want?"

"I want the life of a libertine, committed only to pleasures of the flesh and true freedom. I too believe Rafazi should be the one to lead, but he does not wish it. He is the same as me. We wish to live sensuously and without constraint. He affords me that liberty."

"But Kwadzo must be stopped!"

"Patience, girl. There is a way he can be stopped without me sacrificing my humanity." Lily turned to Rafazi, her face staid, her voice serious. "Do you truly wish to be free of Kwadzo and Jenue?"

He didn't know what his answer would lead her to say next, but he had grown tired of being confined to his bedchamber waiting for Kwadzo to act, despite the joys his harem provided. If he was not going to be respected by the one he had gifted the power of Ramanga to and appointed as leader of the new tribe, there was no need for him to stay. He had done his part for his people. If he decided to blur away, he could do it with a clear conscience.

"Yes," he told her. "I want nothing more than freedom. It's all I've ever wanted."

"Can we live in that freedom together, Master?"

"For as long as you wish."

They kissed again, and Lily smiled at a frowning Penelope.

"You say you wish for freedom, yet you call him 'master.'"

"There is a difference between being mastered and *choosing* to be mastered. Rafazi tells me you will not grow much older in appearance, but perhaps time will teach that distinction to you. Until then, I shall share my plan with you. I propose that our solution lies with Rafazi. He was a member of the first Ramanga Tribe and has walked the earth for over seven centuries. What's more, it is his blood that fueled the victory over Barrow. Anything the people of Lakeside would need to know to combat Kwadzo and his legions, Rafazi could provide. In exchange, we will ask for a place of status for him among us.

One befitting a man who helps them defeat the villain they so detest—his freedom recognized so that he can come and go as he pleases. A house, a horse and carriage, and enough money to live as we so choose."

"Or maybe passage to the Greek Isles," Rafazi said with a smile.

"If you wish it so, Master." Lily smiled back.

"And what if they say no to your demands?" Penelope asked.

"Then they are on their own against the Ramangan power that wiped out their entire leadership. I will go far away from this place and never look back," Rafazi said.

"And I will be by his side as long as he will have me," Lily said. "However, if they recognize the value in his knowledge, then we shall live in any fashion we please, and they will grant us whatever compensation we wish for the privilege. You could even have your army of white immortals if my Master doesn't object, but perhaps he should be the one to sire them."

"But I survive the sunlight. He does not. The blood in my body is superior to his."

Rafazi shook his head. Between the arrogance of both this infant and Kwadzo, he would be glad to take his leave. A new era was dawning that he made possible. He could return to his former luster, before his centuries spent underground avoiding the plague, alone and hungry. With Lily as his emissary, he could rebuild his harem tenfold and indulge his every passion. The world was full of so many delicious amusements. Fighting was for fools.

"I honestly don't care," Rafazi said. "You can have your war. I far prefer carnal delights."

"And you shall have them, Master," Lily said, running a hand over his chest. "Can you make an escape?"

"Of course," he said. "I am still the father of all this. I can take you into the field under the guise of putting you to work after you've displeased me and whisk you away into the night. I can burrow underground with the child and lead her to where she needs to go."

"Burrow underground?" Penelope asked.

"I suppose you were never taught that," Rafazi chuckled. "Just as well. You wouldn't have enough strength to do it on the scarce amount of pig blood they give you."

"You can provide me with human blood?" Penelope's eyes shimmered in delight at the prospect while Rafazi glared at her in annoyance.

"I am so sick of my power being questioned. When night falls, we will make our escape."

"Shh!"

Rafazi became still as he locked eyes with Penelope. They could hear the same thing.

"What?" Lily asked.

"We don't have until nightfall," Penelope warned.

"Then our escape must take shape now," Lily said.

Twenty-Eight

Enemy Within

Kwadzo had transformed the chaos that had broken out after Gertie's return into order. She and Irene were tending to the swollen eye Sarah obtained during the ambush they survived, and his troops seemed more energized than ever after Jenue's tale of Ramangan lineage. He couldn't imagine anyone of the Blood or from his native land not wanting to do all they could to protect what had been started.

What *he* had started.

"Native warriors surround the perimeter, and our strongest men stand guard behind them," Jenue said, stepping in line with him and Seneca as they made their way to the foyer. "Our Ramangan brothers and sisters lay in wait inside. All is as you set have forth."

"Be prepared for anything," Kwadzo said, and they nodded in solemn agreement. He was running through words of encouragement that he might say to his legions when his thought was interrupted by the older man with the French accent and his daughter, Antoinette. He remembered conversing with them before, but their faces remained new.

"Kwadzo," the older man said with a bow as his daughter tugged at his arm in distress.

"Papa, please!" Antoinette cried, but he ignored her.

"The time has come. I wish to take the Blood."

"Do not listen to him, sir," she pleaded. "He speaks without sanity."

"My mind is clearer than it has ever been!" His French accent became more pronounced as he raised his voice. "Hearing the true history of the Blood has filled me with pride and duty. Those of us from the Wilson Plantation are as eager to fight for our freedom as anyone else. We stand grateful to the power of Ramanga, to Irene, to you. I said before I wished for my daughter to see her father as a brave man. I can see no better way to do that now that the enemy is at the gate."

"There is a process through which we deem one who asks worthy of the Blood," Kwadzo said, "but the main requirement is the willingness and commitment to fight—fight to protect our people and our freedom until the end of time. And I see that you do."

"Please." Antoinette was crying now. "Please do not take my father from me."

"Have you no faith in your father, girl?" Kwadzo asked. "Or is it the Blood you doubt?"

"I am afraid," she said, averting her eyes. Kwadzo placed his fingers under her chin, bringing her blue eyes up to meet his.

"Do you not know that fear is the enemy of faith? It claims its victims by requiring of them the same as faith. Belief."

Looking around, he saw that those in the house were watching. "Faith, my people," he called out to them all. "It is our strongest weapon. Faith that the very god that gave us the Blood will allow it to lead us to victory. I have faith that a new era is about to dawn. An era of freedom and prosperity for all our people, and all those who unite with us for this common goal. I have no doubt that, by the Blood of Gamab, we will emerge victorious!"

A deafening cheer went up as Kwadzo took Ramangan form, slit his wrist with a talon, and fed his blood to the older man. He winced from drinking before Kwadzo pulled away.

"Never once as a child in Senegambia could I have imagined this day."

"What is your name?"

"Caesar," the older man said.

"No. Your true name. The name born to you in Senegambia."

Tears filled the older man's eyes. "Madu."

"Welcome to the Blood, Madu."

He gave one final nod as a human before Kwadzo snapped his neck and lay him down. Antoinette yelped and went to her knees.

"Don't worry, child," he told her. "Your father is about to be reborn." Kwadzo rose and waved over a couple of nearby human Alkebulan descendants. "Take Madu to the shed. Make sure there is a hog for him to feed on when he awakes."

Antoinette cried out for her father as he was hoisted up and taken away while other humans led her deeper into the house.

"I have faith, but the wrong skin."

Seneca's comment gave Kwadzo pause, but as he took her hard look in, he realized she was right. All Madu had to do was ask and commit to fighting and he freely gave of the Blood. Yet every time Seneca asked, she, who had helped hunt down Penelope, guard the plantation, cultivate its land, and facilitate the integration of his people with her own, was denied. She was always eager to fight for the cause, but he had even taken offense to her requests.

It was not unlike the way his skin had been the subject of unworthiness ever since his arrival in the New World. He was a leader, *the* leader. He could change the rules. Perhaps there was room for amendment on this one. The battle ahead would tell the true tale.

"What of Penelope?" Seneca asked.

Penelope. In preparation for the predicted offensive from Lakeside, he had completely lost track of her. Had she accomplished her goal right under his nose without his knowing, and now the townspeople of Lakeside were armed with knowledge that would make defeating them all the more difficult?

"She is here."

Carrying a sheet in one hand and Penelope's hand in the other was the blonde white woman Rafazi had brought into the manor. The two descended the stairs with Rafazi in tow. Kwadzo locked eyes with his maker. The snarl of disdain Rafazi gave him was unmistakable. Kwadzo felt his insides churn. Rafazi had no right to be cross with him. He didn't want to be the leader. He wanted Kwadzo to rebuild the tribe, to sire them with his own Blood, to lead the charge. Now that he was doing so, Rafazi had become an infant of a man, throwing tantrums at the slightest provocation. The look in his eyes now though, the sinister smile creeping across his lips—this was something different.

"The whites is comin'!"

The call came from a young, muscular human running into the manor from the front door, armed with a rifle and a look of abject terror. "They's outside, and they looks powerful angry! Just a bunch of white men with rifles and torches! They aims to kill us!"

The young man's face went slack as Kwadzo's eyes pulsed red into his. "You are brave and strong. You will fight valiantly until you prevail. There is nothing to fear."

The young man stood straighter. "If them whip-crackers wants a fight, they's gonna get one!" he said with a renewed sense of strength. "They's gonna get one!"

Rafazi chuckled. "First, you decree there will be no mind bending. Then, you bend the mind of one of your own to suit your needs. A fine leader you will be."

"Come, girl." Kwadzo ignored Rafazi's words to address Penelope directly. "You won't have to go to the town square after all. The town is coming here. You can prove yourself on the front porch."

"She *will* prove herself," Rafazi said. "But not how you think."

Rafazi stood face to face with Kwadzo now. All in the manor crowded them in silence. The thumping of hearts and the rushing of blood were deafening.

"All that you are is because of me," Rafazi said. "A fact you have forgotten. You will never forget it again."

It was then that Kwadzo saw Rafazi was carrying his beige, thick flax cloak, the metal sewn into it clanking with his movement.

"What are you plotting, Rafazi?"

"Oh, so now you seek my thoughts. Suddenly what I think is of value."

"Your value has never escaped me. It's the recklessness of your intentions that could impede our progress if left unchecked that concerns me."

"Well, then. Allow me to alleviate your concern."

Rafazi grabbed the blonde woman and kissed her hard. He ended the kiss in a showy action before staring hard at Kwadzo and placing a hand on Penelope's shoulder.

"Looks like your great white hope has become mine."

"Now, Master?" the blonde woman asked Rafazi, her voice saccharine as she batted her eyes.

"Yes, my pet," Rafazi answered.

She smiled and walked to the front door with Penelope. Kwadzo sped in front of them, blocking their path.

"Where do you think you're going?"

"I'm leaving," the blonde woman said. "Honestly, I thought you would be pleased. You haven't exactly been hospitable toward me."

"I wasn't talking to you."

His eyes were on Penelope, who returned his look with calm eyes.

"When you put silver to Rafazi's neck, you said you would not force anyone. Did you mean that?"

"I cannot allow you to leave here and turn whites with our Blood."

"This blood inside me is mine now. I cannot return it, you said so yourself. That makes it *my* blood, *my* power, to use as I see fit."

His focus on Penelope allowed the blonde woman to rush out onto the porch. The sun hung high in the sky. Kwadzo knew what happened to Penelope in the sunlight would live in the minds of her people far longer than her revival from it. She wouldn't dare leave the manor now. So, he followed the blonde woman onto the covered porch. Natives and Alkebulan descendants formed a human wall between the manor and the Lakeside men who had arrived on the property: thirty, perhaps forty, strong.

At the forefront of this group, Bartholomew and Constance Crabtree sat atop horses.

"Be easy, gentlemen," the blonde woman called out to them all as she stepped down the stairs and into the sun. The Lakeside contingent stared back at her with confusion. "I am unharmed and they cannot survive the sun."

Kwadzo had no idea what Rafazi and the woman were playing at, or what hand Penelope had in their deceit, but he knew it would begin once Rafazi's latest exercise in pleasure reached the men who had besieged the land, *his* land. He reached forward to pull the blonde woman back, but she rushed forward just as he felt a force push his head into the daylight and hold it there. He screamed in torture as the sun's rays burned his face and hair in a most excruciating fashion. Every effort to escape the sunlight was met with powerful opposition that kept him right where he was. Through the sizzle of skin and his own screams, he heard a voice yelling.

"One step more and I will blur across this land and sacrifice your leader to the sun!"

The torment was such that Kwadzo could give no effort to identify the voice. Flames burst out on the top of his head, incinerating his hair as his constitution weakened.

A woman is speaking. Have you no manners?

The voice inside his head was as clear as a bell.

And it belonged to Rafazi.

Hello, old friend.
I can sense you
plotting against me.

Twenty-Nine

Exodus

You dare mock me while you allow every distraction to stop you from your goal. I tell you to lead, yet you refuse to make decisions, but when I finally make one for you, you put silver to my throat? You haven't freed the rest, and you never will, because even with all the power I have bestowed upon you, you are still afraid of the whip-crackers, still a slave to their rules. And now that you have forsaken me, I will make it my business to ensure your failure!

Kwadzo felt his body lift off the porch, swing in midair, and land hard against the wood. The surge of heat in his head slowly began to dissipate as the flames flickered out in the shade of the porch's covering. This was not like being immersed in fire. It was a different sensation entirely. Fire, he could feel synergy with. The sun was like an assault—an invasion of his very being. Had he been left in it, he was certain he would have perished.

However, since he'd been pulled from its deadly rays, all that remained was the pain, and the flames he found he could now absorb without the relentless onslaught of the sun beating down on him. Even in the throes of his searing agony, he could feel the flames enter his veins, strengthening, fortifying him even as he continued to shudder from the sun's trauma. Once he was able to open his eyes, Rafazi appeared, hovering over him covered in his flax cloak. His maker's vicious words held his mind in a vise. Had there been water in his burned tear ducts, Kwadzo felt as though he would have cried.

"You," Kwadzo croaked.

"None among us can escape the sun," Rafazi hissed down at him. "None but your great white hope. Perhaps she is more special than you."

Kwadzo's head was still healing, and his strength was lacking. It was as if his Ramangan makeup was drawing from every source of power within him to repair the damage the sun had done. He wanted to lunge at Rafazi. He wanted to tear his maker's heart from his chest. He wanted to consume all the fire in the world and then rain it down upon Rafazi until he was nothing but dust. The bitter singe of betrayal pained him just as much as his head did.

"Their leader lies in pain, and they do nothing," a smiling Penelope said as she moved next to Rafazi to stare down at him. "Perhaps they fear your maker more than they love you."

With a guttural howl, Kwadzo forced his head to twist through the scorching pain just enough to see the entrance of the manor. Ramangans stood there looking on, their faces covered in shock, their attention divided between him, Rafazi, and the white men who stood at their gate. Only Jenue retained a calm demeanor—still as his man—while he spectated from a distance, almost as if he was entertained, waiting to see what would happen but taking no action to interfere. Forcing his head back the other way, Kwadzo saw the white men—the bulk of whom he imagined to be members of the slave patrol—staring with their jaws slack, flabbergasted by what they had witnessed.

"Extraordinary!" Bartholomew exclaimed.

"As you can see," the blonde woman said, "their fearsome leader is conquered by the light of the sun. They all are. Not a one of them dares step off the porch and into the light, for they would perish."

"And how did you come to be in their presence?" Bartholomew asked. "How did they accost you?"

"All in good time, husband," Constance said. "First things first."

"Quite right. Would you like to be the one to deliver the news, my dearest?"

"It would be my pleasure to." She dismounted the horse. Stumbling a bit and holding her side with a wince, Constance walked past the blonde woman until she was standing before the porch, addressing them all. "Now, then. Your minds may be too feeble to understand this, but understand you must. You will all be punished for the insidious revolt you brought upon this land and its deceased owner. By law, none of you have rights to this land or anything else.

"This law went disobeyed because your savagery wiped out those whose job it was to valiantly uphold the law. The poor citizens of Lakeside were left without leadership to guide them; you left them terrorized to the point that Josiah Browne was coerced into conducting business with your leader, which is lunacy, because he had no right to conduct business in the first place! There is also no doubt that unlawful reading was taught here, which was evidenced by the command of language the leader of the vampyre niggers had when he dared speak to us in the Crown Tavern, a place it was illegal for him to be in. The governor's widow, Sarah Collins, is clearly the culprit. A nigger lover of the highest order and a traitor to her race, she was not above violent assault to cover her crime when she was found out!"

Her last shout caused her pain; she doubled over clutching her side, a spot of red spreading out on her dress from beneath her hand. The scent of the blood awakened Kwadzo's senses through his pain, and he suspected he wasn't the only one. If only she wasn't under the protection of the sun.

"Sarah Collins is guilty of treason," Constance continued. "You will bring her out to face her fate immediately along with the one among you who murdered Gavin Wilson and stole his slaves. Both will hang in the town square for their crimes this night. All of you, nigger and Indian alike, shall vacate this manor and this land. My dear Bartholomew and I will take possession of it just as we have the Wilson Plantation, for we are the only ones with the means to set Lakeside on the path to recovery with a sound economic plan."

The sound of footsteps on the porch caused Kwadzo to turn his head again. Doc and Rebecca Farkus were rushing forward.

"What is the meaning of all this?" Doc Farkus asked.

"That Farkus is a traitor, too!" one of the white men called out. "Him and his nigger-lovin' wife!"

"Doc Farkus, I presume," Bartholomew called out. "It seems your fellow residents believe you have abandoned your own kind for these slaves and savages, but I am inclined to give you the benefit of the doubt, as you are the most skillful doctor the citizens have. I understand you were a guest of the manor when it was attacked."

"I was," Doc Farkus said.

"I was not," Rebecca said defiantly.

"Yes, your nigger-loving status has already been established," Bartholomew spat before refocusing on Doc Farkus. "Now then, I am of the mind that you negotiated this position in order to save yourself from a violent end. If this is true, now is your chance to return to Lakeside and assume your previous position without further consequence."

"And if it is not true?" Rebecca asked, crossing her arms.

"My God, woman! Living among these beasts has made you as ornery as they are," Bartholomew said. "No one is talking to you. Kindly keep quiet so that we can converse with your husband."

Rebecca turned to Doc Farkus, who stepped down the stairs of the porch. "Daniel?"

"It is true," Doc Farkus said. "I feared for my life and offered my services to preserve it and that of my Rebecca."

"But she fell under their spell," Bartholomew said. "As I'm sure was the case with the young lady among them, though she seems to have turned at least one of them to reason."

"It has been my great sadness to witness," Doc Farkus said.

Rebecca unleashed a litany of obscenities in protest of Doc Farkus's words while the blonde woman giggled and Kwadzo suffered yet another sting of betrayal. He cursed the kindness of his nature that allowed the doctor to reside among them, study their physiology, care for Gertie and their child. Anything he knew of them, the mob would know if he followed through with his duplicity.

"Your wife has sealed her fate. You can perish with her, or you can return and share your knowledge of them with us," Constance said.

"I choose to return." Doc Farkus crossed the lawn and took his place among the white men. From his prone position, Kwadzo watched the doctor's eyes search out his own, but he turned away. Doc Farkus was a failure of a decision, and he was suffering from enough disappointment already.

"Now then," Constance said after clearing her throat, "as for the rest of you, I'm sure you believe you can resist us, but know that your crimes against Mister Barrow, his family, and his land, the town of Lakeside, and this very province have been reported to the Crown, and that the British army will be upon you to rid us of your wretched existence should we deem it necessary. Your only course of action is to obey these words I've spoken to you as law and comply by coming along to your fate in a peaceable fashion."

"And what if we don't?"

Kwadzo's eyes followed Rafazi as best they could from his position on the floor of the porch as he moved to the edge of the stairs, a smirk across his lips.

"Surely, by now, you know what just one of us can do," Rafazi continued. "The sun may restrict us, but I suspect none of you have dared to enter these walls because you know you would all be devoured before any of your number could even set foot in the manor. Even more inside have been gifted with the power of my blood, and more still will receive it before your army comes. Your brash words do not ensure your victory here. Mine, however, can."

In the throes of his torment, Kwadzo tried to focus his mind to communicate with the other Ramangans, to ask for their assistance, to make them restrain Rafazi. A feeling of spitefulness grew within him at the fact that not one of them had thought to do the same of their own accord. Penelope's words haunted him.

Perhaps they fear your maker more than they love you.

Amid the pain of healing, Kwadzo was hit with an avalanche of fear. It crashed over him out of nowhere, like a wave in the ocean, and grew deeper and more profound with each passing second, exacerbating the pain coursing through him. It churned the blood within him, and he could sense the source of it—the blood of those he had turned. Just as he'd felt the disruption of the Wretched in his blood, he could now feel the collective blood of those he'd sired bubbling with trepidation. Their concentrated emotion overwhelmed him.

As he lay there on the porch, unable to do much else but reel in pain and this recent sensation, the newness of this Ramangan power he had thrived in dawned on him. Less than two months ago, he was a lowly slave toiling away on the paddy, his back blistered from Monroe's whip after he tried to run. Despite the power they possessed, the stench of slavery was not far removed from him or those of the Blood, not to mention the humans among them. It had only been two hours ago when he'd realized he had been leading them under the shadow of slavery still, placing limitations based on the rules that had been set forth by white society.

Most of those who had taken the Blood after Barrow's fall had been trained for battle but had not yet seen it, and he was certain the idea of having to fight against another Ramangan never entered their minds, much less one whose blood had renewed the ancient tribe. They had not been free long enough for liberation to set in their minds as the default condition of their lives. They were new and in need of their leader. Without one, without him, and in the face of a mighty throng of angry whites bearing down on them in the sunshine, they were lost. Kwadzo needed to heal, and fast, and to do that, he had to relinquish the effort of trying to communicate as much as he could and let the Blood do what it needed to do, and quickly.

"Ladies and gentlemen," Rafazi called out. "I am Rafazi. And while I'm sure you believe Doc Farkus has insight into the nature of what we are, I have walked the earth for over seven centuries. It is my blood that runs through the veins of those you seek vengeance against, and mere mortals are no match for my power. Nevertheless, for the right price and with strict obedience to my tutelage, I can show you the path that leads to victory."

A primal scream brought everyone's attention to the front door of the manor, where Irene, in Ramangan form, launched herself through the air at Rafazi, talons first. Rafazi planted his feet and caught Irene by the neck, then with a pivot, he thrust her into the sunlight and held her in it. Her screams were terrifying as she burned.

"Their power comes from me!" Rafazi hollered over Irene's screams. "But they have yet to even scratch the surface of what they can do. Before that happens, I can expose their weaknesses, their flaws."

Rafazi yanked Irene back from the sunshine and threw her onto the porch floor, where she twisted and lurched, sizzling in pain. The hand he'd held Irene with blistered from the heat, and Rafazi quickly tucked it under his cloak as he slipped the rest of himself under it.

"You see?" the blonde woman said, twisting in the sun, enjoying its warmth. "Rafazi has shown you where his loyalties lie by burning one of his own kind."

"He should've let her burn up all the way!"

Cheers of agreement rose from the crowd before Bartholomew raised his hand, quieting the men.

"Why would you betray your own kind in such a way?" Bartholomew asked.

"Why else?" Rafazi stated. "Money and status. I will go to Lakeside with you and state my terms."

"Terms?" Bartholomew scoffed. "There are no terms for a slave to discuss. You will tell us what we want to know, or you will hang!"

Rafazi was laughing now. "Despite the sun, I could take your life and the lives of ten more and disappear from your sight before you could even blink. Shall I demonstrate?"

Before they could answer, Rafazi's blur, covered by his cloak, zipped across the lawn and returned to the porch. Shrugging off the cloak, steam rose from his head and shoulders as he held a screaming white man in his grasp. Kwadzo's vision went red at the smell of the fearful blood, and he was sure the other Ramangans had experienced the same reaction.

"Shall I return him to you?" Rafazi shouted above the man's earsplitting cries. "Or shall he provide nourishment for my begotten?"

While the man begged for his life, the Lakeside contingent stood in utter shock. They had heard of the power of the Blood, as Kwadzo had shown a slight demonstration of it to them at the tavern, but here, now, they were witnesses to one of their own on the brink of being consumed.

"Send him back," Bartholomew said with a shaken voice. Kwadzo suspected he'd meant to make his statement far calmer. Urine soaked the front of the man's breeches as Rafazi gently released him, and he ran out into the sun to cower behind a horse-drawn carriage that sat amid the delegation.

"Don't think of it as negotiating with a slave. I no longer am a slave. Think of me as a very powerful man offering you extremely valuable information that you will only have access to if my terms are met. If it helps, imagine I am white."

Kwadzo's ears burned more from Rafazi's words now than from the intense heat of the sunlight still throbbing through his head.

"Once those terms are met," Rafazi continued, "I will teach you everything you will need to know. Then, young Penelope and I will select appropriate candidates for the Blood, and together, we can build an eternal army. One that no power on earth can defeat. Or, you could refuse me and perish."

"Ain't no little girl doin' nothin' to me!" a call came from the crowd of men.

"The girl was sent to collect information and bring it back to us," another yelled out. "She failed!"

Hearing the sentiments against Penelope with his own ears did nothing to reconcile the sting of Kwadzo's betrayal.

"Of course, she failed." Rafazi laughed. "You sent a calf into a lion's den. She had no chance of escape here, yet she remains more powerful than any of you, and she possesses a gift none of them carry, not even me. Show them, child."

Penelope took Rafazi's hand, and they stepped into the sunlight. While Rafazi remained secure under his cloak for the time being, he stepped back to the safety of the porch as he let go of her hand. Penelope fell to her knees in the grass with a screech of extreme anguish as the daylight caused her to burn. Gasps of horror swept through the air as she was overtaken by flame. Her hair disintegrated, her eyes boiled and burst. Several of the men doubled over and vomited from the monstrous display.

The fire that consumed her burned away her clothing, and soon, she was charred over from head to toe. Taking the sheet she had descended the stairs of the manor with, the blonde woman placed it over Penelope's incinerated body. They all watched with bated breath, and after a bit of time had passed, her arms were moving under the sheet and pieces of peeled-away charred scabs were flecking out from underneath it.

The Lakeside men murmured in astonishment as the girl sat up holding the sheet against her with one hand while picking away at the char covering her head. As she did, strands of red began to sprout forth and grow. She picked away the black scabs on her face to reveal renewed skin as her hair continued to grow back thicker and stronger at a rapid pace.

"Like the lord and savior you hold dear, this child returns from the dead, while the leader of the ones you fear still trembles in pain!"

Kwadzo's anger at Rafazi's declaration motivated him to push through the pain and rise to his feet. His movement was slow, wobbly, his vision blurry, his knees weak. Still, he moved toward the steps, inching closer to Rafazi. Opening his mouth to speak, Kwadzo could form no words. His vocal cords had not healed enough for him to give voice to his words, but he could still think them.

"You want to know the secrets of Ramanga. I can give them to you. For the right price," Rafazi said as the blonde woman helped the restored Penelope to her feet while the men gawked.

"And you will tell us everything?" Bartholomew asked.

After everything they had been through, all they had endured, they were finally on the verge of freeing all their people. This had all started with the two of them, a scared, desperate slave and a lonely immortal. They had won a revolution together. Rafazi had been a mentor, a friend, a brother.

Now this.

Something inside Kwadzo's heart broke.

"You cannot believe he can be trusted, do you?" Constance asked her husband.

"Judging from the demon's actions against his own kind, I believe he can be about this, my sweet." Bartholomew lowered his voice considerably, but Kwadzo's ears had healed enough for his enhanced hearing to keep him privy to their hushed conversation. "The way he leers at this woman tells me he has defiled her."

"Disgusting!"

"I do not disagree, but the way she leers at him, I suspect she is a willing participant. I also suspect their coupling has caused dissension in the ranks. Besides, you saw what he did. The demon vampyre is right. The men could do battle, but there would be much bloodshed."

"But what of the governor's widow? She must pay for her crimes. So must the one who killed Mister Wilson."

"Yes, yes, but if the knowledge of their traitor proves valuable, it won't matter who killed Mister Wilson. We'll be able to kill them all, and the fate of Sarah and Farkus's wife will be the same as theirs."

"Exactly how long do you two plan on commiserating?" Rafazi asked. "Despite your whispers, I can hear every word. Another power of the Blood, but you would already have known that and much more if you simply made the right decision with haste. I am growing impatient."

Time was short. Kwadzo shut his eyes as tightly as he could and found his focus. He set his mind on Rafazi's.

Please, brother, do not do this, he shouted to his maker in his mind.

It has already been done, came Rafazi's telepathic reply.

"Very well," Bartholomew said. "We shall take advantage of your offer. Just know there is an abundance of fire and silver awaiting you should you choose to lead us astray."

"We shall ride in the coach," Rafazi said. "Open the door to the carriage."

Bartholomew gave a nod, and one of the men opened the door to the carriage. Seconds later, Rafazi's blur rushed inside it, and the blonde woman and Penelope followed him in. The procession started away, and Kwadzo's heavy head filled with Rafazi's echoing voice.

You should have shown me the proper respect, brother. From now on, mind your thoughts.

Thirty

Hate

A singular glass was placed on a table in front of Rafazi. It contained a liquid with a pungent aroma and a rich, brown hue. Surrounded by Lakeside citizens who had packed the Crown Tavern, Rafazi rose the glass to his nose to take in its bouquet.

"What you got there is whiskey," the woman said to him. She'd been introduced to him as Kitty Greer, the owner of this establishment. He could hear the tremble in her voice, smell the fear in her blood. The entire building was filled with fearful blood. The aroma was intoxicating, but there was no need to rush. It had been centuries since he had held court like this. He intended to savor it.

Raising the glass to his lips, he looked up to find every eye in the tavern on him. He was surrounded by white faces, the place chockful of them; even the second-floor balcony and the stairs leading up to it were full of white folks crammed in on top of each other, awaiting his next move. He was the only one seated in the place; Lily and Penelope stood on either side of him, watching him intently like everyone else. He had become the center of attention.

This was more like it.

No one pressing him into action, dismissing his vital contributions, demanding his loyalty, or lording over him. He would be making the demands now. Instead of sipping from the glass, he raised it above his head and into Lily's reach. The tavern was engulfed in silence as Lily took the glass from him and drained it entirely before handing it back to Rafazi. She moaned her satisfaction while wiping two fingers across her lips.

"Thank you, Master," she purred. The male faces in front of Rafazi turned beet red at her addressing of him, and it made him chuckle as he held the glass up again.

"Miss Kitty Greer? Another, if you will."

The tavern owner returned and refilled his glass. Bartholomew leaned on the table and yanked it out of his hand.

"You've been given your drink as you asked for. Start talking."

"You're getting ahead of yourself. We have yet to discuss my terms."

"I knew it!" Constance hollered. "This was just a ruse! Now, you listen to me. Unless you want the wrath of the British army to rain down on you . . ."

She blinked as Rafazi feigned a big, long yawn. He was aware of whose company he was in. He knew they would try to find a way out of negotiating with him, a way of making him talk without compensating him. It didn't matter. He had already come this far. He had turned against his people, against Kwadzo. He couldn't go back. He didn't want to. He wanted to live a life of pleasure. And the people of Lakeside would foot the bill for it with either their money or their blood.

Potentially both, if they became too disagreeable.

"You haven't contacted the Crown, nor will you," Rafazi said, willing to dance this dance with them for the moment.

"How dare you!"

"Your words are many and callous, but they have no weight here. Your finery denotes you've met with success, but ultimately, you are nothing more than farmers. Neither of you hold any position of authority in this town or province, one still under British rule. A province that has lost its governor and council. Not enough time has passed for a meaningful account of what transpired on Barrow's plantation to have been transcribed and sent back to England, so your Queen Anne does not yet know what happened here. However, if she were to learn that slaves have overtaken one of the most profitable plantations in the colony, if word were to spread to the other colonies . . . Well, my understanding is that Britain doesn't lose or shame very well, especially from dissenters."

Constance's cheeks quaked in her anger while Rafazi calmly reclaimed his glass from her husband's grasp.

"My dear, sweet Lily has provided me with a veritable wealth of useful information," he said, taking a sip of the whiskey. One of the men leaned close to whisper in Bartholomew's ear. Rafazi tilted his head slightly and used his superhuman hearing to listen in.

"Queen Anne's war rages on, but Pensacola has been taken," the man whispered. "I am friendly with Colonel Ben Johnston; I can ask his help from the troops that remain."

"Yes," Bartholomew whispered back. "Send someone at once." As the man rushed away, Bartholomew retrained his sights on Rafazi. "You will tell us what you know."

"I must say, I am very disappointed," Rafazi said. To his left and his right, he saw men raising and loading their guns. "I had assumed you British understood how deals work."

"You are surrounded, boy. All the demonic power in the

world cannot make you strong enough to get out of this room alive."

Rafazi chuckled. "I will give you one piece of information for free," he said, taking his time to drain his glass. "Ramangans can smell human blood, and certain emotions alter the scent. Take, for example, fear. The smell of fear in this tavern is overwhelming, and altogether irresistible."

Penelope's eyes were now glowing red, and she began to fidget.

"You see," Rafazi said, pointing her out. "Even this daughter of Lakeside cannot deny the hunger the Blood has given her. She will struggle with restraint. I shall not."

Taking on his Ramangan form, Rafazi leapt from his chair and pulled a man randomly from the mass. To the chorus of gasps and shocked murmurs, his jagged teeth tore into the man's neck and Rafazi drank deeply, dragging the man around the tavern floor as he did so. His goal was to make sure everyone saw what he was doing, but it dawned on him that his blur was moving much too fast for that. Perhaps this was a better display, a violent supernatural act that they could not see or stop but could witness up close.

Rafazi felt the man's heart stop and drank his fill of him before abandoning the lifeless body and rushing to Constance. By the time he had stopped moving, his fangs were at the woman's throat, and she was screaming. Several of the men pointed their weapons at him with wide eyes and shaky arms, including Bartholomew.

"One more free fact," Rafazi called out. "I am dead! I gave my human life for this power! Do you really think your bullets can stop me from draining the life from your beloved? Her mouth is as fat as the rest of her and will bring about the downfall of everyone in this town if my terms are not met! The man I betrayed will only kill when pushed. I will do so indiscriminately!"

A man carrying a sword stepped out from behind Bartholomew. Rafazi felt his blood react to the sight of it right away.

Silver.

"We both know what this does to the likes of you," the man hissed. "So, I'm only gonna tell you this once, nigger. You let her go, or I'll shove this silver all the way up your arse until it kills you dead! You hear me?"

In a blur of speed, Rafazi shifted Constance so that the tip of the silver blade was right under her nose. The man's panic to keep the sword from harming Constance gave Rafazi the short window of time he needed to evade the attack entirely. Leaping over Constance and the man faster than anyone could see, he delivered a lightning barrage of punches to the man's back as Bartholomew pulled his wife out of harm's way. The man hunched forward and dropped the sword; Rafazi swiftly picked it up and pointed its blade at the man's chest.

"But . . . that's silver! How can you touch it?" the man asked, his chest heaving with frantic breath.

"The blade is silver, not the handle, you ignorant fool."

In the haste of the action, the blade had nicked Constance on the tip of her nose, and Bartholomew hurried for a rag to stop the bleeding.

"Shall I go on killing until I've had my fill of blood and disappear, or shall we discuss! My! Terms!" Rafazi roared as he slowly plunged the sword into the man's chest while he wailed in pain. The smell of fright only grew stronger as the crowd watched in horror, but not one of them moved to help the dying man.

"The sun still shines, demon!" Bartholomew said as he tended to a whimpering Constance. "You run; you burn. You may take some of us, but there's enough of us here to tear you limb from limb eventually."

"Not one of you will lay a finger on him," Lily said, embracing him.

"You'll be hanged for this, you nigger-loving slut!" someone in the crowd shouted to several rumblings of agreement.

"How can you align yourself with filth?" another called out, and the angry muttering grew louder.

"I align myself with power!" Lily shouted back at them. "None of you remember me, but I was once a daughter of Lakeside, loyal to a father who held me in little regard, and a betrothed who found pleasure between the legs of anyone but me. The only love that was ever shown to me came from my beloved sister. I fled this place, and she was the only one who searched me out, listened to my woes, put food in my belly, arranged shelter for me when all of you had turned your backs on me. You all *deserved* what happened to you, every one of you!"

"Enough foolishness!" Bartholomew yelled, cutting Lily off and turning to Penelope. "You carry his power, girl! Do not sit idly by while he threatens your people, attack!"

Penelope did not move.

"She will not attack me," Rafazi said, laughing. "She cannot. Unless she wishes to spend the remainder of her eternity as . . ."

With a flick of his wrist, Rafazi yanked the silver blade out of the now-dead man who'd fallen to the floor and poked an unsuspecting Bartholomew in the chest with its bloody tip. The tension in the tavern was so high now, it nearly vibrated the walls.

"The remainder of her eternity as what?" Bartholomew shouted.

"You will learn all you wish once we have discussed my terms!" Rafazi bellowed before effortlessly hurling the sword at a window on the other side of the tavern and shattering it. The sun rays that came through the window were well enough away from him and Penelope that they were no cause for concern.

Constance released a huff of air as she held a bloody rag tightly against her nose, and finally, Bartholomew relented.

"Very well."

Lily clapped and smiled at Rafazi, who sat and extended his hand toward a chair, inviting Bartholomew to do the same, which he begrudgingly did.

"What are your terms?"

"We want a patch of land to call our own," Lily said, sitting on Rafazi's lap. "Enough for us to grow and harvest food for ourselves, but we won't be growing any cash crops."

"No reminders of the past," Rafazi said with a wink.

"A cottage, furnished, of course; a horse and carriage; a cow, chickens . . ."

"My freedom encoded into law, which shouldn't be a difficult task since the one who called himself my master no longer lives. I will suffer no dealings with members of the slave patrol. I will be viewed and respected as a member of this society and treated as such," Rafazi said pointedly.

Constance grunted in the beginning of a response, but Bartholomew's raised hand quieted her. "Is that the extent of your terms?"

"No. In addition to all that's been stated, one thousand pounds," Rafazi stated.

The reactions in the tavern ranged from gasps to laughter, but Rafazi's eyes remained fixed upon Bartholomew.

"One thousand pounds? Are you mad?"

"I'm a monster who gets hungry when he doesn't get what he wants."

"But there isn't enough proclamation money in the province to simply hand you that much. It would be far easier to pay your passage on a ship back to Africa." Bartholomew's eyes widened with a new idea; a smile crossed his lips. "Would you like that? To go back to where you came from?"

"Go back?" Rafazi laughed. "Go back to what? Anything I would have known from the place you call Africa is long gone. Your people saw to that. There is nothing to go back to. You brought us here so you could indulge your laziness. Now, you will pay me to remain, pay for the knowledge that will make your murderous endeavors effective. I have given you two pieces of fact in good faith already. The price for more is everything Lily and I have stated plus one thousand pounds."

Bartholomew's jaw tightened, and Rafazi sighed.

"I suppose I could take a life for every pound if you continue to deny my request. And without my knowledge, you will lose many, many more." Rafazi turned to find Penelope's eyes burning red as her torso heaved. "Or perhaps I should let Penelope do the dirty work. I suspect the abundance of blood in here is driving her mad with hunger."

"It will take some bartering with other landowners, but we shall meet your demands." Murmurs of contention rose from the crowd, but Bartholomew's voice rose above them. "Silence! We have seen what he is capable of. To go against an army of them uneducated is a recipe for our own destruction! Your terms shall be met if we have your assurances that our citizens are safe from your bloodlust."

"Come, now. I do have to nourish myself."

A choir of protest rang out high and loud in the tavern, much to Rafazi's amusement.

"No," Bartholomew said, shaking his head. "The citizens of Lakeside cannot live in constant fear of a demon running loose, killing as he pleases."

"You needn't worry about that." Lily smiled. "I'm sure once the bar maidens have heard of the joys I've experienced, we will rebuild a willing harem to satisfy all of my Master's needs in no time."

Rafazi extended his hand, and Bartholomew reluctantly shook it. The citizens gave voice to their protests in unison, and this time, his shouts could not quiet them. Rafazi jumped from his seat, and his blur zipped through the crowd until it stopped with his talons at the throat of a young man with dark, wavy hair and green eyes that quaked with fear in Rafazi's grasp.

The protests settled at the sight as terror brought about silence. Rafazi inhaled the young man deeply.

"Your fear," he said, "smells better than everyone else's in here."

"No!" Penelope cried. "Don't hurt him!"

Penelope's plea registered with Rafazi, causing him to hesitate. A few of the men in the crowd took the opportunity to rush for Rafazi, but he clasped a hand around the young man's neck before slashing his would-be attackers with his talons, sending them all to the floor, bleeding from his cuts. The groans of the injured men on the ground kept anyone else from making a move, but the young man's lips tightened with courage.

"You're nothing like their leader," he said boldly despite the quiver in his voice. "He showed mercy even when he was attacked. You're a monster who kills for sport."

"Brave words for such a young man whose death is imminent. What is it they call you?"

"Michael Lyon."

"Well, well. There is something to a name after all, young Mister Lyon. Your bold tongue could be compared to that of a lion. But you see, Mister Lyon, I can be merciful, too. When I want to be." He released the young man unscathed and addressed the tavern. "The greatest weapon you have against my kind is hate."

"Hate?" Constance squealed. "You put us through all this just to say the way to stop them is to hate them? He has tricked you, Barty! He has tricked us all! We already have all we need! I hate all niggers immensely! Let us plan our attack against them!"

"Such universal hatred is precisely why it is ineffective," Rafazi said. "General hate, as so many of you carry for my people, is of no use. Barrow nearly won the battle because his chief overseer Monroe hated, but his hate was expressly for Kwadzo. It was a deeply rooted and very specific hate for one Ramangan born out of toil and trouble, of his inability to break him as a slave, of having been conquered by him. Monroe's hate filled his heart and pumped through his blood. That kind of true personalized hate, reserved for a particular Ramangan, can kill that Ramangan. When Barrow learned of this, he sliced Monroe open and let him bleed all over Kwadzo. It nearly conquered him."

"Why didn't it?"

Rafazi paused at Bartholomew's question. There was no turning back. He had intended to teach Kwadzo a lesson about devaluing him, but he had found a pathway back to the way of life he remembered, and he had chosen it over Kwadzo, over his people. A pang of guilt throbbed in his gut. It was something he had felt before, but he'd also learned that with eternity at your disposal, guilt passes. He had done his part. He had no interest in revolution. All he ever wished for was his own freedom. His loyalty was to it and himself.

The life he wished for was but a statement away.

"Find someone who hates Kwadzo the way Monroe did. Find a way to get that person's blood into Kwadzo's system, and you will vanquish him."

The silence loomed for what seemed hours until Lily spoke up.

"I know someone with that kind of hate," she said.

"Who, girl?" Bartholomew asked.

"Me."

Shock swept through the crowd; even Rafazi was taken aback by her admission.

"Charity Barrow was my sister," Lily said. "Big Jim made her miserable, but she wed him at our father's insistence to grow our family's fortune, a fortune he made sure I would never get to share in. But Charity always searched me out and cared for me when no one else would, especially after my father and mother went back to England. When I learned of her death at the hand of her slaves, a fury was born in me, one that led me to the manor to find a way to kill the slave responsible. This was my vow, to avenge my sister. Being inside the manor walls, I discovered that slave was Kwadzo. I've never cared one way or another about the skin a person enters the world with, which was a major point of contention with my father, but my hatred for Kwadzo and desire for his demise never abated. I did not mean to fall under Rafazi's lustful spell, but the acts I subjected myself to for the sake of my mission brought me pleasure beyond any I had ever experienced. I do not wish to give it up, but I still very much wish to avenge my sister."

Lily turned soft, pleading eyes to Rafazi, taking his hands in hers.

"Will you help me, Master?"

This was Kwadzo's fault. If only he had respected his maker's wishes and left him alone to do as he wished, none of this would be happening. He did not wish to do battle and would not. He knew some effort on his part would be necessary if he chose this path. What he didn't count on was hateful blood lying in wait under his nose. This would all happen much faster than he anticipated, but maybe that was a good thing. He could get on with living the existence he wanted all the quicker.

"Yes, my sweet," Rafazi said to Lily. "I will."

"Hateful blood," Bartholomew sighed. "Is there more?"

"Much," Rafazi said. "But first, take me to my parcel of land."

Thirty-One

The New Whites

Kwadzo and Gertie arrived at the balcony that overlooked the foyer, where his troops were armed and falling into formations in preparation for the mission ahead as he had laid it out once he had healed. Four humans gave of their blood to help hasten his physical restoration, but it was Kwadzo's heart that would require far more mending.

For seven centuries, Rafazi had been a Ramangan. Seven hundred years of knowledge and secrets . . . He had no idea how much Rafazi had kept from him. There was so much he still didn't understand, and the existence of Jenue was proof there was much more to know. He racked his brain, rifling through information Rafazi had shared, thinking of ways it could be combated if used against them.

These, however, were minor concerns compared to the agony of Rafazi's betrayal. Jenue attempted to ease his pain, explaining away Rafazi's actions as those of a petulant child with the power of a monster who was simply mad that he hadn't gotten his way—that it had always been his way to cut and run when the pursuit of his wild perversions was impeded. Neither Jenue's man nor woman seemed to be much different, but these were not things he could dwell on now. One of their own was working with their oppressors. The time for action was now.

"My goodness!"

Sarah's exclamation surprised him. Arm in arm with Irene, she stood next to Gertie on the balcony. They both looked much better: Sarah's swollen eye did not seem nearly as inflamed as it had when she arrived, and Irene, in a new set of clothing, looked completely healed from Rafazi's cruelty.

"It's about to begin, isn't it?" Sarah asked.

"It is," Kwadzo said. "Our hand has been forced, but in truth, we should have taken this action long ago."

"Your eye all right?" Gertie asked her.

"Yes. Irene took good care of me."

"And how are you, Irene?" Kwadzo asked her. "What Rafazi did to you . . ."

"He is not who I thought he was." Her jaw was tight, and her eyes were cast downward. Sarah's hand slid over hers, and the two exchanged a furtive glance. "No matter. I'm ready for the fight ahead, thanks to Sarah."

"Thanks to Sarah?"

"Yes." Sarah smiled. "Irene showed me so much kindness, I felt it only right that I return the favor and help her. It was an honor to gift her my blood."

Gertie looked up at Kwadzo, her brows raised, and Kwadzo allowed himself this small amusement. He didn't know when he'd get another one.

Jenue—once again a woman—was moving toward the front door below. She looked up at him with a nod, and Kwadzo descended the stairs with Gertie in tow. Jenue opened the door to a small band of white men and women standing on the porch.

"Kwadzo," Jenue said, putting an arm around the man in front. "I give you my emissary, Jon Paul."

The man—of modest size and elegant dress—removed his three-pointed hat and bowed. "I come with news of your traitor," Jon Paul said.

Kwadzo found momentary distraction from what was sure to be disturbing news in a familiar face among them.

"Missus Kitty Greer," he said, extending his hand to her. Her cheeks went flush as she took his hand, and he kissed it. He ignored the soft huff he heard behind him from Gertie. "What brings you and these others here?"

"Kwadzo," she said, forcing the smile from her face. "I know you have killed because you have suffered, but I believe you to be a man of respect and principle, of justice. The one who left your fold is different entirely. He is a monster. A killer for killing's sake, and still those Crabtrees and the bulk of the residents indulge him. If they prosper, true evil will take hold in Lakeside, and who knows how far and long it will fester?"

"Why does the township embrace the Crabtrees?" he asked. "They have no jurisdiction in Lakeside or anywhere else."

"They're a feckless lot," Kitty Greer responded. "They're much happier to pass the blame for their misfortunes than to take responsibility for them, and you've made for an easy target. But not all of us are so gullible or cruel. So, when I caught this young man slipping out of the tavern, and he told me he was reporting back to you after that despicable display, me and a few of my girls brave enough decided to join your cause."

"You would see the slaves freed?" Kwadzo asked. "All of them?" It was a satisfying sentiment, and one that he couldn't quite bring himself to believe. It wouldn't be the first time a white person had been sent to his front door as a weapon.

"I daresay we'd like to see it come to pass. Our town has seen more than its fair share of blood, and most of it came from your people. Now I admit, I never gave that fact much thought in the past, but listening to the one who betrayed you made me realize just how wicked this slave business is. I don't believe him to be of any good, mind you, but he's got every right to his anger. Just like you do to yours. So, me and the brave among my girls here are with you. These here men, Andrew, Henry, and Michael of the Lyon family, are with you, too," Kitty said, gesturing to the men with her. The one she called Michael stepped forward.

"You don't know me, sir," he said with a shaky breath, "but I am indebted to you. My uncle, Andrew, was part of a militia that came for this house, but you spared his life."

"Yes, I remember," Kwadzo said, eyeing the man.

"My Uncle Andrew is the closest thing me and my brother Henry have to a father. The story of what happened here painted you as pure evil that had to be stopped, no matter the cost. Some of us thought you to be the Devil himself. But it's not you we should be fighting. It's the one who betrayed you. I too believe he has a right to his anger, but he kills without principle. You let my uncle go when you could have easily taken his life. I do not believe that evil and kindness can live together. My family never held slaves, and like Miss Kitty said, none of us ever gave too much thought to the plight of the slave. I reckon there's a part of you that wants to kill us all, and you could. But you didn't. So, if it's freedom you're fighting for, we reckon you deserve it. That's why we're here."

"I done known it," Gertie said to Kwadzo with a smile. "There be good folk in this here world. These here be just like Sarah."

Kwadzo looked them over. This new lot, Sarah Collins, Rebecca, Nez, Seneca, and their people who lived side by side with his people—were the physical evidence of Gertie's words. They were not his people, but he could not detect any deviousness among them, and though they did carry the aroma of fear, it came with sincerity on their faces. He had peered into the eyes of Barrow, Monroe, the Crabtrees. The hatred they carried inside them shone like a beacon. Though his wife remained with them, Doc Farkus had submitted to his will to save himself, but these new faces had each come of their own volition. And while he would remain on guard, he sensed sincerity in their words.

"Then come," Kwadzo said to the group. "Join us."

As they all scurried into the house, Jon Paul hung back, staring up at Jenue with a glint in his eye, as if he were both awaiting permission for something and terribly smitten with the woman.

"Well." Jenue nodded to him. "Go on."

"His request for land was granted. The Crabtrees gathered a contingent to take him to it, and I was among that number at Jenue's instruction."

Kwadzo had never seen a white man subservient to one of his people in such a manner. He raised an eyebrow toward the smiling Jenue, who winked at him in silence.

"Once there, he went about telling them of your plan to free all the slaves and overtake Lakeside and beyond to claim as your own," Jon Paul continued. "He says that though he doesn't know where you will start, he can bend your mind and gain the nature of your thoughts to then report to them. He speaks of the instruments of your demise, including wood from a willow tree. He spoke of the power hateful blood has over you, and the woman who took up residence with him in the manor . . ."

"The blonde woman?"

"Lily is her name. She is the sister of Barrow's wife, Charity. Her purpose for coming to the manor was to find a way to kill you and avenge her sister. She carries the appropriate hate in her blood for it to be lethal to you. They've assigned Doc Farkus to discern the correct amount to extract from her."

"That damn Rafazi!" Gertie muttered. Kwadzo placed a hand on her back to temper her. It wasn't like her to give in to foul language in her anger, but he found it comforting.

"What else?" Jenue asked.

"Members of the British army who remain near these parts after their recent victory in Pensacola are being summoned."

Kwadzo had to execute his plan before he could feel Rafazi's voice in his head, eating away at his resolve, manipulating him to express what he was thinking. He thanked Jon Paul for his report, climbed the stairs to the balcony, and called out to a few of the first Ramangans he'd made to join him. Armed humans of Alkebulan descent and Native warriors, as well as newer Ramangans, came to a standstill, filling the foyer and beyond. Many were distracted by the presence of the whites among them but kept their focus on Kwadzo, Gertie by his side and Irene, Ekow, and Fanna all standing on the balcony with him.

"The time has come," Kwadzo said to them. "We have been betrayed, yes, but we will prevail. Do not be alarmed by the whites among us. Like Rebecca Farkus and Sarah Collins, they have chosen to align with us, to fight for the freedom of us all. Welcome them in and put them to good use. Rafazi has told Lakeside of our intent to begin freeing all the slaves, and the British have notified their army. I believe they will safeguard the most profitable plantations, lying in wait for us. So, I am changing course.

"We will spread out to plantations north of Lakeside, throughout the province and beyond. We will move by night. The main mission of those of us with the Blood will be the turning of the willing slaves we free to grow our number and our reach, plantation to plantation. Word of our victory has most assuredly begun to spread. I doubt you will find much resistance among the enslaved to rescue. The first lesson any new Ramangan must be taught is how to burrow underground to save themselves from the rising of the sun.

"We will also need a contingent of humans and Ramangans to protect this house. The Crimson Manor must not fall. Gertie will gather a group together to help heal the injured. Our number will grow, and grow, until all of us are free. My commanders, who now stand by my side, will form groups and lead you. Use the remaining hours of light to prepare, saddle horses, feed. When night falls, it begins."

A banging on the front door of the manor sent everyone into a fighting stance. It was consistent and loud. Urgent. Kwadzo nodded to a Native warrior close to the door to open it, and in strode a sweaty white man, haggard and out of breath. His eyes darted around frantically.

"Willie!" he called out, searching through the crowd of people. "I must speak with Willie!"

"Willie was the name they gave me because they refused to pronounce Kwadzo," Kwadzo said. The man moved toward the staircase but was blocked by humans. Kwadzo expected the man to resist, but instead, he stepped back.

"Forgive me, Kwadzo. My name is Robert Callowhill," the man said. "I was in this very house the night you took it."

Recognition took hold of Kwadzo. "You were the one who led me to where Barrow was cowering."

"Yes! You spared my life, and I have never forgotten it."

"'I do not agree with this,' you said to me. 'Your people suffer unjustly.'"

"I fled for the North that very night. I received word from a friend of the aftermath of that fateful night, but I saw firsthand the power you possess. It is my belief that you wish to free the rest of the slaves in Lakeside, in all the colonies."

"Are you not concerned with the welfare of your wife and daughter?"

"She is no daughter of mine, and her mother is a traitorous whore."

"She is dead."

Robert blinked in shock as Kwadzo descended the stairs once again to face the man.

“Killed by her daughter who stole the Blood,” Kwadzo explained.

“Stole the blood?”

“Mister Callowhill!”

He seemed shocked to find Rebecca Farkus approaching him with a smile.

“Goodness gracious!” she exclaimed. “It is good to see your face again!”

“And I am shocked to see yours. How did you come to be here? Didn’t your husband plot against them by commissioning silver to be used against them?”

“Daniel continues to plot against them,” she said. “He lied to save his skin, then betrayed us all. But enough talk of him. I thought you had absconded to the North.”

“I had . . .”

“Word, it seems, travels fast,” Kwadzo said, cutting the reunion short. “I am sure you have a great deal of questions, Mister Callowhill, but I’ve no time to answer them.”

“I understand that you seek to free the slaves in the South,” Robert said. “I can help you achieve the same in the North. Your people suffer there as much as they do here. I’ve traveled here by coach, and it is large enough to carry several of your men North to carry out what you will be achieving here in the South. However, there are more who are opposed to slavery in the North, and I believe I can help you even more effectively there without such violent means.”

Another white helper, and given his words, the North was just as treacherous as Carolina. Kwadzo thought of Charlie. Perhaps he would have ended up dead even if they had made it to the North. If only he had lived long enough to have taken the Blood.

Charlie’s fate, however, had already been determined, and now this man stood before him, understanding the power of Ramanga enough to align himself with it. If only the other citizens of Lakeside had been so wise, perhaps Rafazi would never have betrayed him.

"How so?" Kwadzo asked Robert.

"The story of what you have done, told by you, with all who hear it bearing witness to your power; I believe the North would be hard-pressed to deny you and your cause. We could put an end to slavery in all the colonies by the power of law if we are persuasive enough."

Conquering the North and the South simultaneously. The thought stirred excitement within Kwadzo.

"Whatever you need, I shall do my best to accommodate," Robert said, "but we must hurry. No one in Lakeside knows I'm here. Leaving with you and those you choose to join you before they do would be most advantageous."

"I believe this could be a beneficial strategy, Kwadzo," Jenue said. "Your goal could be reached all the quicker and with less bloodshed."

Kwadzo was inclined to think the same, but he had been tricked by white skin before. "Were we to travel with you and you revealed yourself to be insincere . . ."

"I know firsthand what you are capable of and know I am no match for your power. I assure you, I've no intention of gambling with my life."

Kwadzo looked to his original scions, racking his brain for whom to choose. They would all be so vital to accomplish the mission, but any of the others he felt were too new in the Blood to leave. The most basic instinct to feed naturally led to the fight, but Robert's words led Kwadzo to think that more finesse would be needed in the North. But who to spare for it? His eyes flashed red and went wide.

Hello, old friend.

Rafazi's voice in his head.

I can sense you plotting against me. What is your plan? Which plantation will you attack first?

"No!"

Kwadzo grasped his head, stumbling back. The voice that had led him to freedom now echoed in his head as the agent of the enemy. "Mind your thoughts," Rafazi had told him just before he left. He fought to stop the thinking in his mind.

"Kwadzo? What? What wrong with you?" He focused on Gertie's voice, hoping it would keep the pain building in his head at bay.

"Rafazi, in my head," he groaned. "Keep talking, Gertie. I don't want to think."

"He cannot read your thoughts," Jenue said. "He can only communicate."

"I'm afraid of my thoughts mixing with my words. There are so many things I want to say, but I don't want him to hear me."

Don't want to talk? Shall I make you?

A coarse holler escaped Kwadzo as he shut his eyes tight and fell back against the wall. A maniacal hum vibrated in his mind that he could not stop. It overpowered his hearing, and the pain tore through him like flame through wood. He squeezed his head to no avail, sliding down the wall in a helpless heap. His legs kicked from the torture that was being inflicted upon him.

Looking up at the concerned group before him didn't help any. He could see the worry on their faces, smell the fear in the blood of the humans bearing witness to this invisible attack on his senses. Their lips moved in the way screams and shouts were emitted, they fell to their knees, and he could feel their arms around him, but he could no longer hear them. Just the hum—the incessant hum rumbling so that he thought it would melt his brain. He felt the matter in his head shaking, as if it were bouncing off the walls of his skull, threatening to break free from it. His vision grew hazy.

I cannot read your mind. Rafazi's voice broke through the hum, causing his brain to quake even harder. *But I can rattle it. Not even Jenue knows this little trick. I suppose I have a special power, after all.* He heard Rafazi's laughter through the hum, and he felt his heart shudder.

He felt possessed by true evil at the sound of it.

I can rattle your brain until you go mad, or you can answer my questions. The choice is yours.

He fought the impulse to communicate back as Jenue kneeled in front of him. Her eyes pulsed red as she took Ramangan form. His vision got clearer with each pulse.

"What are you hearing?"

He could barely make out the words she shouted, but it was enough for him to hear and understand.

"A loud hum," he shouted back, pain throbbing through his crown. "Vibrating!"

She turned to Gertie and muttered something he could not hear before bearing her fangs. She held her lips in place, her eyes pulsing, until he could see venom begin to coat her jagged teeth. With each pulse, the venom's volume increased, growing increasingly more viscous until it was dripping from the upper row to the bottom and pooling in her mouth. Then, her mouth was attacking his, her tongue pushing the venom into his orifice. Their tongues swirled against each other, mixing saliva with venom until Kwadzo was forced to swallow. In seconds, the hum disintegrated, and silence returned to his head. The pain was gone and so was Rafazi, freeing his mind once more. His vision cleared completely, and his muscles relaxed.

From the frown on Gertie's face, Kwadzo could only assume that Jenue's advanced apology did nothing to quell her displeasure. She pushed Jenue away and took her place in front of him.

"Kwadzo, is you all right?"

He nodded to her with relief before she barraged him with kisses and a tight hug, her breath short and her heart beating fast. "I was so scared!"

"Whatever he did to you was as painful as it was because he is still relatively close," Jenue said. "You must go to the North now. Before he tries again."

Kwadzo nodded. He was still getting his bearings and had yet to choose the right Ramangan, or Ramangans, to accompany him, but he now knew he had to go if he had any chance of continuing to lead the charge. There was also a sinking feeling growing in the pit of his stomach at the thought of being so far away from Gertie. The thought of leaving her and their child behind for the North brought back painful memories of how this all began. In a manner of speaking, they had been within arm's reach of each other since they met, and now war was imminent. He wanted nothing to come between them.

"Jenue right. And you need to take Irene with you."

Rising to his feet, Kwadzo faced her, his brow furrowed. Gertie's assertion surprised him. There was no hesitation and not a hint of doubt in her voice.

"No," he told her. "*You* have to come with me."

"I cain't go, Kwadzo. I gots work to do here. You say this here house need protectin', well, I gots to protect the ones protectin' it. You done gave me that task and I aims to do it."

In his concern, Kwadzo was second-guessing his decision.

"But how? Without Doc Farkus . . ."

"The good doctor has abandoned us," Rebecca said, "but we have no need of him. I will assist Gertie in any way I can for the good of Crimson Manor." She took Gertie's hand in her own, and the two smiled in solidarity. It was a gesture Kwadzo appreciated considering what Doc Farkus had done.

"I ain't sittin' on the side no more," Gertie told him. "I's doin' my part just like you doin' yours. 'Sides, we's gonna need this here ancient one helpin'." Gertie gave Jenue's back a slap.

"Pardon?" Jenue asked her.

"You done shoved all that venom in Kwadzo's mouth and freed him from pain. If'n it do that for a Ramangan, ain't no tellin' the good it gonna do humans."

"Gertie," Kwadzo said. "Jenue isn't here to help. She doesn't want to."

"Well, too bad. She gonna. And you gonna take Irene. Outta ev'rybody, she done as much as you done. She freed Wilson's slaves, come back from the dead after he slit her throat, turned her mama and got control of them two poor souls that look stronger than any of the others."

"I shall go with her!" Sarah called out as the Wretched pushed through the crowd, making a pathway for her and Cecilia. Irene embraced her mother as Sarah faced Gertie and Kwadzo, bumping her clenched fists against one another nervously. "I was raised in the North; I think I can be of greater assistance there. I fear my continued presence here could put this stronghold in jeopardy. If I am gone, they've one less reason to attack this place."

"A woman of Missus Collins's station would go a long way in changing minds," Robert chimed in, his voice shaky, his quaking eyes glued to the Wretched ones.

Kwadzo nodded, but he was not blind to the deep eye contact being made between Irene and Sarah. Charlie the bloodhound entered the room barking, distracting Kwadzo from the women. The dog rushed up to Gertie, raising his front legs on her insistently. She pet him with a giggle.

"No, no, Charlie," she told the dog. "You gots to stay here with me. I needs me some protectin' of my own."

Kwadzo took her in his arms and kissed her.

"Go on, get 'way from here and keep Rafazi out your head. Charlie here, and Fanna, and plenty others here, they all gonna protect this here house till you get back."

"Your victory is ours, too," Seneca said as she stepped up to Kwadzo with Nez by her side. "Our people come in many tribes, and they have all been persecuted in the North as well as the South. Your power must protect them."

Only one side of Seneca's face smiled. Her sadness shone through her eyes, but her stance was strong, one of determination and fearlessness. He knew then exactly what to do.

"You are right. This power protects and unites us," he said. "There is no reason it should not run through your veins."

Tears welled in Seneca's eyes as her face curved in a true smile. Kwadzo bit into his wrist to draw his blood, and Seneca tilted her head back and opened her willing mouth.

"No!"

Nez's face was scrunched in anger. He was tugging his sister away from Kwadzo.

"Power may come from a god," he said, glowering. "But not *our* god!"

"I don't care!" Seneca said, yanking away from her brother. "This is what I want!"

"You cannot! What of Great Spirit?"

"They used their blood to liberate our land and push off our common enemy. If we can celebrate that with them, I can celebrate in the Blood with them."

She grabbed Kwadzo's wrist, still dripping with his blood, and sucked, drinking as deeply as she could. Nez and the Native warriors present frowned at her action, but she remained undeterred. Kwadzo eased his arm out of her grasp.

"The unity between our two peoples remains," he said to Nez. "This only strengthens it. It links us, bonds us together in brother and sisterhood, and when we rise victorious from this, our bounty will be great." Nez stayed silent but made no attempt to stop what was coming next.

"You will be my newest commander," Kwadzo said to Seneca as she swallowed his essence. "Gather a troop and start into the next town over when darkness falls."

"I'll see to her." Ekow's hand on Kwadzo's shoulder cemented Seneca's acceptance. "We will join forces."

"We will meet again in victory," Seneca said to Kwadzo, wiping tears from her eyes. "Thank you, Kwadzo." She turned to her brother, who took a step back from her now. "When next I see you, brother," she told him with a blissful smile, "I will be reborn."

But Nez walked away from Seneca as Kwadzo snapped her neck.

Fighting mortals
cannot prepare you
to face an opponent
of the Blood.

Thirty-Two

Rise of a Goddess

The coach was sizable, but with all its passengers, it was cramped. Two horses pulled the oversized coach, guided by Robert Callowhill's man in the box. Kwadzo spent the bumpy ride answering Robert's inquiries, filling in the blanks left in the letter he'd received about the aftermath of the battle for the manor—the fates of the Barrows, the town, his wife, the girl he raised, the ones he'd known as slaves. He measured the man as they conversed, studying his face for any indication that Robert could not be trusted. All he found was wide-eyed sincerity.

"She possesses the same power as you?" Robert asked.

"Yes," Kwadzo said of Penelope. "Though she has the ability to survive the sunlight."

"And you do not."

Kwadzo shook his head as Robert's eyes drifted to Irene, then Cecilia, then out the window of the carriage, where he saw one of the Wretched running alongside the carriage. Robert's breath caught at the sight and the knowledge that the second one was keeping pace on the other side of the carriage.

"You've nothing to fear from them," Irene said, "but you would do well to calm your fear. They can smell it."

"Can you smell fear as well?" Robert asked.

"Yes. The blood carries it."

"Is that a special power like Penelope's ability that Kwadzo spoke of?"

"No. All of us can smell certain emotions carried in the blood: fear, hate, love. Blood is extra special sometimes," Irene said. "Some of us gain special powers, some don't."

"Do you have any special powers, Irene?"

"No. I'm just a regular Ramangan."

"There's nothing regular about you," Kwadzo told her. "You did what I should have been doing. You led a charge, saved your mother, increased our number."

"But I did it all wrong."

"Who's to say which way is wrong or right? I've made many mistakes. You shouldered your responsibilities, and, in the end, you freed our people. That has always been the goal. And with the Wretched, you taught us more about our kind."

Irene's smile softened, and her wet eyes told Kwadzo of her gratitude for his words, his acceptance of her. Her mother pulled her close and kissed her cheek.

"Kwadzo's right," Cecilia said. "You saved me from a fate worse than death, and now, I get to spend eternity with you."

"The Wretched?" Robert asked. "That is what you call the ones running alongside the carriage? Will you all become like them?"

"Only if we feed from one another," Kwadzo said. "The Wretched are abnormal among us, but they are part of us just the same. These were sired from Irene's blood, so they are fiercely loyal to her. She can communicate with them, command them, but only through the mind. They are stronger and faster than the rest of us."

"Are there such creatures loyal to Penelope?"

"No. She is new in the Blood, but I fear it is being used to give the whites our power."

"I fear Penelope cannot be trusted," Robert insisted. "She is an obstinate girl. This power in her hands, it could be catastrophic."

"That's why we need to free and turn as many as we can," Kwadzo said, nodding. "We won't force anyone, but if enough of us have the Blood, we can combat anything that comes at us. Even white Ramangans."

A gasp from Sarah brought the conversation to a stop. She looked through the coach window, and Kwadzo followed her gaze. In the distance, a mass of slaves stood in a field. A large fire burned, and shabby huts stood behind them. In the center of the space, a white man, presumably an overseer, was whipping a slave viciously. The slave's screams rang in Kwadzo's ears, and his vision went red with extreme focus. It was a female slave, a barely blossoming young woman. Tied to a post, her brow and eyes were scrunched in pain and her mouth wide and drooling, sending her cries out into the night.

"Stop the coach."

With a wooden cane, Robert tapped on the roof of the coach three times, and the coach rolled to a stop. "Why are we stopping?"

"We're freeing those slaves."

"Now? But once we make it to the North and you tell your story, we can free all of them lawfully."

"Yet they suffer now," Kwadzo said. "Your future law won't spare this woman the beating she is getting tonight. What good is a law that goes into effect only after she is killed? We are the new law, Mister Callowhill. The law of now."

Kwadzo maneuvered his way out of the coach, and they all followed suit. He had taken on his full Ramangan form, his eyes set on the whipping taking place. While he considered Robert's plan a good one and knew he had troops moving through the southern plantations, he wondered how many of their people they had passed who were still suffering.

"With all due respect," Robert said to Kwadzo, "it is best if we keep going."

"You continue on. We will catch up to you."

"But you don't know the trail. And what of the daylight? Should you get caught, you will burn. The shade over the coach's window will keep you all safe."

"I can remain with them," Sarah said. "I know this trail; I've traveled it many times with my parents. I can guide them back."

"Missus Collins, surely you will not be on the plantation land as they attack. A woman alone on this road . . ."

"I will protect her."

Kwadzo took note of the fierce determination in Irene's response as her eyes went red. Sarah took in the sight of her with raised brows, shaking hands, and a smile, something that caught Kwadzo's attention as well. It was clear something had transpired between the two when they tended to each other's wounds.

"Yes," Sarah said. "Yes, Irene will protect me. I will guide them to the coach before the dawn once their business is done."

"Very well." Robert returned to the coach, and it took off into the night as the slave's screams echoed louder across the sky.

"Keep yourself hidden," Kwadzo said to Sarah. "I will take more of your blood. This will allow me to communicate with you mentally." He stepped toward her, but she stepped back.

"No," she said. "When you took my blood before, it did something to me. Something I don't quite understand, but it felt intimate, and it feels wrong to engage in such a manner with you. Any intimacy you have belongs to Gertie. I shall give my blood to Irene." The young Ramangan's cheeks were flush as Sarah moved in front of her. "You can communicate with me like he can, yes?"

Irene looked to Kwadzo, and after receiving his nod, Sarah tilted her neck, offering herself to Irene. But instead, Irene took Sarah's arm. Taking full Ramangan form, Irene's eyes became redder and brighter than Kwadzo had ever seen. The eyes of the Wretched burned with an equal brightness now, until Sarah was awash in red as all three stared at her. She stared back at Irene with awe, and the two women held their look as Irene sank her teeth and fangs, dripping with venom, into Sarah's forearm. The brightness in Irene's eyes began to pulse at the rate of Sarah's heartbeat, and the Wretched's eyes matched the pulsing.

Sarah's eyes glazed over as Irene drank from her. What he was witnessing was something he'd never seen before, but he felt his own blood quake. He could sense that something more was going on, something deeper than anything he had ever experienced in the Blood, and somehow, the Wretched were intensifying whatever Irene was doing to Sarah. Whatever it was, however, it was taking too long. The slave was still crying out in the distance. There was no telling how big the farm was or how many slaves needed to be freed, but every moment counted if they were to successfully stabilize whatever the situation was that awaited them.

"That's enough, Irene," he said, tapping her shoulder, but Irene's eyes only burned brighter into Sarah's.

"Irene!"

With a final pulse, Irene dislodged from Sarah. The brightness decreased from both Irene and the Wretched, and Sarah's eyes dripped with tears. Kwadzo's head was spinning with what had just happened, but the wails of the slave beckoned.

"Hide yourself; do not let yourself be seen," Kwadzo said to Sarah, who could only nod, even as she began to sob. "We will find you."

What did you do to her? he asked Irene telepathically.

I don't know, came her answer.

He would question her later. The night was all they had, and its minutes ticked away.

The five Ramangans blurred toward the farm, stopping in the trees just a few feet away from the atrocity before them. Kwadzo, Cecilia, and Irene reverted to their human forms, and he instructed Irene to have the Wretched hide behind trees. Close to what Kwadzo believed to be seventy slaves were being forced to watch one of their own get whipped by the light of the fire. The white man doing the whipping dripped with sweat while a second man, one of wealthy dress, walked among the slaves, a pistol in his hand.

"Do you see what you get when you disobey?" the gun-toting man screamed at the slaves, all cowering in his presence. "This one here forgot the golden rule with all that humming she was doing. I want complete silence on my farm! I never need to hear a peep out of any one of you, and if I do, this is what you'll get!"

"I suppose that means we three are in trouble."

The gun-toting man and his whip-cracker shifted their focus as Irene and her mother began humming a tune in unison as they approached with Kwadzo.

"Well, well, well," the gun-toting man said. "What are you three doing out there? Did you think you could run away?"

"We stopped running a long time ago," Kwadzo said amid the humming.

The gun-toting man moved closer to them, his pistol aimed squarely at Kwadzo's chest. "Well, aren't you an ornery one? Where in the hell did you get those clothes? Y'all stole from me, didn't you? I'd rather not blow holes into my clothing."

The man was so callous he didn't even know he wasn't talking to his slaves. This was how little they meant. It would all change.

"Untie the girl," Kwadzo said.

The gun-toting man cracked with laughter right along with the whip-cracker.

"You hear the mouth on this boy, Edgar?" He retrained the pistol at Kwadzo's head. "I reckon I could live with a little blood getting on my clothes if it teaches all you slaves a lesson; and stop that goddamn humming! Now, you got any more smart words to say before I blow your nigger head clean off?" The hammer of the pistol was cocked, and its barrel was placed on Kwadzo's forehead. Irene and Cecilia had ceased their humming and were now sharing a smile with Kwadzo.

"You shouldn't have used that word," Kwadzo said.

Now, he then said to Irene telepathically. The white men stumbled back, their mouths agape when her eyes went red, and before they could speak, the Wretched sprang out at them. The gun and whip were dropped as the Wretched lifted the men off the ground by their necks, impairing their efforts to scream. The assembled slaves gasped in horror.

"Now then," Kwadzo said, his voice calm. "First and foremost, the word you used in reference to my head is never to be uttered again. For having used it, your tongue will be taken. And secondly, these people you call slaves, the ones you beat and torture, they are no longer slaves. From this day forward, they are free."

"Says who?" the man who'd held the gun managed to croak out.

"Kwadzo Okoro from the Crimson Plantation."

He looked around at those who had been oppressed, quaking in fear. They were sons and daughters of Alkebulan deserving of so much more. "We do not wish to alarm you," he said as he untied the woman from the post. "We wish to bring you freedom. How big is your number?"

"There be sixty-two of us," the beaten female said after a long silence, the only sounds being the gurgling of the white men struggling for air against the grip of the Wretched.

"Then there are sixty-two free descendants of Alkebulan on this land. We are of the Crimson Order. We, like you, were once shackled in bondage to slave owners who brought us to this land against our will, but we have been rescued by the Blood of Gamab, the blood of Ramanga."

Gasps rippled through the former slaves again, and there was a wave of shuffling in the dirt as they backed away in fear. "Perhaps there are some among you who have heard the legend of Ramanga," Kwadzo continued. "The power of their Blood is not a myth. Its purpose now is for the freeing of all our people throughout the colonies. There are whites who know of this power and have taken it from us. What we ask is that a portion of you consider taking the Blood and joining us. Our collective freedom will not come without a fight, but I have no doubt the power of the Blood in enough of the right hands will lead us to victory and a new dusk across this New World."

With a nod to Irene, the Wretched dropped the white men and hovered over them with menace as the men coughed and fought for their breath.

"You goddamn nigger!" the man who'd held the gun said just before Cecilia sped to him and slammed her fist against his forehead, causing his mouth to gape open in pain. Cecilia took the opportunity to reach in and rip the tongue from his mouth.

"You were told never to use that word," she said as he released a garbled scream and blood shot up from his mouth. Placing her mouth over his, she sucked, gorging herself on the fountain of blood his maw produced. She then rose in full Ramangan form, sending a third round of gasps through the former slaves.

"It's true!" one of them called out.

"It is very true," Kwadzo said. "This power can belong to anyone who wants it. You can use it to take back this land from the men who have profited from your labor. We can build a new world together, one of freedom and justice for every one of us."

"You won't get away with this!" the man who'd held the whip called out. "My blacksmith and stable boys will bring their guns out here and kill y'all dead! Walter!"

"I wants the power," the girl who was being beaten said to Kwadzo, her dress torn in shreds that hung from her, dirt on her face. "This here man don't never tire of beatin' on me. I reckon I'd like to beat on him."

"What is your name, child? Your real name."

"Hadiza," she said.

"You will drink from me, Hadiza, and I will end your mortal life. You will awaken immortal and forever be a part of the new Ramanga Tribe." Kwadzo slit his wrist with a talon and offered it to her.

"Wait!"

Hadiza hesitated as Irene stood between her and Kwadzo.

"Let it be my blood."

"Why?" Kwadzo asked Irene.

"If it's my blood, I think I can show her everything she needs to know, everything you taught me, in an instant. When the Wretched ones fed on each other after they both fed from me, it felt like they knew everything I did, even though they couldn't speak. And when I took Sarah's blood, I wanted her to see me, all of me."

"What exactly did you do?"

"I don't know; there was just something about her blood. It smelled of . . . not love, I wouldn't know the scent, but something akin to it. It smelled of compassion, honesty. I've known so little of either, but I wanted to know it from her for some reason, and it made me reveal myself, and I think she saw me,

Kwadzo. It felt like she did. I could feel the Wretched in my mind, helping to make sure she did. I can't exactly explain it, but I feel stronger now, and I think I can do the same with her without having to take her blood."

"How would that even be possible?"

"I don't know, but I can hear them in my head, telling me it is so. If they are right . . ."

Realization washed over Kwadzo. She was speaking of the Wretched. *They* were Irene's special power. They amplified her abilities and served as powerful bodyguards for her and anyone she commanded them to be. Was it possible that, though new to the Blood, their condition inherently unlocked an even deeper knowledge of its power than even he had?

"Kwadzo?"

Her words must have trailed off because of the trance of his thoughts he had felt himself enter. The miracles of the Blood, it seemed, were unending.

"Bless her with your blood," he said to Irene with a smile.

Irene cut her wrist and offered it to Hadiza. The girl's eyes jerked between Kwadzo and Irene. "It's okay," Irene said. "It will be just like Kwadzo said. We will celebrate freedom until the end of time."

Kwadzo nodded and Hadiza drank. Her eyes were still wide when Irene snapped her neck, and they remained that way when she fell to the ground facing her captors. The one who was still capable of screaming did so as they both scrambled to get away from Hadiza while the former slaves watched with rapt attention. Cecilia moved to the white men, kicking them in the backs of their heads, forcing them to face the girl they had been torturing mere moments ago.

"Get her away from me, you monsters!" the man who'd held the whip screamed. "You evil monsters! Y'all will hang!" He struggled against Cecilia to no avail until finally, Hadiza's transformation began. Her wounds began to heal, and her eyes opened. They were bright red and staring directly into the man's eyes, which were filled with terror. He screamed again, and gunfire rang out. The former slaves dove for cover as three more white men ran toward them, firing rifles.

"We gonna kill you niggers dead!"

With just a nod from Irene, the Wretched dropped to a stance on their four paws. They ran for the men, using all four limbs to do so, like wild beasts would. They took a barrage of bullets from the men, but not one slowed their pace. The men retreated, screaming their fright, but it was futile.

The Wretched pounced on the three men, tearing their limbs from their bodies and feasting on their blood. It was a most violent display; the men's insides were slurped up by the Wretched: intestines, hearts, livers, kidneys. Despite the carnage, the Wretched behaved like animals at play. Their barbarity took seemingly no effort at all. The men were disemboweled, their limbs scattered across the ground, their heads torn from their bodies, their bodies turned upside down, their blood gushing down on the Wretched as they drank and played in the fluid like pigs in mud.

Several of the former slaves voided their stomachs at the grotesque spectacle while the whip-cracker kept his wits about him enough to slide across the dirt and reach for the fallen pistol. Turning it upward, he aimed at Kwadzo, but Cecilia stomped on his wrist, causing a horrible crack. He hollered out as she lifted him by his broken joint, slashed across his neck, and drank her fill of him.

Hadiza broke from her haze amid this, and her eyes found Irene. She ran her hands over her face, her body.

"I's alive," she whispered. "*Is* I alive?"

"Better." Irene took her hands and the Wretched, covered in blood, rushed to their master's side. Mutters of shock swept through the former slaves as red blasted from the eyes of Irene and the Wretched, drenching Hadiza in a crimson hue as her own eyes pulsed red. It was as brilliant a red as Kwadzo had ever seen. When the final bright flash of red throbbed from Irene, Hadiza closed her eyes, stumbling back and holding her head before she straightened, her eyes once again clear.

"I understand," she said, her voice sure. "I knows what to do and how to show them."

Kwadzo smiled at the joy on Irene's face. She stood tall and firm, in her power. This girl, subjected to ridicule and violation because of the way she looked, had now risen above superficial appearances to embrace the glory of the divine Blood that ran through her veins. Twice now, she had used it to free their people, and she was stronger than he had ever seen her.

"It worked," she said to him.

"Of course it did." He smiled with pride. "Never doubt a goddess's blood."

The last white man alive garbled out something loud but unintelligible as he climbed to his knees, blood still seeping from his mouth. Kwadzo assessed by his tone that whatever he'd meant to say was something angry and could tell by his clothes and haughty demeanor, despite all he'd witnessed and suffered, that he had considered himself the owner of this land and these people. Hadiza bending to grab him by the throat all but confirmed his suspicion. His eyes became saucers as Hadiza lifted him off the ground with just one sure hand, digging her talons into his neck deep enough to draw blood. She was in full Ramangan form now, and her former master trembled in her grasp.

"Your evil come to an end this here night," she told him. "We *your* masters now." Her grip tightened slowly, her talons cutting deeper into his skin and causing his blood to spurt out onto Hadiza's face. Licking the essence from her lips, her red eyes pulsed, and she pulled him in close before digging her teeth and fangs into his neck roughly, drinking heartily until the life left him. Pulling away, she yanked his throat from his neck, and his body fell with a dull thud.

With his severed larynx in her hand and covered in blood, Hazida's eyes shut tightly and she stumbled as if she'd gone dizzy. Moments later, she opened her eyes and smiled assuredly.

"That was the most delectable thing I've ever tasted!" she said with a clear voice before licking away at the blood on the ripped-out flesh tuber she held.

"This power is for all of our people," Kwadzo said to the former slaves, who thrilled at Hazida's display of dominance, "but not all have to partake of the Blood. We need to continue on in the natural way, and those of us of the Blood will serve as the guardians of our human brothers and sisters for the decades and centuries to come."

Several were now stepping forward, asking to take the Blood. Kwadzo, Irene, and Cecilia helped Hadiza turn those who wished for the Blood while the humans among them were instructed to bring livestock for the newly turned to feed on. At the same time, Hadiza relayed to them the events of the battle for the Barrow Manor, as Irene had projected them onto her mind and explained how to apply the same techniques while they moved forward to conquer other plantations.

"Secure this place," Kwadzo told her. "Then send others to the plantations nearby. Free them, share the Blood with them, teach them. All through the South, our people are being liberated. Landowners in Carolina are amassing against us, and more will as word of our revolution spreads."

"Our army needs to outgrow theirs, and it will," Hazida said. Her face was firm with confidence, her eyes as sure as Irene's with the very same knowledge.

"Safeguard yourselves, exact your vengeance, and listen for our call," Kwadzo said, pointing to his head, then to hers.

"Thank you, Kwadzo, and thank you, Irene."

And as fast as the five Ramangans arrived on the land, they disappeared into the night as darkening clouds loomed above.

Thirty-Three

The New Ramangans

Ever since night had fallen, a tense stillness loomed over the Crimson Plantation, despite the increased speed of the wind and the thickening clouds above. Under the soft orange glow provided by candles and lanterns in every corner of the manor and the dark sky that now hung outside of it, all had readied themselves for a fight that had not come. Gertie had no idea where Kwadzo was.

Her concern for him had grown quite complicated ever since he had taken the Blood. His physical safety, she realized, had become much less of a concern. What worried her more was him being undone by his own rising grandeur. She had watched him acclimate to his greatness quickly, and a sense of superiority had led to the ruination of many a man. His vanity caused him to ignore his moral compass and had allowed that wicked little Penelope to enter this house and betray them all, right along with Rafazi.

What he had set out to do was noble, but success would make him the leader of every African, or rather, Alkebulan, as she had learned had been explained by Jenue, living or dead, in the New World, and quite possibly beyond. Women already clamored to gift him their blood now, and more were choosing to take the Blood, something she knew she would never do.

She wondered if she would shrink in his vision as his dominance grew.

"Is the little one kicking so soon?"

Gertie hadn't realized her hand was against her belly when Jenue approached her with a glass jar half-filled with clear liquid.

"What this here?" she asked as the ancient Ramangan—still in her female form—handed her the jar.

"Venom," Jenue said. "Use it sparingly. It has a very powerful effect on humans. Too much will create a highly intoxicating result. In the event that you run out, have someone send for me, and I shall produce more. Our venom is like your saliva. I'll never run out."

"Wait," Gertie said, grabbing Jenue's hand. "Where you goin'?"

"You wanted my help." Jenue chuckled. "This is me helping. Now, I shall retire to a bedchamber and reward my emissary for a job well done. Perhaps I'll take Rafazi's. He's relinquished use of it."

"You just gonna go lay with that man? What 'bout the fight?"

"In, I suppose, an attempt to shame me, you boisterously declared that I was to help. Foolish but brave, even mildly impressive. For that reason, I have gifted you my venom. Any Ramangan can produce it, but seeing as every Ramangan here is an infant and given my advanced age, my venom is far more potent and will do the job of healing far quicker. You may remember your beloved telling you I did not want to help. He did not lie. This freedom crusade of Kwadzo's is valiant and entertaining, most of the time, but it is *Kwadzo's*. I've been on this earth long enough to know that pursuing anything other than pleasure is almost always wasted effort."

"And how long that been?"

"Beg your pardon?"

"How long you been livin' empty?"

Jenue cocked her head to the side, and Gertie shook her own. This Ramangan could end her in an instant, but she stood firm in her conviction, as she always did. It removed fear from her.

"You made Rafazi, and he seven hundred years old. So, what is you? A thousand? More? And in all that time, you ain't found one thing worth fightin' for? I knows from lookin' at you, you ain't never had to suffer no toil."

"How would you know that, Gertie?"

"I ain't be 'live thirty years yet, and here you is, thousands of years old, look younger than me, and ain't got nary a scratch on you."

"Maybe not thousands of years old." Jenue laughed. "Just one thousand. And a half. As for my appearance, the time of my demise and the Blood determine that, but obviously, I was quite young and attractive."

"This blood they ain't had it but a minute compared to you. They need you," Gertie said, ignoring Jenue's glibness.

"Ten white men is outside!"

The call from one of the human warriors moved Gertie, with Charlie the bloodhound and Jenue in tow, along with several others to the porch of the manor. More warriors—Alkebulan-descended and Native—stood ready while ten white men approached the manor, their heads high and their chests pushed out.

"We're givin' you niggers ten seconds to surrender. That's one second from each of us. That's all you get," their leader called out, and a smattering of laughter broke out among the warriors guarding the manor.

"You ain't but ten," one of the warriors said. "There be more of us than you."

"That may be, darkie, but we still have the upper hand. Right, boys?"

On his call, all ten white men took on Ramangan form. Twenty eyes burned red on the manor, and Gertie's hand went to her mouth in shock. Penelope was nowhere to be seen, but there was no doubt this was her work. Hers and Rafazi's. It rendered the warriors stunned.

"Y'all thought you could keep this power to yourselves?" the leader yelled with a maniacal laugh. "Anythin' y'all get belongs to us! It's in better hands anyway. We were above you as humans—we'll be above you as demons. And by the way, them ten seconds is up! C'mon, boys!"

Undeniably fueled by Ramangan Blood, the ten white men became blurs just as fierce rain began pouring, descending on the human warriors outside the manor. Blood shot out in all directions as the reserve warriors rushed out to fight back. Soon, several human warriors were strewn across the grounds, suffering from wounds as Gertie watched in horror.

The rain poured and the wind howled. She watched as Nez bravely attacked one of the white Ramangans directly, only to have his face and chest slashed before being thrown to the ground. Gertie shuddered at the sight of him shaking and bleeding into the muddy earth.

"Jenue," she pleaded, "help me bring them wounded back into the manor. And call them other Ramangans!"

Jenue's glare did nothing to intimidate Gertie. The knowledge of Jenue's power never left her, but there was something far greater at stake, something bigger than both of them. She pushed past the ancient Ramangan and shivered as a gust of wind splashed rain from the storm across her face.

"Never mind," Gertie scoffed, sucking her teeth in disdain. "I do it myself." She felt a firm hand grip her arm and pull her back from the steps of the porch just before Jenue's blur shot past her. She was barely able to get her bearings before she was bumped into from behind.

"Pardon me, ma'am!"

Gertie moved to the side as the three Lyon men—Andrew, Henry, and Michael—rushed the porch, rifles in hand as the quickening wind splattered water across the porch floor. They fired their guns into the fray, but the white Ramangans moved too fast to be hit by their bullets. When Michael's shot hit one of the Native warriors in the back, Gertie pulled his arm back.

"Stop!" she hollered at him. "You shootin' our people!"

"I didn't mean to!" Michael responded. "They're just so fast!"

"We need them of the Blood!"

Andrew and Henry rushed back into the house to escape the bloodshed, but Michael dropped his gun and unsheathed a sword of silver.

"This silver will stop them!" Michael ran for the steps and Gertie followed him, tugging at his shirt.

"Boy, get back here! You gonna get yourself killed!"

In seconds, they were both face to face with the leader of the white men, his face ashen, drenched in water and blood. The veins bulging in his face were even more visible than they were on the Alkebulan Ramangans, and the wet, pale skin of his engorged brow crested over his red, pulsing eyes with his tongue licking away at the fresh blood on his lips made his appearance all the more menacing.

"Well, well, well," he said. "Michael Lyon, you nigger-loving traitor. Did you think you could get a taste of their master's woman?" His eyes shifted to Gertie. "Penelope told us all about you. I bet that baby in your belly will be delicious!"

He reached for Gertie, but Michael thrust his silver blade between them, stabbing it into the man's shoulder. He cried out and stumbled back in pain. Smoke hissed out from the wound the sword created. Michael pushed Gertie behind him.

"You take your men and leave this place," he said to the white Ramangan. "These people didn't come after you. Leave them be."

"I'll take you with me!" The white Ramangan swiped his talons across Michael's chest just as the young man pulled his blade back and thrust it through the man's abdomen. The dual action sent both men to their backs as Alkebulan Ramangans finally raced past in their blurs to join in the fight and prevent the manor from being fully invaded.

Gertie dropped to her knees and held up Michael's head. He bled profusely from three gashes across his chest and stomach, gasping for air, for life.

"You hold on, now," Gertie pleaded with him. "Just hold on!"

"Papa, don't!"

A beautiful dark-skinned young woman with tears in her bright blue eyes was standing above them watching the battle.

"My father," she whimpered. "He went out into the fight, into the storm . . ."

"Girl, if he blurred past, he done took the Blood, he gonna be fine. I need you to help me get this one back into the manor! Come on, now!"

Gertie was pushing the white Ramangan off Michael's body. Unable to retract the silver sword, the white Ramangan's form bled and quaked. His eyes turned black as coal and his skin turned gray before he disintegrated to dust. Witnessing this cause the blue-eyed young woman to void her stomach, but Gertie had already begun tearing away Michael's shirt and holding the scraps of material against his wounds. It was an atrocious thing to see, but again, Gertie's mind was set on the bigger picture.

"Is you fine now?" Gertie asked the girl, who nodded weakly as the fight around them escalated. "All right, then? Come on now . . ."

The blue-eyed young woman reached under Michael's arms and pulled him into the manor with Gertie carrying his legs.

The salon room had been made into a makeshift sick house. Mattresses, tables, and chaise longues were being used to hold wounded human warriors. Kitty Greer and her bar maidens, along with some Alkebulan and Indigenous women, were tending to the injured, wrapping up wounds and passing the jar of Jenue's venom between them to give to the men as Gertie and the blue-eyed woman placed Michael on a chaise longue. Jenue was hovering over a bleeding man on a table, her mouth covering his.

"She is kissing the men? At a time like this?" the blue-eyed woman gasped as Jenue raised up, her lips dripping with a clear, viscous liquid. The man below her moved off the table, still worse for the wear but on the mend, and the bar maidens put a young Native man in his place.

"That there's venom in her mouth, child! Ain't you seen what Jenue can do?" Gertie asked.

"No, I've been so concerned for my father . . ."

"Where you from? Wilson's farm?"

"Yes. And you are Gertie, right? Kwadzo's intended."

"What they call you?" Gertie asked with a nod.

"Antoinette."

"Antoinette," Michael said adoringly, gazing up at her in a haze. "You are so beautiful . . . I love you."

"He is delirious!" Antoinette exclaimed with panic.

"Go get some venom from Jenue for this here one. He need it bad and fast!"

Antoinette hurried to follow Gertie's order as Michael began to convulse. Gertie knelt closer, taking his face in her hands.

"No, you stop that, now! You gonna be all right, now; you just hang on just a lil' while longer, you hear?"

Michael's eyes rolled to the back of his head as he shook. Gertie ran a hand through his hair, shushing him, comforting him.

"Don't you fret none. You gonna make it. You come on back to Ol' Gertie, now, you hear me?"

His eyes began blinking sporadically; he opened his mouth to speak, but only the gurgle of blood came out. He was nodding his head forward now as he tried to focus his eyes, looking past her, behind her.

"Hi, Gertie. Miss me?"

Gertie knew the voice in an instant, but in the chaos, she was never able to alert anyone before a small, damp hand clamped around her mouth and she was snatched away in a Ramangan blur.

Thirty-Four

The Mad and the Bad

Sarah Collins was crying when they found her. Hidden in the thick grass, chin resting on her knees, her arms wrapped around her legs, rocking herself back and forth as the rain beat down on her, drowning her and her sobs. Kwadzo was perplexed by this until she saw the look she gave to Irene. It was full of knowing; it was similar to the look Hadiza had given Irene after having had her mind imbued with the knowledge necessary for her to continue their crusade, only this look was deeper, more intimate. Sarah stood before Irene, fighting to control her breathing. She never bothered to look at anyone else.

"I'm so sorry," Sarah said to her, her voice quaking, "for every snide remark, every dirty look, every violation, every act of violence, every injustice you have suffered."

As Sarah's sobs overtook her once more, Irene's power was reiterated to Kwadzo. With the help of the Wretched, she had shared her innermost thoughts with Sarah without a full understanding of how she'd done so. It left Kwadzo's mind reeling as the wind howled, whipping rain all around them as the storm picked up speed.

Irene shot a look toward him, then turned her eyes away, keeping them low before addressing Sarah. "I'm sorry. I knew I had made you see it, but I didn't . . ."

"I didn't just see it, Irene," Sarah said, stepping closer to Irene as the wind swirled almost violently. "I felt it. I never knew a person could feel so horribly alone."

Irene frowned. "I did not mean for you to see all that you did."

"But you wanted me to see."

"I do not wish for your pity."

"I don't pity you, Irene," Sarah said, taking another tentative step toward her. She reached out for her hand but pulled it back, as if thinking better of the action. "I am in awe of you. You are the strongest woman I have ever known. You never need feel alone again if you do not wish it."

The softness between the two women moved Kwadzo, calling Gertie to his mind, but there was little time to indulge the feelings or the power that had led to their expressions.

"We must press on," he said. Sarah's shoulders shook, her focus on Irene having been so singular it was as if the sound of his voice startled her.

"Yes, of course. Forgive me. We can continue along this road. There is an inn and horse stables about twenty miles north. Mister Callowhill will most likely have stopped there to switch horses and rest before traveling on."

Irene glanced up at Kwadzo, her eyes seeking approval. It was not a look he believed necessary.

"Irene will carry you." Kwadzo smiled. "You will lead us."

A small smile crept across Irene's lips as she hoisted Sarah into her arms and the woman gasped. Kwadzo heard her heartbeat increase at Irene's display of strength.

"Don't be afraid," Irene told her. "It will be very fast, but I won't drop you."

"I know you won't," Sarah said. "Just follow this road forward."

"If we come across another plantation along the way," Kwadzo called out, "we will stop. We will do all we can before sunrise."

Sarah's hands gripped the back of Irene's neck tight, and the Ramangans blurred forward.

The storm raged on as Kwadzo, Irene, Cecilia, and the Wretched blurred toward Robert's coach after having freed slaves from yet another plantation. An even larger number of them were eager to take the Blood, and Kwadzo could feel them rampaging across the land, sharing the power of Ramanga as they went. He could feel all of those who were of his blood, expanding, conquering. There would be untold ground to cover and many plantations to overthrow, but if their number continued to grow, there would be no stopping them.

The storm had not let up for hours, and the downpour had washed away the copious amounts of blood that the five of them had collected on their persons during their plantation battles. Diligence was vital. He was certain Penelope, and possibly even Rafazi, would share of their blood with white men who would then descend on the manor. Irene had reminded him of the formidable force he'd put in place to defend it, the training he had given them, but still, fret ruled his heart for Gertie and his child.

The five of them had blasted through three plantations so far. He was sure that night had turned to day, though thanks to the dark gray clouds filling the sky and the relentless downpour that the brisk squall whisked around them, there was no sunlight to be found. Kwadzo knew they were operating on borrowed time, but the storm didn't seem to be letting up, which allowed for those they had sired to continue their conquests, and so, too, they would continue to press on.

"We're getting close to Virginia," Robert called out to Kwadzo, opening the door to the coach as the Ramangans grew close. "I do know of another plantation on the province border due east, but I think we'd fare better if we concentrated our focus on getting back to Philadelphia. Surely those you have freed and turned will spread across Carolina without you having to stop at every plantation along the way."

"The storm has blessed us with cover from the sun," Kwadzo shouted back, "but I've no doubt that Penelope has turned white men who wish us dead. We need to ensure as many as we can to combat whatever forces are being built against us with our own power."

"What if the storm lets up and the sun breaks through the clouds?"

"We know what to do if that happens. Safeguard yourself and Sarah. This storm can make travel treacherous."

Robert nodded as the coach was brought to a stop. Sarah took his place at the door, reaching out to grab Irene's hand.

"I would give you my blood, but I doubt you're in need of it," Sarah said to her.

"I would never turn away the gift of your blood."

Sarah leaned her head into the rain and tilted her neck.

"Then have it."

Sarah closed her eyes and cradled Irene's head as the Ramangan bit into her. The moan of pleasure the human emitted once again brought Gertie to the forefront of Kwadzo's mind. He yearned to return to her victorious, to shut himself in the master bedchamber with her for hours on end, but there was work to do first.

"I smell fearful blood due east," Cecilia said.

"We must make use of the storm before it subsides" was his gentle call to Irene. She dislodged from Sarah, but the two women remained locked in a warm, amorous gaze.

"Do be safe," Sarah whispered before taking Irene's face in her hands and kissing her with passionate abandon for a few precious moments before Kwadzo tapped the back of the coach. Sarah reluctantly ducked back inside, and the coach rode on.

"You disapprove," Irene said, lowering her head. Kwadzo raised her chin.

"How could I? She has proven herself to be beyond their culture of skin. I can hear her heart every time she looks at you, and I can feel yours. Now, let's make the world a place that will embrace your love like any other."

The five Ramangans created a massive blur that charged through the wilderness in search of the next plantation. Their speed caused the rain to whip across their faces, the gusts of wind becoming even faster in their wake. Kwadzo thought he could detect the faint sounds of voices in the distance when he fell to his knees and out of pace with the others. A familiar humming ripped through his brain, and his eyes shut from the pain. He couldn't move.

Where are you, brother?

Rafazi.

He could hear Irene and Cecilia calling out to him, but the pain coursing through his brain made it impossible to open his eyes.

"Go!" he grumbled out to them. "Find the plantation ahead! Rafazi is tracking me. I won't allow him to slow us down."

"No!" he heard Irene shout. "We cannot leave you!"

"Go! Before he finds us all!"

Seconds later, he heard the rush of wind carry them away as he fell to his back, fighting against Rafazi.

Go away, he thought. *Let me be.*

The words entered his head involuntarily. He hoped against hope Rafazi hadn't heard them.

Not until you show me where you are.

Kwadzo's eyes involuntarily shot wide open, but all he saw was black. He felt his eyes moving, rotating in his head; he felt his head twist and turn. Neither movement was against his will. He could feel Rafazi in his head, invading it, and realized that his sight was now under Rafazi's control.

His maker was accessing the area around him.

You keep forgetting the power of a maker, Rafazi hissed into Kwadzo's brain. *You cannot escape me. I will find you.*

Slamming his hands against his head, Kwadzo was struck by such intense pain that he could no longer move. He was barraged with a series of emotions that were not his own. At least, they should not have been his own: anger, resentment, vengeance. He had no desire to take revenge against Rafazi; he wished for them to be on the same side. He wanted his maker to come to his senses, to be fighting with him, not against him.

It was then that he realized the depths at which Rafazi's invasion resided in his mind. His ability to differentiate between his own thoughts and those of Rafazi's was slipping. The more he fought against the thoughts he didn't believe belonged to him, the longer they persisted. Still, he had to rally in opposition to them, to *him*.

You made your choice, Kwadzo screamed into the silence of his mind, resigning himself to the blind chaos in which he'd been thrust. *You got what you wanted. What do you want with me?*

An ominous growl hovered over him now, and within seconds, Kwadzo felt an immense pressure on his torso and the feel of great paws pushed against his stomach. His shaking hand reached up and filled with a wet, coarse mass of fur that covered the muscular frame of a wild animal. The beast gave a roar, as did Kwadzo, when he felt sharp fangs sink into the skin of his chest. He could feel the animal's tongue lash across his fresh wound, consuming the blood that spurt forth from him.

And he could hear Rafazi's wicked laughter in his head.

Kwadzo reached up and twisted the animal's head, forcing its great teeth out of his flesh. Howling from the attack, he kept twisting the beast's head until he heard a horrible crack. Throwing the animal free of him, he got to his hands and knees, and once he had, his sight returned. He blinked as the pounding in his head lifted. Rising from the soaked earth, Kwadzo shook his head and found it clear of Rafazi. His hand went to his ruptured chest, coating his fingers in his own blood as his flesh began healing itself. He took in the wild jaguar that lay slain at his side.

Though relieved from the physical pain, his eyes went red with anger. Betrayal was one thing, but now he was being hunted. Maker or not, he was tired of Rafazi's games. He wanted to face the one who made him. His efforts were being thwarted by the one who set him up to be a leader. He no longer cared why.

He just wanted it to end.

"Show yourself!" Kwadzo wailed out into the storm, getting to his feet. "Face me!"

A rattling roar sounded behind him. Kwadzo jumped from the noise, and his eyes went wide at the sight before him—the jaguar had risen and doubled in size. The spotted wild cat's golden fur had taken on a reddish-brown hue, and it was now nearly ten feet long from nose to tail, standing close to four feet tall. It roared again, and Kwadzo thought it was more akin to a lion's than its own subspecies. The jaguar's mouth had stretched and grown to accommodate its bigger teeth and fangs.

And its eyes burned red.

Training his own glowing red eyes on the big cat's, Kwadzo moved toward it. He knelt, getting level with the jaguar. In response, it moved its large face right up to Kwadzo's, snarling, its red eyes pulsing.

"You took my blood," Kwadzo whispered to the jaguar. The face of the big cat softened, yawning its jaw wide before lapping its tongue across Kwadzo's wet face. The cat shook the excess water from its body even as the rain continued to pour, then let out a short, loud burst of air through its nostrils and bumped its snout against Kwadzo's nose in an affectionate manner.

Kwadzo was reminded of his first encounter with Charlie after the bloodhound had taken his blood.

He took the jaguar's face in his hands while it gave a series of short chuffs, breathy snorts that were followed by another bump of its snout and a quick period of rolling its snout along Kwadzo's face. Their eyes pulsed at each other, and Kwadzo could feel his mind walking around in the big cat's, bending its mind to become one with his own.

Just like it happened with Charlie.

Only this time, he was more aware of what was happening.

"You know what you are now, don't you?" The jaguar gave Kwadzo's face another large lick, and the Ramangan smiled. "I'm going to call you Ruby," he said, instinctively knowing the cat was female. He nuzzled his new pet, so fully engrossed with the animal that he'd almost forgotten about Rafazi's cruel invasion. Their red eyes constantly pulsing at each other, through each other, collecting information. All else but the wind and the rain seemed to slip away—until their connection was interrupted by the sound of barking echoing in Kwadzo's mind. It grew louder, urgent.

Familiar. Charlie's bark.

Ruby the jaguar grunted and cocked her head, as if she could hear Charlie's bark, too. Kwadzo wondered if connecting with the animal shifted his focus to the bloodhound. The insistence of the barks grew stronger, and Kwadzo came to understand their meaning and why he was hearing them—Charlie was communicating to him mentally that Gertie was in danger. He refocused his mind on the mother of his child and pulsed his eyes at Ruby the jaguar, sending mental images to her. She grunted and growled.

"Help Charlie, Ruby. Help him find Gertie," he said, and stood as Ruby the jaguar took off at a speed unnaturally fast given her engorged size. She became a blur and disappeared into the storm as if she were light as air. With Gertie weighing heavily on his heart, Kwadzo contemplated joining Ruby to ensure his love's safety, but his mission was far from complete. The rain pounded him, its persistence urging him to come to a decision.

"I know that look."

Kwadzo spun and grimaced at the sight of Rafazi, no longer in his head but standing before him. His calm but cold stare, the small smirk of arrogance across his lips. He wore a chain around his neck that held a small vial of blood.

Blood he could smell the hate in.

His maker seemed wholly unaffected by the rain, and once again, he felt Rafazi's thoughts commingle with his own and the pain in his head returned.

He could not tell where his thoughts ended and Rafazi's began.

"Torn between two options, unsure which to choose," Rafazi said. Kwadzo could feel his blood burning. The man he once held in his heart as a brother stood in opposition to him, taunting him.

"More often than not, it's Gertie who puts you in these conundrums. Second-guessing your choices, making you weaker." Rafazi chuckled. His progeny looked so lost in his sudden presence. He found Kwadzo's pout to be priceless. The man he had rescued from permanent death had repaid him with disrespect. That would be righted.

He realized he didn't need Kwadzo, or Jenue, or a new Ramanga Tribe. He didn't need to be a part of anything else, didn't need to belong. He was a centuries-old, all-powerful, immortal being. The plague was gone; the world was new. He could do whatever he wanted and answer to no one, especially an ungrateful infant of a Ramangan.

"She strengthens me more than you do," Kwadzo said, shaking his head clear, trying to reclaim his own thoughts. Rage ripped through him, but he was as sad as he was angry. Rafazi had left him alone in his new position, all because he had been asked to fulfill his part of a plan he had instituted. He had been clear about not being a leader, but even so, Kwadzo was hesitant to lash out against him. Rafazi was here now. Perhaps he wasn't beyond reason.

"Does she?" Rafazi asked him. "Was it her blood that gave you strength and speed beyond human capability? The power to overtake your enslaver? Immortality itself? If she had gotten her way, you both would be dead by now!"

"She remained loyal despite her objections!" Kwadzo hollered back. "She opened her heart to the Blood, saw it for the righteousness that it truly was, and embraced it, embraced me, though I had become a monster!"

"*She* saw a monster. I made a god!"

"And then abandoned him! Set him on a path, then retreated to the very people who are hell-bent on obstructing it! I was, am, but a babe in the Blood. You are my maker. You were supposed to guide me. Instead, you kept information from me, lied to me, and reduced yourself to tantrums. Our people, the entirety of our race, hangs in the balance. I asked you to pull yourself away from your orgy of lust and blood long enough to protect it, and you respond by deserting me, your very blood, and for what? What did they give you? A few shillings as tribute for your treachery against your own kind?"

"I never wanted to lead a revolution, Kwadzo. I told you that before I gave you the gift of my blood, before I reminded you of your true name. You were the one who wanted the fight, to get revenge against the whip-crackers."

"Yes, you told me you were a deserter. You told me you cared for nothing but your own survival. But you took my blood and *stayed*; said you didn't want to be alone anymore, that you wanted me as your *brother*. You said we would make the colonies our own. Together! Where did that man go?" Kwadzo was grateful for the rain, as it hid his tears. "If this is all that you are, why did you not just take my blood and leave?"

Rafazi ran a hand over his face, clearing it of water, only to have it drenched again. Thus was their situation. No matter what the two of them said to each other, they would always arrive back at the same place. To him, freedom meant freedom from responsibility, from rules, even from his own statements. The freedom to change his mind and act on his whims, to choose whatever pleasurable impulse suited him, without Jenue forcing him into doing her bidding. His maker had left him in the dark about so many things as well—he never even knew of her intersex power—disappearing for years at a time, leaving him to his own devices, to learn things on his own, only to return out of the blue to force a degrading task upon him for her own sick amusement.

It was in that neglect that he found true freedom—freedom that the plague had stripped away. He had done what was necessary to get it back, but he had no intention of being beholden to those actions. Kwadzo, a father, a de facto husband, would never understand true liberation. He had traded it away before the two had ever met. Continued arguments would be futile. Rafazi had made his choice. He had chosen himself and his own freedom. Even if Kwadzo didn't survive, the Blood would change the world enough for him. One last task to collect his treasure was all that was required, and he could blur away to a new adventure.

"All I want is complete freedom," Rafazi told Kwadzo. "Freedom from having to consider the tribe, our people, you. I want what I want when I want it, no good, no bad, just choice, my choice, and the only way to have it is to be alone. To not care, one way or another, for anyone or anything other than myself, and to have the power to enjoy every pleasure that infinite time brings. I can think of nothing else as glorious as that."

Kwadzo's heart grew hard against Rafazi. He questioned if he would have taken the Blood at all if he knew what he did now. He wondered if this frame of mind was somehow a condition of having the Blood for so long; if after centuries of killing to survive, a Ramangan lost all sense of humanity the way Rafazi seemed to. He pondered if his presence had brought Rafazi back from the bleak pit of apathy and into the light of compassion, only for him to fall back again. He queried his own heart, asking if the same would happen to him once Gertie was gone. He decided it would not. He vowed never to abandon what he had started and to let nothing stand in the way of its completion, not even the one who made its birth possible.

"This is a rarity for us," Rafazi said, turning his face up to the sky, catching raindrops on his tongue. "These are daylight hours, but the storm keeps the sun and its rays hidden. We walk in the day yet. Savor it. I don't think you will see it again."

Kwadzo cursed his heart for softening again. If he were to hold on to his humanity, it would have to extend to anyone, even his maker.

"I am your Blood," Kwadzo said, ashamed of the pleading in his voice but using it just the same. "You are my maker. This does not have to be the way. We could come to a better understanding of one another. You could find your way back to us, and your riches and freedom could grow beyond measure. I would take no joy in battling you, brother, but you have allowed things that cannot stand. You cannot stop what your Blood has started. Nothing and no one will."

"I have never ended one of my own kind," Rafazi said. "Let alone one I have created. Any return would be met with animosity and contempt. I would be an outcast among my own kind and better off alone anyway. I deeply regret that it has come to this, but come to this it has."

"So be it."

Taking on their Ramangan forms, they hurled themselves through the air at each other, their glowing red eyes piercing through the darkness of the storm. Screaming out his rage, Kwadzo swung an arm at Rafazi in attack, but the older Ramangan caught it in mid-air. He bent it back until the bone cracked, then hurled Kwadzo to the ground before landing behind him.

Rafazi stomped on Kwadzo's broken arm, but with a guttural groan, Kwadzo blurred back to his feet and charged for Rafazi again. This time, the elder Ramangan simply pivoted out of Kwadzo's path, forcing him to stop short and circle Rafazi.

"You carry hateful blood around your neck," Kwadzo said to him.

"The elixir of your demise."

Kwadzo righted his footing. "Was it your intent to end me when you brought the sister of Barrow's wife into the manor?"

"Don't worry. I've been instructed not to exterminate you. They want that burden for themselves."

"So, you've traded my rules for theirs. Doesn't sound like freedom to me."

"Unlike slavery, I'm getting paid to complete this task."

"How much is my return worth?"

"One thousand pounds. Once I have it, my freedom will truly begin."

"Your power is greater than theirs. Why not just snatch it from them and run? Why betray me? Your people?"

"Your anger conveniently paints me the villain." Rafazi laughed. "Ramangan power cannot be stopped. Only led. I am not fit to do so. Perhaps you aren't either."

Kwadzo was tumbling to the wet ground before Rafazi finished speaking. His jaw still throbbed from the impact of Rafazi's punch. He fought the pain and stood again, focusing on the vial around Rafazi's neck. He had to find a way to get the vial away from Rafazi and spill its contents onto the wet earth.

The Ramangans circled each other again. Kwadzo dove headfirst at Rafazi, launching himself through the air and ramming his maker into the trunk of a tree. He reached for the chain, but Rafazi threw his palm into Kwadzo's chin, which left him airborne until he landed hard on his back. No sooner had he gotten back to his feet than Rafazi was upon him, unleashing a staggering barrage of punches, powerful blows across his face and torso that came at an alarming rate of speed. Rafazi's attacks were so fast that they left no room for Kwadzo to retaliate and left him incredibly weakened.

In all the whippings and beatings he'd endured at the hands of overseers, he had never felt the force of what Rafazi was unleashing upon him. His chest felt as if it were caving in, and his entire upper body pulsated in an excruciating ache.

"Fighting mortals cannot prepare you to face an opponent of the Blood," Rafazi said, laughing. "Especially one with seven centuries of existence."

Kwadzo slumped to his knees, and as he watched the tension in Rafazi's muscles relax, he summoned all the power he had left. He thrust a fist into Rafazi's chest, ripping the chain from his neck in the process. Rafazi fell backward, and the vial went flying across the clearing, collecting mud as it rolled away from them both. Kwadzo took off in his blur to grab hold of it, using his red vision to search the muddy ground. But seconds after he spotted and reached out for the vial, it lifted from the mud and flew out of Kwadzo's reach, seemingly of its own volition. He turned to find it sailing back into Rafazi's outstretched hand.

"You can move things with your mind?" Kwadzo asked him, slack jawed.

"After a century or so, so will you," Rafazi said. "Well, you would have. Had you a century left."

There was not enough energy left in Kwadzo to escape the approach of Rafazi's blur. He looked up at his maker, whose knee on his chest pinned him to the ground. He watched Rafazi open the vial with quaking eyes.

"Do not do this," came his final plea.

"I will paint you as a martyr in the years to come and speak fondly of you to your child."

"If you take me from my child, you will stay away from him!"

"As you wish."

A punch to the throat made Kwadzo's mouth yawn open, and Rafazi held the open vial over Kwadzo's maw. Only a few drops sent Kwadzo into convulsions as the hateful blood made its way into his system. The agony was all too familiar. He lost the ability to speak and felt as if a fire like no other coursed through him, one he had no control over. He jerked and seized in indescribable pain as he felt Rafazi lift him over his shoulder and use his blur to speed them away in the storm.

We can't have him
dying before we've
had our fun.

Thirty-Five

From Afar

Gertie slid across the cold wooden floor of an abandoned cabin as the wind flapped its door open and shut. She slammed against the wall so hard it set off a ringing in her head that clouded her vision. She shook her eyes clear to find Penelope standing over her, her smile wide and wicked.

"You stay 'way from me!" Gertie screamed, one hand rubbing the back of her head, the other covering her pregnant belly.

"Don't you worry." Penelope grinned. "I'm not killing you until your murderous intended comes to find you. I'm going to watch his face while I rip the child from your belly and kill you both. An eye for an eye, just like the Good Book says."

"Your daddy would still be alive if he ain't come to kill Kwadzo first! He the murderer!" Gertie growled back. Penelope stood unfazed and Gertie glared back. How satisfying it must feel to believe you were born right, no matter the facts, Gertie thought to herself. This girl, this child, so committed to her revenge that nothing, not even Ramangan Blood, could compel any change in perspective, wasn't worth an ounce of sympathy. After everything she had been through, everything she had lost, everything she had done, she was an unrepentant traitor and murderer. Kwadzo had done all that anyone could for the girl.

"You watch your mouth with me, Negress," Penelope warned. "I said I wouldn't kill you until he came. I didn't say I wouldn't put a hurting on you."

"Hurt me, kill me, what it gonna do for you? Huh? Killin' me gonna make your daddy come back to life? It gonna make you unkill your mama?" Gertie stood her ground as Penelope's eyes widened in shock. "That's right. I already know you's a killer. Kwadzo done told me ev'rythin'."

"You call for him."

"When you gonna learn, child?"

"I said call for him!"

"All this be on you! You the one took Fanna's blood. You the one who reject Kwadzo when your own people turn you 'way."

"They didn't turn me away! They sent me on a mission!"

"A mission you failed! You wouldn't be here now if'n they ain't throw you out again. What happen? You turn them men and they ain't show you no mind, did they?"

"They know nothing of the powers I possess!" Penelope glowered, her eyes burning red. "I should have been the one to lead the fight. I am the one who survived the enemy. I am the one with the power, not them! Instead, they took my blood and cast me aside! I did what they asked of me. I did what none of them could have done and it was nothing to them! *I* was nothing to them!"

"They ain't got no respect for you, in spite of you havin' the blood," Gertie said, keeping her voice low. Penelope was a child, but she was still a Ramangan, one capable of killing her. If she could commiserate with the girl and show her reason, perhaps she could save herself. "You thought you was too good for us when Kwadzo tried to pull you to his bosom. Now you done took me here thinkin' my demise gonna win they's favor. It ain't. They's don't care 'bout me no more than they's care 'bout you now that you got what they's call 'demon nigger blood' in your veins."

"Don't you pity me, nigger! We are *not* the same! But I will tell you this: It doesn't matter that they rejected me. I can still do what they can't do, what the Lord wants done. The reason He made me His vessel with this wicked blood, is so I can take that evil nigger down by killing you. Once I've conquered him, my rightful place and all you niggers have taken away from me will be restored."

"So, you wants to kill me 'cause you think it gonna make you take Kwadzo down and give you back the life you lost? You ain't lost it, child; you threw it 'way when you stole that blood outta Fanna! When you ate up your own mama!"

"You shut up! And stop saying Kwadzo! That's not even his name!"

"It's the name his mama give him, not his master."

"I said shut up!"

"Your revenge ain't brought you nothin' but pain. That all it ever gonna bring."

Penelope blurred right up to Gertie's face, her red hair plastered to her red cheeks that were almost as red as her eyes.

"*My* revenge? It was *his* revenge that started all of this! If he had just stayed in his place and been grateful to his master, none of this would have happened! You niggers wanted more than you deserved, more than what was intended for you, including this power. You all having it was never in the Good Lord's plan. You all need to go back to the dirt where you belong!"

Penelope's attempt at intimidation seemed to have the inverse effect on Gertie. A certain calm washed over her as the words spit out of the girl's mouth—words of ignorance, words without meaning. Even without him consuming her blood at the time, Gertie felt in her bones that it was their love that caused Kwadzo to hear her calling out to him when Barrow locked her in the hot box. She didn't feel the need to call to him now, not for this. Not for *her*. Penelope was a cancer, yes, but one that was easily cured. She was not a problem. Not anymore. Her fear of the girl's blood was dissolving. Penelope was no one to fear. Gertie had come to believe that the Blood was only as effective as the person who possessed it, and this girl had been carrying around a trail of failure since she had stolen it.

She could be dealt with.

And Gertie could be the one who dealt with her.

"No lord that's good would ever do to people what y'all done to us. Kwadzo ain't fightin' for revenge. He fightin' for freedom, freedom y'all took 'way, freedom for a whole race of people. Your skin don't give you no dominion over nobody. Yours come off easy as mine, and the only thing 'neath either of us is blood. But I guess ain't nobody bother to teach you that."

With an agonized scream, Penelope took on full Ramangan form and slashed her talons across Gertie's cheek, drawing blood. Gertie shrieked in pain as Penelope then bit into her cheek, sucking in her blood. She pulled back and spit the blood back into Gertie's face.

"I will leave you on your dyin' breath until he shows, you bitch," Penelope hissed. "Now I know you two are connected by the love in your blood, so you call to him now, or I will put my fist through that nigger brat in your belly and bite the rest of . . ."

Vicious barking turned both their heads to the door where Charlie the bloodhound—his Ramangan eyes glowering at Penelope and his mouth foaming—was launching himself at Penelope, his jowls snapping. Penelope swiped at Charlie as the hound tackled her to the floor. Biting into the arm Penelope held up to defend herself, the hound gave a wicked growl in response to her painful howl. She punched Charlie off her, then rolled and continued her assault of the dog, slamming the fist of her unharmed arm into him repeatedly.

"You mutt traitor!" she yelled at Charlie as he whimpered in pain. The crack of bone shook the walls of the cabin with each of Penelope's punches. Gertie got to her feet and rushed to Penelope, wrapping her arms around Penelope's waist as she struggled to pull the girl away from Charlie.

"You leave him be!" she yelled just before a new growl, a sinister one, sounded from the doorway. Once again, they looked to the open door where the glow of two red orbs hovered in the darkness outside the cabin. Abandoning the whimpering Charlie, Penelope knocked Gertie aside before grabbing her by the throat and stalking slowly toward the open door.

"Come on in, you black bastard," Penelope called out. "Come watch your wife and child die!"

Both women jumped as the doorway cracked and groaned to accommodate the largest jaguar they had ever seen. The huge cat's growling never stopped as its red eyes pulsed at them in what Gertie sensed to be recognition. She could feel Penelope's body shaking in terror against hers and used her fear to break herself free from the girl's grasp. Sucking in air, Gertie took a step toward the oversized jaguar, and the cat mimicked it, licking its tongue out and releasing a series of chuffs at her. Gertie smiled.

Even without having to call on him, Kwadzo was looking after her.

"You knows me, don't you?" she asked the cat, then stepped to the side, leaving its path to Penelope unobstructed. The great cat's growl became a roar that rattled the cabin and sent Penelope leaping and crashing through the cabin window to escape. The giant jaguar chased after her, breaking the wall around the window through which the storm now made its way in. Gertie moved to the whimpering Charlie, pulling him into a corner of the structure to avoid the wind and rain that continued to invade it, holding him for both comfort and warmth.

"We just need to ride out this here rain, Charlie," she said to him. Gertie could hear the grinding of the bloodhound's bones as the Blood slowly mended him. Struggling to move, Charlie positioned his nose to Gertie's belly, sniffing and licking it. Gertie pet his head gently.

"She all right. You gonna be all right, too."

Gertie grimaced as she reached for a shard of broken glass and used it to slice her forearm. She presented her blood for Charlie's needy tongue to lap up.

"We's all gonna be all right."

Gertie's lips curled ever so slightly into a smile.

She knew that they would be.

Thirty-Six

Fade Away

The swirling howl of wind was all Kwadzo could hear, and falling rain whipped across his face. He could still feel his body seizing from the effect of the hateful blood Rafazi had put into his system. It stunted his healing and left him feeling as weak and sickly as Monroe's had. Barrow's cowardly act of cutting Monroe open had been one thing. To be defeated by the one who made him was quite another. Nothing had ever made him feel so useless, crushed.

Beaten.

His head pounded and his mind was an excruciatingly hopeless fog. Each attempt he made to focus his mind or determine who the tainted blood had come from resulted in an unbearable throbbing. When Monroe's blood debilitated him during the manor battle, only Gertie's blood had the power to restore him, knowledge he was sure Rafazi hadn't shared with the townsfolk. He was missing her more than ever, and in his weakened and agonizing condition, he began to wonder if he would ever see her again.

All of this, of course, was compounded by Rafazi's attacks. They had left him drained both physically and emotionally. With each blow came the repeated confirmation that Rafazi was lost to him, perhaps for the remainder of his existence, a thought far more painful than the violence his maker had doled out. For the first time since he had taken the Blood, Kwadzo felt the cloud of finality, and it was winning the battle against the Ramangan Blood that sustained him.

An eternity seemed to pass before he felt his body being flung from his maker's shoulder and landing hard on the wet ground. Voices whirled back and forth over him. Actual words were hard to decipher, but he felt as if his fate were being decided without him. This was not why he took the Blood. He was not supposed to give his people a small, short taste of freedom only for it to be cut short by way of the mysterious, hateful essence raging through his veins.

This would not stand.

He was a god.

It could not stand.

He accepted the blurriness of his vision and shut his eyes. Fighting through the fog in his mind, he pushed his thoughts toward those he had made: Ekow, Fanna, Irene. Even Tussy. They and all the others who helped take Barrow Manor. *Crimson* Manor. The ones he turned and trained in the plantation fields in the wake of their victory. The ones he turned on the road North, the ones they turned as they spread across the land. He had given them strength. Now he needed strength from them.

Slowly, he began to feel them again. He still couldn't focus on any one of them in particular, couldn't bend his own mind to project his thoughts onto any of theirs, but he was starting to sense their collective presence. Though it was slight, he could feel that presence growing, and it made him feel just a little less weak.

The horrific haze of pain remained, but after its repeated use, Kwadzo heard the word "money" bandied about. Reopening his eyes to squint, his hazy vision could make out Rafazi pointing down at him, then putting his hand out toward a man who seemed to be Bartholomew Crabtree. There were other figures hovering above him as well, but the face that became clear was the one that leaned down to get right in front of his.

"So, this is what my blood does to you, huh, Willie?"

The sound of his slave name scorched Kwadzo's ears, and his insides stirred horribly as the blonde woman in front of him laughed at his pain. She was the one Rafazi had brought into the manor, the one he had defiled himself with. He caught her scent, and it was as rancid as Monroe's had been.

It was her blood.

Had Rafazi known of her all along? Had his maker orchestrated his demise?

"Have a little more." She poked her finger with a small blade, grabbed Kwadzo's jaw, and squeezed more droplets of her blood into his open mouth with a gleeful grin. Kwadzo fought to move his head away from the bloody finger, but he was still too weak to stop even this violation.

"That will be all, Lily," Kwadzo heard a voice call. "We can't have him dying before we've had our fun."

Lily. Hate this lethal took every fiber of his being to survive without the benefit of blood filled with love, Gertie's blood. He fought to concentrate his thoughts on her, and thankfully, Lily moved away from his face. He hacked and spit, trying to release what little blood of hers had managed to slip past his tongue. A new wave of agony began to set in, however, and the surge of hopeful energy the thought of Gertie and his brethren and sistren in the Blood brought faded.

"That's just a taste," he heard Lily say. "I wouldn't have given a damn if you had only killed the fat bastard Barrow, but you took my sister Charity from me, and she never hurt a soul. You will pay for what you did. I'm glad it was my blood that brought you to your knees!"

The irony was such that, had he the energy, he would have laughed. Even from beyond the grave, Barrow reached for his downfall. Spittle landed on his face, adding insult to injury.

"We're gonna make you suffer, boy," Bartholomew said. "As soon as this storm lets up, we're all gonna watch you burn."

Kwadzo winced and growled as he was pushed onto his side and felt a new sting of pain in his back—a thin, sharp blade was being driven deep into his flesh. He tried to summon the strength to fight, to blur, to do anything that would release him from the unseen clutches that held him, but Lily's blood and the injuries inflicted upon him by Rafazi were still too much.

"By now, the British army will have descended on the manor you desecrated with red paint and burned it, and everybody in it, to the ground. Your reign of terror is over," came Bartholomew's voice again.

He wanted it to be a lie. He *needed* it to be a lie. And though white men spoke lies all the time, they were accompanied by an acceleration in the blood, no matter how calm their speech was. He could sense no such acceleration now. There was nothing he could do now to save his people, to save her. He had tasted Gertie's sweetness many times, but she had never so much as sampled his blood, so there was no way for him to sense her. He wished for more strength and offered silent supplication to Gamab that he could find some semblance of focus, some way to rise from the depths that had befallen him. All he could do now, though, was hope and shut his eyes to keep his tears from escaping them.

Irene stood at the edge of yet another plantation, watching those she'd turned lay waste to a patch of overseers and take over the house of their former master. The rain, which was beginning to show signs of letting up, had kept her, her mother, and the Wretched from being coated in blood, though the taste was still fresh on her tongue. She had lost count of the plantations they had overthrown under the cover of the storm, but she knew they had traveled far.

What disturbed her was the fact that she could no longer feel Kwadzo. She had never wondered about her sense of him and remained focused on the task at hand. He was her maker and the strongest of them all, even by Rafazi's own account. She was sure that whatever he could dish out, Kwadzo could overcome. Still, she had focused her mind on his several times to alert him of their location and received no answer back, as if her connection to him had faded away.

She had not shared this information with her mother, but the masking of her concern was weighing on her. She hated the very thought of it, and she worried that somehow Kwadzo had been extinguished. The thought that Rafazi himself may have carried out the evil deed only made her feel worse, so she chose continually to push such thoughts away. Kwadzo was well somewhere.

Somehow.

She kept going. She knew he would want them to continue freeing slaves, but they would need a leader. They would need *him*. If he wasn't there, a new leader would have to emerge.

Irene wondered if she could be up for the task.

"One of the turned said that we are just a few miles south of the Province of Delaware. Just over yonder."

Splattered with fresh blood, Cecilia had blurred up to Irene, who could barely nod at the news.

"Still can't feel him?" She felt her mother's hand on her back as she turned to Cecilia with wide eyes.

"You're my daughter," she said. "Still my flesh and blood. I know Kwadzo had removed all the trouble from your mind, but I can see its return in your eyes. There is only one conclusion I could reach." Irene shook her head, her eyes now glassy with tears.

"He's going to be all right," Cecilia said. "You've got to have faith, child."

Irene looked up at the sky. The wind had settled, and the rain had reduced itself to wisps of water. The darkness told her that night had fallen once more. The storm had allowed them to survive the day, but the sun would be making its return. She wondered where they would be by then, where Kwadzo would be.

"The only faith I've ever had was that which he gave me," she said. "If he's gone, what do I have left?"

"You've got me," her mother said. "You've got every one of our people you've set free, Blood or no Blood. We must always remember that our people are resilient. All that they've done to us, all that they've taken from us, our homes, our names, our native land, and still our native blood found a way to give us the strength to survive, to rise up. To build kingdoms and empires again here, just like our ancestors did in Alkebulan. Don't give up on Kwadzo just yet. Use the Wretched to make your call to him stronger."

It had never occurred to Irene to do so. "Help me find Kwadzo," she said to them before closing her eyes and focusing her mind on her maker. She reopened them, and her eyes were glowing a bright, brilliant red. The Wretched's eyes glowed just as brightly, and Irene's vision went completely red. She could feel the tears running down her cheeks from the sheer emptiness her mind was accessing, made even more pronounced by the enhancement of her power from the Wretched.

And then, in a distant recess, she could hear labored moaning, the clank of a chain, the sizzle of skin.

Kwadzo? she called out in her mind.

Irene? It seemed like an eternity before the response came. It was weak and strained, but it was Kwadzo. Irene felt a sob of joy escape her throat.

Kwadzo! Thank Gamab! I thought you were lost to Rafazi.

I was. I am. They have sent forces against us.

Then we must fight! Where are you?

Captured. They have fed me hateful blood.

No matter. You must press on.

No! We will come back and rescue you!

No, Irene. I am but one. I am not more important than freedom. You must beat them back. Do not let up. Do not let them stop our goal. No matter what. Fight on.

But what will happen to you? His voice vanished from Irene's mind, along with her sense of him. *Kwadzo? Kwadzo!*

Their connection was gone again. The emptiness returned as she lost all sense of him. Her eyes burned and pulsed red now with an urge for vengeance, as did the eyes of the Wretched.

"What did he say?" Cecilia asked.

Irene gritted her teeth. She balled her hands into fists, and the blood in her veins pulsed with urgency as she took on her Ramangan form.

"He said to fight."

"Then fight we must."

"And fight we will. For him."

Your fear. It smells
simply divine.
And here I am,
famished.

Thirty-Seven

Bound to Fire

The rattling of chains pulled Kwadzo from his haze. Above him stood a gaggle of whites that included the Crabtrees, Lily, and the traitorous Doc Farkus. The one dark face among them was Rafazi's. A few of them carried lit torches, helping the lanterns on the ground to illuminate the space. The room he was in was made of brick with an iron door. The clothes he had worn were replaced with slave rags made of Negro cloth, though he didn't remember being stripped down.

He shifted his legs back and forth as much as he could, an effort to alleviate the itch the fabric left on his skin. The condition caused his skin to become chafed. It had taken so little for his skin to become accustomed to better materials.

The pain from Lily's blood remained, though it had diminished itself to a dull ache throbbing through him from head to toe. There was a soft sizzling in the distance, but he could not discern what was causing it. The shackles confining him limited his movement; he had been placed on his back on the cold dirt floor of the room.

His arms and legs were outstretched and attached to long iron chains that were embedded into the brick, silver cuffs burning the skin around his wrists and ankles keeping him painfully bound. The singe of the silver concerned him since he hadn't had any reaction to silver after his fire-absorbing power manifested, but he assumed it was a side effect of the hateful blood he could still feel flowing within him.

The communication he'd managed to share with Irene had sapped what little energy he had left. Closing his eyes, he again tried to focus his mind on his progenies and their power, hoping to extract more of it for himself. He was rewarded with painful spasms ricocheting in his head for the effort. The same happened when he turned his thoughts to Gertie, when he tried to think at all. He feared the dull ache translated to the numbing of all his senses, and he was terrified that it was becoming permanent.

A deluge of foul liquid was poured over his face. Kwadzo shook and spit the liquid from his lips, gagging at the stench.

"What's the matter, slave? Too good for a drink of piss?"

The white folks laughed at the question, but he could not make out who had asked it. His eyes cleared again as Rafazi knelt in his face.

"Well, old friend. This is where I take my leave of you."

Kwadzo could feel his limbs shaking in his maker's presence. There were so many things he wanted to say, but he could not bring himself to utter a word.

"They have paid me handsomely; I doubt you'll ever see me again, or anyone else. Their aim is to end you by sunlight. For a brief moment, though, you were magnificent. So few get to be so, no one remains so."

"No one but you," Kwadzo croaked through the pain, his voice low and weak.

"Not me. What I am is shrewd and self-serving. Consider yourself lucky. If it weren't for me, you would have died on your knees as Willie, a forgotten slave. Now, you will die a hero. I suspect your demise will become the stuff of legend in the years to come."

"Why did you make yourself my enemy?"

"Because I made you my equal, and you wished me to be your servant. I placed you above me and you lorded it over me. Power, Kwadzo. 'Tis a tricky thing. I suppose that is your final lesson."

"What of those of the Blood now? What of our people?"

"I believe you have far more immediate concerns."

"Come, Master." Lily joined Rafazi in front of him now, a wicked smile across her face. "There is better use of your time waiting in our new home between my legs." She licked Rafazi's cheek before turning to spit on Kwadzo. "Besides, he stinks of piss."

Kwadzo felt the wind of Rafazi's blur rushing away as the remaining people came into focus. Bartholomew and Constance Crabtree walked along either side of him—she, dragging a long sword behind her, and he, kicking at Kwadzo's leg while carrying a long metal rod with a branding iron on the end of it. The iron was burning bright orange and seemed to him to form the letters *BC*.

"This is more like it," Bartholomew said. "Parading around in your master's clothes, defiling them. The Negro cloth is far more becoming. Your last hours are upon you, nigger. The storm has lifted, and night prevails. When the sun comes up tomorrow, you will burn in it for all to see."

Kwadzo felt his blood churn with a growing rage. Fighting through the pain, he placed his focus on Gertie and his child and gained a modicum of might. He shifted against the chains and felt himself transform, albeit far slower than he'd grown accustomed to. The deep red that usually coated his vision in his Ramangan state was barely a light pink in his damaged condition.

"Pity," Bartholomew said. "It doesn't have nearly the same effect when you are chained up and weak with Lily's blood debilitating you."

Kwadzo coughed through the phlegm in his throat. "My blood has spread beyond this township, beyond this province," he said, feeling his anger fueling his speech. "I saw to it myself. I feel it within me still."

"Do you feel this?"

Constance raised her sword high and swung it downward, leaving Kwadzo screaming in agony as his right arm was severed from his torso. The light red in Kwadzo's eyes began to flicker from the sudden loss of blood.

"How about this?"

Constance repeated the action on Kwadzo's right leg, then kicked the limbs aside. Kwadzo bellowed, gritting his teeth in torture as he caught sight of Doc Farkus collecting his severed limbs out of the corner of his eye. The cloud of haze returned to his mind and his vision as even more of his essence spilled from him.

"Your maker, as he called himself, was quite informative," Bartholomew said just before Kwadzo unleashed a third horrific howl of pain as Constance switched sides with her husband and sliced off his left arm.

"The part I found of particular interest," Bartholomew continued over Kwadzo's screams, "was how you misled the other slaves into thinking that you were some kind of savior and the faith you tricked them into giving you. If Rafazi is to be believed, it is he with the centuries-old power. You are no better than any of them, certainly no wiser. You're just an ornery slave given an evil gift that you couldn't utilize to any effective degree."

"Ol' Barrow might beg to differ," Kwadzo huffed.

"Battles are won and lost every day. Most are forgotten. It's the victors of wars that history remembers. Great Britain is not named great for nothing. Victory is our birthright. It is written in our blood. There is nothing written in yours but servitude and death."

Constance's sword cut Kwadzo's left leg off, and his blood now spilled out in all directions. He was being drained. He felt cloth wrap around his bloody stumps as he felt himself fading, but he was awakened by the horrific pain of Bartholomew stomping the burning iron on his chest. Kwadzo cried out as the brand burned through his shirt and emblazoned the initials onto the skin of his chest, leaving him helplessly twisting in agony.

"A gentle reminder of who brought you to your doom. *Nigger*," Bartholomew hissed before walking away.

"Keep him alive until we come for him, Doctor," Constance said.

"Technically, he's already dead," Doc Farkus said. "This ancient blood reanimates them, though I've yet to discover how or why. But if I can, it could be the key to immortality. I thank you for the opportunity to study him."

"Learn as much as you can as quickly as you can," Bartholomew said. "When the sun comes up, alive or dead, he will burn under the light of God's glory."

One by one, the room cleared out save for Farkus, who was on his knees hovering over Kwadzo, wiping away the spittle and urine from his face.

"How little you must think of me," Doc Farkus whispered as he cleaned Kwadzo up and continued tending to his wounds. "I am not a brave man. I am quick to fear and seek to preserve myself at all costs." The scent of fear coming off him was undeniable. "I learned very much about your kind on the land you reclaimed. It would take decades to unlock the mysteries your blood possesses, decades I do not have. It should come as no surprise to you that I am fearful of my own demise as well, and while I learned nothing I could truly make use of from Ramangan power, two results of taking the blood seem abundantly clear: courage and immortality. Two things I am sorely lacking in.

"You've been vehemently opposed to anyone having the Blood who wasn't African, so the mob descending on the manor presented me with an opportunity I could not pass up. I could see how this would play out. I envisioned you being left to die alone, though I did not suspect they would cut off your limbs. Still, I took the occasion to turn events toward my favor. I would let them think I had been taken against my will and ask for a final chance to examine you alone before they sealed your fate. Once unaccompanied, I would strike a deal with you."

Despite his situation, Kwadzo found himself chuckling at Farkus. He knew exactly the deal he wished to make.

"You wish for the Blood."

"I suppose I am not as cunning as I believe myself to be."

"So, why ask? It was you who cut into my back to take my blood, was it not? Why not simply drink it and leave me to die?"

"As I've said, I am a coward. Every one of your people you turned from human to vampyre had to be killed for the change to occur. Drinking your blood would have given me some benefits; I saw small abrasions on Clarence's hands and arms heal themselves faster than they would have on any other human, albeit slower than the healing that occurs on full Ramangans. But I suspect simply having the Blood in one's system is healing in and of itself. Still, I would be too terrified to end my mortal life on my own to gain the full effect. I took your blood as a ruse to make the Crabtrees think I could find secrets in it to benefit them."

"So, you wish to take my blood and have me kill you? How would I?"

"Blood fuels and restores you, does it not? I am willing to give you my blood in exchange."

There was no way of knowing how much healing Farkus's blood would provide. Blood continued seeping from his wounds, and the hateful blood of Lily continued to linger wickedly in his veins. He was but one man, and as weak as Kwadzo felt, he was certain he would drain him if given the chance. Still, there was one permeating thought he was sure the doctor would point out.

"I am the only choice you have."

It was true. Farkus's blood was the only available to him, and he was in desperate need of it. Even Rafazi sustained himself with the blood of rodents to survive. Refusing Farkus wasn't a chance he could take, not with everything at stake, not when he was so close to achieving true freedom.

"You've required a commitment to do battle as a condition of giving someone your blood," Farkus said. "I've no doubt drinking yours would come with courage, but I still would not wish to fight. Instead, I would vow to remain loyal to Ramanga and you, and to do all in my power to discover how the Blood can benefit mankind, starting with the humans among your people. Having Ramangan Blood running through my veins I suspect would hold me to my promise."

"You say you lack courage," Kwadzo said, "yet you pose a dangerous bargain. In my state, I could drain the life from you were you to present your neck to me."

Farkus pulled a short, thick knife from his coat. "Silver to your heart should the drink become too much. Do not consider it an affront to you. As I've mentioned, self-preservation."

"So, you have."

"Have we a deal?"

Red flickered in Kwadzo's eyes as he smelled the fear in Farkus's blood rise to a fever pitch, his heart racing. There was no other option. Kwadzo opened his mouth and bared his fangs. Even in his weakened condition, he could feel the venom dripping from them. His hunger demanded satiation. Farkus gasped audibly at the sight.

"The venom," he said. "Does it truly make the bite pleasurable?"

"Feel for yourself."

Farkus began an agonizingly slow crawl toward Kwadzo, who took on his Ramangan form. His vision grew a bit darker in anticipation of the blood to come. At long last, the man's neck hovered over the Ramangan's maw, his silver blade at the ready. Kwadzo bit into the man's flesh and immediately felt vitality surge through his system. The red of his vision was restored fully in an instant, and he felt the full force of his Ramangan form take hold.

His muscles flexed as fresh blood coursed through him, fusing with the Ramangan Blood left in him to fight against the damage Rafazi and Lily's blood had done. As his mind cleared, he refocused, and one by one, he began to feel the force of the ones he'd turned along the trail north. The number kept growing, along with the strength they collectively contained. He could feel the distance that they had already crossed, that they continued to stretch out even farther. He felt a new one turn, and another, and then another, their power trickling into his consciousness.

He closed his eyes, savoring Farkus's flavor as the man's hand pushed down on his chest. Kwadzo clamped his jaw down just a bit tighter.

Just a little more.

Farkus gasped in pain and raised his blade high just before Kwadzo released him. He could hear the man fall over and cough, but he was far more focused on the sensation of rejuvenation that was now flowing through him. There was a tingling in his extremities, and he felt his very flesh pushing against the cloth Farkus had wrapped around his stumps.

"Unwrap me!"

Farkus was still coughing and bleeding from the wound Kwadzo left in his neck as he crawled to Kwadzo's left leg stump and removed the cloth.

His eyes went wide, and he backed away from what he saw: Kwadzo's bone, tissue, muscle, flesh, and skin were actively moving, reshaping themselves to take their original forms.

The stump pulsed and grew, and Farkus could only stare in slack-jawed wonder.

"Extraordinary . . . !"

Kwadzo could feel himself getting stronger; he needed more, but it was no longer blood that he craved. His veins cried out for something else.

"Set me on fire."

"No! You will burn, and they will have my head for taking the pleasure from them!"

"You took that pleasure from them when you agreed to gift me your blood. Now, use the lanterns and set me on fire!"

"You will protect me from them? Promise me!"

"You will have the strength to protect yourself."

"Give me your blood first."

"I am still not whole. Do you wish my weakened blood, or do you wish for eternity?"

Farkus cursed as he went about gathering the lanterns in the room.

"You must remove my clothing."

Farkus used his blade to do so and placed the lit lantern candles onto Kwadzo's skin. He winced in pain as the flickers grew into larger flames, something Kwadzo now knew his body was doing. His veins not only ached for blood.

They ached for fire.

He felt the temperature of his blood increase, and his skin grew hot. The flames engaged his blood and grew thicker, hotter, higher. He could feel blood and fire communing throughout his entire being. The fire raged across his skin, burning away Bartholomew's brand. The pain he experienced the last time he was engulfed had vanished. His body now welcomed the fire, accepted that he would absorb it, and that it would become a part of him, that he could harness it however he wished, that he could expel what he wanted and hold onto what he needed with the knowledge that his blood would ignite the fire in his veins when it needed to.

Every fiber of his being told him that the fire would become a permanent part of him from this day forward. The flames covered him completely and burned ferociously. They sank deep beneath his skin, racing though his organs, burrowing below his stomach and forming a pit of their very own. Kwadzo was reminded of the times he'd died and found himself bathed in the Red, lying in peace and calm as his system rejuvenated himself. The same was happening now. The fire raged, yet he was at peace, reveling in his body restoring itself. From the pit, he felt the fire grow and shoot through his veins, racing through the whole of him, and as it moved, there was regeneration throughout his entire form.

Kwadzo could feel his limbs rebuild under the power of blood and flame, faster and faster until he was once again intact. The flames absorbed into his body, and the room grew dark as orange-and-red cracks covered the surface of his skin, emitting a soft glow. His eyes glowed bright orange. He rose to his feet, inspecting his hands and arms, his legs, his feet. He reveled in his full Ramangan glory. Farkus stood before him, holding his slave clothing up to him.

"I have never witnessed such a spectacle in all my days," Doctor Farkus said breathlessly. "I shall drink from you directly."

Kwadzo smiled, and with a talon, slit his wrist.

Thirty-Eight

Before the Sun

Gertie and Charlie stepped out of the abandoned cabin, the earth still soaked beneath their feet and paws. The hound had been fully restored with the help of her blood, and she had torn a piece of fabric from her frock and held it against the wound on her cheek. Reaching down to pet Charlie, the dog gave her what she took as an appreciative bark in response. Kwadzo and Charlie: the men in her life. Both had saved her from Penelope's vengeance. In the distance, she could still hear the echoing roars of the great jaguar that was chasing the wayward Ramangan away.

She wondered how far Kwadzo had ventured, where he had come across the jaguar, how many he had freed. She wondered if he would be able to find proper shelter once the sun came up now that the storm had broken. The battles were the hardest on her. Not knowing where or how he was, scared that someone, somewhere, would find a way to destroy him. Now, that someone was Rafazi in her mind.

Though she vowed to never take the Blood for the sake of their child, it was in times like these when she would imagine doing so. She envisioned his blood running through her veins, making their already strong bond all the greater, cementing their union for all time. She would visualize blurring with him, fighting by his side, never again feeling the fear that seemed to grip her human heart at every turn in his absence.

She shook the fear from her mind. The jaguar was evidence that there was always an indescribable, unbreakable connection between them already. No matter how far away from one another they were torn, he was always watching over her. The thought firmed her resolve, straightened her back, and raised her head. He would prevail.

Charlie's barking pulled Gertie out of her thoughts. He was in full Ramangan form, barking loudly, his tail wagging wildly.

And his eyes were glowing red and orange.

"Charlie? Is you all right?"

She hesitated before she moved to him; he had become spastic in his movement, but Charlie jumped up at her and she pulled him in. He licked her face enthusiastically and she laughed.

"What done got into you, Charlie?" She took the hound's face in her hands and took closer note of his eyes. They had never been orange before. "Charlie . . . Kwadzo?" Charlie barked and whipped his tail even faster.

First through the big cat.

Now, through Charlie.

Kwadzo was letting her know that he was okay. That he could make sure she would be, too.

"Gertie!"

Spinning and gasping, she found Jenue standing before her.

"Jenue!" she exclaimed. "You 'bout scared the skin off me!"

"Apologies, but I have been looking for you ever since the manor fell."

"What you mean the manor fell?"

"British soldiers came after you disappeared. Between them and the white men with the Blood, they burned the house to the ground. There were those who got away, but many of our people were murdered, including many Natives. Others were captured and taken to Lakeside as prisoners."

"What happen to Michael Lyon? He got to shakin' somethin' awful . . ."

"Venom settled him for a while, but in the chaos, Caesar turned Antoinette to protect her, though she protested. When Michael found out, he begged her to turn him; said he could not live without her."

"He was still that bad off?"

"Turns out our Michael was already acquainted with Miss Penelope. He divulged to me that they'd been carrying on an affair in secret for months."

"Really? Did she turn him?"

"Don't know. Once the flames became too much, I made my escape and haven't seen either of them since. Why did you run?"

Gertie's breath caught, but she would not allow herself to question who had survived and who had perished. She feared answers would send her into deep despair.

"Ain't run. Penelope took me," she said instead. "Brung me out here to kill me to gets revenge 'gainst Kwadzo. How you find me?"

"Your smell."

"You can smell my blood from that far?"

"My sense of smell has grown quite sensitive over the millennia. Right now, I need to get you to safety with the others who got away, or Kwadzo will go on a rampage when he returns. There is a cottage at the border of Lakeside and Bedshire owned by Miss Kitty Greer. Those who made it away with their lives have taken refuge there. That's where we'll go." Jenue's brow crinkled at Gertie's smile. "Perhaps you don't fully grasp the situation."

"You say you ain't care 'bout nothin', but here you is, rescuin' me for Kwadzo's sake."

"I never said I didn't care about anything," Jenue said.

"You know where he be?"

"No, but I do know that something's happened to him."

"What? What happen?

"Something entirely phenomenal. I believe he's become more powerful than he thought possible."

Gertie had no doubt.

Irene raced across the wilderness in her blur with a vengeance. She considered her communication with Kwadzo a distress signal. He had been captured. He was weak and alone. Even as her blur picked up speed, fueled by the power of the Wretched, she could still feel those of her blood spreading. She had no idea the number she had turned, but one thing was certain: Nothing could stop what had started.

What Kwadzo had started.

The man who saved her life and gave her power and immortality. She thought it noble that he was willing to sacrifice himself for the mission of freedom, but there was no way she would let that happen. He could be angry with her for going against his order. He could scream and yell. That she could take. What she would not abide was his destruction.

"Irene!"

Cecilia—not fast enough to keep pace with the accelerated pace the Wretched provided Irene—had fallen behind. Irene had no time to marvel at the astonishing display of speed she exhibited with the help of the Wretched or the fact that with them she was becoming like three Ramangans in one. She just needed to get to Kwadzo. Mentally, she sent one of the Wretched back to pick her mother up and carry her forward. She couldn't lose her pace. Every second she wasn't there, he could be closer to extermination. Then, without warning, she was struck by an invisible force that brought her to a screeching halt. It was a powerful surge of strength and heat unlike anything she had ever felt before. Her whole body seized up, out of her control. Her head flew back, and orange seeped into her red vision. Then, like rolling thunder, a voice echoed in her head.

My brothers and sisters in the Blood! Our time has come. Let nothing stop you until every one of us is free. Our power is eternal! Our freedom is eternal!

Kwadzo's voice.

Clear and strong.

For a short moment, she felt as if she were imbued with all his power, a greatness too magnificent to even describe. A divine intensity that made her smile brighter than she ever had and brought tears to her eyes. She turned to the Wretched one who remained with her and found it to be frozen in place as well, its eyes glowing with the same orange and red as her own. Kwadzo was communicating with each one of the Blood at once. They thought they had conquered him, but whatever they'd done to him, he had only emerged stronger than ever.

He's back, Irene thought, and she couldn't have been happier as his voice rumbled forth in her head again.

The sunrise looms. There are those who are fighting the British north of us. I can feel them, see them, hear their cries. But fighting is not our true purpose. We are here to free our people from their shackles. I feel our numbers growing and the power along with it. Our presence is undeniable. So, press on. Free as many as you can in the few hours left before the day returns. Each one of you of the Blood must burrow underground before the sun's rise, and when night falls, we will emerge, and I promise you, by the Blood of Gamab, we will emerge victorious.

Irene felt herself stumble forward and realized her body was once again under her own control.

"That was amazing!" Cecilia said as she and the Wretched one Irene sent back for her blurred up.

"We are eternal, Mother," Irene said joyfully as the orange left her vision. "Nothing can stop us. We must return northward."

Taking visual stock of where they were, Irene felt her heart drop at the sight in the distance—Crimson Manor. It had fallen. Had she not been so familiar with the land, it would have been unrecognizable. The manor had been crushed and burned down to its foundation, and much of the land had been scorched. Farther in the distance, the squat round houses had been torn down. The place was barren and devoid of people. How many had gotten away? How many had perished?

Which group had Gertie been in?

In an instant, Irene was sent tumbling several feet forward by an unexpected force. Its scent registered as Ramangan, which made no sense. What Ramangan would attack another at such a crucial moment? Especially after experiencing the glory of Kwadzo's return?

She was pushed from the blur that had entrapped her and rose in her own Ramangan form, ready to battle, her jaw stiffening with resolve. The blur separated, and two emerged: Clarence and Derby. Her shoulders dropped and shook with her amusement. The two of them, so against Kwadzo even after his actions freed them, so diametrically opposed to the Blood and all it stood for, now stood before her as the very beings they hated. Perhaps the Blood had shown them the error of their ways.

"That's right," Clarence said. "Y'all wanted me to be as evil as y'all, and now, I am!"

Perhaps not.

"Them British soldiers found me in the cellar when they took the manor. I told them I wanted no part of what Ol' Willie was doin' . . ."

"His name is Kwadzo," Irene corrected.

"His name is Willie! That's the name Massa was kind enough to give him, and he turn his back on it. See? None of y'all ever been grateful for what Massa give you, so y'all let Willie take away any chance you had for grace. This here world need to be rid of all you! That's what I told them soldiers. I told them I was already doomed so they could kill me and I could use this here power for good, and that's just what I done. I found Derby and turn him, and we ate us some good-for-nothin' niggers, and thank the white lord, them soldiers told us if we's keep killin' for them, we's get spared. So now, we's gonna eat you."

Clarence. Disloyal to his people even in death. Even anointed by the power of their Blood.

She found Derby's silence odd; he seemed to be far more enthralled with himself than Clarence and his rhetoric, which made sense, considering he was still Derby. As usual, he was shirtless, and his muscularity seemed even more defined, a by-product of the Blood, she was sure. Despite her annoyance with him, his dark skin was stunningly rich and luminous, a trait she'd taken note of in her own skin when she transformed. At any rate, he was in no way prepared to fight, but Clarence was.

He charged for her, but Irene dropped her hands. Clarence never saw the Wretched slam into him from behind. The sight of them sent Derby blurring away into the woods while Clarence got to his feet and traded vicious punches with the Wretched. It wasn't long before they had overpowered him, tossing him back and forth between them and stabbing their thick claws into his flesh before slamming him to the ground. One of the Wretched dropped to continue the attack, but Clarence yawned open his jaw and bit into the Wretched.

He immediately fell back and began to mutate, screaming out as he took on the same form as the Wretched. The screams stopped when the transformation was complete. Calmly, the Wretched pushed him onto his stomach, and the one who used to be Clarence stood up on its haunches and released a wrathful roar before standing with the other two before Irene in subservience.

Irene moved to the one who used to be Clarence and pet him on the head, an affection he welcomed. "Perhaps Rafazi was right," she said with a chuckle. "In death, you will find your usefulness."

She took one final look at the ruins of the manor. It had been so crucial before, the ultimate symbol of their victory, and while she mourned the lives lost at the site, the manor itself didn't seem to matter anymore. There was so much more waiting for them.

And Kwadzo would lead them to it.

Thirty-Nine

When Day Breaks

All through the night, Lakeside town square was alive with music and merriment. It was packed with citizens and British soldiers, all in the height of their joy. Minstrels filled the streets playing music, singing, and dancing. Children chased each other with glee, and ale and wine overflowed in cups and goblets. The only ones not enjoying themselves were the ones chained up to each other in the middle of it all, the captured prisoners of war, Alkebulan descendants and Indigenous peoples, who were being used as target practice. They were littered with rotten produce; some men even went so far as to urinate on them to rousing cheers.

It was the celebration of a victory over him, this Kwadzo knew. Still, he was grateful for this as it allowed him to move among them undetected. Doc Farkus had provided him with modest clothing and a long black cloak before disappearing to go in search of his wife with his newfound power. He'd given the doctor instructions not to share the Blood with anyone, not even his wife, without his permission. He wasn't concerned that the doctor would be disobedient. The Blood may have given him power and courage, but the remnants of his human blood still smelled of fear.

While the sky was still dark, Kwadzo felt a sweltering heat bearing down on him, telling him the sun would make its appearance in less than an hour's time. At any moment, the Crabtrees would go to the cell he was supposed to be held in to find it empty and Doc Farkus gone. They would learn that their efforts to destroy him had failed.

His Ramangans were just below the surface, lying in wait for night to fall. He would face the citizens, tell them of their folly directly, and give them the coming daylight hours to change their minds and mend their ways to create a lasting peace for all. If not, Ramangan power—which had expanded considerably throughout the colonies and would continue to do so—would rise and there would be nothing they could do to stop it.

First, however, he would free those who had been captured. With the cloak wrapped over his head, not a single soul moved to stop him as he knelt before the prisoners and went about breaking the chains and cuffs that held them. He assumed the liquor they consumed led them to believe he was assaulting them for pleasure somehow, just as they were. As the captured eyed him with recognition, he spotted Nez among them. Nodding to the Native man, Kwadzo put a finger to his lips and Nez nodded in response. The action kept them all quiet.

"GODDAMMIT!"

The shout echoed off the town square buildings, bringing the music and jubilation to a halt until the only sound to be heard was that of metal breaking and falling to the ground.

"That goddammit doctor betrayed us and freed that vampyre nigger!"

Bartholomew's voice was loud and clear now and followed by the clicking of a myriad of rifle hammers behind Kwadzo.

"Show yourself!" one of the soldiers standing behind him called out as Bartholomew and Constance came running. Calmly, Kwadzo stood, dropping his cloak and exposing himself, stretching his arms high above his head and standing as tall as his legs would allow. The Crabtrees gawked in wonder, as did the Lakeside citizens.

"How?" Constance croaked.

"Did I ruin the celebration?" Kwadzo chuckled, addressing the citizens. "Had you all been told that my limbs had been severed from my body? Had you been summoned for a nightlong revelry to end with my burning in the sun? I am sorry to disappoint. Ramangan Blood and fire have restored me, and now, Lakeside, you have a choice to make. Daylight is nearly upon us, and you will have all its hours to make your decision.

"Even as I stand before you, the power of Ramanga stretches throughout the colonies, North and South. I feel the immortal might of each one within the blood I house. There has been a shift. The descendants of Alkebulan you brought here against their will and the people native to this land will no longer be subjected to your violence and cruelty. A new society will be built, one that honors all of us. You can choose to be a part of it, or you will perish."

Kwadzo shifted uncomfortably and looked up to the sky. It had become lighter and would continue to do so. He would have to burrow underground soon, safe in the knowledge that any who came after him would face the waiting Ramangans he would be joining.

"What are you all waiting for?" Bartholomew cried out at the top of his lungs, his cheeks red with fury. "KILL HIM!"

The soldiers standing before him answered the call by opening fire on Kwadzo, sending the town square into pandemonium. He saw the citizens charge him in a collective fury as those he freed from their chains launched themselves into the battle.

As the bullets ripped through Kwadzo, he closed his eyes and focused on his blood and each one it had spread to.

Great Gamab, he said in silent prayer as chaos raged around him, *strengthen me as my blood has strengthened them.*

He felt his blood rumble in his veins and the bullets in his body collect in them. He felt his internal fire rush through them, searching for escape. His eyes transformed into balls of fire as he opened them and his mouth to release multiple torrents of flame. Once the soldiers were incinerated, there was a flock of citizens rushing him.

Taking on Ramangan form, the veins in Kwadzo's arms, neck, and face bulged orange and red as he blurred through them, his talons extended and his teeth and fangs out for blood. His blur was moving faster than it ever had, and he could feel his power being boosted by those he had sired; wherever they were, they were sending him their strength, and it fueled him forward. Blood and bone shot up into the air from the cloud of battle he had become, rolling through the citizens who would not let up in their attack.

Blades, bullets, sticks, and fists, he endured them all, but it was getting hotter. The sky had gotten even lighter, and a single ray of sunlight broke through the morning clouds and struck him in the shoulder with such pain that he cried out and fell to the ground. The attacking citizens took advantage of this eventful turn and unleashed their violence on him tenfold. Swords and blades were stabbed into him, and bullets were shot down at him at point-blank range as vitriol was shouted at him. The crush of them was great, and with the sun rising, he lacked the power to push himself free.

"Leave him! Leave him!"

The call made the mob back away from him as Bartholomew and Constance pushed through the crowd.

"You see? The sun that causes nature to bloom weakens you." Bartholomew smiled down at him with evil glee. "Your very existence is an affront to our Lord. You are destined to die just as everyone like you is. You are a blight on humanity, a wicked abomination to be wiped out and forgotten. There will never be a place in this world for you."

Kwadzo felt the immense heat of the rising sun boil his blood as his exposed skin began to smoke and sizzle. Bartholomew and Constance laughed as they pushed the crowd back to leave him vulnerable to the sun.

"This is it!" Bartholomew shouted. "Just as we promised! Watch the vampyre nigger burn to nothing! We won't have to lift a finger!"

Kwadzo's limbs began to shake as he tried to fight against the sun to no avail. The skin on his cheeks cracked and smoked, and the crush of true death hovered over him once more.

That was when a massive roar sounded in the town square, louder than anything Kwadzo had ever heard, loud enough to distract him from his pain, and everyone else from him. Multiple gasps of fright erupted from the crowd as Ruby, in her Ramangan form, huge and terrifying, opened her jowls and unleashed a second roar that sent the crowd into a fearful panic as she lunged directly into the middle of them. Her teeth and paws tore through several of them before she hovered over Kwadzo, giving him enough shade to heal, even as flames broke out across her back and she growled out in anguish.

It didn't take long for Kwadzo to heal under her cover. Once he had, he gave Ruby a nod and the massive cat launched toward a group of men standing in front of a shopfront. While they screamed, she stretched her front limbs and tackled them all into the shop. Kwadzo could hear her devouring them under the cover of the store's interior. As he sat up, the sun began to inflict its damage on him again, though it was slightly less intense. The citizens were running away in all directions, but he was seeking out only two.

Bartholomew and Constance Crabtree.

Spotting them running for the large building with two crossed boards atop it, Kwadzo set his sights on following them inside. Getting to his feet, he pushed his blur toward them, his eyes burning red. As he moved, he watched his blur turn red and jolt him forward so fast he could no longer see anything but red. It was the fastest he'd ever moved, and he wasn't sure his feet were even touching the ground anymore. He was engulfed in red, but he had not been ended. This was a different red than the one that rebirthed him.

In an instant, he willed himself to stop. His sight returned, and he found himself inside the building he intended to follow the Crabtrees into, but it was empty. It took a few minutes for him to collect himself from the shock of his movement, but when the Crabtrees came running into the building, they stopped cold.

"Fret not," Kwadzo said to their stunned faces. "I will personally see to the freeing of those you call your slaves, but I suspect they have already been liberated."

"How did you . . . ?"

They were the last three words Constance spoke before Kwadzo blurred to her and—mimicking the woman's first attack on him—slammed his fists against the sides of her head until they touched, smashing the woman's skull, brain, and the blood they contained to mush.

"CONSTANCE!" Bartholomew bellowed as he dropped to his knees and sobbed. Kwadzo knelt next to him and took in his scent.

"Ah, there it is," Kwadzo said, sniffing of the man deeply.

"What?"

"Your fear. It smells simply divine. And here I am, famished."

Bartholomew never had the chance to scream before Kwadzo was upon him, using the full power of his bite to crush the man's neck and feed on his blood until there was none left. Satiated, he sat back and took stock of the events that had led him to this point and everything that now lay ahead. The moment was bittersweet. The last time he tasted triumph, his maker was by his side. Now, Rafazi had made himself an enemy of the very tribe his blood had created.

Kwadzo shook the thought free of his head as best he could. He could feel all those of his blood pulsing with energy, lying in wait beneath the surface throughout the colonies. Once the sun had set, a new era would dawn. They would rise from the earth and continue spreading freedom across the vast land. Victory was theirs. There was much to look forward to, but nothing took precedence over holding Gertie again.

She is itching to meet her daddy.

Forty

Blood and Gold

The night breeze was warm and calm on Kwadzo's face. The sound of the ocean in his ears and the feel of the sand on his feet soothed him as he rested across Gertie's legs, his ear to her protruding pregnant belly. While Charlie the bloodhound and Ruby the jaguar roughhoused playfully along the beach in their Ramangan forms, Kwadzo listened to the heartbeat of the child he would soon meet.

The path west had been more treacherous than he had thought it would be. It had taken months. He was left with little choice after meeting with the Pennsylvania Provincial Council. Robert Callowhill and Sarah Collins had made a compelling case for the abolishment of slavery, but nothing spoke louder than the Ramangan force that emerged from the earth after his conquering of Lakeside. Their power had become too vast to be denied.

Not only could slavery no longer be enforced with so many Ramangans and plantations overthrown, but the Crown had also granted the colonies their freedom. Word had spread to England of their victory, causing the Queen herself to relinquish all stake in the colonies on the condition that the military already on this land remain and none of the colonists ever return or ask the Crown for support of any kind. There was no longer anything that could be done for Kwadzo's people that they could not do for themselves.

A mass exodus from the colonies began, one that included many more white folks than he anticipated. Kwadzo chose to travel west, but no one was forced to follow. There were those of his race who stayed behind, ever loyal to their fallen masters. Several Native tribes stayed to reclaim their lands while Seneca, Nez, and young Chev, among others, took their place in the Crimson Order. Kwadzo sent Fanna with a contingent of Ramangans to hunt the white Ramangans Penelope had sired. Though they were all found and destroyed, Penelope remained unaccounted for.

Ultimately, Kwadzo decided she was a problem for another time and called Fanna and the others back to join their trek westward. If she used the Blood to mobilize whites against them again, they would be ready. The same was true for any and all enemies they would face, including Rafazi.

Wooden coffins with steel lids were made for the Ramangans to travel in during the daylight hours. Gertie told Kwadzo that vultures would circle above during the day, presumably smelling the dead below. Prey was hunted but scarce, as was blood. There were willing humans among them, but Kwadzo and his commanders had to make sure feeding was rationed. Illness was kept to a minimum thanks to Ramangan venom, and passage through Indigenous lands was negotiated with as little battle as possible. Peace remained Kwadzo's goal, especially with those native to the land, but the smell of sea air taunted his nostrils, and he was determined to settle only after they'd made it to the beckoning sea. They made their new home on the land right by the ocean, working with the native peoples there to begin the creation of a new, just, and joint society.

Now, in the spring of the year 1711, that society was slowly taking shape. A system of trade was being established, food was being grown, different cultures were becoming acquainted with one another, and Kwadzo had finally given Gertie her wish, their own house where they grew their own food on their own property and raised a family consisting of the two of them, Fanna, young Chev, who they had taken in as their own, and the one set to make his—or her—appearance, the one who still called Gertie's belly home.

His life, their life, was their own.

And it came with an ocean view.

"'And even to this day the tomb is to be seen; so that among the monuments that in Verona been, there is no monument worthy of the sight, than is the tomb of Juliet and Romeus her knight.'"

Gertie closed the book she'd read from with a huff and tossed it onto the sand.

"You didn't like it?" Kwadzo asked.

"Those two were far too young to be in the throes of love like that. And then they just end up dead?"

"Well, it is called 'The Tragicall Historye of Romeus and Juliet.'" Kwadzo chuckled as Gertie glowered. "That means it's a tragedy."

"Why would you teach me to read if this was what you were going to give me to read? We lived through tragedy. I don't need to read about it, too."

"So, you didn't like it?"

"No, I did not. I've got a good mind to throw this copy out into the sea so that no one else can read this, this . . ."

"Drivel?"

"What's that mean? Drivel?"

"It means you didn't like it."

"Then I should throw this drivel into the sea."

Kwadzo kissed her belly and chuckled. He closed his eyes and reveled in the feel of her hand rubbing his head.

"This time tomorrow," she said, smiling down at him, "you are going to be my husband."

"That is if this little one doesn't decide to come first."

"She is itching to meet her daddy." Gertie grunted and moved her hand to her belly just as Kwadzo felt movement against his cheek.

"Kicking again?"

"I thought the sound of the ocean might put her to sleep, but it's not working."

"Should we go to the creek?"

"Yes. That always works."

She stood, and Kwadzo scooped her up in his arms.

"Don't blur too fast," she said. "I get cold. Better yet, do the thing where you just get us there."

Kwadzo took but one step in speed, and he and Gertie were engulfed in a brilliant red for what was but a moment. Like all the others, this new power of his had been getting stronger ever since nothing but a thought transported him from Lakeside town square to the inside of a building. The red was glorious, made all the more special with her being in it with him. He kissed her tenderly, and then the red was gone, and water was rushing around his feet. They were surrounded by gorgeous mountains, greenery, and huge rocks, smoothed out from years of the creek water rolling over them. Kwadzo set Gertie down on one of them and they sat together, enjoying the sound of the water rushing beneath them.

Gertie placed Kwadzo's hand on her belly and covered it with her own.

"I think it's working."

He kissed her belly. "Sleep well, little man."

She slapped his shoulder playfully. "Little *woman*. Sleep well, little woman. It's a girl."

"If you say so."

Gertie's brow crinkled playfully before her eyes shifted to focus on something below the water's surface.

"Kwadzo, what is that? It looks shiny."

His curiosity piqued, Kwadzo moved across the creek and made his vision red to see clearer. Squinting, he discovered something sparkling through the red. Reaching under the water, he picked up the source: a gray rock encased by thick, jagged strands of brilliant, shiny yellow. He examined it closely until recognition set in, and once it did, he found himself laughing. It was the kind of laughter that only came from stumbling upon the improbable.

"What are you laughing at?" Gertie asked him as he turned and held up his find.

"Do you know what this is?"

The shimmering in her wide eyes as she moved closer to take it in was answer enough.

"That's gold ore!" she exclaimed. "Just like from back home, like the white folks killed for!"

Kwadzo handed the ore to her and moved back to the slab of rock in the water where he'd found it. He punched into the rock with all his might, first with one fist, then with both at extraordinary speed. When he was done, chunks of gold ore were floating in the rolling creek, giving it a golden hue that illuminated many more slabs of rock also containing gold ore. He heard Gertie laughing and clapping behind him, and soon, he was joining her. His quest for freedom had come with an additional reward.

Gold.

Discussion Questions

1. *Blood Rising* opens with Penelope alone in the woods after having just killed her mother, and throughout the book, she is hellbent on vengeance. Do you think her feelings are justified? What would you do if everything you had ever known was suddenly gone?

2. Though certainly not devoid of violence, *Blood Rising* has considerably less violence than *Blood Slaves*. Did that enhance your reading experience or detract from it? And why?

3. As the Natives and Africans (or Alkebulans) celebrate their newfound freedom with a lavish feast, Nez tells Kwadzo that his people had tried to feast with the colonists before and that it hadn't gone well, an obvious nod to Thanksgiving. Does the celebration of the holiday ever give you pause, considering the history behind it?

4. As the new leader of the Ramanga Tribe, Kwadzo struggles with how to move forward and butts heads with Rafazi on the right methods to use. Have you ever been thrust into a position of power you weren't ready for? Was your power challenged? How did you handle it?

5. A major plot point in the book is the contention between Kwadzo and Rafazi, which leads to Rafazi betraying Kwadzo. Have you ever been betrayed by someone close to you? What did you do about it?

6. How did you feel about Rafazi becoming the villain in *Blood Rising*?

7. Jenue, Rafazi's long-thought-expired maker, shakes up the manor not just by their presence but also by the ability to shift genders. What benefits do you think Jenue's existence has had due to being both male and female? What female attributes could men benefit from and vice versa?

8. Irene becomes much more powerful in the book, liberating her mother, Cecilia; finding love with Sarah Collins; and inadvertently spawning a different species of Ramanga, the Wretched. Did you enjoy her transformation? Do you think she would make a better leader than Kwadzo?

9. The Natives have a much larger presence in this book, most notably the new character Seneca, who overshadows her brother, Nez, in the story by making her desire for the Blood and her admiration for Kwadzo known. What did you think of Seneca's boldness? Was she out of line for how she spoke of Kwadzo in front of Gertie?

10. Gertie left readers divided in *Blood Slaves*. Did you find her to be more agreeable in *Blood Rising*? Do you think she is Kwadzo's moral compass or that she gets in the way of progress?

11. Clarence, who was against Kwadzo's rebellion in *Blood Slaves*, ultimately becomes one of Irene's Wretched. Do you think this was a just development for his character? If so, why?

12. It is gravely important for Kwadzo to find Penelope, who is now a Ramangan, and change her way of thinking to be in support of their cause and embrace her as one of their own because of the Blood they share. Do you think his desire for unity with her was productive or counterproductive? Is

there a point where you no longer believe harmony with enemies is attainable or worth pursuing?

13. SPOILER! At the end of the book, Kwadzo and Gertie discover the gold that would have triggered the California Gold Rush in 1848, another historical event that will never happen in the timeline of the series. What do you think they will do with the gold? What would you do with it if you found it? How important do you believe the creation of generational wealth to be?

14. Now that Doc Farkus has the Blood, do you think he can be trusted?

15. What do you think of Kwadzo's turning Ruby the jaguar? How do you feel about animals being given the Blood? Would you let your pet take it?

Acknowledgments

How 'bout that discovery of gold, huh? What's going to happen next? I so wish I could tell you, but the good people at Kensington Publishing say you have to wait until 2027, so I hope you stay with me until then!

Blood Rising would not have been possible without the incredible support *Blood Slaves* received, and that support slipped over during the crafting of this second novel of the Blood Saga series. Most significant, however, is the continuous support I receive from my wife, Isis Heuser. Not only has she put up with my nonsense for far longer than anyone should have to, but she has given me a family that now includes grandchildren; thanks to Ryan, who devoured one of the first copies of *Blood Slaves* with enjoyment despite it being written by his stepdad, and his wife Mika, the parents of said grandkids. To Jeremy, who seems to get more philosophical by the day, and Eric, perhaps the most genuine person I've ever known. Isis also had to mourn the death of a character she loved, the aforementioned Michael Lord in the dedication, for this series to launch. I'm sorry, honey. I will find a way to pay restitution. Thank you for choosing me.

I also want to thank the kind folks at my agency, The Rights Factory, and Jennifer Chevais in particular, who handles my work with so much care and elevates it at every turn. In fact, it was Jennifer who came up with the title *Blood Rising*, which solidified the branding of this series. Because of her, the word "blood" will be in every title of the series. Sam Hiyate continues to lead the charge toward adaptation and is always quick with a kind word, as is the in-house social media team that shouts out and reposts everything they can to help get the word out.

And of course, the good people of Kensington Publishing, who believed in this series from the jump and decided it was worth bringing to you. From my fearless editor Leticia Gomez, who gives me both guidance and trust, to Michelle Addo and Vida Engstrand, the publicists who find me the coolest events to participate in, to my publisher, Jackie Dinas, who, despite spearheading an entire publishing house with hundreds of authors and several imprints, somehow finds the time to respond to my emails. Double props for the out-of-this-world Twisted Retreat Exclusive Edition of *Blood Slaves* that she made happen along with Twisted Retreat's owner Melanie McKnight. If you've seen the book, you know what fire it is.

Speaking of fire, I would be remiss if I didn't publicly give thanks to Kensington's art director, Kristine Mills, for her brilliant cover design of both *Blood Rising* and *Blood Slaves*. Just . . . wow. From Andi Paris, Kristin McLaughlin, Larissa Ackerman, Alexandra Nicolajsen, Cassandra Farrin, Leah Marsh, Catherine Kenny, Kait Johnson, and even Steven Zacharius, the CEO, who graciously followed me back on social media, my heartfelt thanks to the entire Kensington team.

It would also be impossible not to acknowledge the dear folks of Black Cat Books & Oddities in Medina, Ohio. I had never met Alicia or Max Frazier before the preorder launch of *Blood Slaves*, but when they heard there weren't enough preorders through Barnes & Noble for the retailer to carry the book, Alicia and Max did something unheard of: They offered discounts at their indie bookstore to folks who preordered *Blood Slaves* through B&N. I was blown away.

I had the pleasure of meeting Alicia and the fantastic staff at Black Cat, including Tatum, Schuyler, Celiah, Emily, Kendra, and Katie, who created some amazing artwork of Irene and Charlie the bloodhound in full Ramangan mode. Each one of these women has lifted my spirits at every turn as not only supporters of this series but fans of it. Thank you all. If you ever find yourself in Medina, Ohio, go to Black Cat Books & Oddities. Seriously. It's an experience.

I also want to thank the authors I've met on this journey, all skillful storytellers, and some of whom you might recognize from that very prestigious list out of New York, who did nothing but offer encouragement even as they were embarking on and advancing their own literary careers. Here is but a sample of the kindhearted novelists who extended their kindness to me: Shalini Abeysekara, Liann Zhang, Alex Gonzalez, Tatiana Schlote-Bonne, Clay Cane, Tlotlo Tsamaase, I.V. Marie, Veronica Bane, Jihyun Yun, LaDarrion Williams, Nicholas Belardes, Isabel Cañas, Kristen Berry, Xan Kaur, Molly O'Sullivan, Rachel Phan, Hien Nguyen, Jenni Howell, Maria Tureaud, Amy Kaufman, Michelle McGill-Vargas, Brendan Slocumb, and Rebecca Rowland.

There were more as well, like Kelsie Sheridan Gonzalez, who not only lent support during her own launch, but introduced me to Bri Busby (@bribwriter on TikTok), who then introduced me to Sophia Dean (@piasreadz), and the two of them turned their white-hot passion for books onto mine and made videos of praise on TikTok, which then kicked off a firestorm of support on the platform, that spread to Instagram. Not only am I incredibly thankful to them for their support but also the others who followed suit. So many of you made videos shouting out the book and the raw emotions it made you feel, and I've no doubt it all built the anticipation for *Blood Rising*. There were also those with podcasts, like 3 Sistas 1 Bookclub Podcast, who streamed the book out to their following and even held giveaways for their book club. There were folks on YouTube like Veena Ms. WOC Reader, who made several videos in support of the book.

And then, there is Tananarive Due. I honestly can't believe that I get to say this, but the release of *Blood Slaves* led to me gaining support from the Queen of Black Horror herself, and I remain shook. Thank you for giving a nod to this newbie.

And then, there were the readers. The folks who heard the preamble, bought the book, and joined me in the Blood. So many, too many to name here, made posts, sent personal messages about what the book meant to them, how it affected them emotionally, how it helped them cope through current events. To each and every one of you, I say thank you.

I'd like to take a moment to give appreciation to the multitudes of Black readers out there. There's been a lot of talk disparaging Black intellect and readership as I write this, but I would like to declare publicly that Black readership is strong, passionate, massive, and wildly insightful. *Blood Slaves* received some of its best, most thought-provoking and deep-diving reviews from Black readers, both from those who loved it and from those who didn't exactly love it. I can't wait to hear what you all think of this one.

Of course, there was the artistry of others who helped me through the writing process. This time around, my go-to was the music of Laufey. How I wish my dad had lived to hear this young woman bring back the art of bossa nova. She went hand in hand with Samara Joy, whose voice and lyrics have invigorated jazz music. Much gratitude to you both for helping me along.

As always, Singaporean television remains in my thanks as *Emerald Hill*, the sequel to the brilliant Little Nyonya series, did not disappoint. Ferlyn Wong stole the show for me. Thank you to the cast and crew for giving me a rich historical world to disappear into when I needed it.

Lastly, my mother, Thelma, who reached the milestone of ninety years during the editing of this book. Thanks for reminding me that stories are worth telling.

Until 2027, folks.